TABLE OF CONTENTS

CHAPTER 1

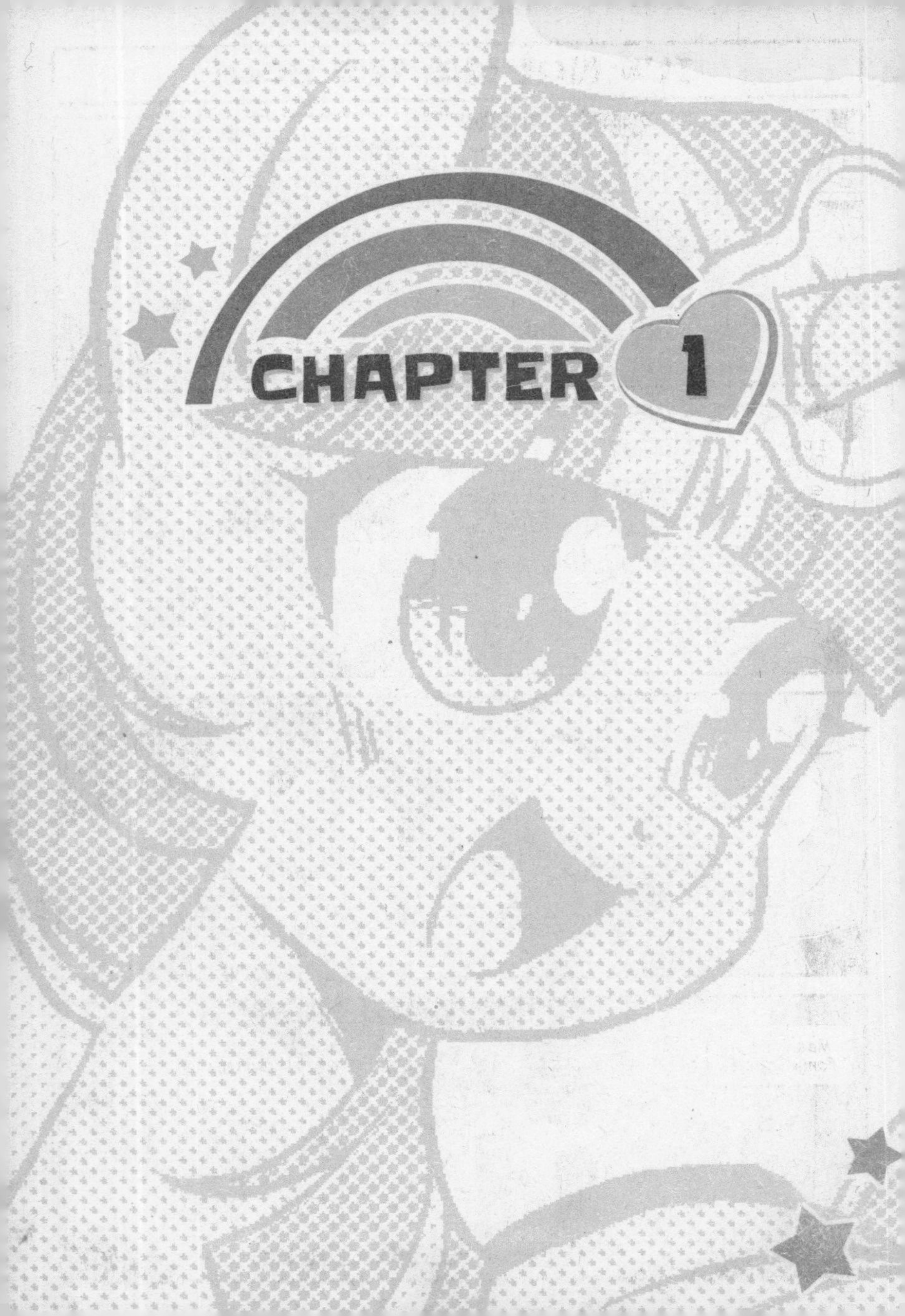

It's Not Me, It's You!

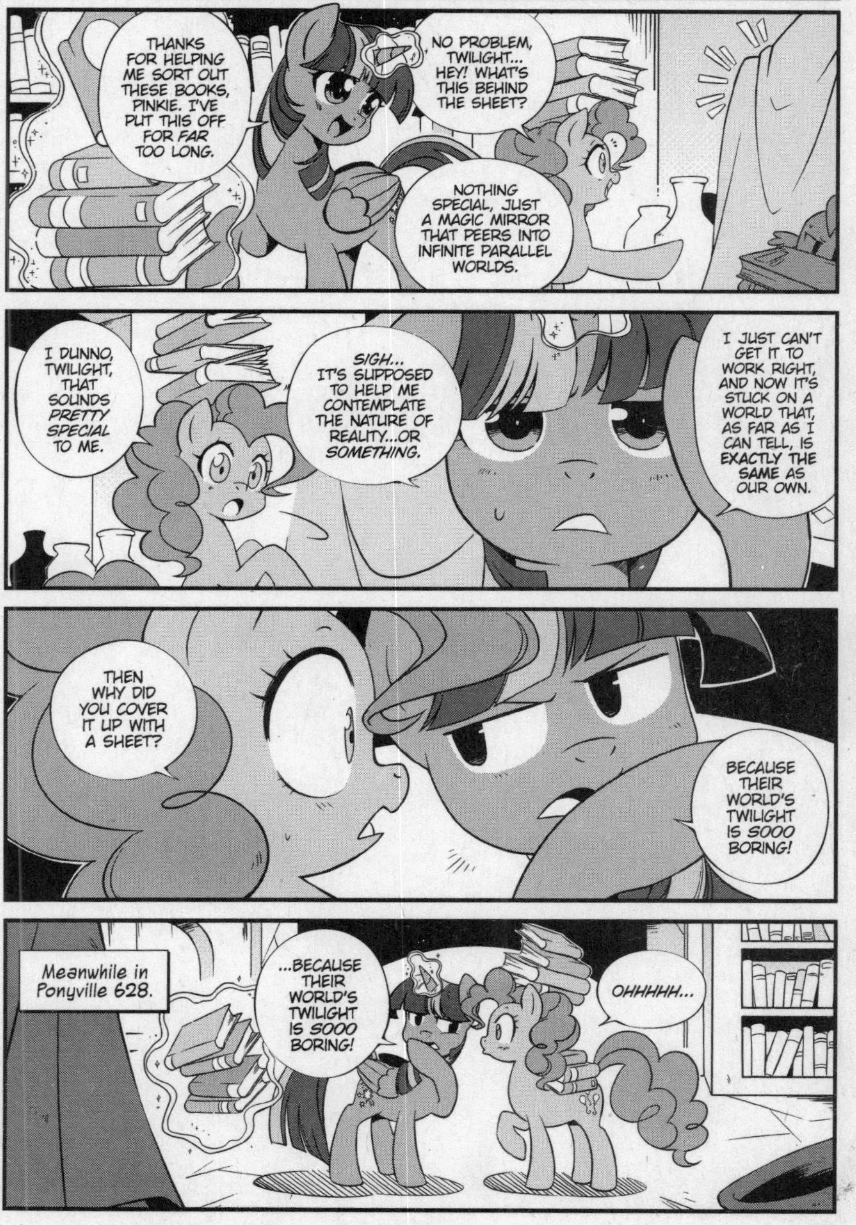
THANKS FOR HELPING ME SORT OUT THESE BOOKS, PINKIE. I'VE PUT THIS OFF FOR *FAR* TOO LONG.
NO PROBLEM, TWILIGHT... HEY! WHAT'S THIS BEHIND THE SHEET?
NOTHING SPECIAL, JUST A MAGIC MIRROR THAT PEERS INTO INFINITE PARALLEL WORLDS.
I DUNNO, TWILIGHT, THAT SOUNDS *PRETTY SPECIAL* TO ME.
SIGH... IT'S SUPPOSED TO HELP ME CONTEMPLATE THE NATURE OF REALITY...OR *SOMETHING.*
I JUST CAN'T GET IT TO WORK RIGHT, AND NOW IT'S STUCK ON A WORLD THAT, AS FAR AS I CAN TELL, IS **EXACTLY THE** SAME AS OUR OWN.
THEN WHY DID YOU COVER IT UP WITH A SHEET?
BECAUSE THEIR WORLD'S TWILIGHT IS *SOOO* BORING!
Meanwhile in Ponyville 628.
...BECAUSE THEIR WORLD'S TWILIGHT IS *SOOO* BORING!
OHHHHH...

Me, Myself, and Pie

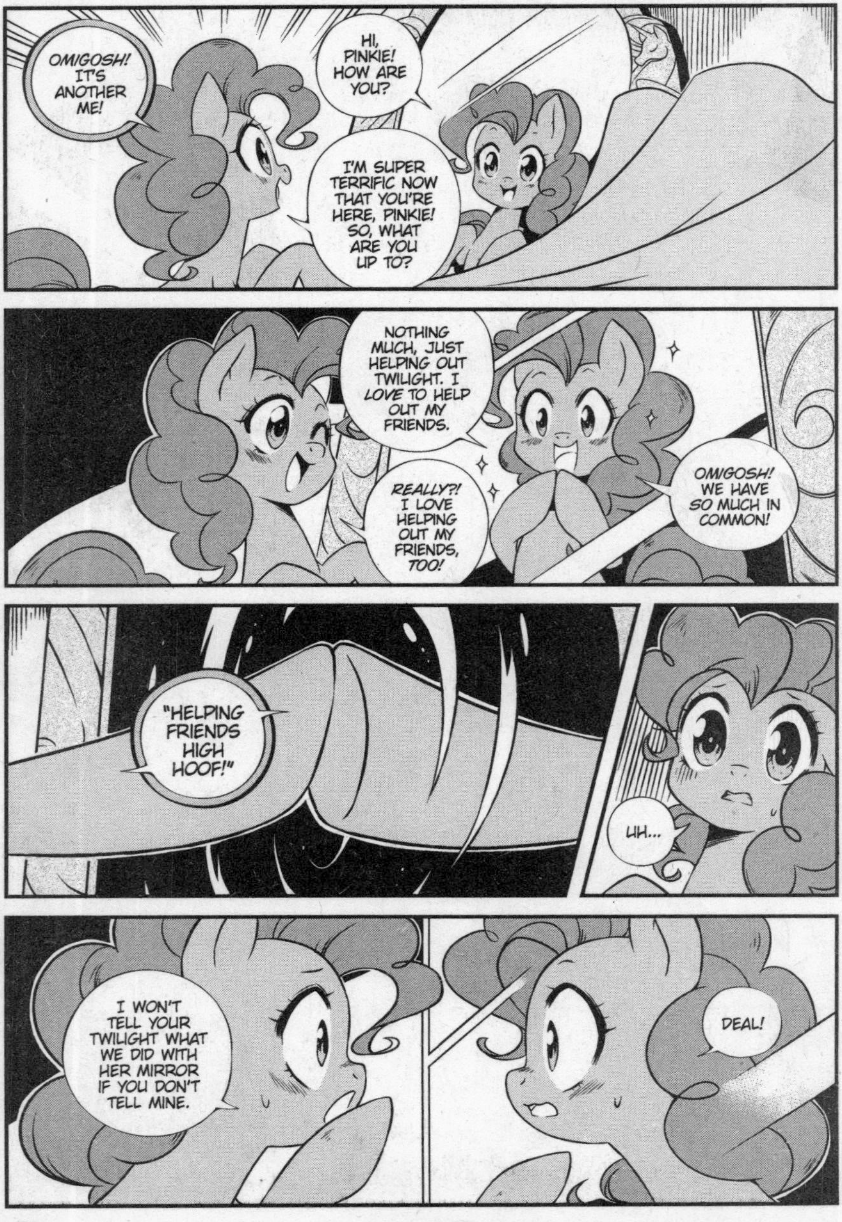
OMIGOSH! IT'S ANOTHER ME!
HI, PINKIE! HOW ARE YOU?
I'M SUPER TERRIFIC NOW THAT YOU'RE HERE, PINKIE! SO, WHAT ARE YOU UP TO?
NOTHING MUCH, JUST HELPING OUT TWILIGHT. I *LOVE* TO HELP OUT MY FRIENDS.
REALLY?! I LOVE HELPING OUT MY FRIENDS, *TOO!*
OMIGOSH! WE HAVE SO MUCH IN COMMON!
"HELPING FRIENDS HIGH HOOF!"
UH...
I WON'T TELL YOUR TWILIGHT WHAT WE DID WITH HER MIRROR IF YOU DON'T TELL MINE.
DEAL!

Vive La Difference!

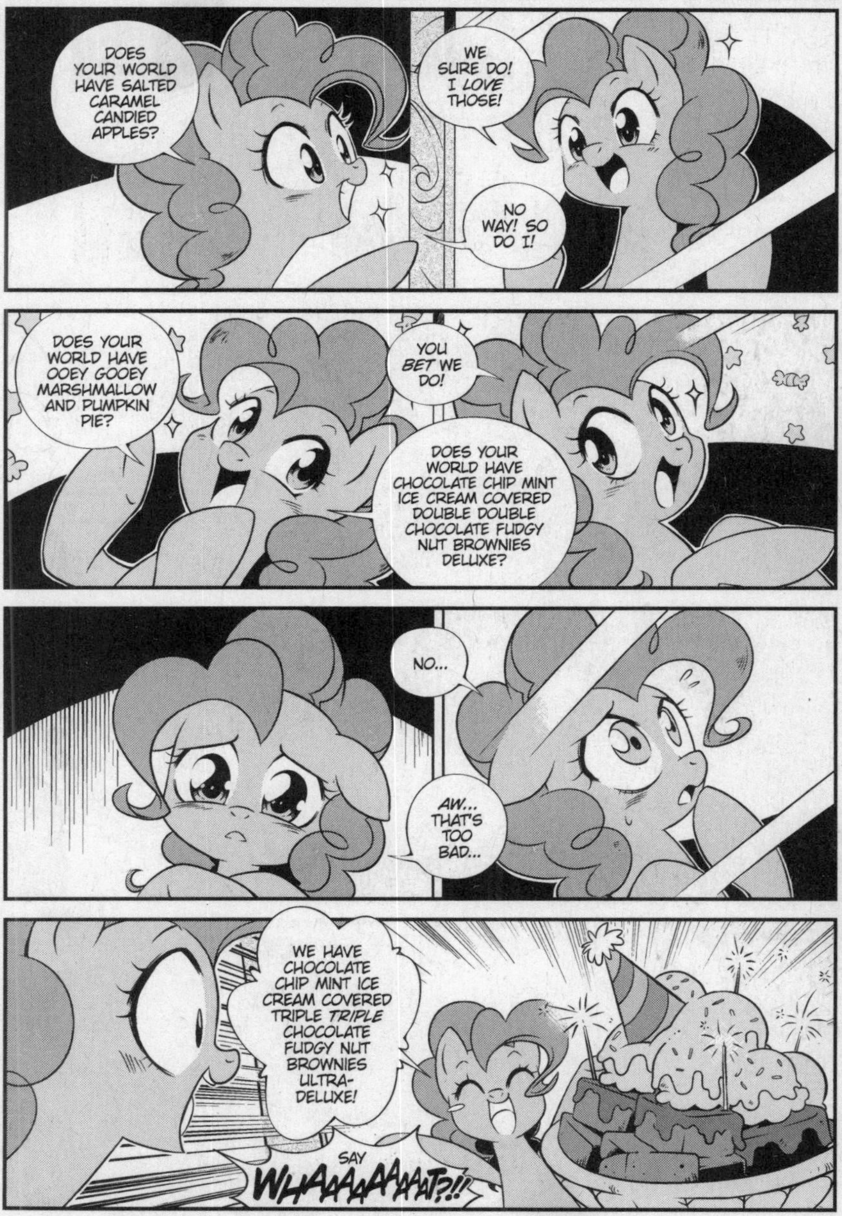
DOES YOUR WORLD HAVE SALTED CARAMEL CANDIED APPLES?
WE SURE DO! I *LOVE* THOSE!
NO WAY! SO DO I!
DOES YOUR WORLD HAVE OOEY GOOEY MARSHMALLOW AND PUMPKIN PIE?
YOU *BET* WE DO!
DOES YOUR WORLD HAVE CHOCOLATE CHIP MINT ICE CREAM COVERED DOUBLE DOUBLE CHOCOLATE FUDGY NUT BROWNIES DELUXE?
NO...
AW... THAT'S TOO BAD...
WE HAVE CHOCOLATE CHIP MINT ICE CREAM COVERED TRIPLE *TRIPLE* CHOCOLATE FUDGY NUT BROWNIES ULTRA-DELUXE!
SAY
WHAAAAAAAAAT?!!

Late for Dinner

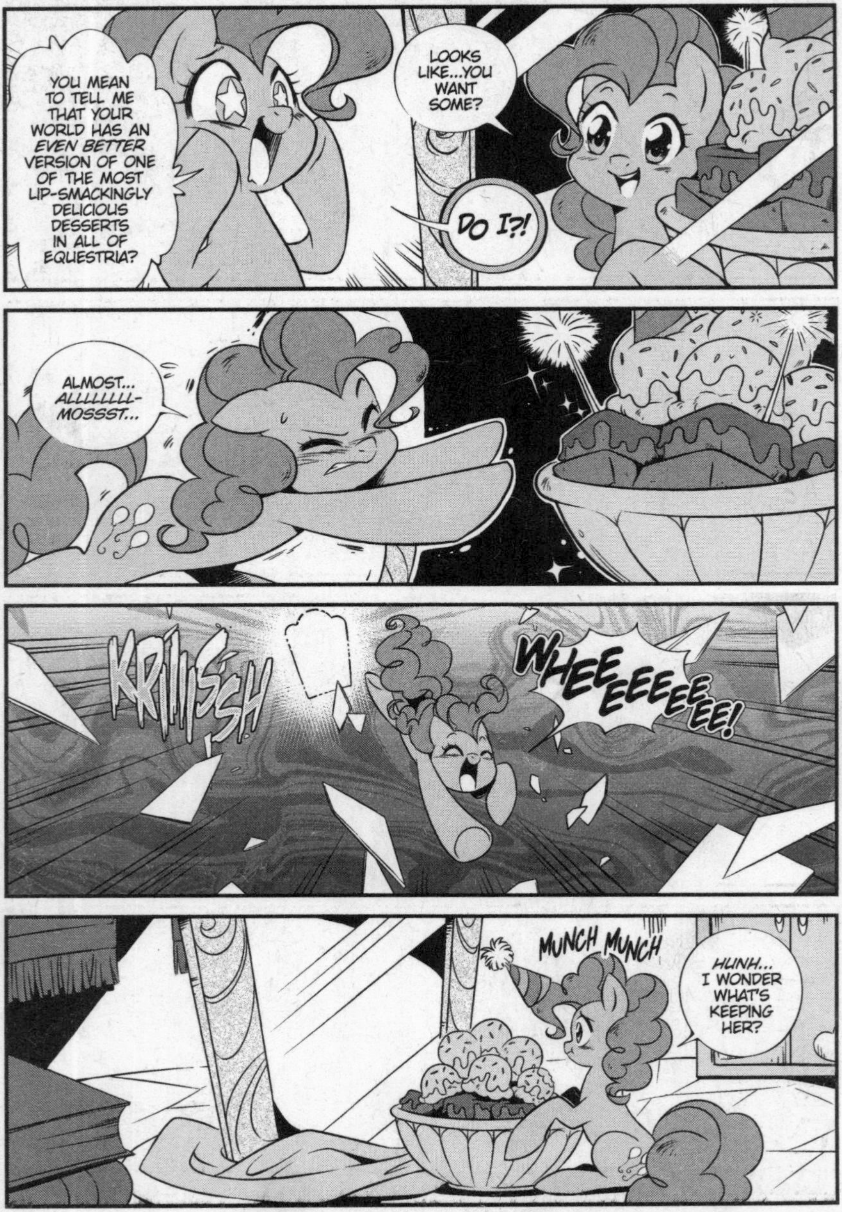

YOU MEAN TO TELL ME THAT YOUR WORLD HAS AN *EVEN BETTER* VERSION OF ONE OF THE MOST LIP-SMACKINGLY DELICIOUS DESSERTS IN ALL OF EQUESTRIA?
LOOKS LIKE...YOU WANT SOME?
DO I?!
ALMOST... *ALLLLLLLL-MOSSST...*
KRIIIISSH
WHEEEEEEEEEEEE!
MUNCH MUNCH
HUNH... I WONDER WHAT'S KEEPING HER?

Zombie A-clop-olypse

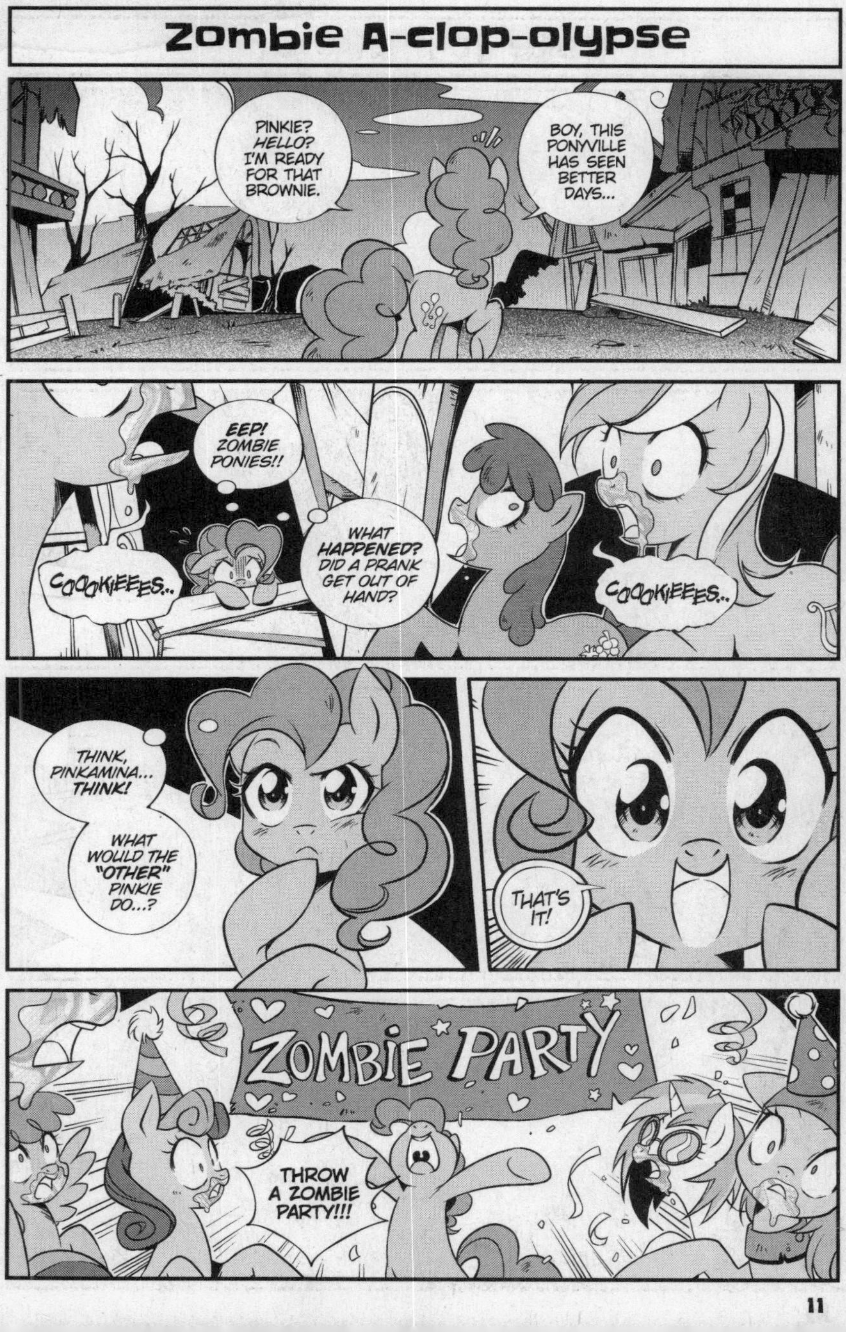

PINKIE? HELLO? I'M READY FOR THAT BROWNIE.
BOY, THIS PONYVILLE HAS SEEN BETTER DAYS...
EEP! ZOMBIE PONIES!!
COOOKIEEES...
WHAT HAPPENED? DID A PRANK GET OUT OF HAND?
COOOKIEEES...
THINK, PINKAMINA... THINK!
WHAT WOULD THE "OTHER" PINKIE DO...?
THAT'S IT!
ZOMBIE PARTY
THROW A ZOMBIE PARTY!!!

Fear the Prancing Dead

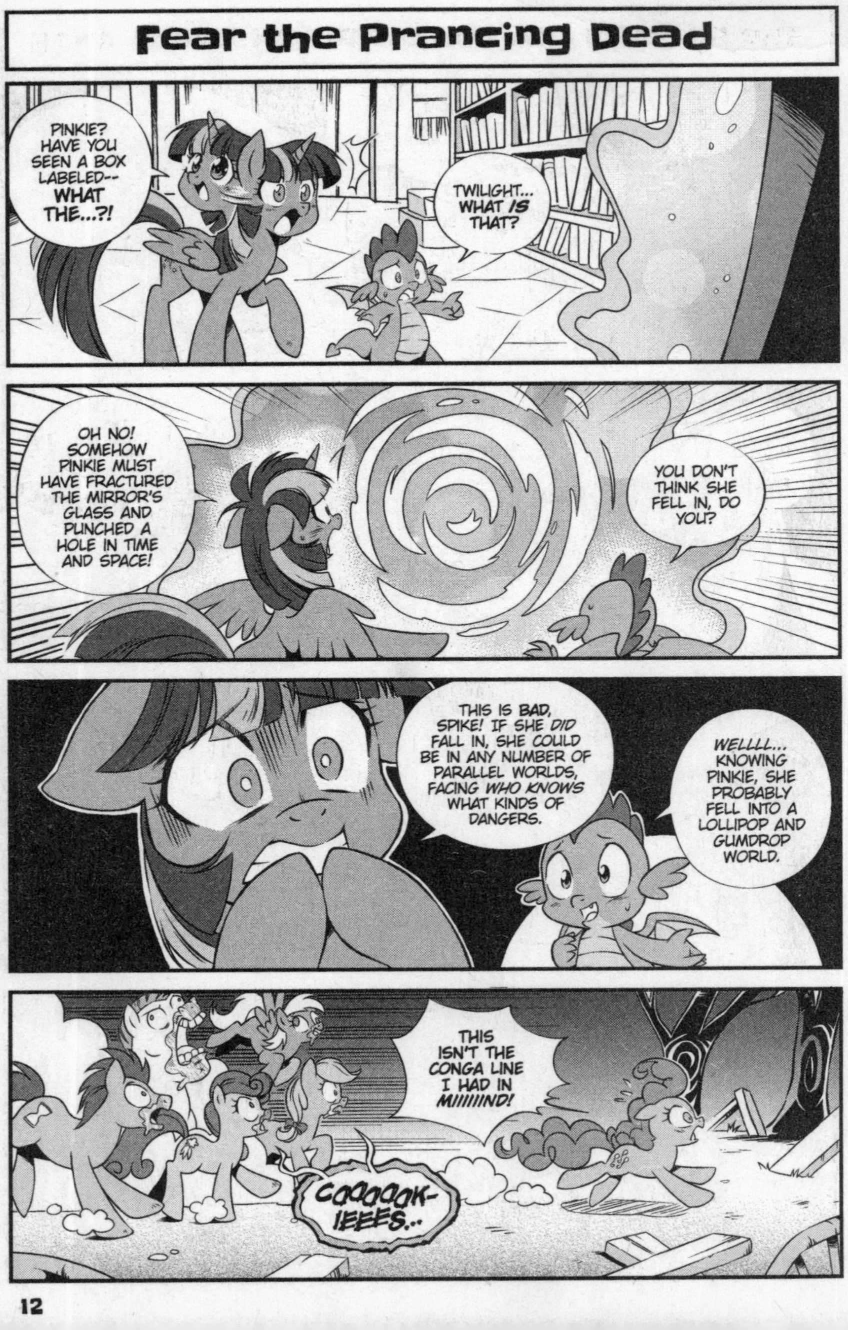
PINKIE? HAVE YOU SEEN A BOX LABELED-- WHAT THE...?!
TWILIGHT... WHAT *IS* THAT?
OH NO! SOMEHOW PINKIE MUST HAVE FRACTURED THE MIRROR'S GLASS AND PUNCHED A HOLE IN TIME AND SPACE!
YOU DON'T THINK SHE FELL IN, DO YOU?
THIS IS BAD, SPIKE! IF SHE *DID* FALL IN, SHE COULD BE IN ANY NUMBER OF PARALLEL WORLDS, FACING *WHO KNOWS* WHAT KINDS OF DANGERS.
WELLLL... KNOWING PINKIE, SHE PROBABLY FELL INTO A LOLLIPOP AND GUMDROP WORLD.
THIS ISN'T THE CONGA LINE I HAD IN *MIIIIIND!*
CAAAAAK- IEEES...

The Portal Giveth, and the Portal Taketh Away

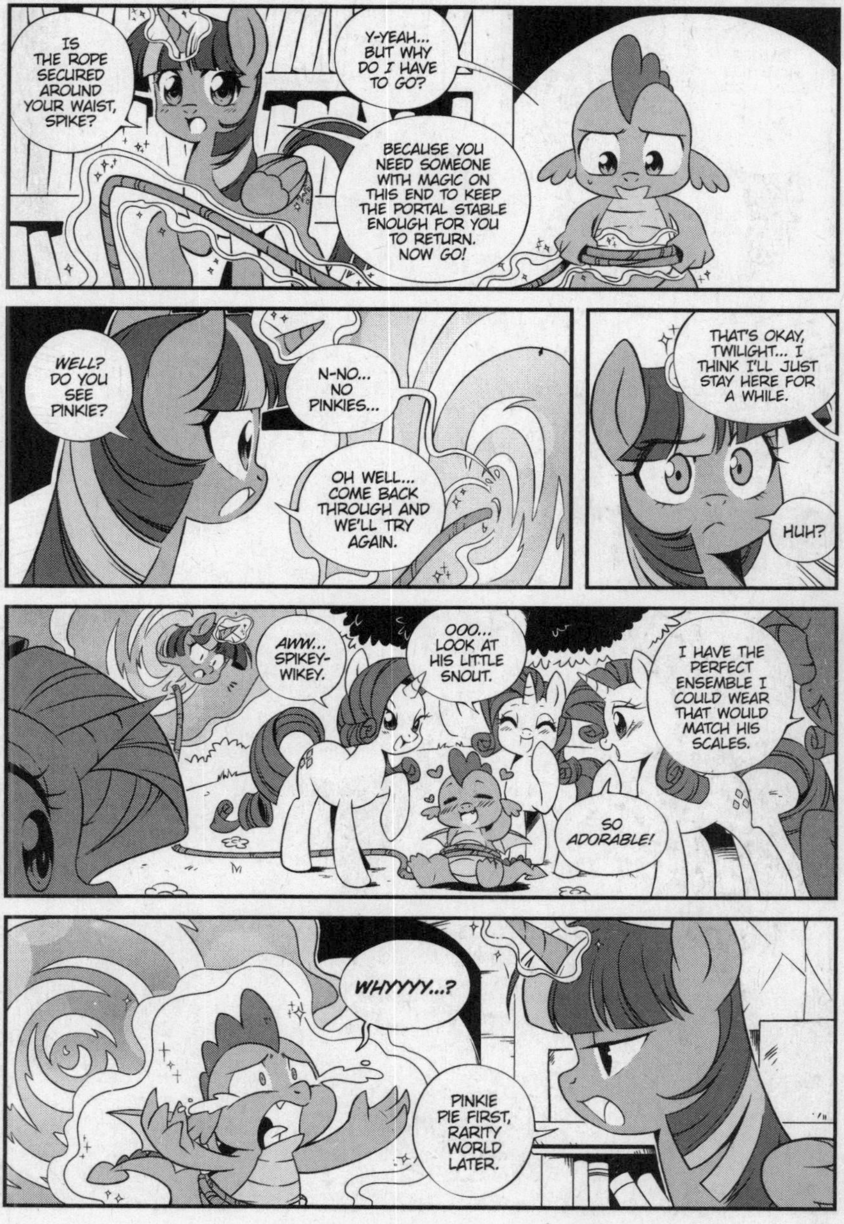
IS THE ROPE SECURED AROUND YOUR WAIST, SPIKE?
Y-YEAH... BUT WHY DO I HAVE TO GO?
BECAUSE YOU NEED SOMEONE WITH MAGIC ON THIS END TO KEEP THE PORTAL STABLE ENOUGH FOR YOU TO RETURN. NOW GO!
WELL? DO YOU SEE PINKIE?
N-NO... NO PINKIES...
OH WELL... COME BACK THROUGH AND WE'LL TRY AGAIN.
THAT'S OKAY, TWILIGHT... I THINK I'LL JUST STAY HERE FOR A WHILE.
HUH?
AWW... SPIKEY-WIKEY.
OOO... LOOK AT HIS LITTLE SNOUT.
I HAVE THE PERFECT ENSEMBLE I COULD WEAR THAT WOULD MATCH HIS SCALES.
SO ADORABLE!
WHYYYY...?
PINKIE PIE FIRST, RARITY WORLD LATER.

Where No Spike Has Gone Before

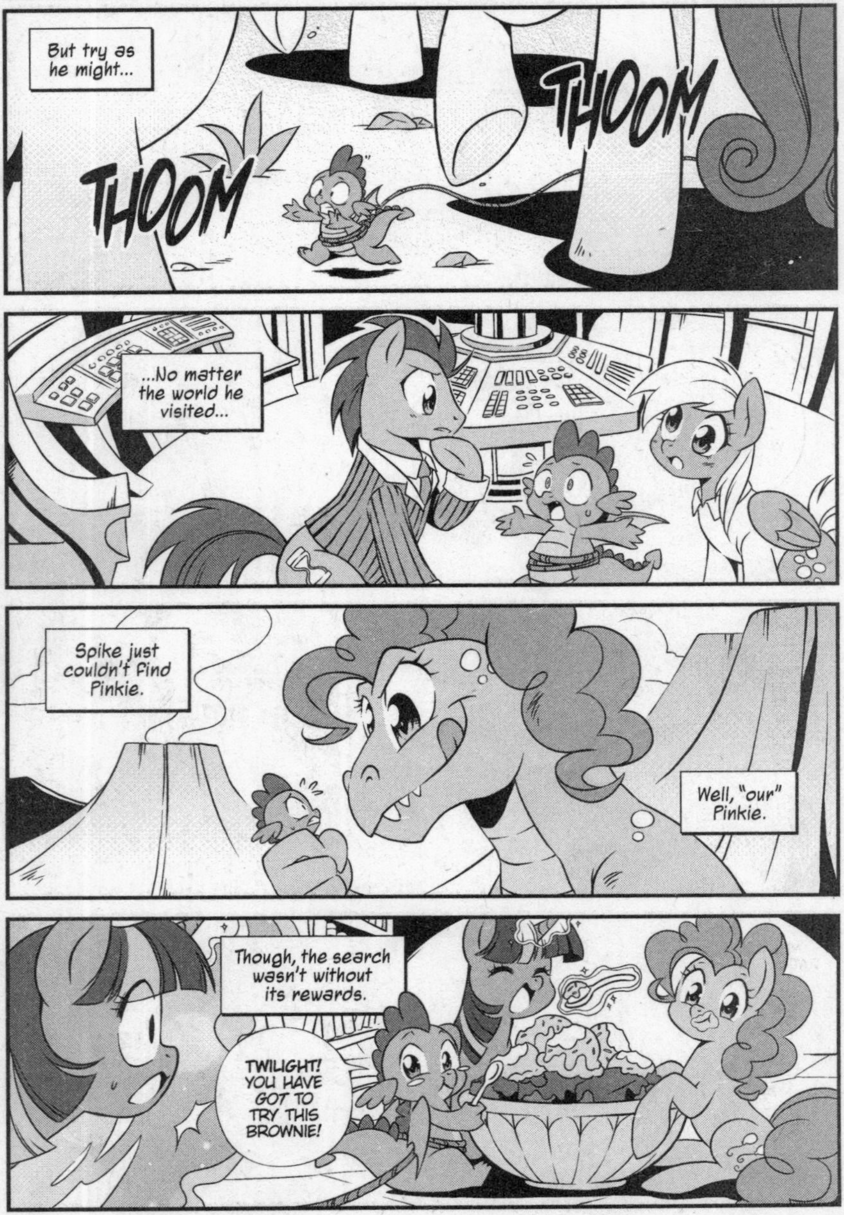

But try as he might...
THOOM
THOOM
...No matter the world he visited...
Spike just couldn't find Pinkie.
Well, "our" Pinkie.
Though, the search wasn't without its rewards.
TWILIGHT! YOU HAVE GOT TO TRY THIS BROWNIE!

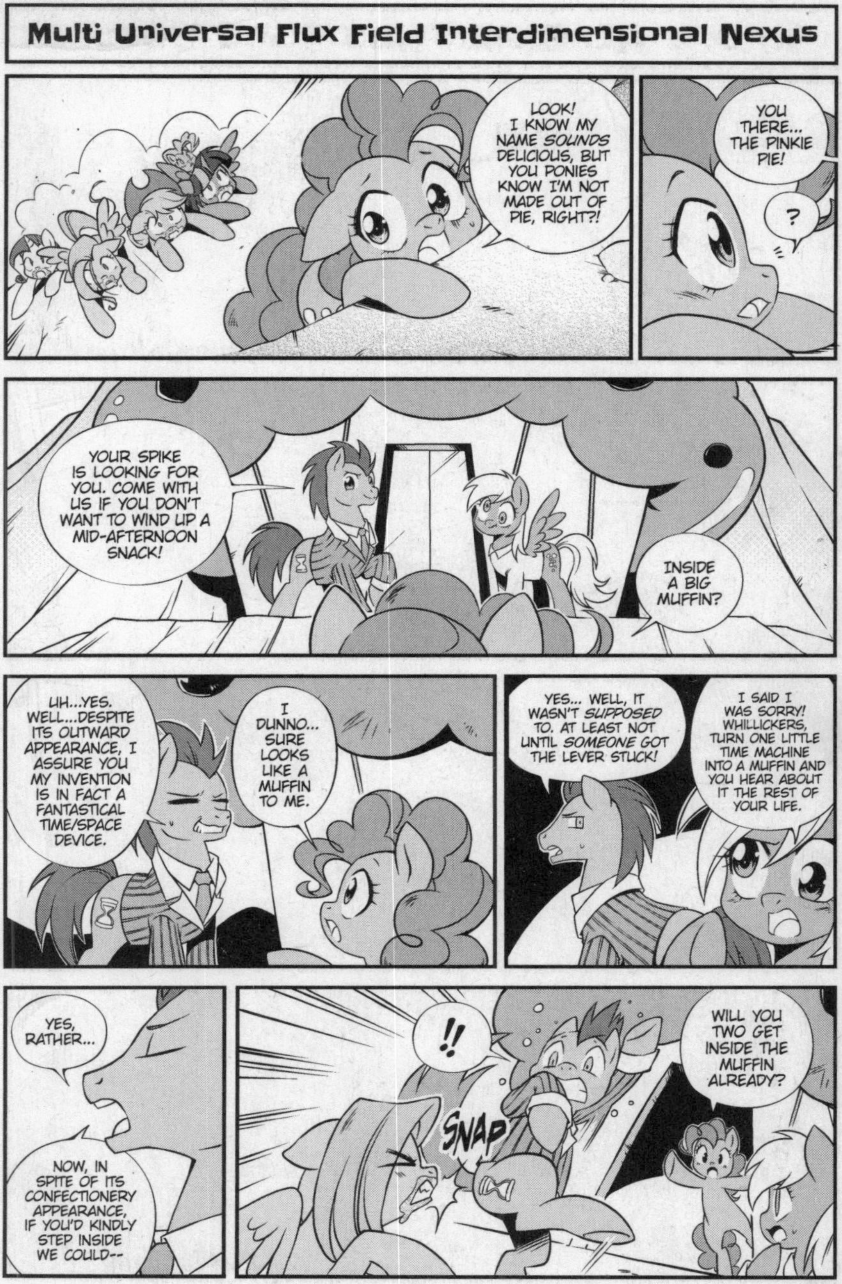
Multi Universal Flux Field Interdimensional Nexus
LOOK! I KNOW MY NAME *SOUNDS* DELICIOUS, BUT YOU PONIES KNOW I'M NOT MADE OUT OF PIE, RIGHT?!
YOU THERE... THE PINKIE PIE!
?
YOUR SPIKE IS LOOKING FOR YOU. COME WITH US IF YOU DON'T WANT TO WIND UP A MID-AFTERNOON SNACK!
INSIDE A BIG MUFFIN?
UH...YES. WELL...DESPITE ITS OUTWARD APPEARANCE, I ASSURE YOU MY INVENTION IS IN FACT A FANTASTICAL TIME/SPACE DEVICE.
I DUNNO... SURE LOOKS LIKE A MUFFIN TO ME.
YES... WELL, IT WASN'T *SUPPOSED* TO. AT LEAST NOT UNTIL *SOMEONE* GOT THE LEVER STUCK!
I SAID I WAS SORRY! WHILLICKERS, TURN ONE LITTLE TIME MACHINE INTO A MUFFIN AND YOU HEAR ABOUT IT THE REST OF YOUR LIFE.
YES, RATHER...
NOW, IN SPITE OF ITS CONFECTIONERY APPEARANCE, IF YOU'D KINDLY STEP INSIDE WE COULD--
!!
SNAP
WILL YOU TWO GET INSIDE THE MUFFIN ALREADY?

A Face Full of Pie

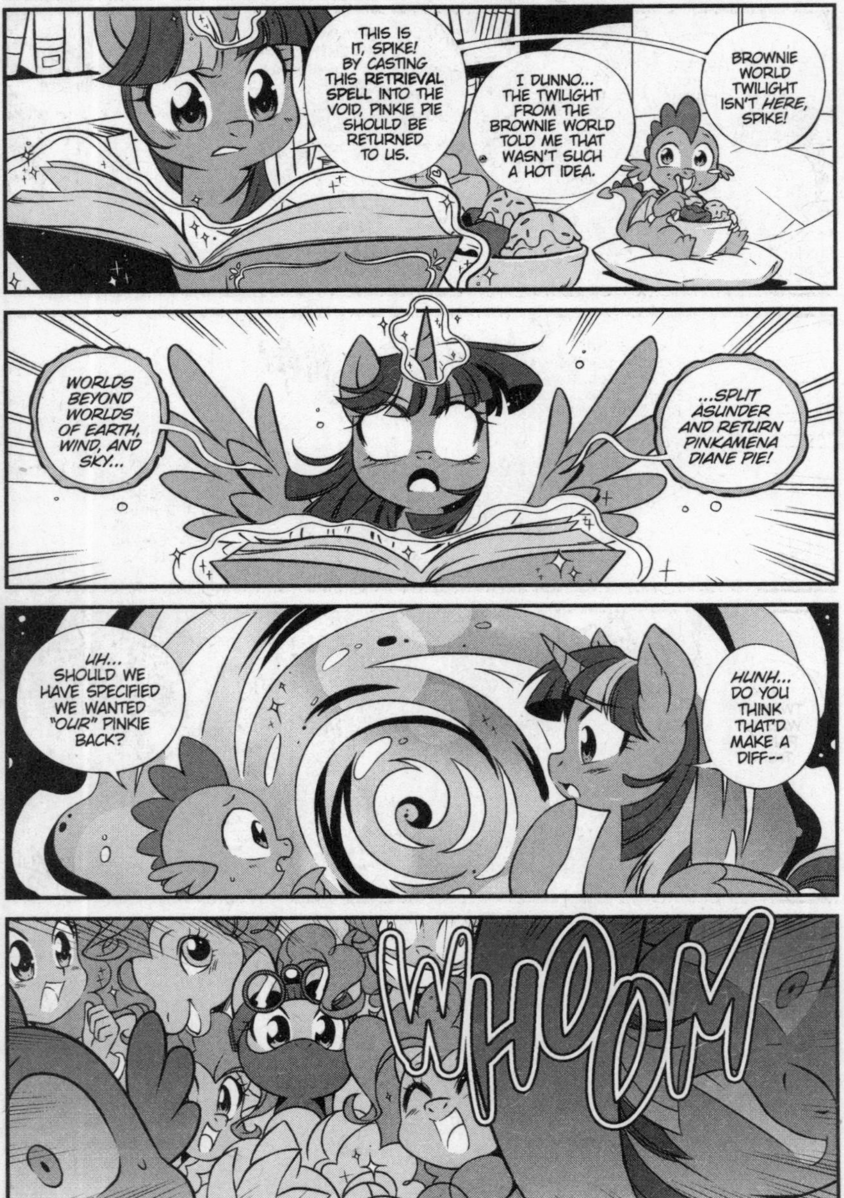
THIS IS IT, SPIKE! BY CASTING THIS RETRIEVAL SPELL INTO THE VOID, PINKIE PIE SHOULD BE RETURNED TO US.
I DUNNO... THE TWILIGHT FROM THE BROWNIE WORLD TOLD ME THAT WASN'T SUCH A HOT IDEA.
BROWNIE WORLD TWILIGHT ISN'T *HERE*, SPIKE!
WORLDS BEYOND WORLDS OF EARTH, WIND, AND SKY...
...SPLIT ASUNDER AND RETURN PINKAMENA DIANE PIE!
UH... SHOULD WE HAVE SPECIFIED WE WANTED *"OUR"* PINKIE BACK?
HUNH... DO YOU THINK THAT'D MAKE A DIFF--
WHOOOM

That's Pinkie All Over

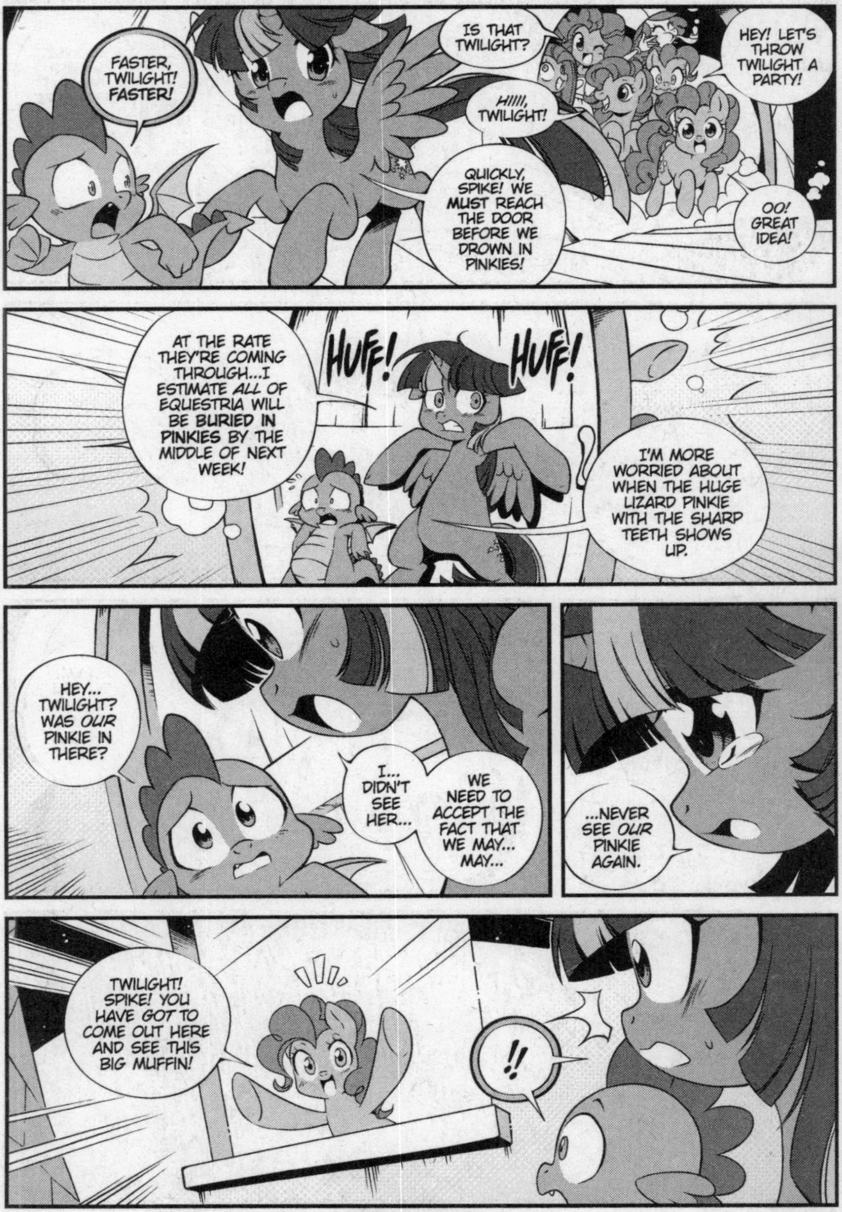

FASTER, TWILIGHT! FASTER!
IS THAT TWILIGHT?
HIIII, TWILIGHT!
QUICKLY, SPIKE! WE MUST REACH THE DOOR BEFORE WE DROWN IN PINKIES!
HEY! LET'S THROW TWILIGHT A PARTY!
OO! GREAT IDEA!
AT THE RATE THEY'RE COMING THROUGH...I ESTIMATE ALL OF EQUESTRIA WILL BE BURIED IN PINKIES BY THE MIDDLE OF NEXT WEEK!
HUFF!
HUFF!
I'M MORE WORRIED ABOUT WHEN THE HUGE LIZARD PINKIE WITH THE SHARP TEETH SHOWS UP.
HEY... TWILIGHT? WAS OUR PINKIE IN THERE?
I... DIDN'T SEE HER...
WE NEED TO ACCEPT THE FACT THAT WE MAY... MAY...
...NEVER SEE OUR PINKIE AGAIN.
TWILIGHT! SPIKE! YOU HAVE GOT TO COME OUT HERE AND SEE THIS BIG MUFFIN!
!!

Bye Bye, Pies

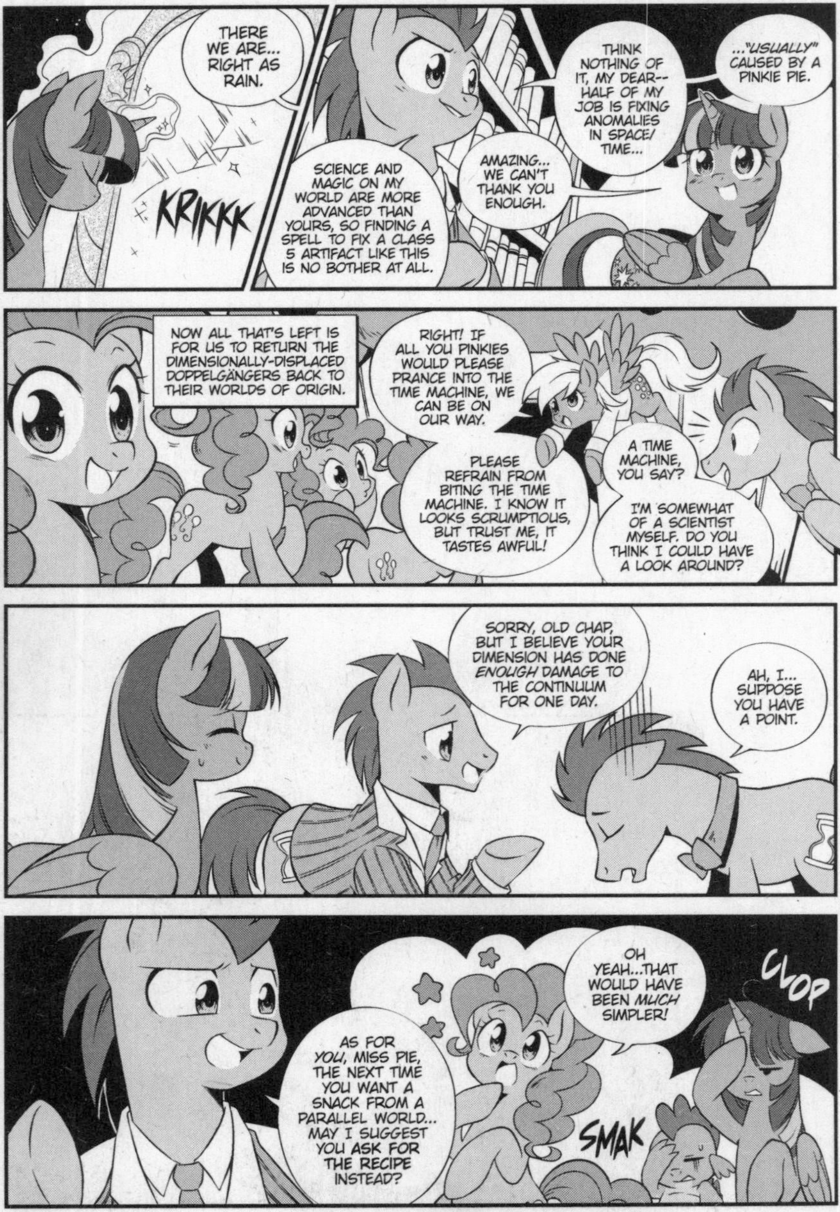
THERE WE ARE... RIGHT AS RAIN.
KRIKKK
THINK NOTHING OF IT, MY DEAR-- HALF OF MY JOB IS FIXING ANOMALIES IN SPACE/ TIME...
..."*USUALLY*" CAUSED BY A PINKIE PIE.
SCIENCE AND MAGIC ON MY WORLD ARE MORE ADVANCED THAN YOURS, SO FINDING A SPELL TO FIX A CLASS 5 ARTIFACT LIKE THIS IS NO BOTHER AT ALL.
AMAZING... WE CAN'T THANK YOU ENOUGH.
NOW ALL THAT'S LEFT IS FOR US TO RETURN THE DIMENSIONALLY-DISPLACED DOPPELGÄNGERS BACK TO THEIR WORLDS OF ORIGIN.
RIGHT! IF ALL YOU PINKIES WOULD PLEASE PRANCE INTO THE TIME MACHINE, WE CAN BE ON OUR WAY.
PLEASE REFRAIN FROM BITING THE TIME MACHINE. I KNOW IT LOOKS SCRUMPTIOUS, BUT TRUST ME, IT TASTES AWFUL!
A TIME MACHINE, YOU SAY?
I'M SOMEWHAT OF A SCIENTIST MYSELF. DO YOU THINK I COULD HAVE A LOOK AROUND?
SORRY, OLD CHAP, BUT I BELIEVE YOUR DIMENSION HAS DONE *ENOUGH* DAMAGE TO THE CONTINUUM FOR ONE DAY.
AH, I... SUPPOSE YOU HAVE A POINT.
AS FOR *YOU*, MISS PIE, THE NEXT TIME YOU WANT A SNACK FROM A PARALLEL WORLD... MAY I SUGGEST YOU ASK FOR THE RECIPE INSTEAD?
OH YEAH...THAT WOULD HAVE BEEN *MUCH* SIMPLER!
CLOP
SMAK

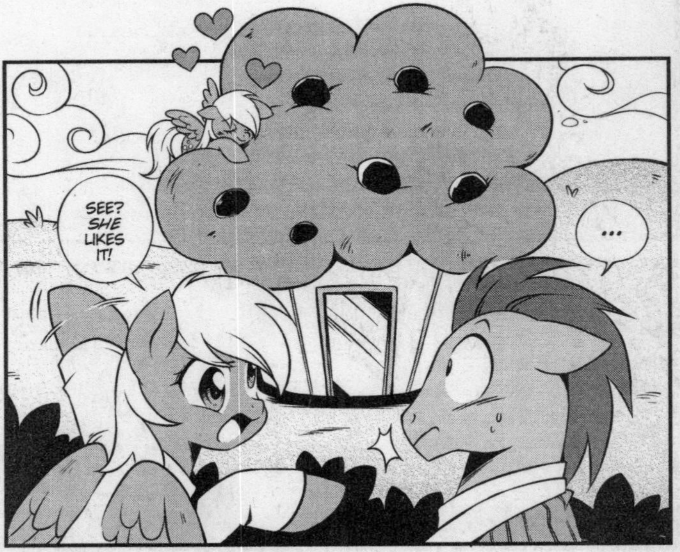
SEE? SHE LIKES IT!
...

CHAPTER 2

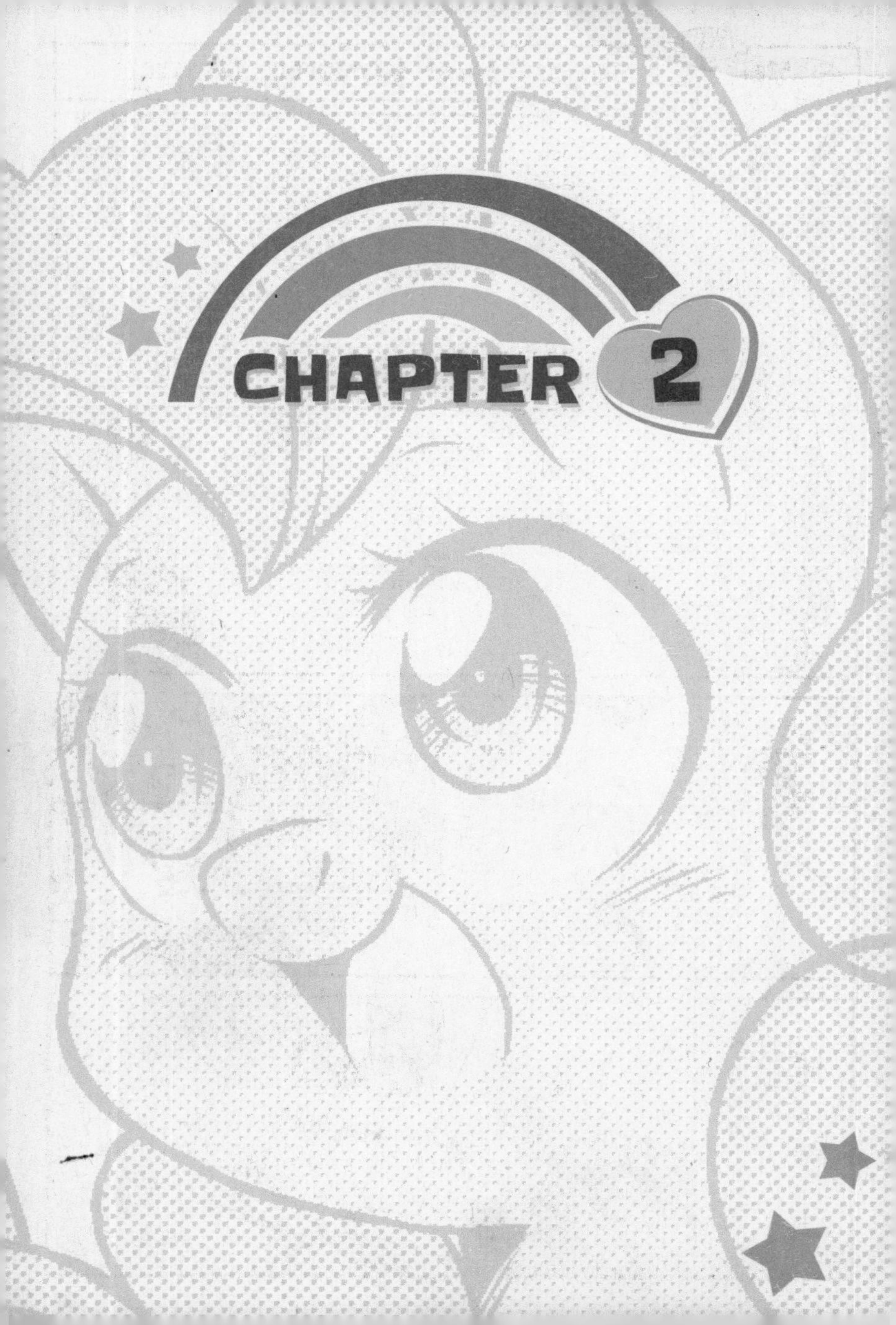

The Case of the Wrong Pony

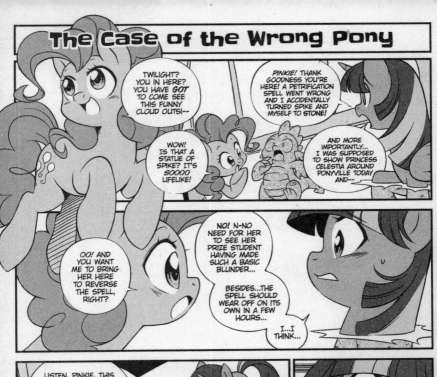

TWILIGHT? YOU IN HERE? YOU HAVE *GOT* TO COME SEE THIS FUNNY CLOUD OUTSI--

PINKIE! THANK GOODNESS YOU'RE HERE! A PETRIFICATION SPELL WENT WRONG AND I ACCIDENTALLY TURNED SPIKE AND MYSELF TO STONE!

WOW! IS THAT A STATUE OF SPIKE? IT'S *SOOOO* LIFELIKE!

AND MORE IMPORTANTLY... I WAS SUPPOSED TO SHOW PRINCESS CELESTIA AROUND PONYVILLE TODAY AND--

OO! AND YOU WANT ME TO BRING HER HERE TO REVERSE THE SPELL, RIGHT?

NO! N-NO NEED FOR HER TO SEE HER PRIZE STUDENT HAVING MADE SUCH A BASIC BLUNDER...

BESIDES...THE SPELL SHOULD WEAR OFF ON ITS OWN IN A FEW HOURS... I...I THINK...

LISTEN, PINKIE, THIS IS *VERY IMPORTANT*... SOMEONE STILL NEEDS TO SHOW PRINCESS CELESTIA AROUND PONYVILLE. I NEED YOU TO GO FIND RARITY AND TELL HER--

TELL HER NOT TO WORRY, BECAUSE YOU WANT *ME* TO GIVE HER THE TOUR FOR YOU?

EXACTL--

WHAT? NO! TELL RARITY SHE NEEDS TO GIVE THE TOU--

DON'T WORRY ABOUT A THING, TWILIGHT! PRINCESS CELESTIA AND I ARE GOING TO PAINT THE TOWN PINK!

YOU JUST RELAX AND ENJOY BEING A STATUE!

KRIKK

...

All Shook Up

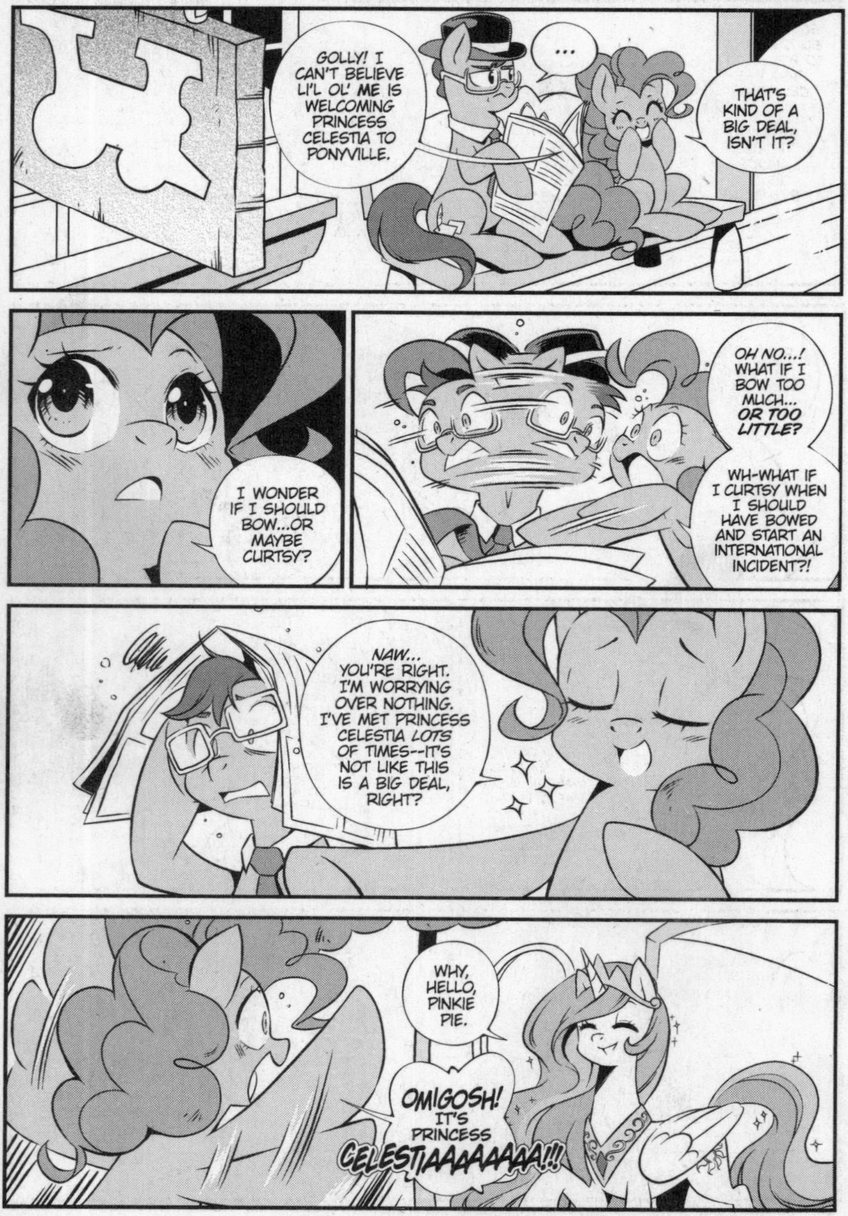
GOLLY! I CAN'T BELIEVE LI'L OL' ME IS WELCOMING PRINCESS CELESTIA TO PONYVILLE.
...
THAT'S KIND OF A BIG DEAL, ISN'T IT?
I WONDER IF I SHOULD BOW...OR MAYBE CURTSY?
OH NO...! WHAT IF I BOW TOO MUCH... OR TOO LITTLE?
WH-WHAT IF I CURTSY WHEN I SHOULD HAVE BOWED AND START AN INTERNATIONAL INCIDENT?!
NAW... YOU'RE RIGHT. I'M WORRYING OVER NOTHING. I'VE MET PRINCESS CELESTIA LOTS OF TIMES--IT'S NOT LIKE THIS IS A BIG DEAL, RIGHT?
WHY, HELLO, PINKIE PIE.
OMIGOSH! IT'S PRINCESS CELESTIAAAAAAAA!!!

Can't Touch This

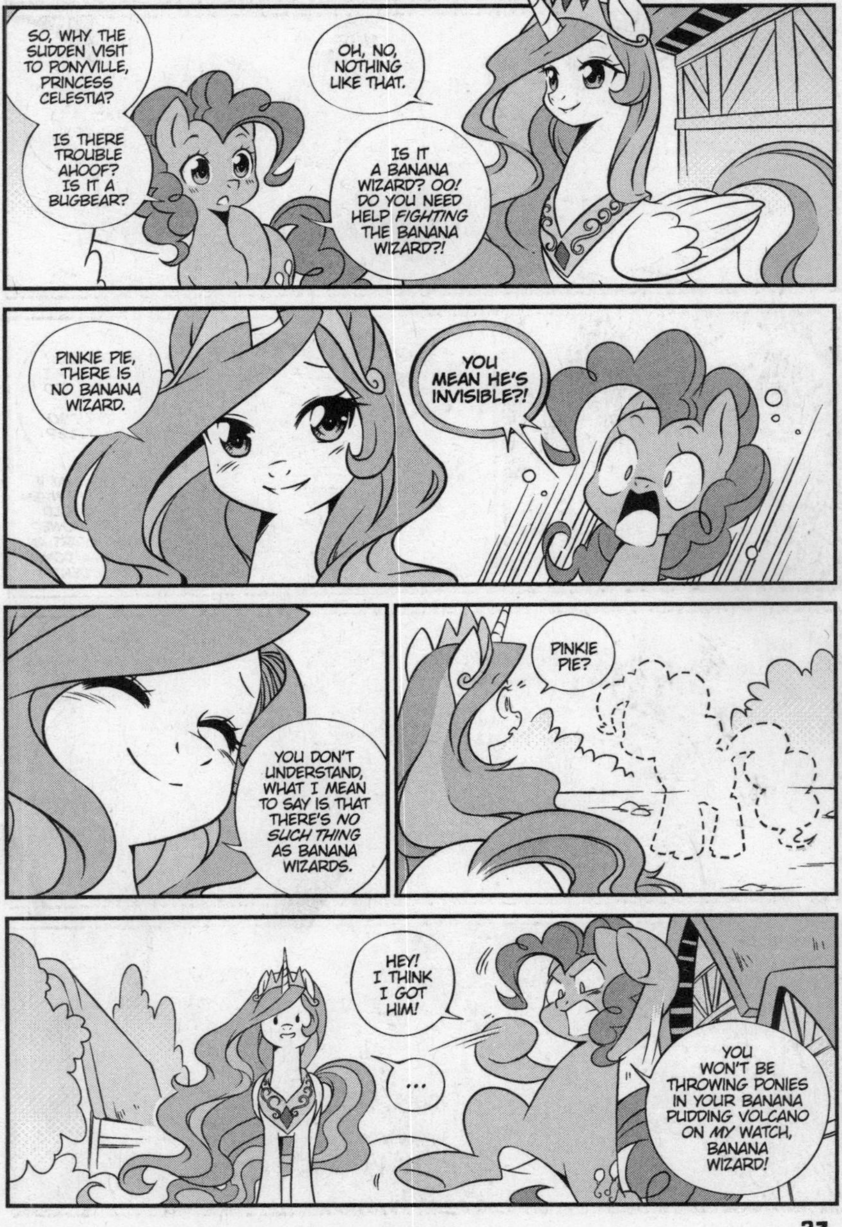

SO, WHY THE SUDDEN VISIT TO PONYVILLE, PRINCESS CELESTIA?
IS THERE TROUBLE AHOOF? IS IT A BUGBEAR?
OH, NO, NOTHING LIKE THAT.
IS IT A BANANA WIZARD? *OO!* DO YOU NEED HELP *FIGHTING* THE BANANA WIZARD?!
PINKIE PIE, THERE IS NO BANANA WIZARD.
YOU MEAN HE'S INVISIBLE?!
YOU DON'T UNDERSTAND, WHAT I MEAN TO SAY IS THAT THERE'S *NO SUCH THING* AS BANANA WIZARDS.
PINKIE PIE?
HEY! I THINK I GOT HIM!
...
YOU WON'T BE THROWING PONIES IN YOUR BANANA PUDDING VOLCANO ON *MY* WATCH, BANANA WIZARD!

The Stone Cold Truth

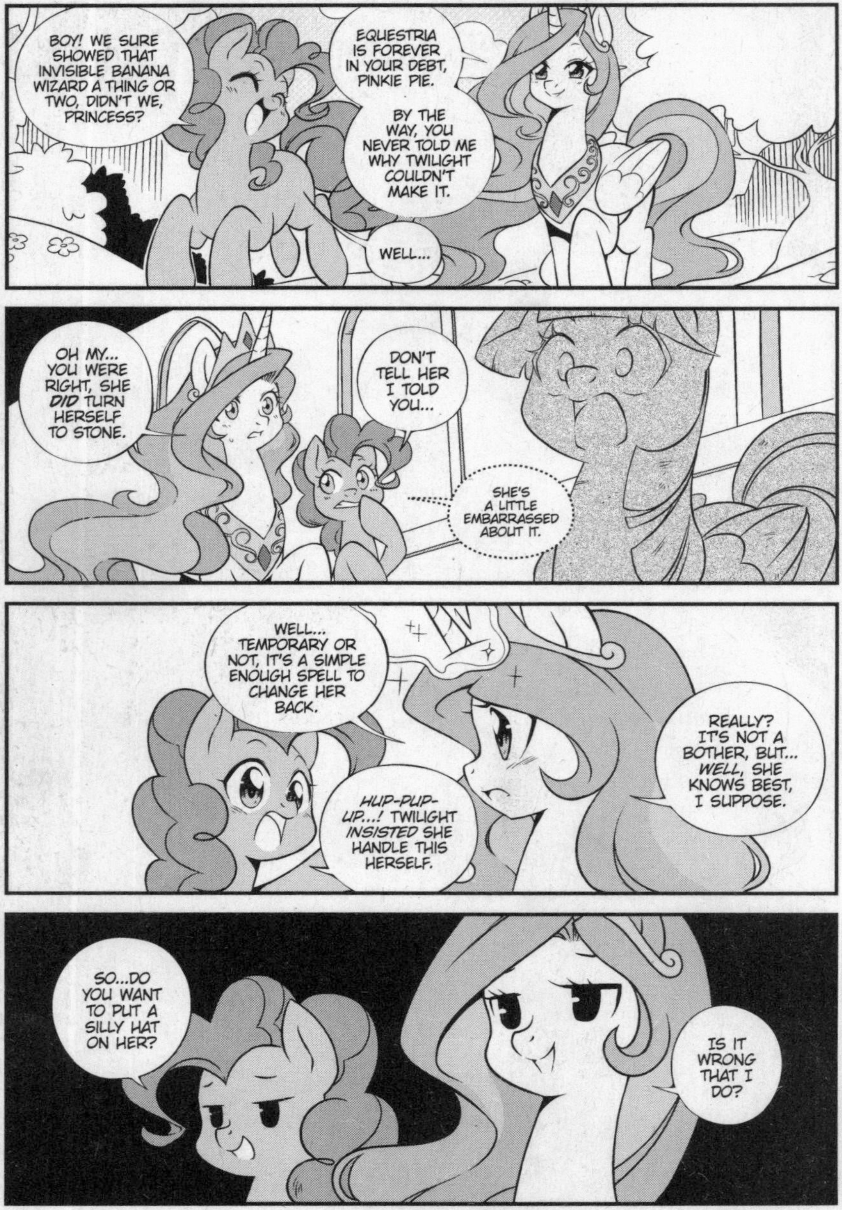
BOY! WE SURE SHOWED THAT INVISIBLE BANANA WIZARD A THING OR TWO, DIDN'T WE, PRINCESS?
EQUESTRIA IS FOREVER IN YOUR DEBT, PINKIE PIE.
BY THE WAY, YOU NEVER TOLD ME WHY TWILIGHT COULDN'T MAKE IT.
WELL...
OH MY... YOU WERE RIGHT, SHE *DID* TURN HERSELF TO STONE.
DON'T TELL HER I TOLD YOU...
SHE'S A LITTLE EMBARRASSED ABOUT IT.
WELL... TEMPORARY OR NOT, IT'S A SIMPLE ENOUGH SPELL TO CHANGE HER BACK.
HUP-PUP-UP...! TWILIGHT *INSISTED* SHE HANDLE THIS HERSELF.
REALLY? IT'S NOT A BOTHER, BUT... *WELL*, SHE KNOWS BEST, I SUPPOSE.
SO...DO YOU WANT TO PUT A SILLY HAT ON HER?
IS IT WRONG THAT I DO?

Model Pony

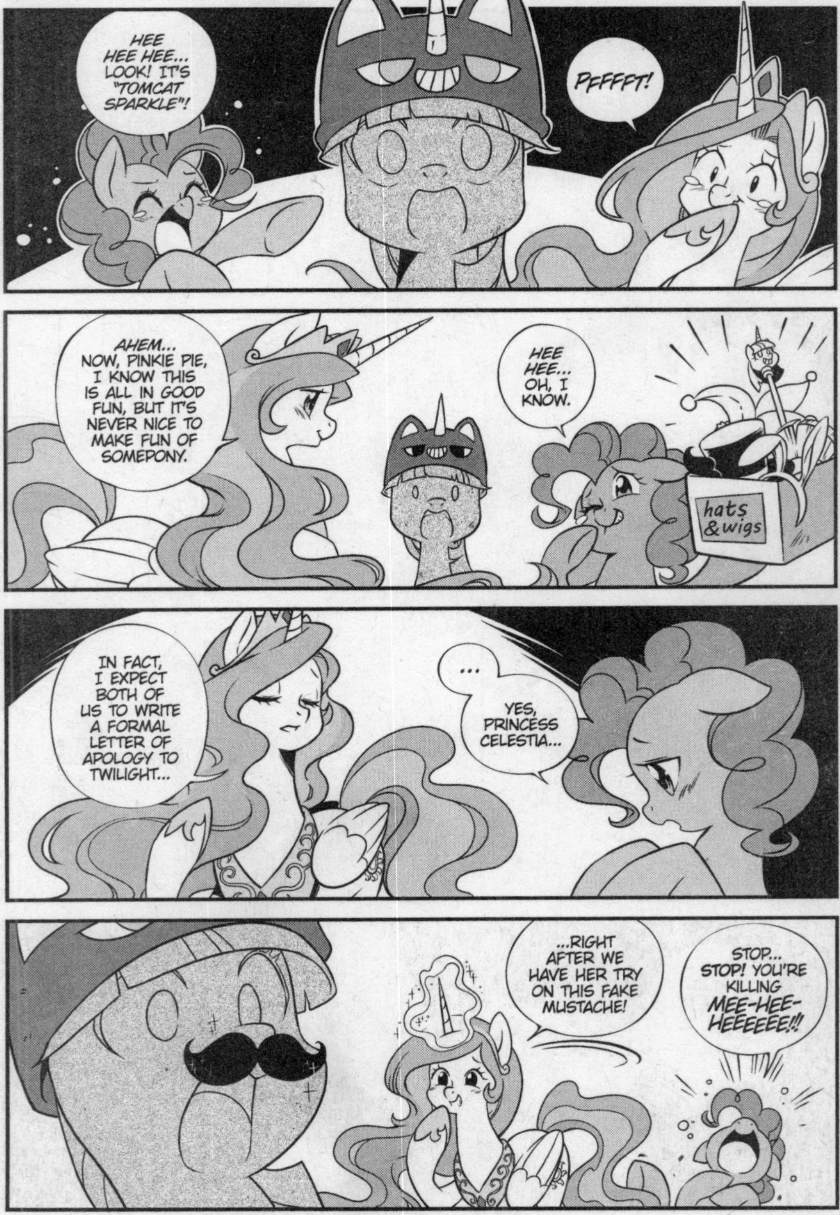
HEE HEE HEE... LOOK! IT'S "TOMCAT SPARKLE"!
PFFFFT!
AHEM... NOW, PINKIE PIE, I KNOW THIS IS ALL IN GOOD FUN, BUT IT'S NEVER NICE TO MAKE FUN OF SOMEPONY.
HEE HEE... OH, I KNOW.
hats &wigs
IN FACT, I EXPECT BOTH OF US TO WRITE A FORMAL LETTER OF APOLOGY TO TWILIGHT...
...
YES, PRINCESS CELESTIA...
...RIGHT AFTER WE HAVE HER TRY ON THIS FAKE MUSTACHE!
STOP... STOP! YOU'RE KILLING MEE-HEE-HEEEEEE!!!

Oh, These Are the Ponies in Your NEIGHborhood...

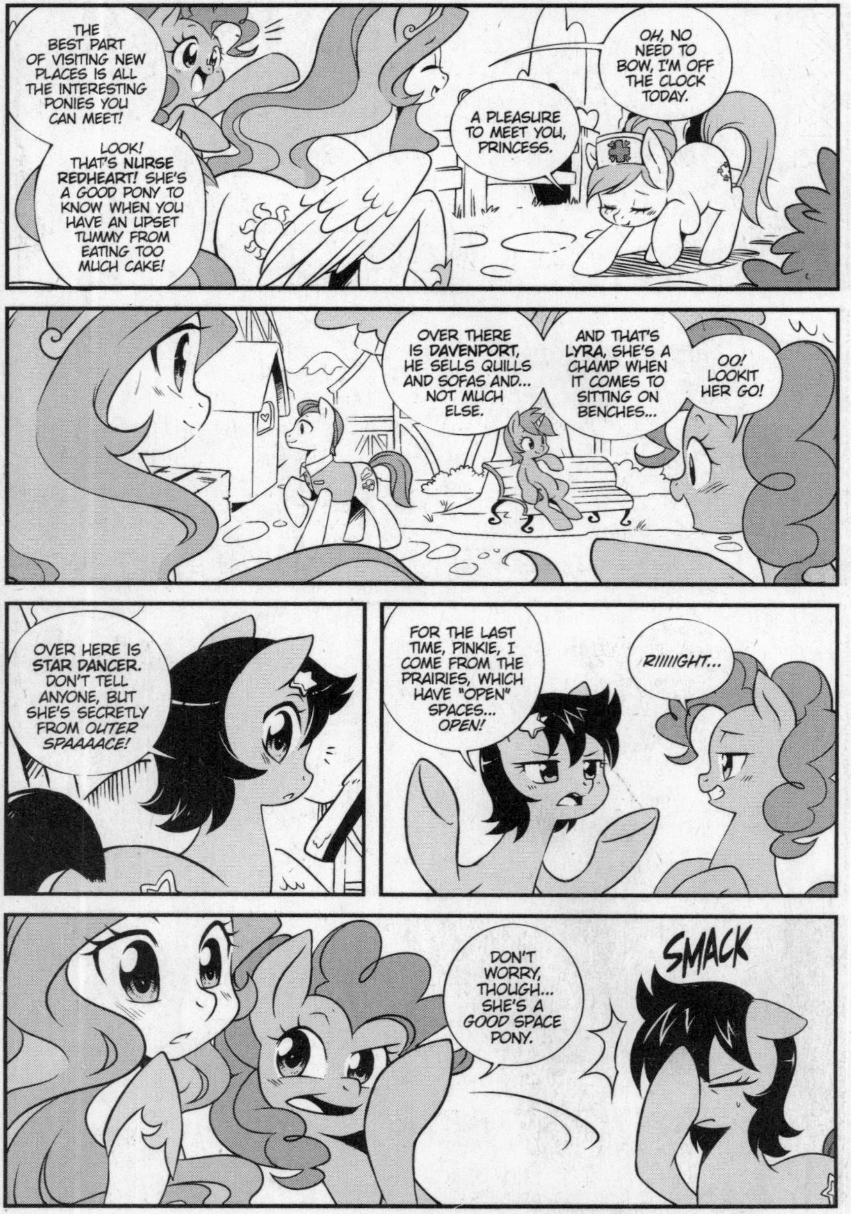
THE BEST PART OF VISITING NEW PLACES IS ALL THE INTERESTING PONIES YOU CAN MEET!
LOOK! THAT'S NURSE REDHEART! SHE'S A GOOD PONY TO KNOW WHEN YOU HAVE AN UPSET TUMMY FROM EATING TOO MUCH CAKE!
A PLEASURE TO MEET YOU, PRINCESS.
OH, NO NEED TO BOW, I'M OFF THE CLOCK TODAY.
OVER THERE IS DAVENPORT, HE SELLS QUILLS AND SOFAS AND... NOT MUCH ELSE.
AND THAT'S LYRA, SHE'S A CHAMP WHEN IT COMES TO SITTING ON BENCHES...
OO! LOOKIT HER GO!
OVER HERE IS STAR DANCER. DON'T TELL ANYONE, BUT SHE'S SECRETLY FROM OUTER SPAAAACE!
FOR THE LAST TIME, PINKIE, I COME FROM THE PRAIRIES, WHICH HAVE "OPEN" SPACES... OPEN!
RIIIIGHT...
DON'T WORRY, THOUGH... SHE'S A GOOD SPACE PONY.
SMACK

The Truth Is Out There

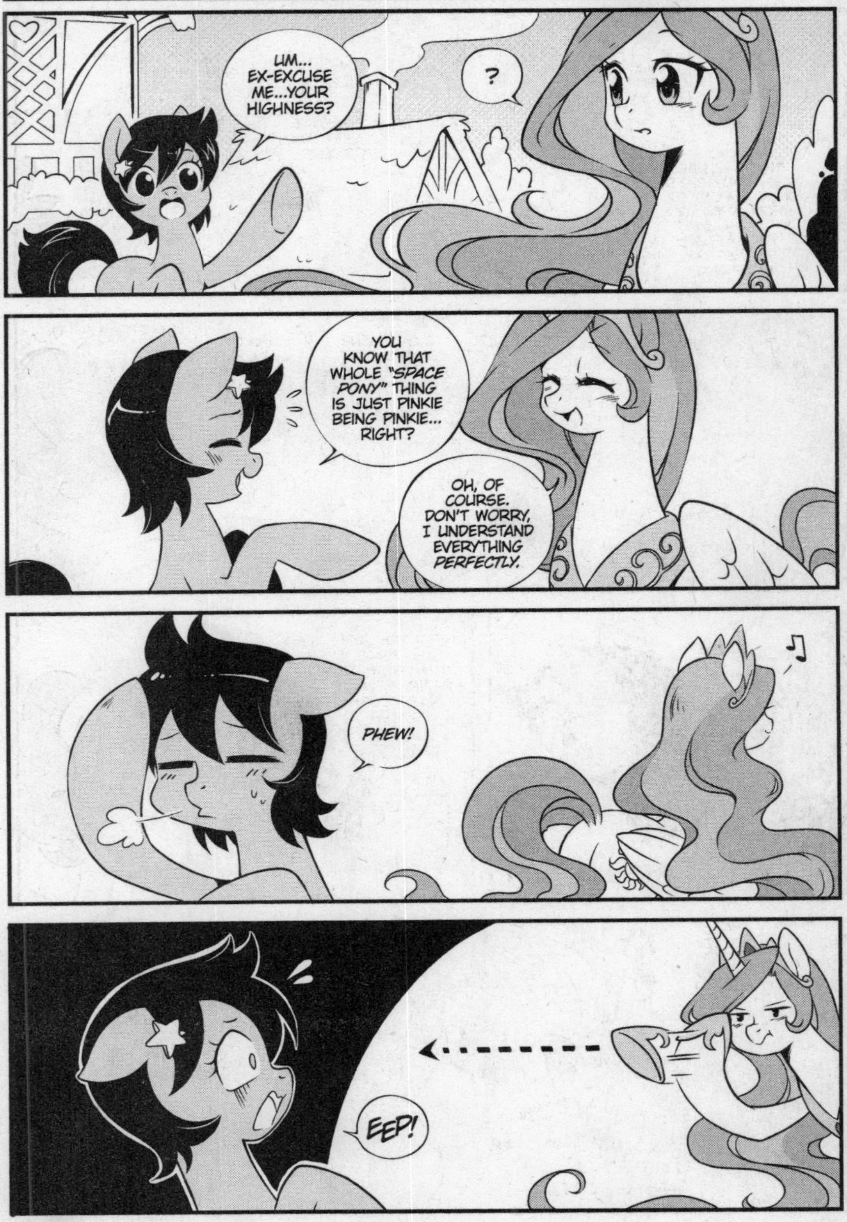
UM... EX-EXCUSE ME...YOUR HIGHNESS?
?
YOU KNOW THAT WHOLE "SPACE PONY" THING IS JUST PINKIE BEING PINKIE... RIGHT?
OH, OF COURSE. DON'T WORRY, I UNDERSTAND EVERYTHING PERFECTLY.
PHEW!
EEP!

Ponyville Theatre: Now with Air Conditioning

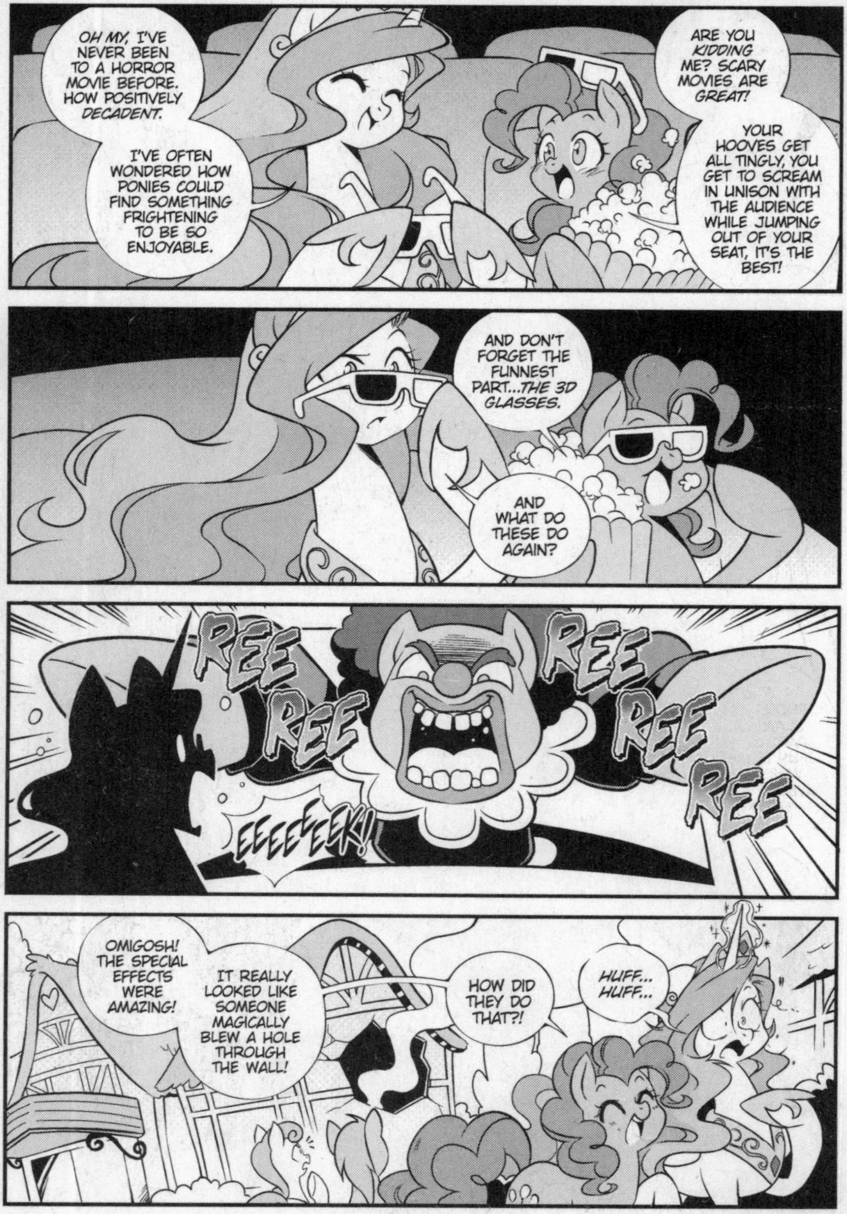
OH MY, I'VE NEVER BEEN TO A HORROR MOVIE BEFORE. HOW POSITIVELY DECADENT.
I'VE OFTEN WONDERED HOW PONIES COULD FIND SOMETHING FRIGHTENING TO BE SO ENJOYABLE.
ARE YOU KIDDING ME? SCARY MOVIES ARE GREAT!
YOUR HOOVES GET ALL TINGLY, YOU GET TO SCREAM IN UNISON WITH THE AUDIENCE WHILE JUMPING OUT OF YOUR SEAT, IT'S THE BEST!
AND DON'T FORGET THE FUNNEST PART...THE 3D GLASSES.
AND WHAT DO THESE DO AGAIN?
REE REE
REE REE REE
EEEEEEEK!
OMIGOSH! THE SPECIAL EFFECTS WERE AMAZING!
IT REALLY LOOKED LIKE SOMEONE MAGICALLY BLEW A HOLE THROUGH THE WALL!
HOW DID THEY DO THAT?!
HUFF... HUFF...

Gotta Catch 'Em All

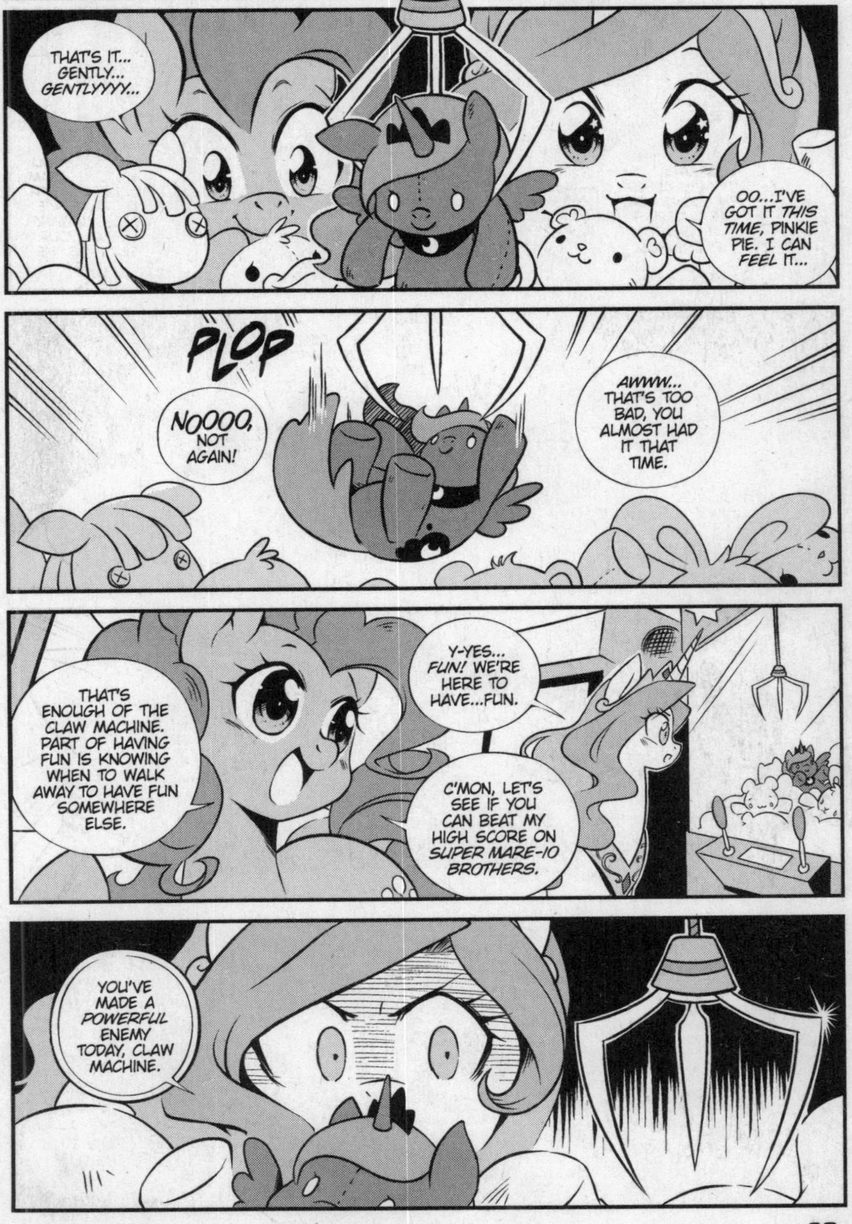

THAT'S IT... GENTLY... GENTLYYYY...
OO...I'VE GOT IT THIS TIME, PINKIE PIE. I CAN FEEL IT...
PLOP
NOOOO, NOT AGAIN!
AWWW... THAT'S TOO BAD, YOU ALMOST HAD IT THAT TIME.
THAT'S ENOUGH OF THE CLAW MACHINE. PART OF HAVING FUN IS KNOWING WHEN TO WALK AWAY TO HAVE FUN SOMEWHERE ELSE.
Y-YES... FUN! WE'RE HERE TO HAVE...FUN.
C'MON, LET'S SEE IF YOU CAN BEAT MY HIGH SCORE ON SUPER MARE-IO BROTHERS.
YOU'VE MADE A POWERFUL ENEMY TODAY, CLAW MACHINE.

Outta This World

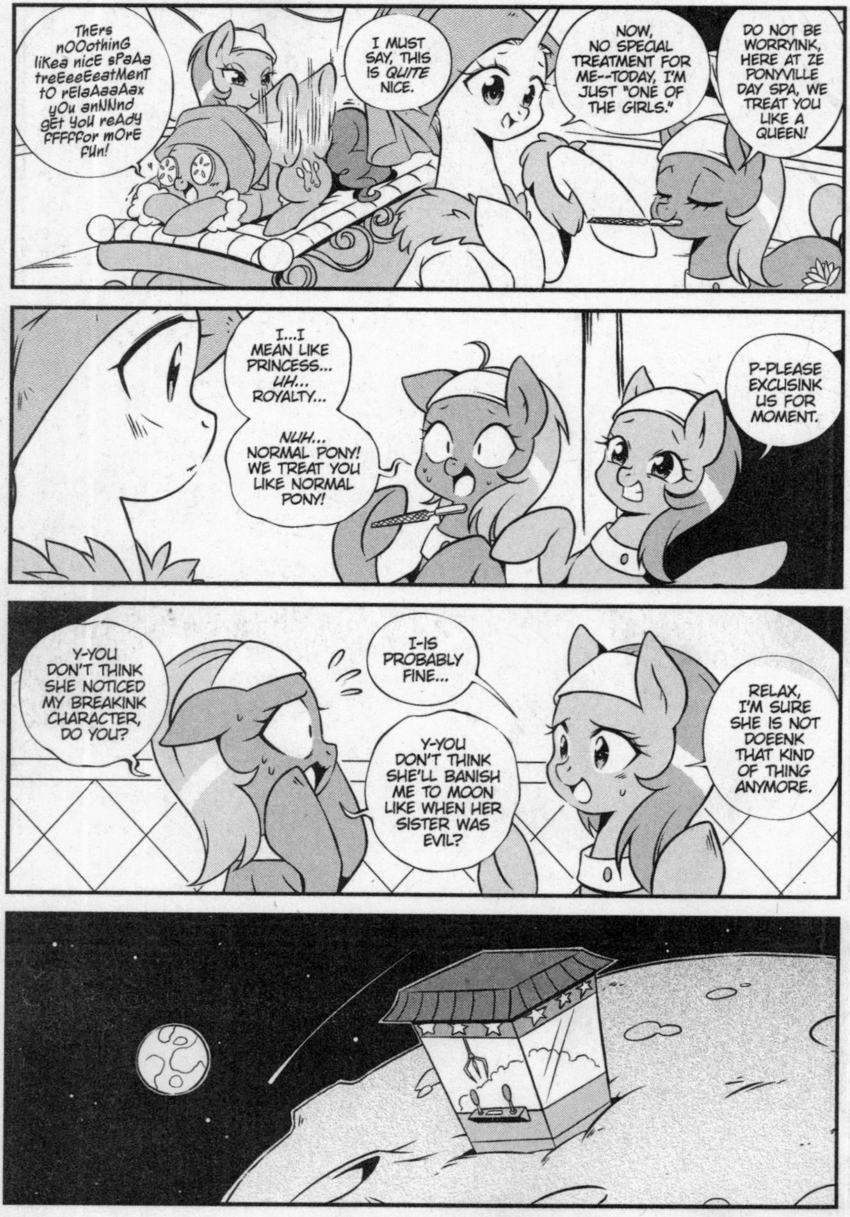

ThErs nOOothinG liKea nicE sPaAa treEeeEeatMenT tO rElaAaaAax yOu anNNNd get YoU reAdy fFFFFor mOrE fUn!
I MUST SAY, THIS IS *QUITE* NICE.
NOW, NO SPECIAL TREATMENT FOR ME--TODAY, I'M JUST "ONE OF THE GIRLS."
DO NOT BE WORRYINK, HERE AT ZE PONYVILLE DAY SPA, WE TREAT YOU LIKE A QUEEN!
I...I MEAN LIKE PRINCESS... *UH*... ROYALTY...
NUH... NORMAL PONY! WE TREAT YOU LIKE NORMAL PONY!
P-PLEASE EXCUSINK US FOR MOMENT.
Y-YOU DON'T THINK SHE NOTICED MY BREAKINK CHARACTER, DO YOU?
I-IS PROBABLY FINE...
Y-YOU DON'T THINK SHE'LL BANISH ME TO MOON LIKE WHEN HER SISTER WAS EVIL?
RELAX, I'M SURE SHE IS NOT DOEENK THAT KIND OF THING ANYMORE.

Sugar Rushed

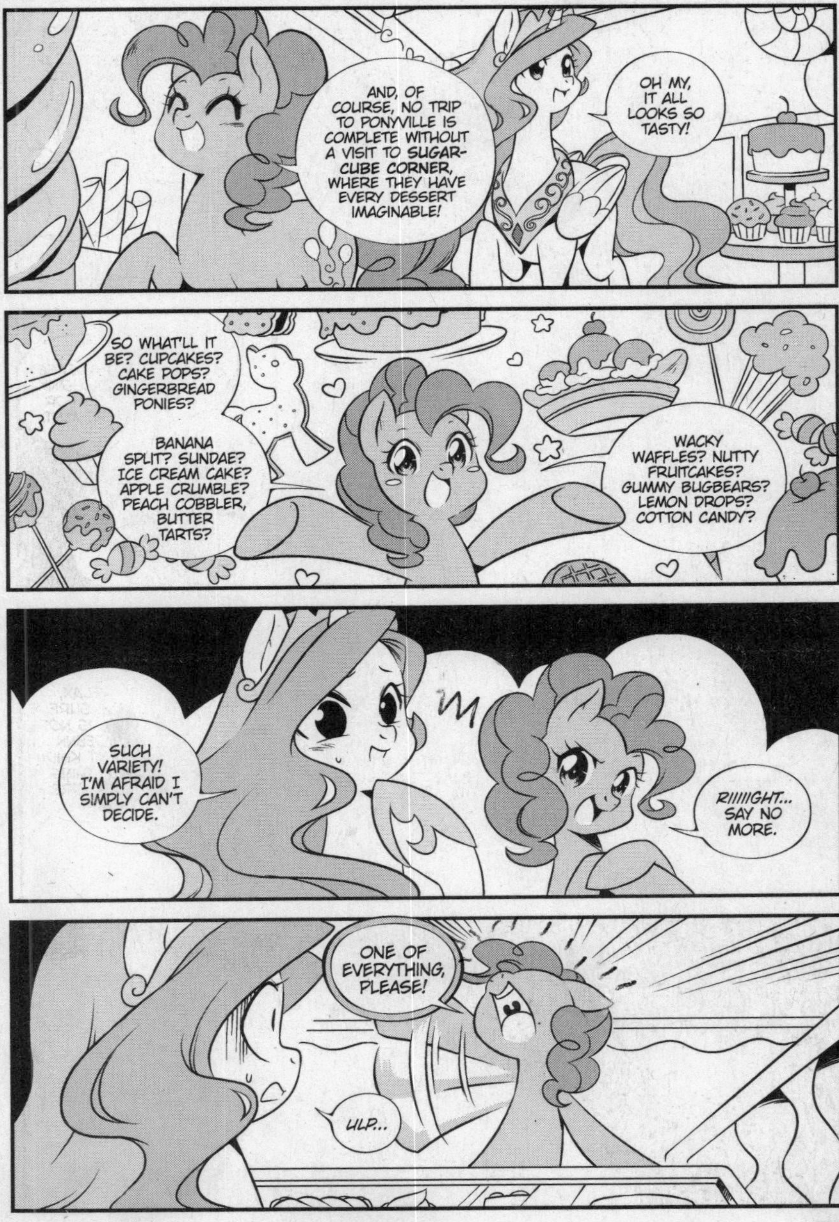

AND, OF COURSE, NO TRIP TO PONYVILLE IS COMPLETE WITHOUT A VISIT TO SUGAR-CUBE CORNER, WHERE THEY HAVE EVERY DESSERT IMAGINABLE!
OH MY, IT ALL LOOKS SO TASTY!
SO WHAT'LL IT BE? CUPCAKES? CAKE POPS? GINGERBREAD PONIES?
BANANA SPLIT? SUNDAE? ICE CREAM CAKE? APPLE CRUMBLE? PEACH COBBLER, BUTTER TARTS?
WACKY WAFFLES? NUTTY FRUITCAKES? GUMMY BUGBEARS? LEMON DROPS? COTTON CANDY?
SUCH VARIETY! I'M AFRAID I SIMPLY CAN'T DECIDE.
RIIIIIGHT... SAY NO MORE.
ONE OF EVERYTHING, PLEASE!
ULP...

It Was Right in Front of You the Entire Time

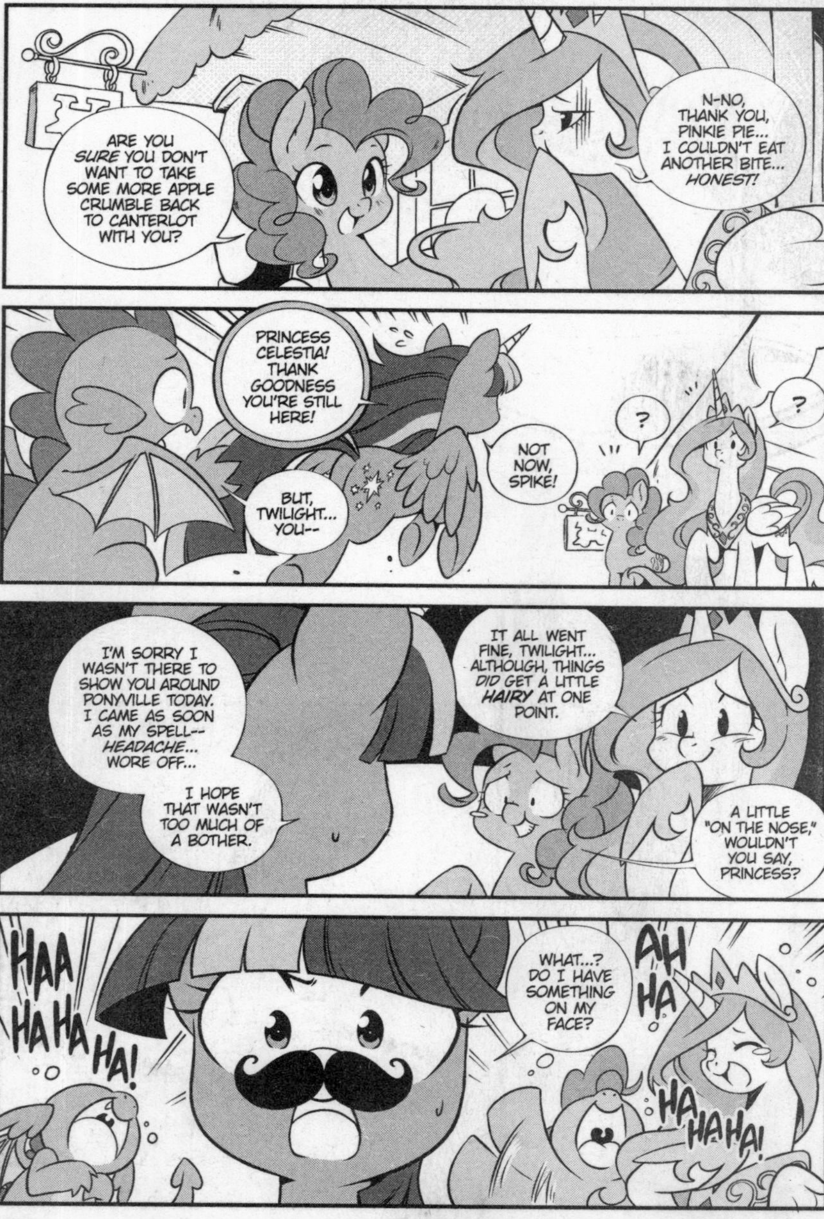
ARE YOU *SURE* YOU DON'T WANT TO TAKE SOME MORE APPLE CRUMBLE BACK TO CANTERLOT WITH YOU?
N-NO, THANK YOU, PINKIE PIE... I COULDN'T EAT ANOTHER BITE... *HONEST!*
PRINCESS CELESTIA! THANK GOODNESS YOU'RE STILL HERE!
BUT, TWILIGHT... YOU--
NOT NOW, SPIKE!
?
?
I'M SORRY I WASN'T THERE TO SHOW YOU AROUND PONYVILLE TODAY. I CAME AS SOON AS MY SPELL-- *HEADACHE*... WORE OFF...
I HOPE THAT WASN'T TOO MUCH OF A BOTHER.
IT ALL WENT FINE, TWILIGHT... ALTHOUGH, THINGS *DID* GET A LITTLE ***HAIRY*** AT ONE POINT.
A LITTLE "ON THE NOSE," WOULDN'T YOU SAY, PRINCESS?
HAA HA HA HA!
WHAT...? DO I HAVE SOMETHING ON MY FACE?
AH HA
HA HA HA!

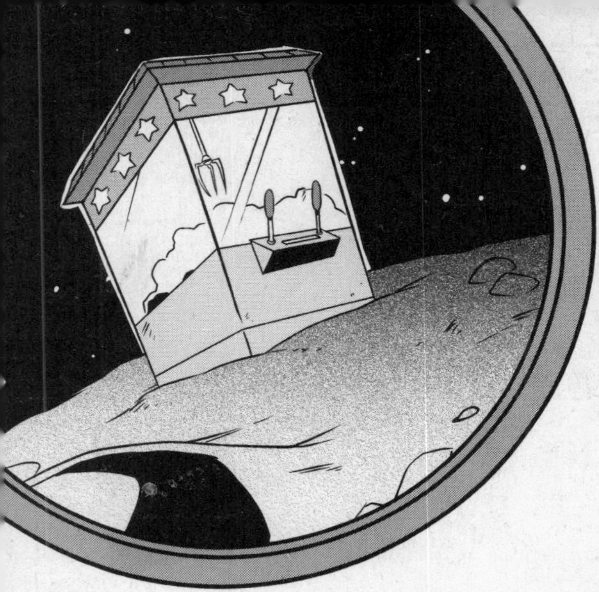

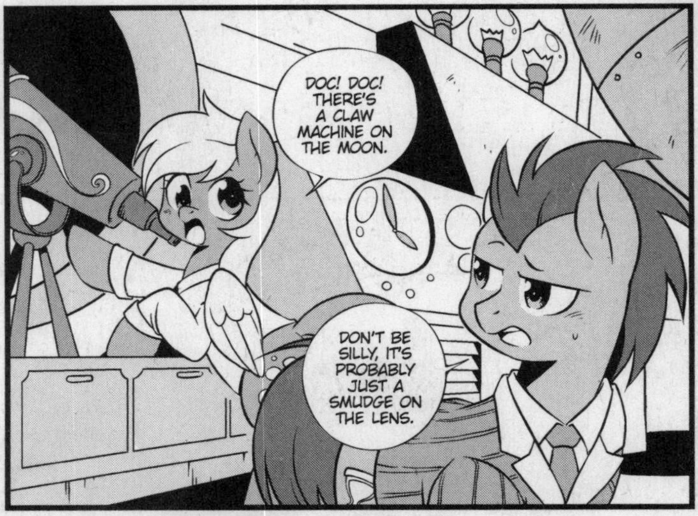
DOC! DOC! THERE'S A CLAW MACHINE ON THE MOON.
DON'T BE SILLY, IT'S PROBABLY JUST A SMUDGE ON THE LENS.

CHAPTER 3

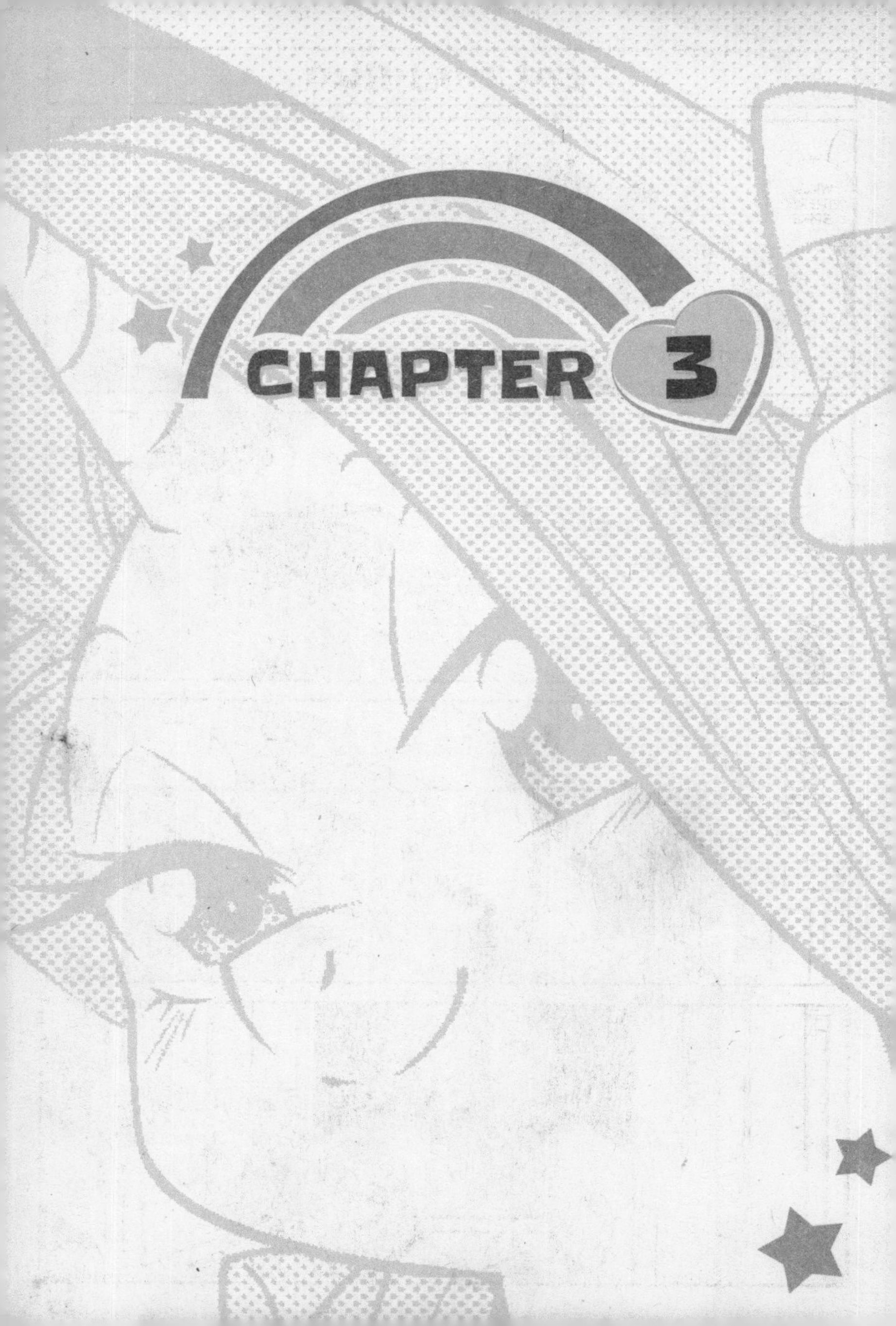

Eat and Run

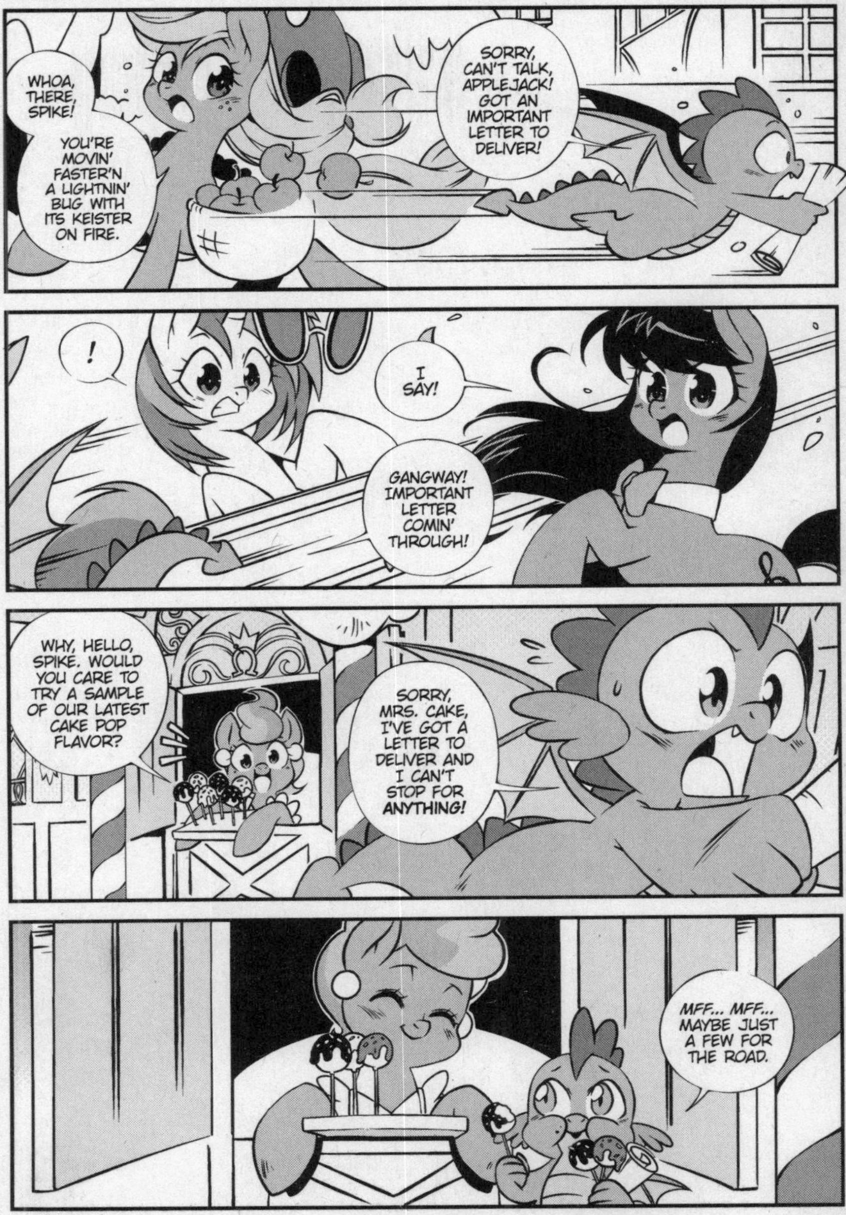
WHOA, THERE, SPIKE!
YOU'RE MOVIN' FASTER'N A LIGHTNIN' BUG WITH ITS KEISTER ON FIRE.
SORRY, CAN'T TALK, APPLEJACK! GOT AN IMPORTANT LETTER TO DELIVER!
!
I SAY!
GANGWAY! IMPORTANT LETTER COMIN' THROUGH!
WHY, HELLO, SPIKE. WOULD YOU CARE TO TRY A SAMPLE OF OUR LATEST CAKE POP FLAVOR?
SORRY, MRS. CAKE, I'VE GOT A LETTER TO DELIVER AND I CAN'T STOP FOR ANYTHING!
MFF... MFF... MAYBE JUST A FEW FOR THE ROAD.

Fashion Self-Conscious

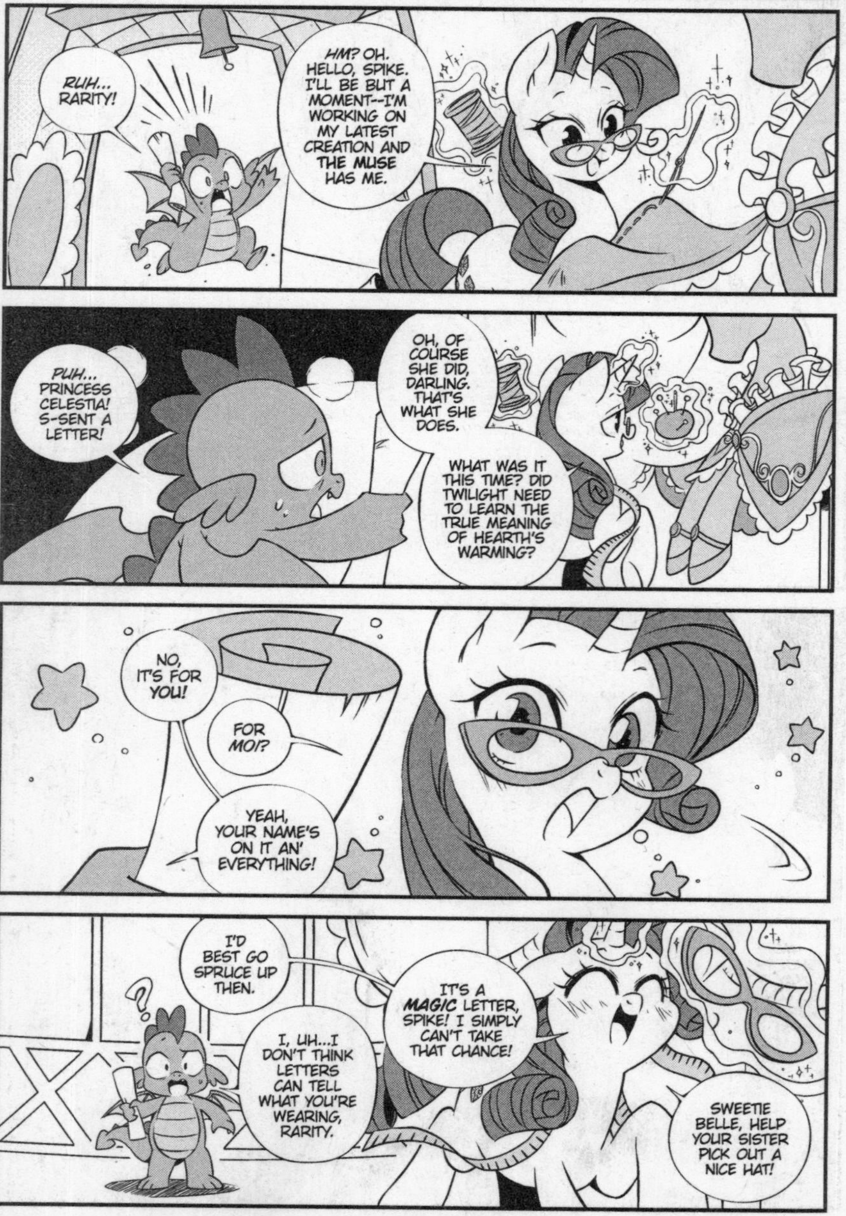
RUH... RARITY!
HM? OH. HELLO, SPIKE. I'LL BE BUT A MOMENT--I'M WORKING ON MY LATEST CREATION AND THE MUSE HAS ME.
PUH... PRINCESS CELESTIA! S-SENT A LETTER!
OH, OF COURSE SHE DID, DARLING. THAT'S WHAT SHE DOES.
WHAT WAS IT THIS TIME? DID TWILIGHT NEED TO LEARN THE TRUE MEANING OF HEARTH'S WARMING?
NO, IT'S FOR YOU!
FOR MOI?
YEAH, YOUR NAME'S ON IT AN' EVERYTHING!
I'D BEST GO SPRUCE UP THEN.
I, UH...I DON'T THINK LETTERS CAN TELL WHAT YOU'RE WEARING, RARITY.
IT'S A MAGIC LETTER, SPIKE! I SIMPLY CAN'T TAKE THAT CHANCE!
SWEETIE BELLE, HELP YOUR SISTER PICK OUT A NICE HAT!

Fancy Letter Readin'

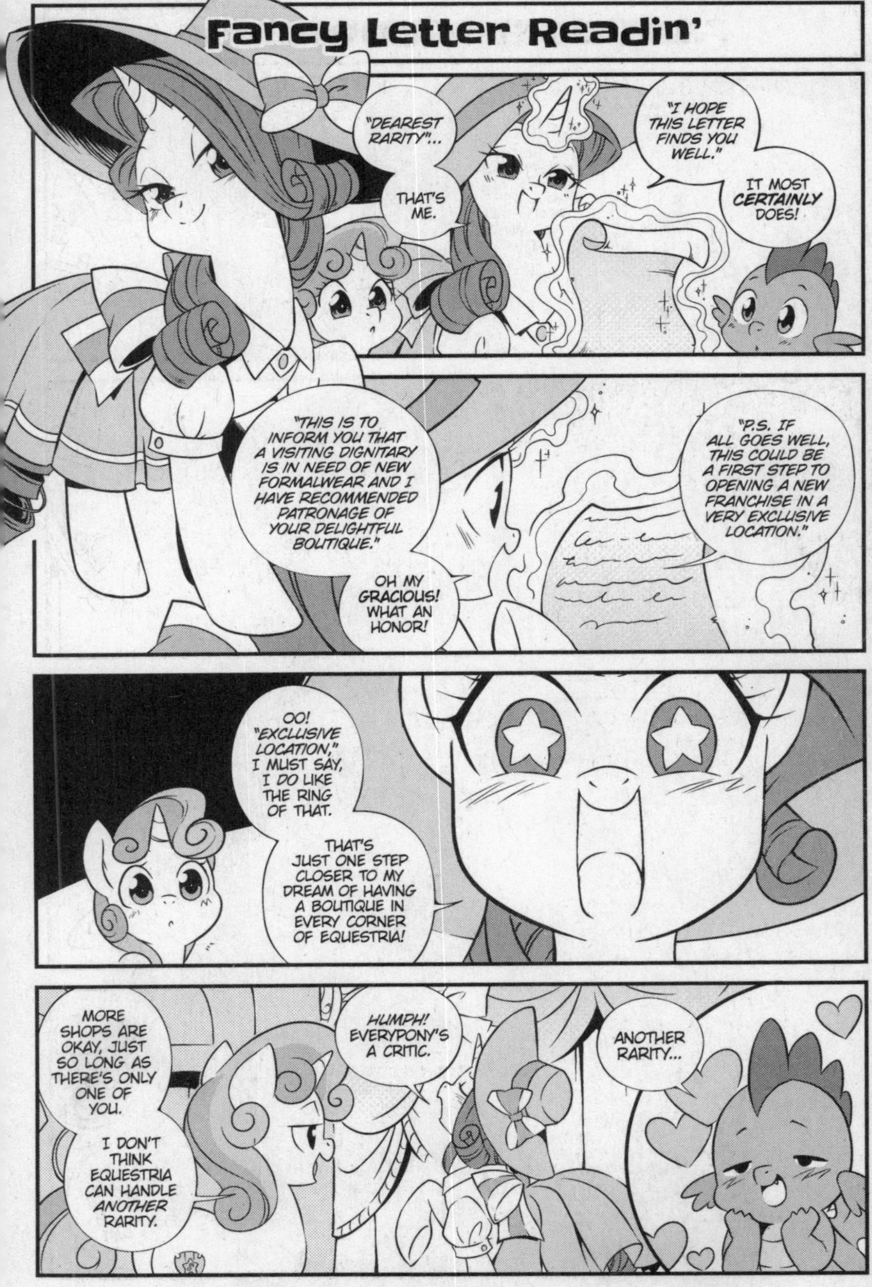
"DEAREST RARITY"...
THAT'S ME.
"I HOPE THIS LETTER FINDS YOU WELL."
IT MOST CERTAINLY DOES!
"THIS IS TO INFORM YOU THAT A VISITING DIGNITARY IS IN NEED OF NEW FORMALWEAR AND I HAVE RECOMMENDED PATRONAGE OF YOUR DELIGHTFUL BOUTIQUE."
OH MY GRACIOUS! WHAT AN HONOR!
"P.S. IF ALL GOES WELL, THIS COULD BE A FIRST STEP TO OPENING A NEW FRANCHISE IN A VERY EXCLUSIVE LOCATION."
OO! "EXCLUSIVE LOCATION," I MUST SAY, I DO LIKE THE RING OF THAT.
THAT'S JUST ONE STEP CLOSER TO MY DREAM OF HAVING A BOUTIQUE IN EVERY CORNER OF EQUESTRIA!
MORE SHOPS ARE OKAY, JUST SO LONG AS THERE'S ONLY ONE OF YOU.
I DON'T THINK EQUESTRIA CAN HANDLE ANOTHER RARITY.
HUMPH! EVERYPONY'S A CRITIC.
ANOTHER RARITY...

A Spike in Housework

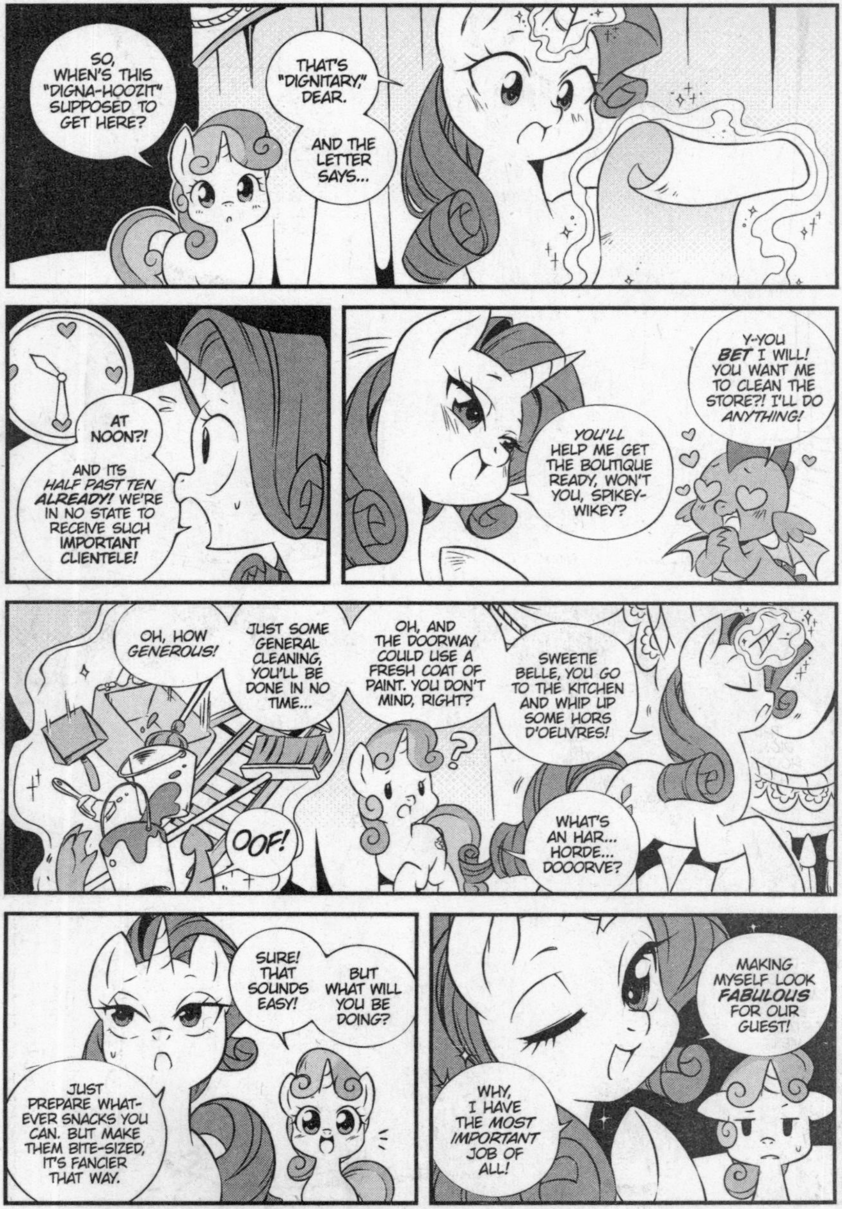
SO, WHEN'S THIS "DIGNA-HOOZIT" SUPPOSED TO GET HERE?
THAT'S "DIGNITARY," DEAR.
AND THE LETTER SAYS...
AT NOON?!
AND ITS *HALF PAST TEN ALREADY!* WE'RE IN NO STATE TO RECEIVE SUCH IMPORTANT CLIENTELE!
YOU'LL HELP ME GET THE BOUTIQUE READY, WON'T YOU, SPIKEY-WIKEY?
Y-YOU ***BET*** I WILL! YOU WANT ME TO CLEAN THE STORE?! I'LL DO *ANYTHING!*
OH, HOW *GENEROUS!*
JUST SOME GENERAL CLEANING, YOU'LL BE DONE IN NO TIME...
OH, AND THE DOORWAY COULD USE A FRESH COAT OF PAINT. YOU DON'T MIND, RIGHT?
SWEETIE BELLE, YOU GO TO THE KITCHEN AND WHIP UP SOME HORS D'OEUVRES!
OOF!
WHAT'S AN HAR... HORDE... DOOORVE?
JUST PREPARE WHAT-EVER SNACKS YOU CAN. BUT MAKE THEM BITE-SIZED, IT'S FANCIER THAT WAY.
SURE! THAT SOUNDS EASY!
BUT WHAT WILL YOU BE DOING?
WHY, I HAVE THE *MOST IMPORTANT* JOB OF ALL!
MAKING MYSELF LOOK ***FABULOUS*** FOR OUR GUEST!

I Can Never Read This Guy

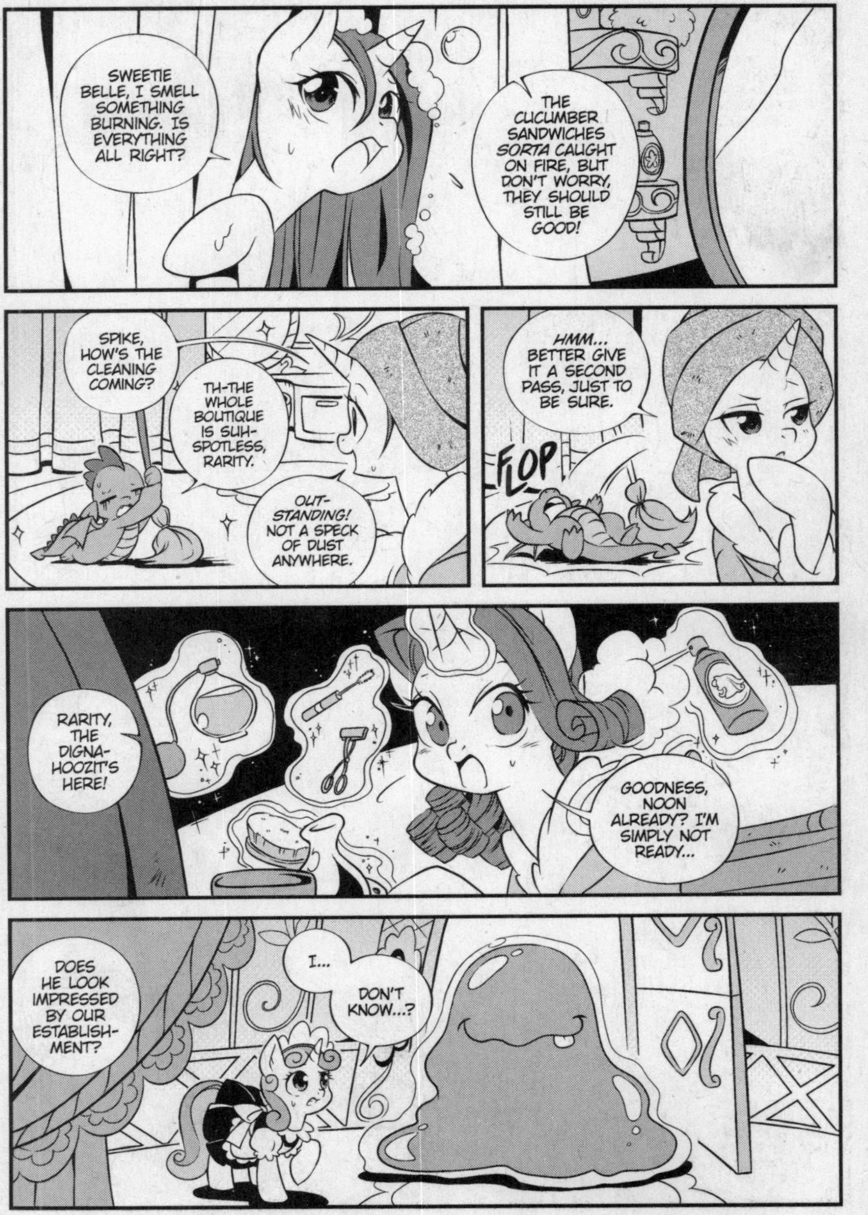
SWEETIE BELLE, I SMELL SOMETHING BURNING. IS EVERYTHING ALL RIGHT?
THE CUCUMBER SANDWICHES *SORTA* CAUGHT ON FIRE, BUT DON'T WORRY, THEY SHOULD STILL BE GOOD!
SPIKE, HOW'S THE CLEANING COMING?
TH-THE WHOLE BOUTIQUE IS SUH-SPOTLESS, RARITY.
OUT-STANDING! NOT A SPECK OF DUST ANYWHERE.
HMM... BETTER GIVE IT A SECOND PASS, JUST TO BE SURE.
FLOP
RARITY, THE DIGNA-HOOZIT'S HERE!
GOODNESS, NOON ALREADY? I'M SIMPLY NOT READY...
DOES HE LOOK IMPRESSED BY OUR ESTABLISH-MENT?
I...
DON'T KNOW...?

One Slimy Customer

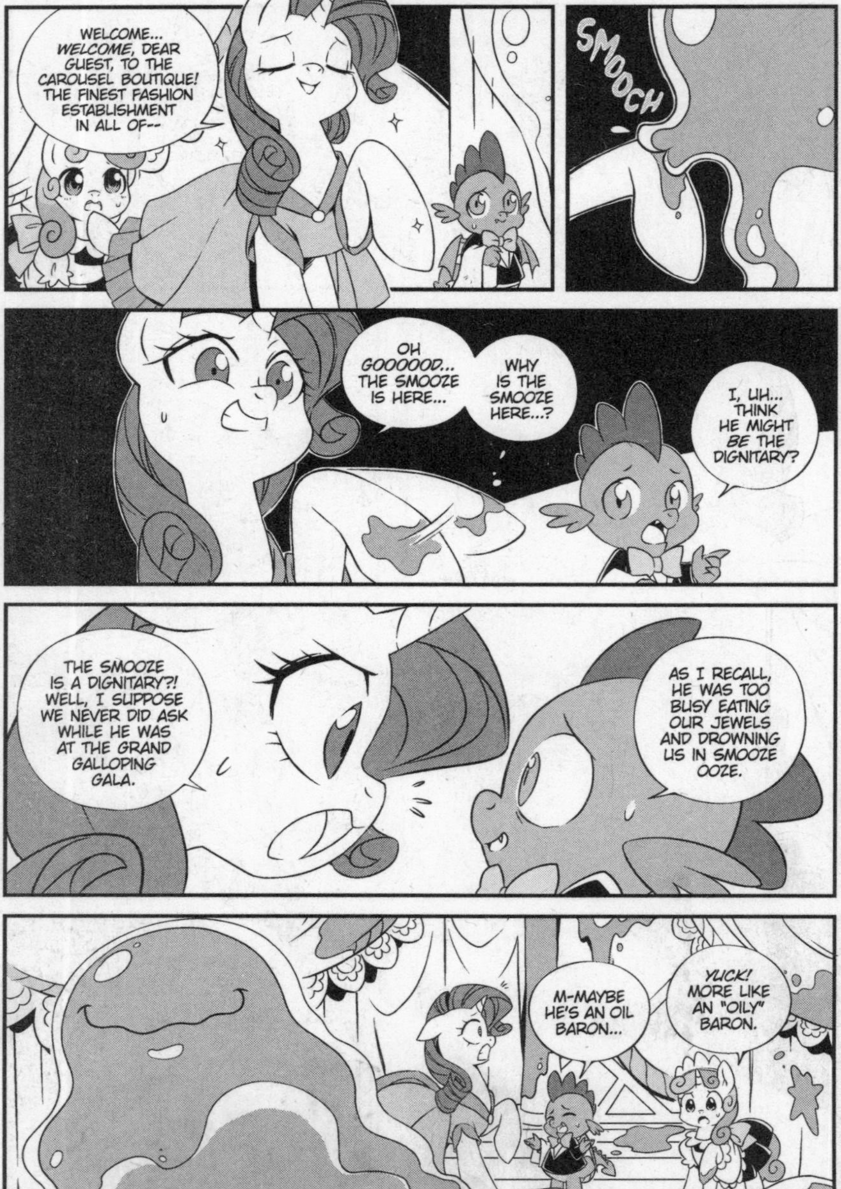
WELCOME... *WELCOME*, DEAR GUEST, TO THE CAROUSEL BOUTIQUE! THE FINEST FASHION ESTABLISHMENT IN ALL OF--
SMOOCH
OH *GOOOOOD*... THE SMOOZE IS HERE...
WHY IS THE SMOOZE HERE...?
I, UH... THINK HE MIGHT *BE* THE DIGNITARY?
THE SMOOZE IS A DIGNITARY?! WELL, I SUPPOSE WE NEVER DID ASK WHILE HE WAS AT THE GRAND GALLOPING GALA.
AS I RECALL, HE WAS TOO BUSY EATING OUR JEWELS AND DROWNING US IN SMOOZE OOZE.
M-MAYBE HE'S AN OIL BARON...
YUCK! MORE LIKE AN "OILY" BARON.

Sticky Situation

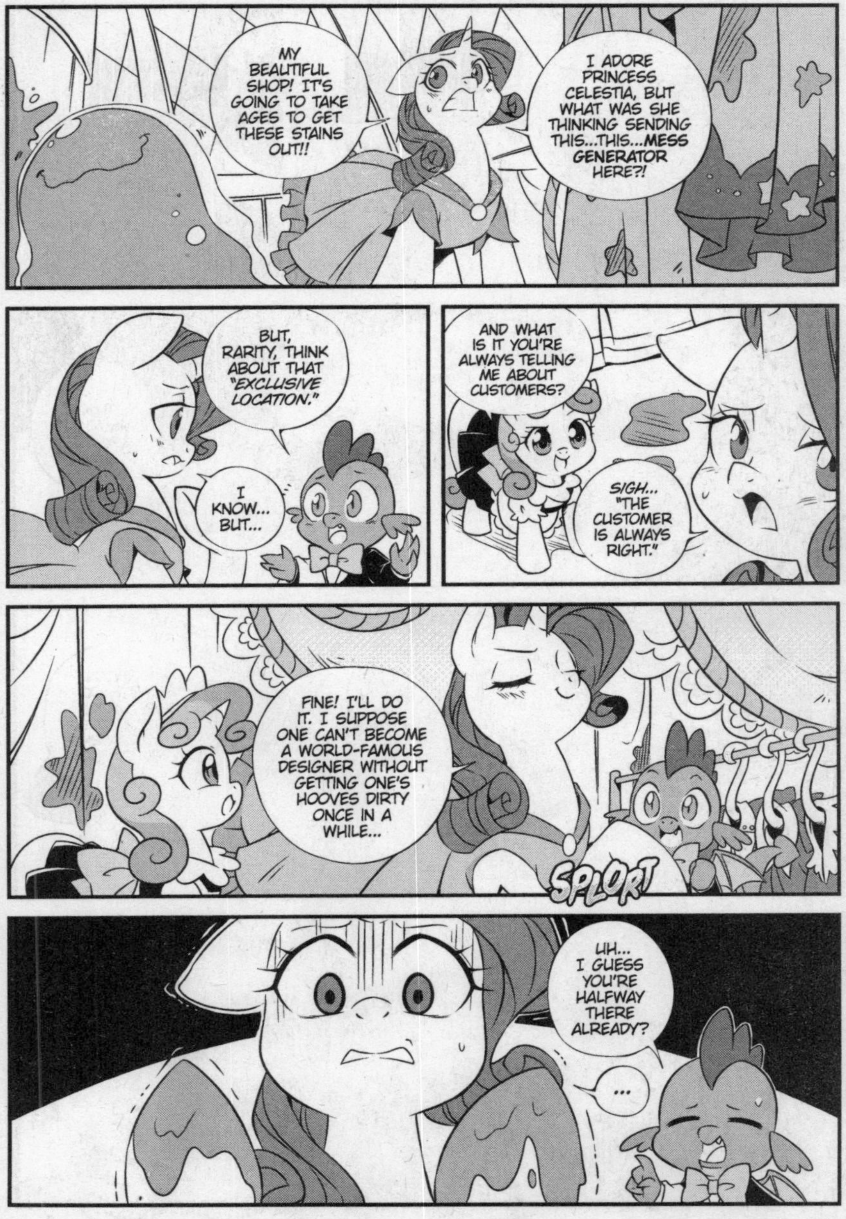

MY BEAUTIFUL SHOP! IT'S GOING TO TAKE AGES TO GET THESE STAINS OUT!!
I ADORE PRINCESS CELESTIA, BUT WHAT WAS SHE THINKING SENDING THIS...THIS...MESS GENERATOR HERE?!
BUT, RARITY, THINK ABOUT THAT "EXCLUSIVE LOCATION."
I KNOW... BUT...
AND WHAT IS IT YOU'RE ALWAYS TELLING ME ABOUT CUSTOMERS?
SIGH... "THE CUSTOMER IS ALWAYS RIGHT."
FINE! I'LL DO IT. I SUPPOSE ONE CAN'T BECOME A WORLD-FAMOUS DESIGNER WITHOUT GETTING ONE'S HOOVES DIRTY ONCE IN A WHILE...
SPLORT
UH... I GUESS YOU'RE HALFWAY THERE ALREADY?
...

He's a Growing Blob

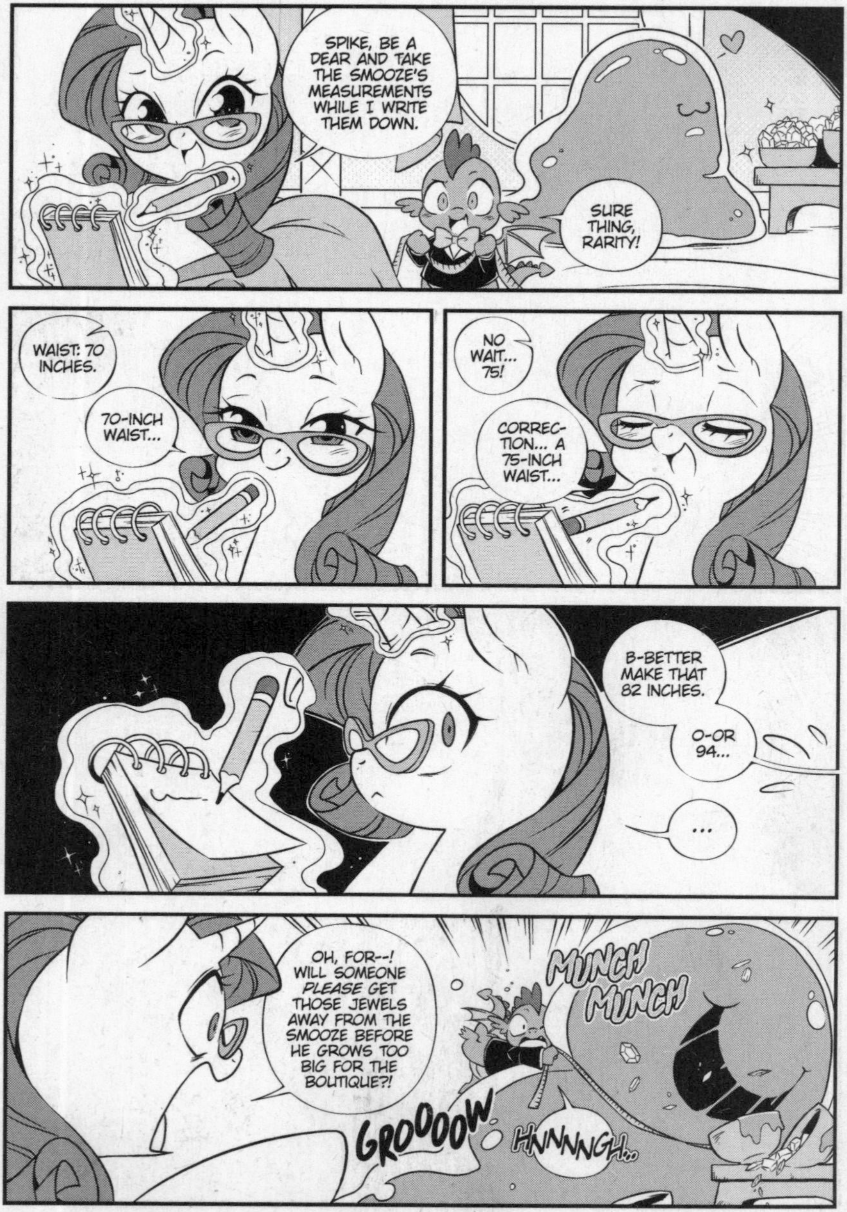
SPIKE, BE A DEAR AND TAKE THE SMOOZE'S MEASUREMENTS WHILE I WRITE THEM DOWN.
SURE THING, RARITY!
WAIST: 70 INCHES.
70-INCH WAIST...
NO WAIT... 75!
CORRECTION... A 75-INCH WAIST...
B-BETTER MAKE THAT 82 INCHES.
O-OR 94...
...
OH, FOR--! WILL SOMEONE *PLEASE* GET THOSE JEWELS AWAY FROM THE SMOOZE BEFORE HE GROWS TOO BIG FOR THE BOUTIQUE?!
MUNCH MUNCH
GROOOOW
HNNNNGH...

In Your Face!

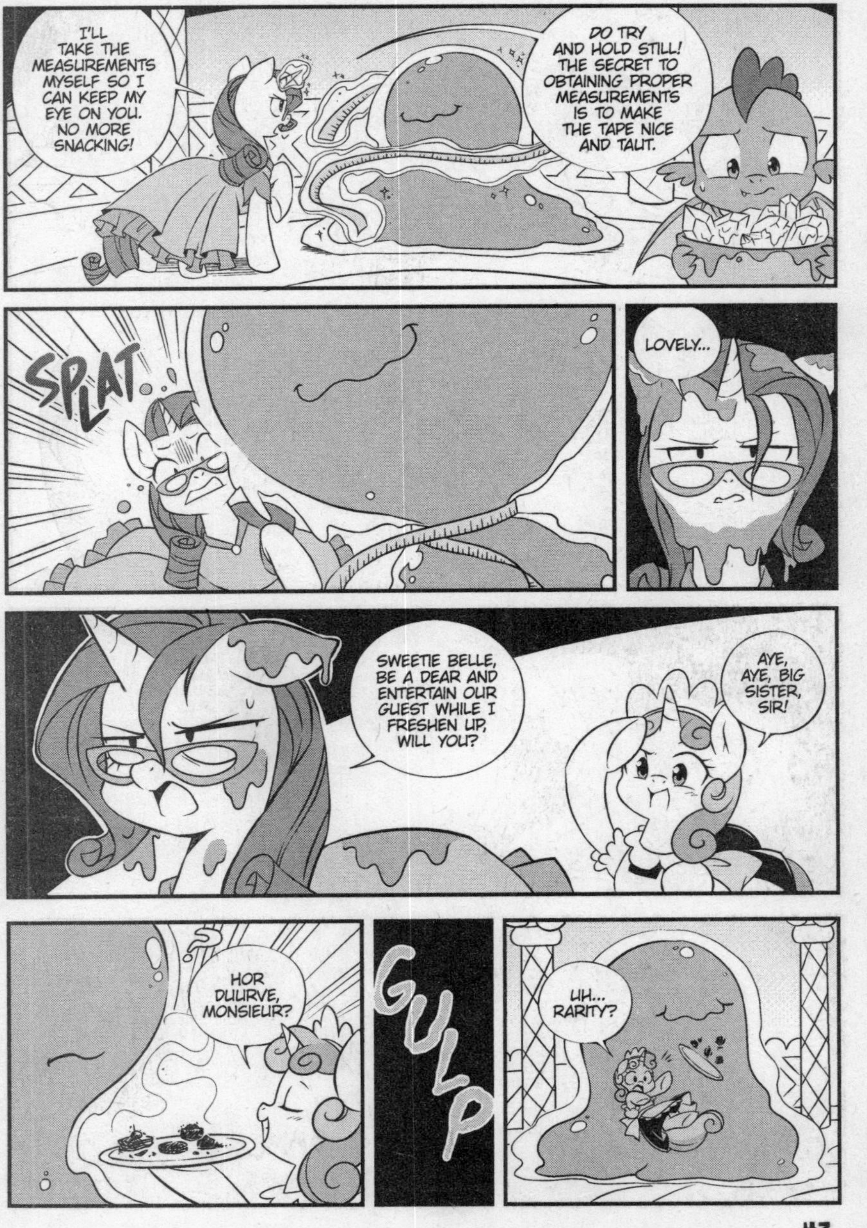
I'LL TAKE THE MEASUREMENTS MYSELF SO I CAN KEEP MY EYE ON YOU. NO MORE SNACKING!
DO TRY AND HOLD STILL! THE SECRET TO OBTAINING PROPER MEASUREMENTS IS TO MAKE THE TAPE NICE AND TAUT.
SPLAT
LOVELY...
SWEETIE BELLE, BE A DEAR AND ENTERTAIN OUR GUEST WHILE I FRESHEN UP, WILL YOU?
AYE, AYE, BIG SISTER, SIR!
HOR DUURVE, MONSIEUR?
GULP
UH... RARITY?

That Sinking Feeling

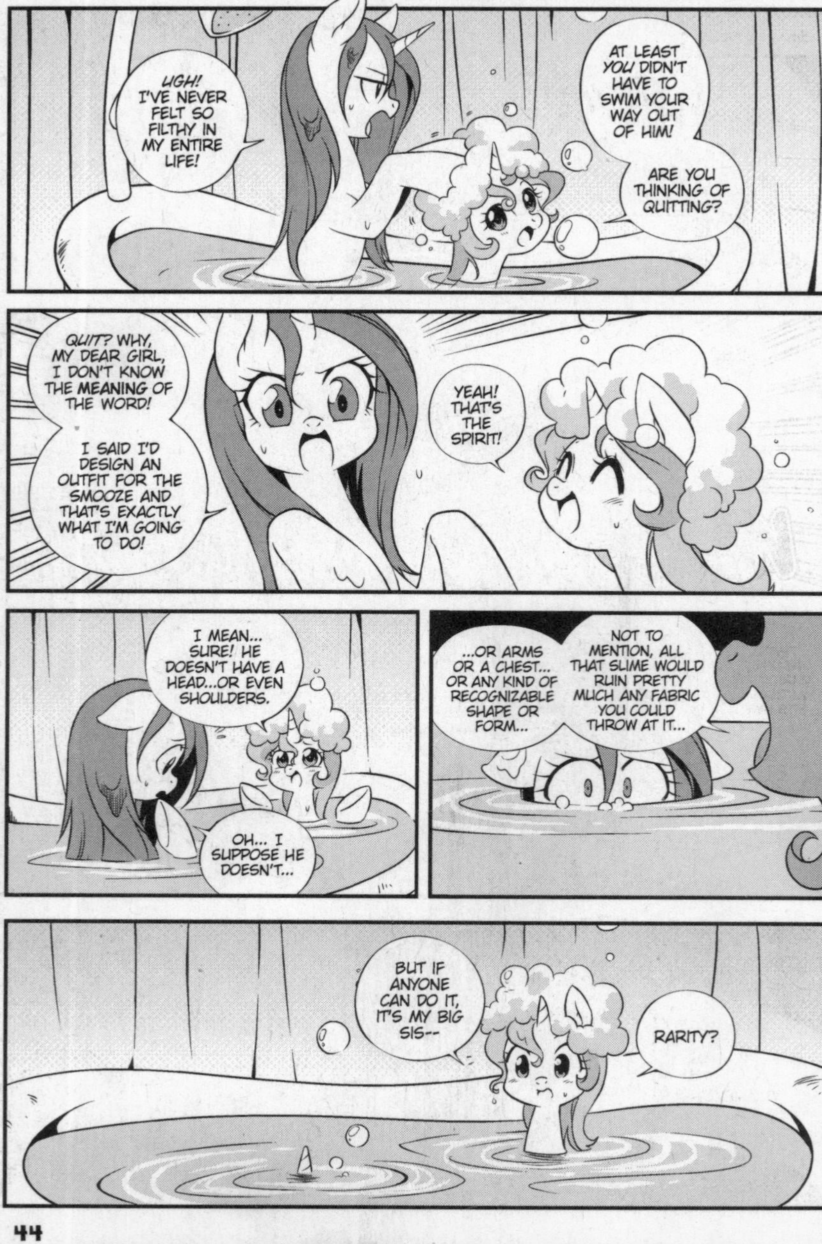
UGH! I'VE NEVER FELT SO FILTHY IN MY ENTIRE LIFE!
AT LEAST YOU DIDN'T HAVE TO SWIM YOUR WAY OUT OF HIM!
ARE YOU THINKING OF QUITTING?
QUIT? WHY, MY DEAR GIRL, I DON'T KNOW THE MEANING OF THE WORD!
I SAID I'D DESIGN AN OUTFIT FOR THE SMOOZE AND THAT'S EXACTLY WHAT I'M GOING TO DO!
YEAH! THAT'S THE SPIRIT!
I MEAN... SURE! HE DOESN'T HAVE A HEAD...OR EVEN SHOULDERS.
OH... I SUPPOSE HE DOESN'T...
...OR ARMS OR A CHEST... OR ANY KIND OF RECOGNIZABLE SHAPE OR FORM...
NOT TO MENTION, ALL THAT SLIME WOULD RUIN PRETTY MUCH ANY FABRIC YOU COULD THROW AT IT...
BUT IF ANYONE CAN DO IT, IT'S MY BIG SIS--
RARITY?

Belle of the Blob

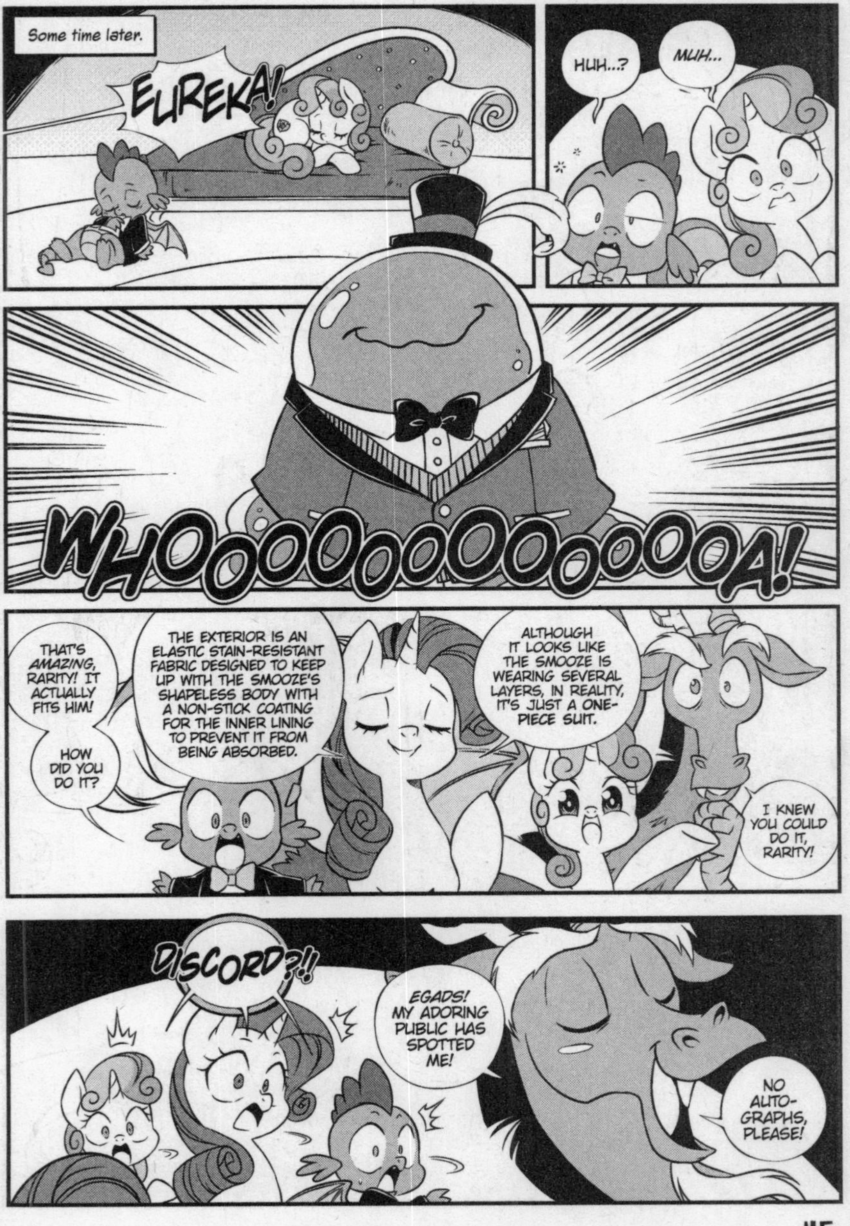

Some time later.
EUREKA!
HUH...?
MUH...
WHOOOOOOOOOOOOOOA!
THAT'S *AMAZING*, RARITY! IT ACTUALLY FITS HIM!
HOW DID YOU DO IT?
THE EXTERIOR IS AN ELASTIC STAIN-RESISTANT FABRIC DESIGNED TO KEEP UP WITH THE SMOOZE'S SHAPELESS BODY WITH A NON-STICK COATING FOR THE INNER LINING TO PREVENT IT FROM BEING ABSORBED.
ALTHOUGH IT LOOKS LIKE THE SMOOZE IS WEARING SEVERAL LAYERS, IN REALITY, IT'S JUST A ONE-PIECE SUIT.
I KNEW YOU COULD DO IT, RARITY!
DISCORD?!!
EGADS! MY ADORING PUBLIC HAS SPOTTED ME!
NO AUTO-GRAPHS, PLEASE!

Be Careful What You Wish For...

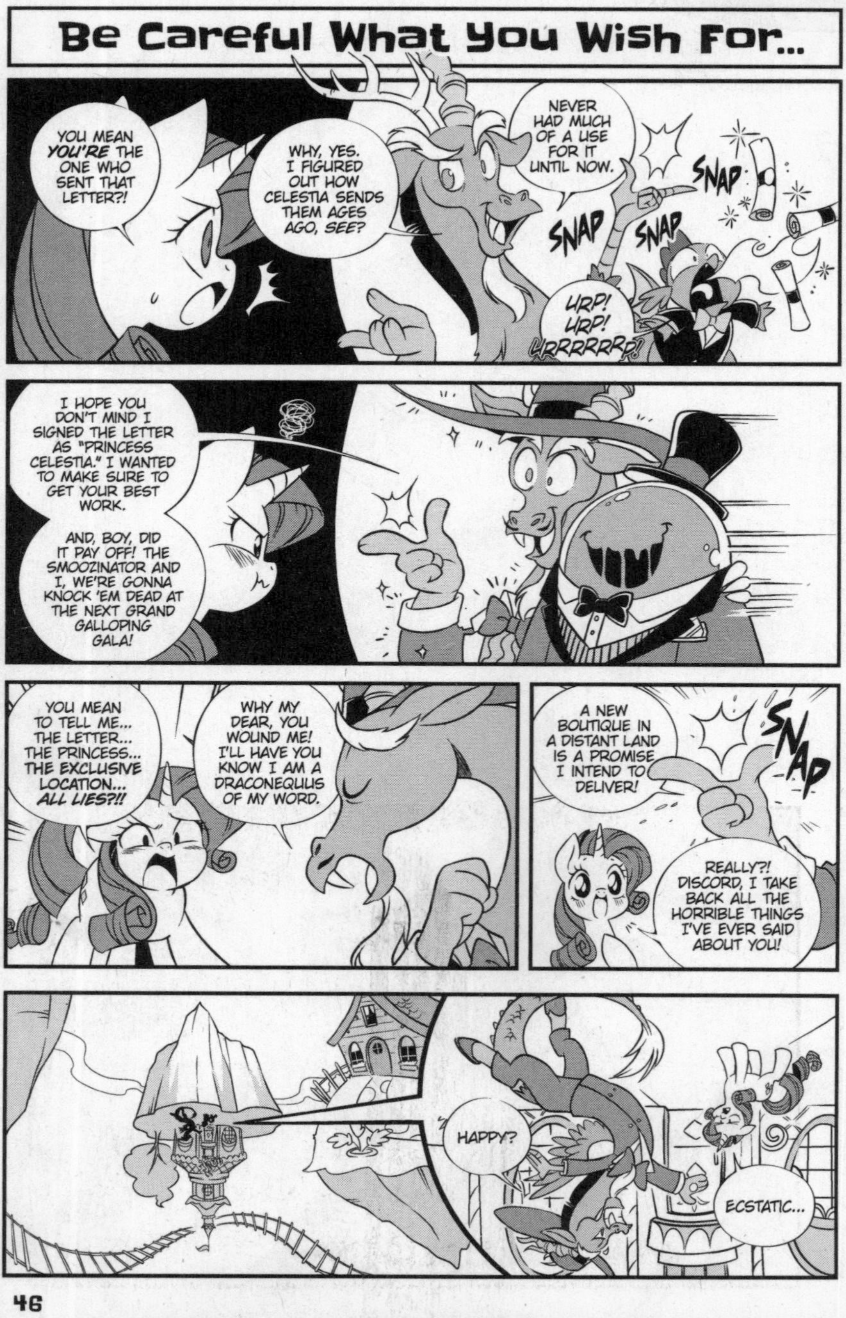
YOU MEAN YOU'RE THE ONE WHO SENT THAT LETTER?!
WHY, YES. I FIGURED OUT HOW CELESTIA SENDS THEM AGES AGO, SEE?
NEVER HAD MUCH OF A USE FOR IT UNTIL NOW.
SNAP
SNAP
SNAP
URP! URP! URRRRRRP!
I HOPE YOU DON'T MIND I SIGNED THE LETTER AS "PRINCESS CELESTIA." I WANTED TO MAKE SURE TO GET YOUR BEST WORK.
AND, BOY, DID IT PAY OFF! THE SMOOZINATOR AND I, WE'RE GONNA KNOCK 'EM DEAD AT THE NEXT GRAND GALLOPING GALA!
YOU MEAN TO TELL ME... THE LETTER... THE PRINCESS... THE EXCLUSIVE LOCATION... ALL LIES?!!
WHY MY DEAR, YOU WOUND ME! I'LL HAVE YOU KNOW I AM A DRACONEQUUS OF MY WORD.
A NEW BOUTIQUE IN A DISTANT LAND IS A PROMISE I INTEND TO DELIVER!
SNAP
REALLY?! DISCORD, I TAKE BACK ALL THE HORRIBLE THINGS I'VE EVER SAID ABOUT YOU!
HAPPY?
ECSTATIC...

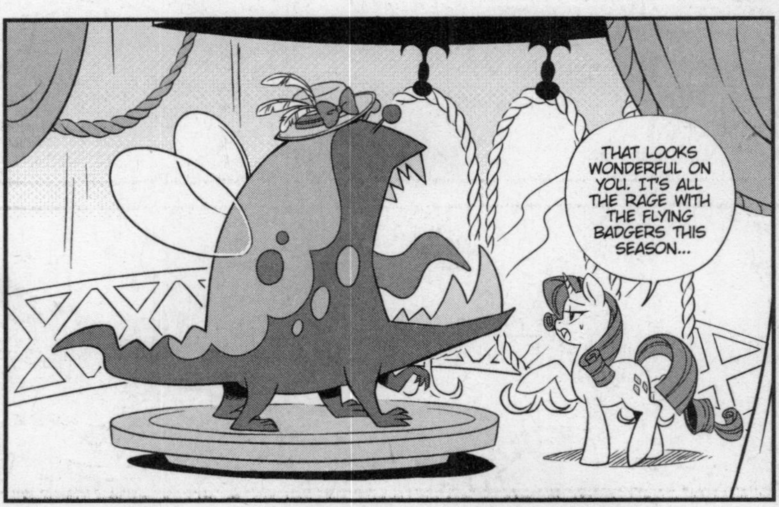
THAT LOOKS WONDERFUL ON YOU. IT'S ALL THE RAGE WITH THE FLYING BADGERS THIS SEASON...

CHAPTER 4

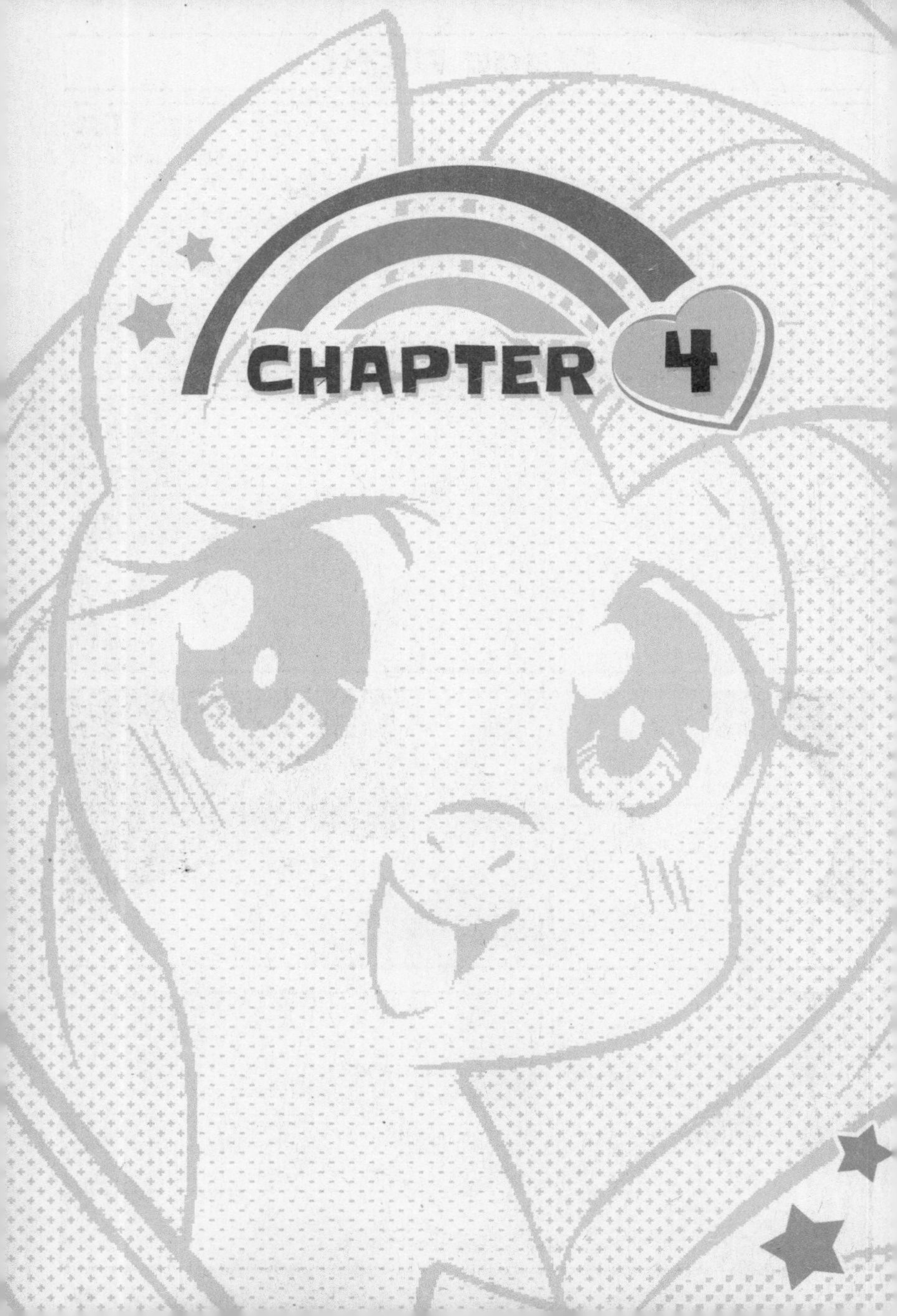

Stage Flight

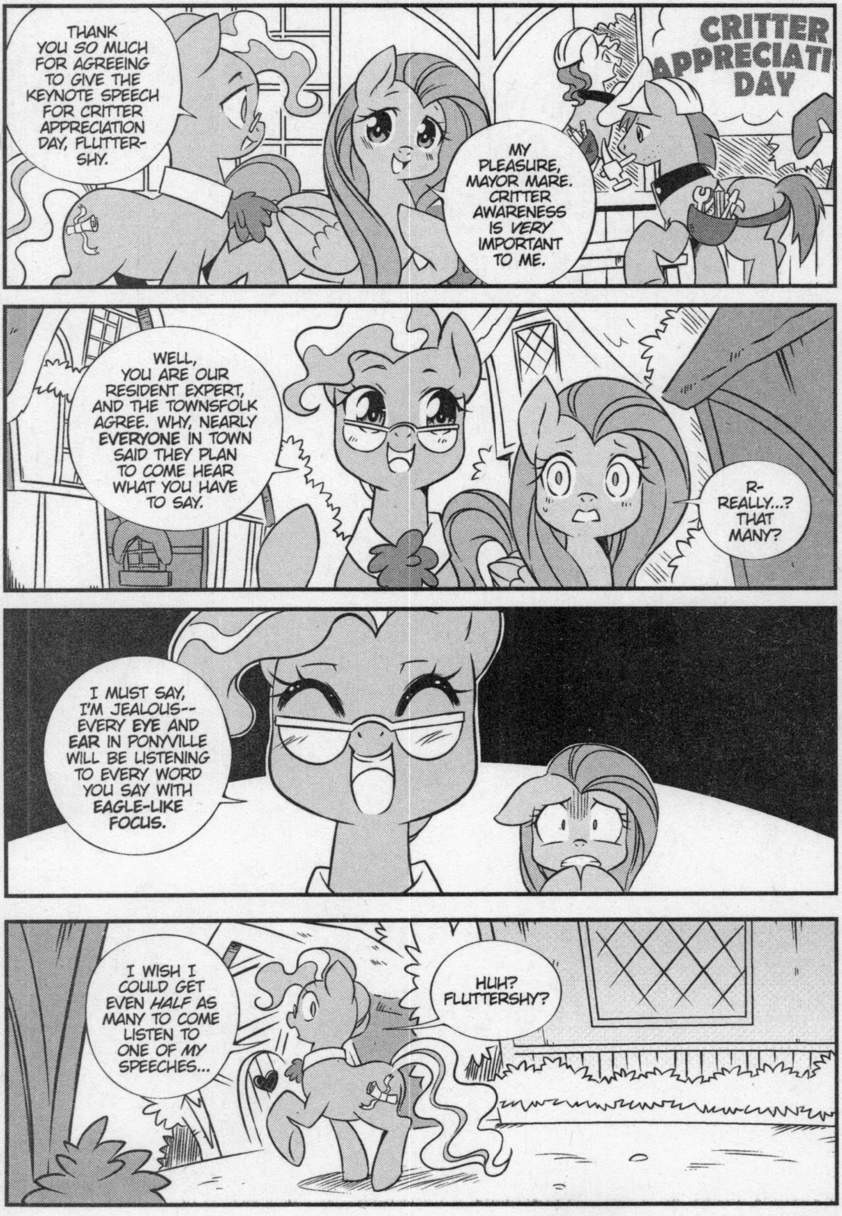
THANK YOU *SO* MUCH FOR AGREEING TO GIVE THE KEYNOTE SPEECH FOR CRITTER APPRECIATION DAY, FLUTTER-SHY.
MY PLEASURE, MAYOR MARE. CRITTER AWARENESS IS *VERY* IMPORTANT TO ME.
CRITTER
APPRECIATI
DAY
WELL, YOU ARE OUR RESIDENT EXPERT, AND THE TOWNSFOLK AGREE. WHY, NEARLY **EVERYONE** IN TOWN SAID THEY PLAN TO COME HEAR WHAT YOU HAVE TO SAY.
R- REALLY...? THAT MANY?
I MUST SAY, I'M JEALOUS-- EVERY EYE AND EAR IN PONYVILLE WILL BE LISTENING TO EVERY WORD YOU SAY WITH EAGLE-LIKE FOCUS.
I WISH I COULD GET EVEN *HALF* AS MANY TO COME LISTEN TO ONE OF *MY* SPEECHES...
HUH? FLUTTERSHY?

Shed Some Light on This Mystery

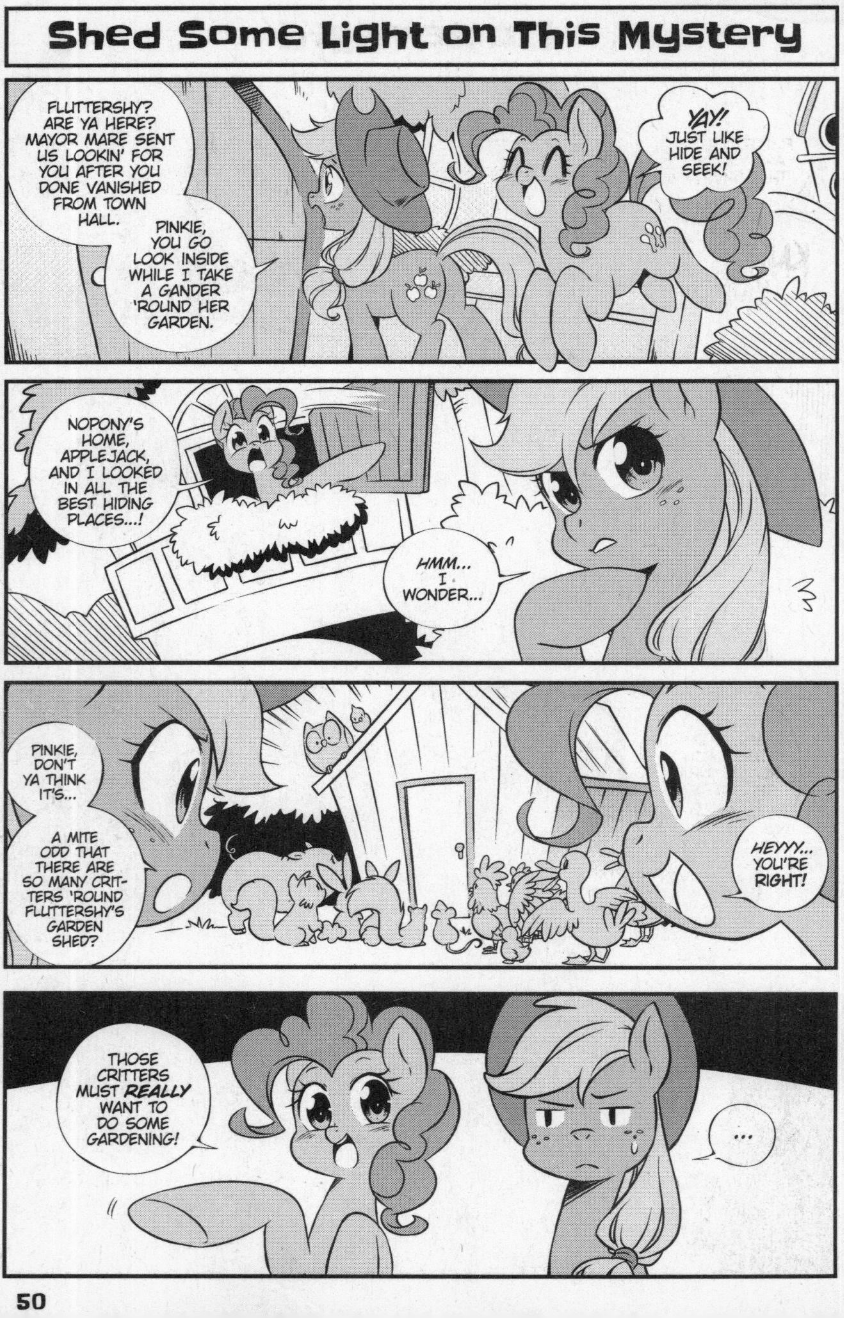
FLUTTERSHY? ARE YA HERE? MAYOR MARE SENT US LOOKIN' FOR YOU AFTER YOU DONE VANISHED FROM TOWN HALL.
PINKIE, YOU GO LOOK INSIDE WHILE I TAKE A GANDER 'ROUND HER GARDEN.
YAY! JUST LIKE HIDE AND SEEK!
NOPONY'S HOME, APPLEJACK, AND I LOOKED IN ALL THE BEST HIDING PLACES...!
HMM... I WONDER...
PINKIE, DON'T YA THINK IT'S...
A MITE ODD THAT THERE ARE SO MANY CRITTERS 'ROUND FLUTTERSHY'S GARDEN SHED?
HEYYY... YOU'RE RIGHT!
THOSE CRITTERS MUST REALLY WANT TO DO SOME GARDENING!
...

Fluttershed

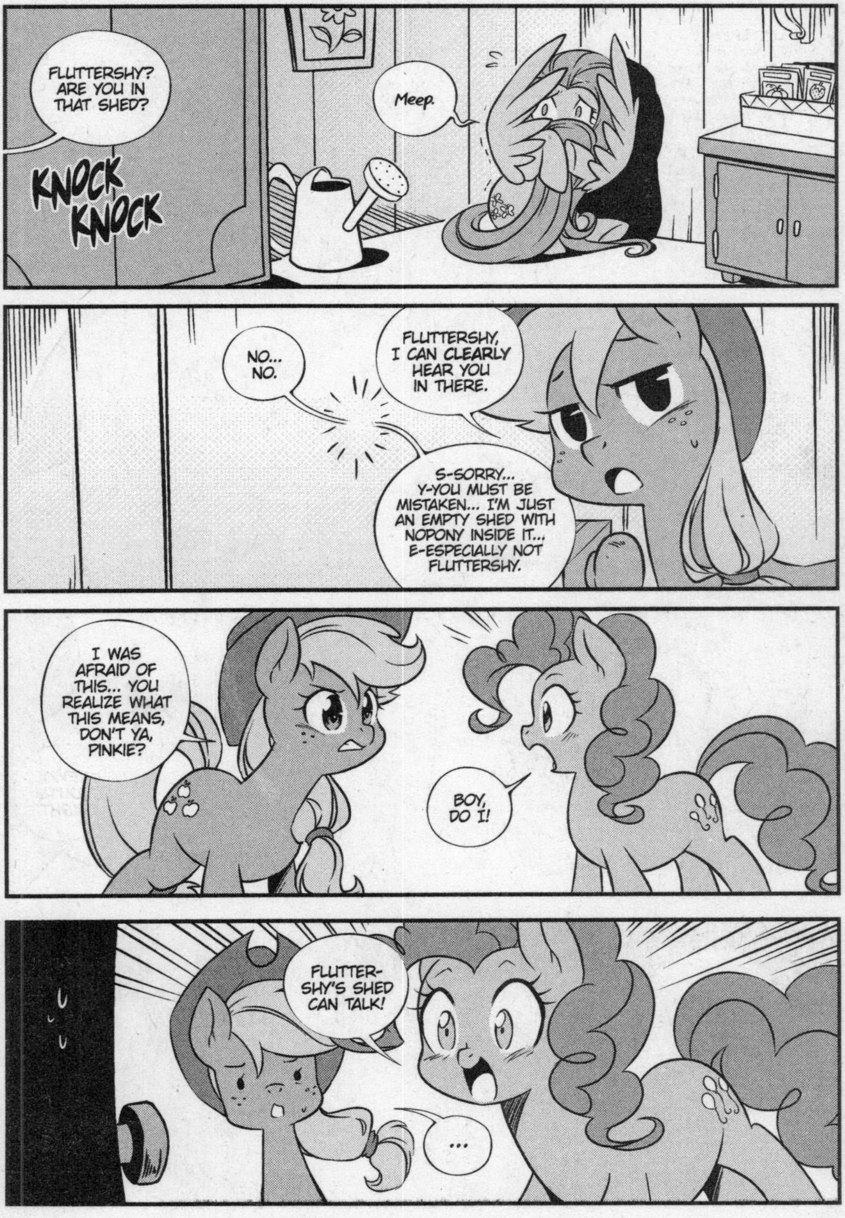
FLUTTERSHY? ARE YOU IN THAT SHED?
KNOCK KNOCK
Meep.
NO... NO.
FLUTTERSHY, I CAN CLEARLY HEAR YOU IN THERE.
S-SORRY... Y-YOU MUST BE MISTAKEN... I'M JUST AN EMPTY SHED WITH NOPONY INSIDE IT... E-ESPECIALLY NOT FLUTTERSHY.
I WAS AFRAID OF THIS... YOU REALIZE WHAT THIS MEANS, DON'T YA, PINKIE?
BOY, DO I!
FLUTTER-SHY'S SHED CAN TALK!
...

Hungry Hungry Critters

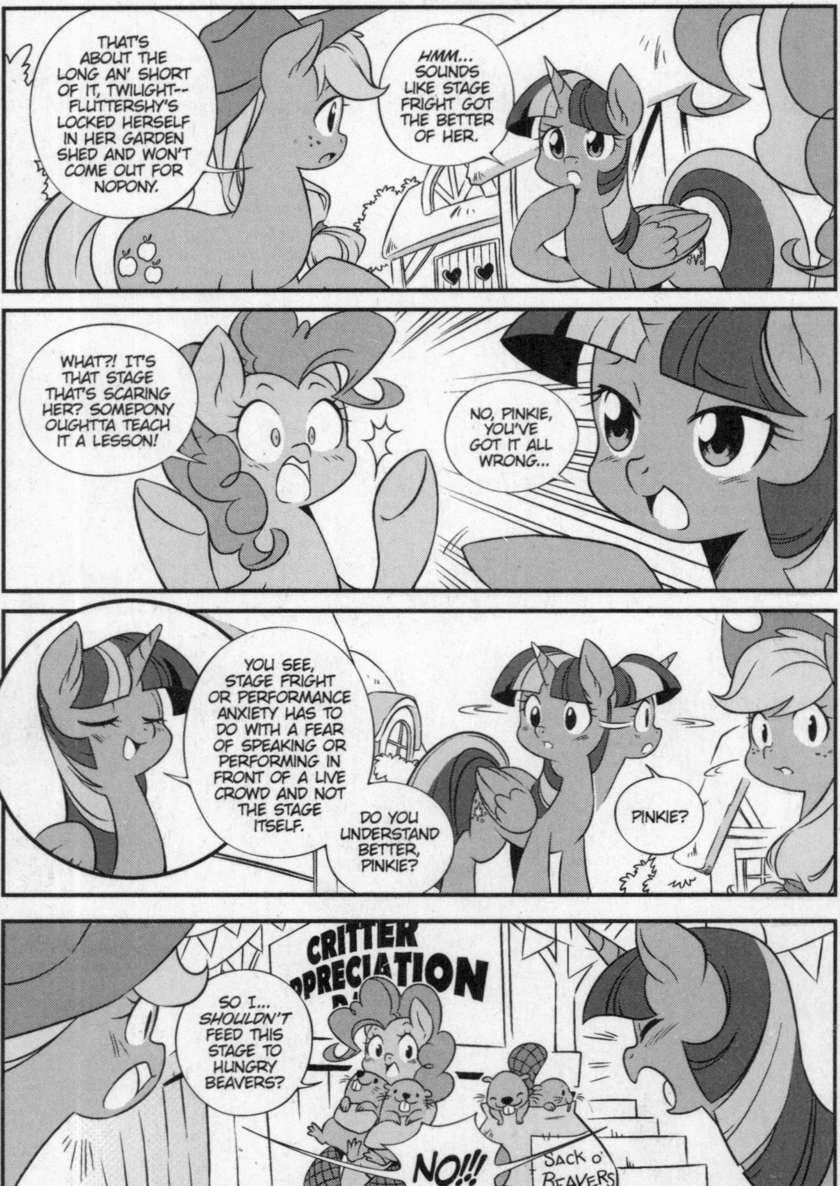

THAT'S ABOUT THE LONG AN' SHORT OF IT, TWILIGHT--FLUTTERSHY'S LOCKED HERSELF IN HER GARDEN SHED AND WON'T COME OUT FOR NOPONY.
HMM... SOUNDS LIKE STAGE FRIGHT GOT THE BETTER OF HER.
WHAT?! IT'S THAT STAGE THAT'S SCARING HER? SOMEPONY OUGHTTA TEACH IT A LESSON!
NO, PINKIE, YOU'VE GOT IT ALL WRONG...
YOU SEE, STAGE FRIGHT OR PERFORMANCE ANXIETY HAS TO DO WITH A FEAR OF SPEAKING OR PERFORMING IN FRONT OF A LIVE CROWD AND NOT THE STAGE ITSELF.
DO YOU UNDERSTAND BETTER, PINKIE?
PINKIE?
CRITTER
PPRECIATION
SO I... *SHOULDN'T* FEED THIS STAGE TO HUNGRY BEAVERS?
NO!!!
SACK O' BEAVERS

A Dash of Finesse

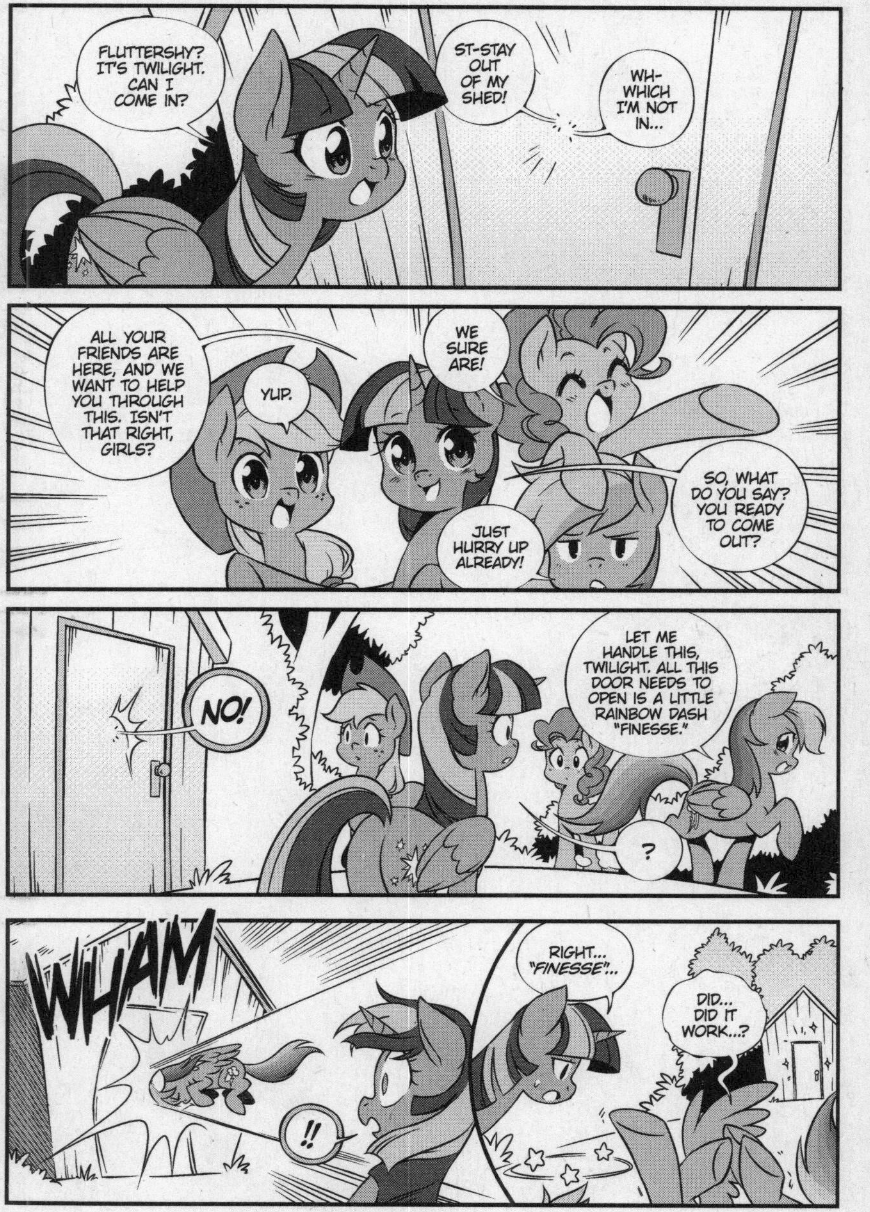
FLUTTERSHY? IT'S TWILIGHT. CAN I COME IN?
ST-STAY OUT OF MY SHED!
WH-WHICH I'M NOT IN...
ALL YOUR FRIENDS ARE HERE, AND WE WANT TO HELP YOU THROUGH THIS. ISN'T THAT RIGHT, GIRLS?
YUP.
WE SURE ARE!
SO, WHAT DO YOU SAY? YOU READY TO COME OUT?
JUST HURRY UP ALREADY!
NO!
LET ME HANDLE THIS, TWILIGHT. ALL THIS DOOR NEEDS TO OPEN IS A LITTLE RAINBOW DASH "FINESSE."
?
WHAM
!!
RIGHT... "FINESSE"...
DID... DID IT WORK...?

A Sequins of Unfortunate Events

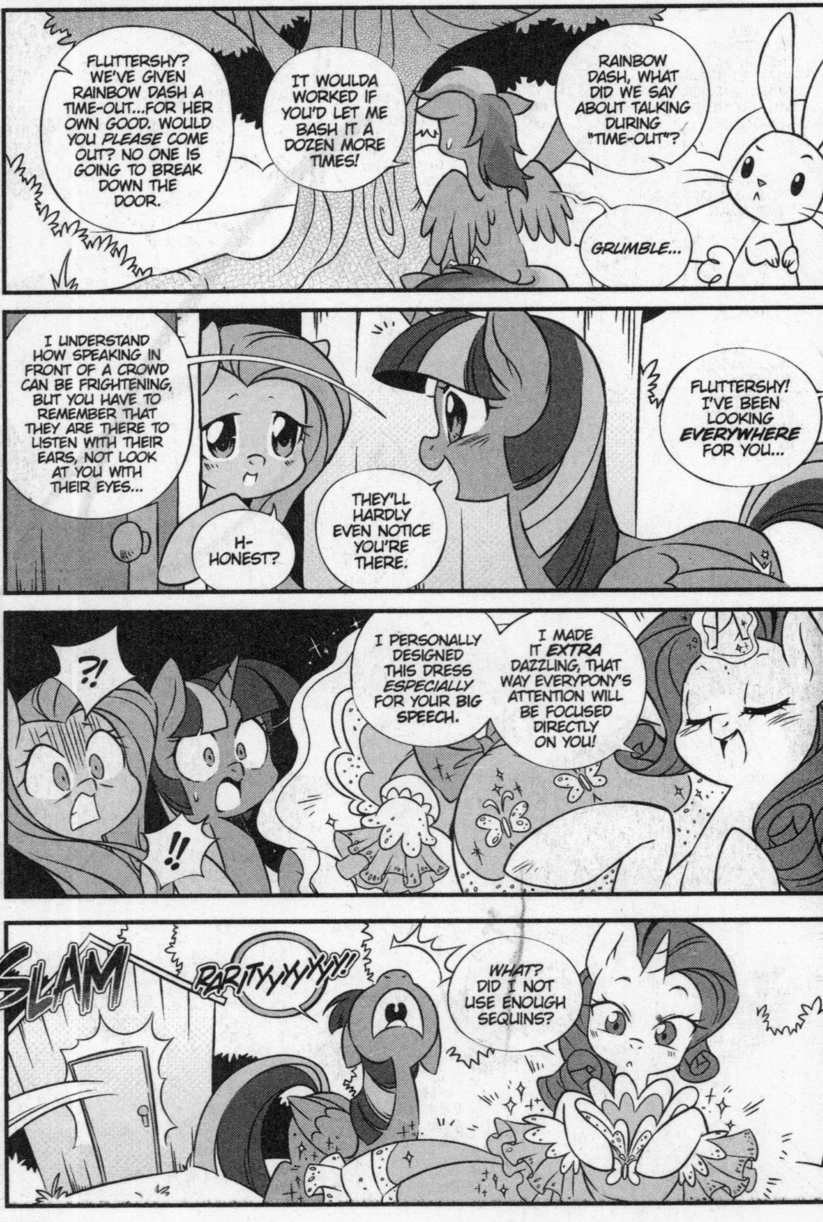

FLUTTERSHY? WE'VE GIVEN RAINBOW DASH A TIME-OUT...FOR HER OWN GOOD. WOULD YOU *PLEASE* COME OUT? NO ONE IS GOING TO BREAK DOWN THE DOOR.
IT WOULDA WORKED IF YOU'D LET ME BASH IT A DOZEN MORE TIMES!
RAINBOW DASH, WHAT DID WE SAY ABOUT TALKING DURING "TIME-OUT"?
GRUMBLE...
I UNDERSTAND HOW SPEAKING IN FRONT OF A CROWD CAN BE FRIGHTENING, BUT YOU HAVE TO REMEMBER THAT THEY ARE THERE TO LISTEN WITH THEIR EARS, NOT LOOK AT YOU WITH THEIR EYES...
H-HONEST?
THEY'LL HARDLY EVEN NOTICE YOU'RE THERE.
FLUTTERSHY! I'VE BEEN LOOKING ***EVERYWHERE*** FOR YOU...
?!
!!
I PERSONALLY DESIGNED THIS DRESS *ESPECIALLY* FOR YOUR BIG SPEECH.
I MADE IT ***EXTRA*** DAZZLING, THAT WAY EVERYPONY'S ATTENTION WILL BE FOCUSED DIRECTLY ON YOU!
SLAM
RARITYYYYYY!
WHAT? DID I NOT USE ENOUGH SEQUINS?

The Itsy Prickly Spider

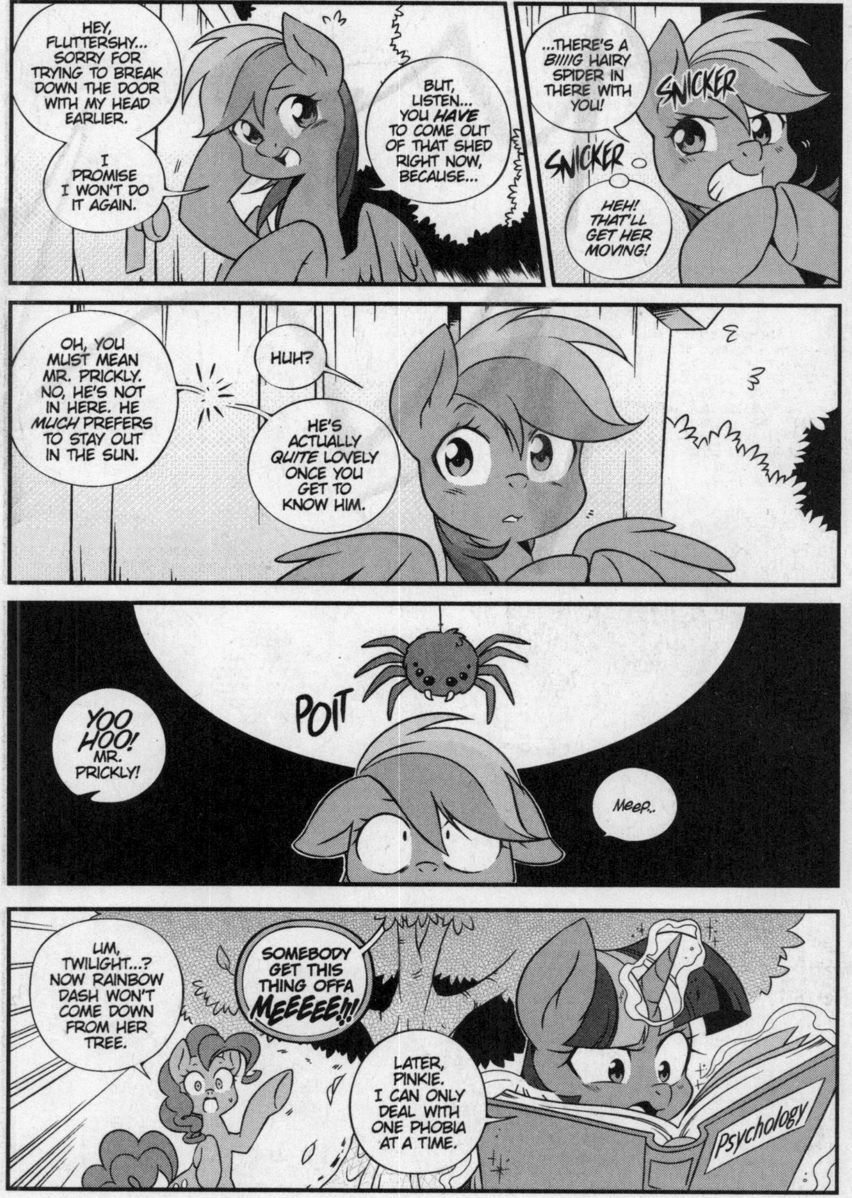
HEY, FLUTTERSHY... SORRY FOR TRYING TO BREAK DOWN THE DOOR WITH MY HEAD EARLIER.
I PROMISE I WON'T DO IT AGAIN.
BUT, LISTEN... YOU *HAVE* TO COME OUT OF THAT SHED RIGHT NOW, BECAUSE...
...THERE'S A *BIIIIG* HAIRY SPIDER IN THERE WITH YOU!
SNICKER
SNICKER
HEH! THAT'LL GET HER MOVING!
OH, YOU MUST MEAN MR. PRICKLY. NO, HE'S NOT IN HERE. HE *MUCH* PREFERS TO STAY OUT IN THE SUN.
HUH?
HE'S ACTUALLY *QUITE* LOVELY ONCE YOU GET TO KNOW HIM.
YOO HOO! MR. PRICKLY!
POIT
Meep..
UM, TWILIGHT...? NOW RAINBOW DASH WON'T COME DOWN FROM HER TREE.
SOMEBODY GET THIS THING OFFA MEEEEE!!!
LATER, PINKIE. I CAN ONLY DEAL WITH ONE PHOBIA AT A TIME.
Psychology

Crumbling Your Fears

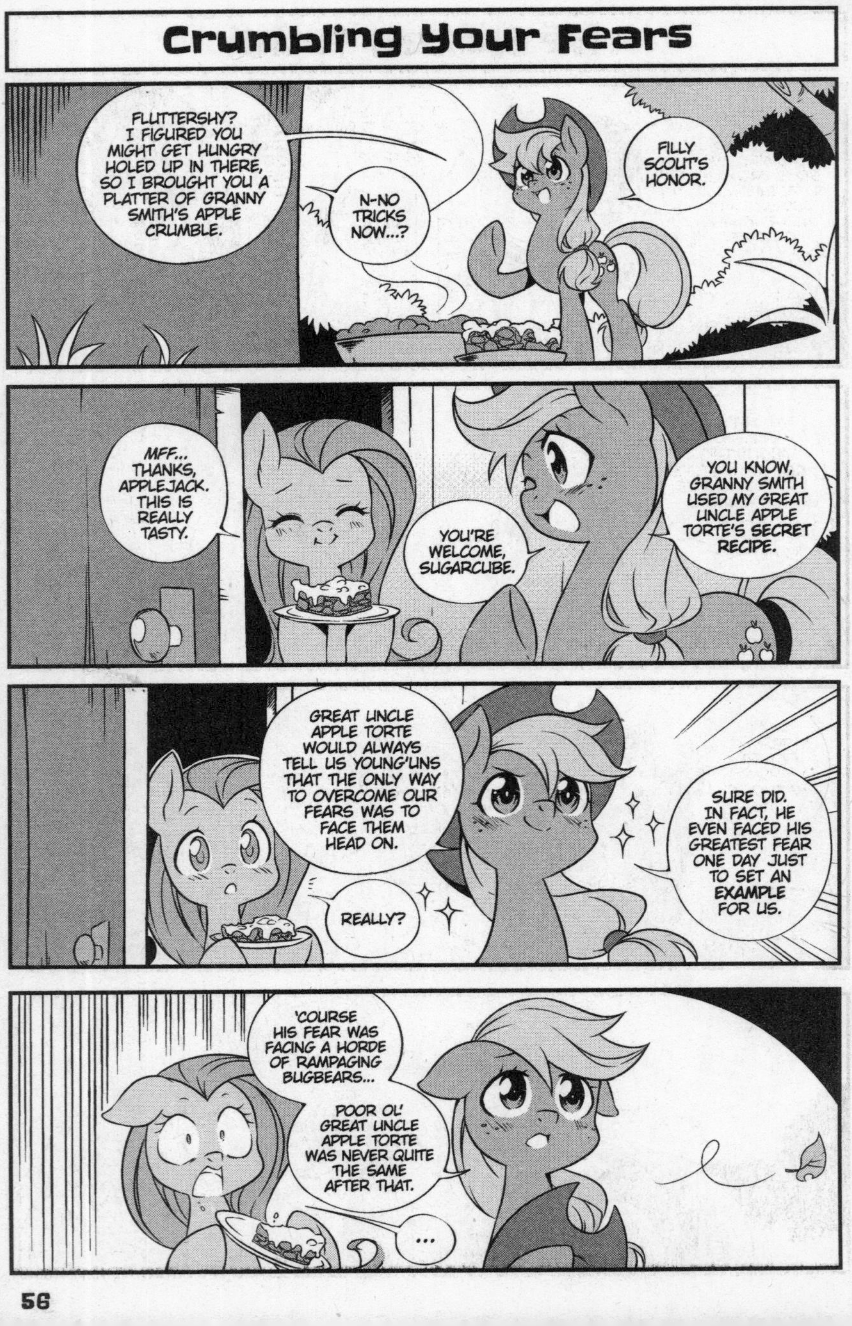
FLUTTERSHY? I FIGURED YOU MIGHT GET HUNGRY HOLED UP IN THERE, SO I BROUGHT YOU A PLATTER OF GRANNY SMITH'S APPLE CRUMBLE.
N-NO TRICKS NOW...?
FILLY SCOUT'S HONOR.
MFF... THANKS, APPLEJACK. THIS IS REALLY TASTY.
YOU'RE WELCOME, SUGARCUBE.
YOU KNOW, GRANNY SMITH USED MY GREAT UNCLE APPLE TORTE'S SECRET RECIPE.
GREAT UNCLE APPLE TORTE WOULD ALWAYS TELL US YOUNG'UNS THAT THE ONLY WAY TO OVERCOME OUR FEARS WAS TO FACE THEM HEAD ON.
REALLY?
SURE DID. IN FACT, HE EVEN FACED HIS GREATEST FEAR ONE DAY JUST TO SET AN EXAMPLE FOR US.
'COURSE HIS FEAR WAS FACING A HORDE OF RAMPAGING BUGBEARS...
POOR OL' GREAT UNCLE APPLE TORTE WAS NEVER QUITE THE SAME AFTER THAT.
...

The Naked Truth

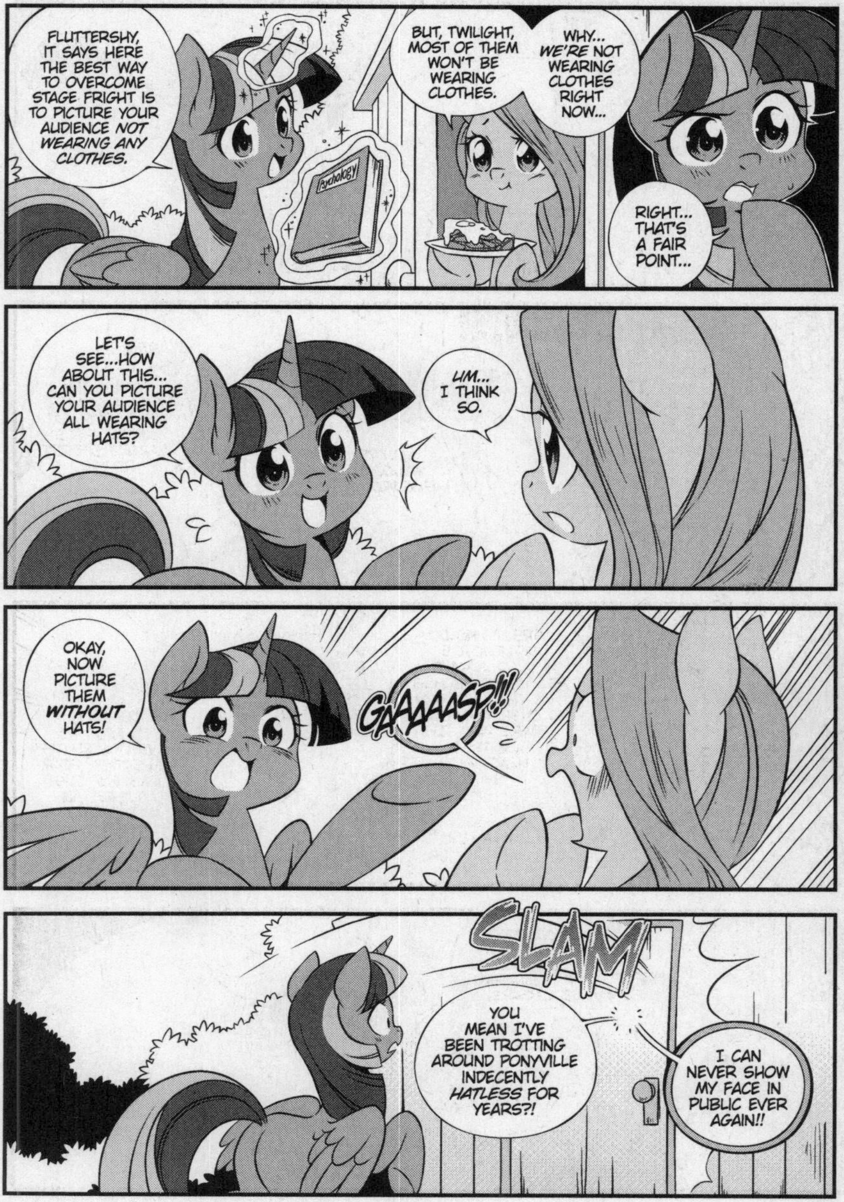

FLUTTERSHY, IT SAYS HERE THE BEST WAY TO OVERCOME STAGE FRIGHT IS TO PICTURE YOUR AUDIENCE *NOT* WEARING ANY CLOTHES.
Psychology
BUT, TWILIGHT, MOST OF THEM WON'T BE WEARING CLOTHES.
WHY... *WE'RE* NOT WEARING CLOTHES RIGHT NOW...
RIGHT... THAT'S A FAIR POINT...
LET'S SEE...HOW ABOUT THIS... CAN YOU PICTURE YOUR AUDIENCE ALL WEARING HATS?
UM... I THINK SO.
OKAY, NOW PICTURE THEM ***WITHOUT*** HATS!
GAAAAASP!!!
SLAM
YOU MEAN I'VE BEEN TROTTING AROUND PONYVILLE INDECENTLY *HATLESS* FOR YEARS?!
I CAN NEVER SHOW MY FACE IN PUBLIC EVER AGAIN!!

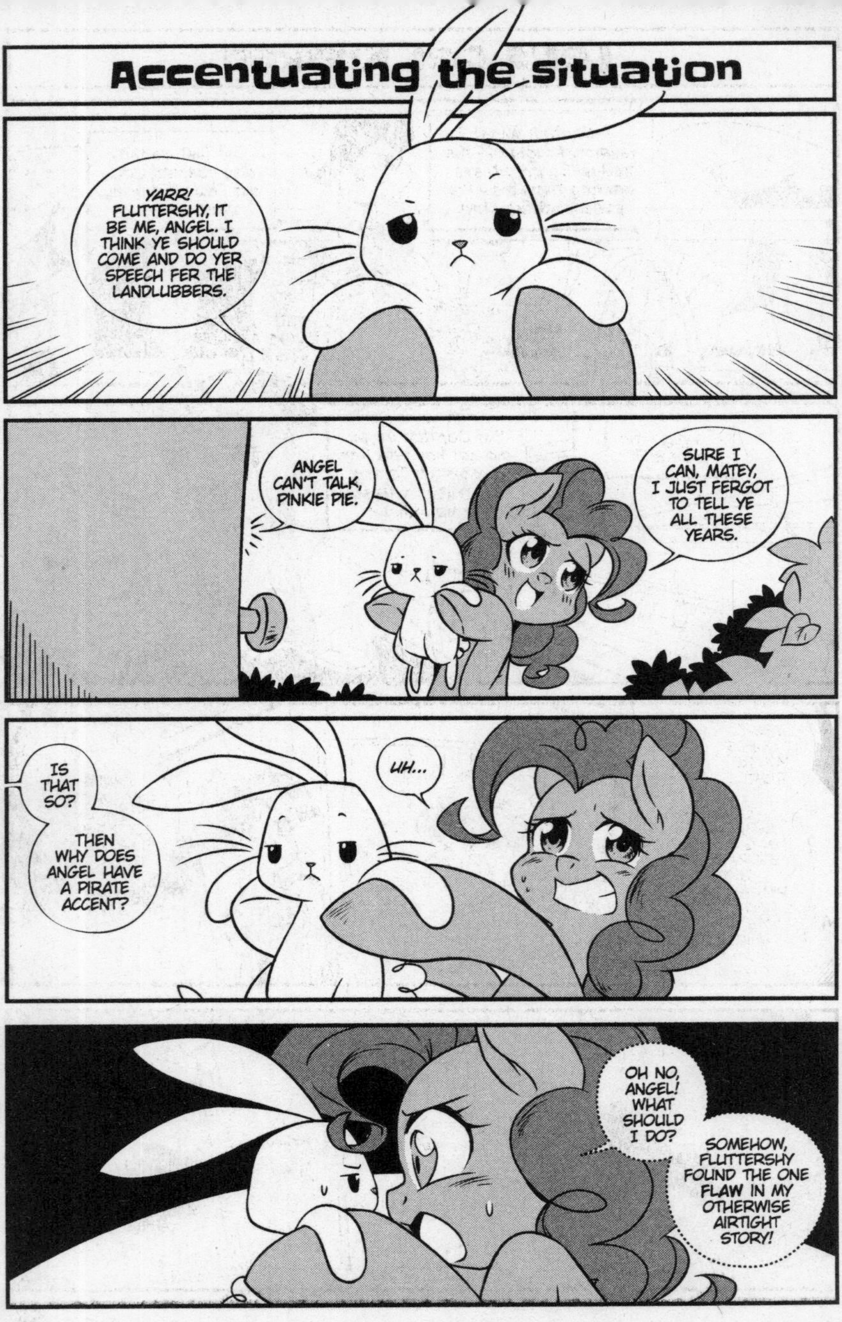
Accentuating the situation
YARR! FLUTTERSHY, IT BE ME, ANGEL. I THINK YE SHOULD COME AND DO YER SPEECH FER THE LANDLUBBERS.
ANGEL CAN'T TALK, PINKIE PIE.
SURE I CAN, MATEY, I JUST FERGOT TO TELL YE ALL THESE YEARS.
IS THAT SO?
THEN WHY DOES ANGEL HAVE A PIRATE ACCENT?
UH...
OH NO, ANGEL! WHAT SHOULD I DO?
SOMEHOW, FLUTTERSHY FOUND THE ONE FLAW IN MY OTHERWISE AIRTIGHT STORY!

Let's Get Kraken

--Captain Angel valiantly fought off the hedgehog privateers, meeting them blow for swashbuckling blow.

But just as the day seemed won, out from the briny deep arose...

...a gigantic KRAKEN!!!

But Captain Angel did not hesitate for a moment! Taking his trusty cutlass in hand he--

PINKIE... I DON'T THINK THIS IS WORKING.

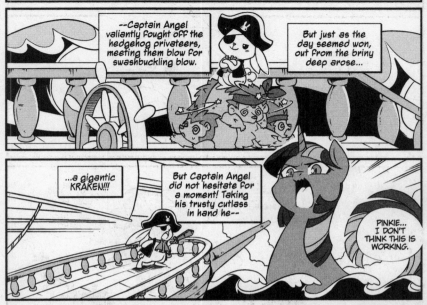

YEAH... I GUESS YOU'RE RIGHT...

I JUST GOT SO WRAPPED UP IN GIVING A BACK STORY AS TO WHY I GAVE ANGEL A PIRATE ACCENT THAT I FORGOT WHAT I WAS DOING IN THE FIRST PLACE.

THAT'S OKAY, WE'LL THINK OF SOMETHING ELSE. GOOD TRY, THO'.

S-SO, WHAT DID CAPTAIN ANGEL DO NEXT...?

H-HELLO...?

59

Shed it All Onstage

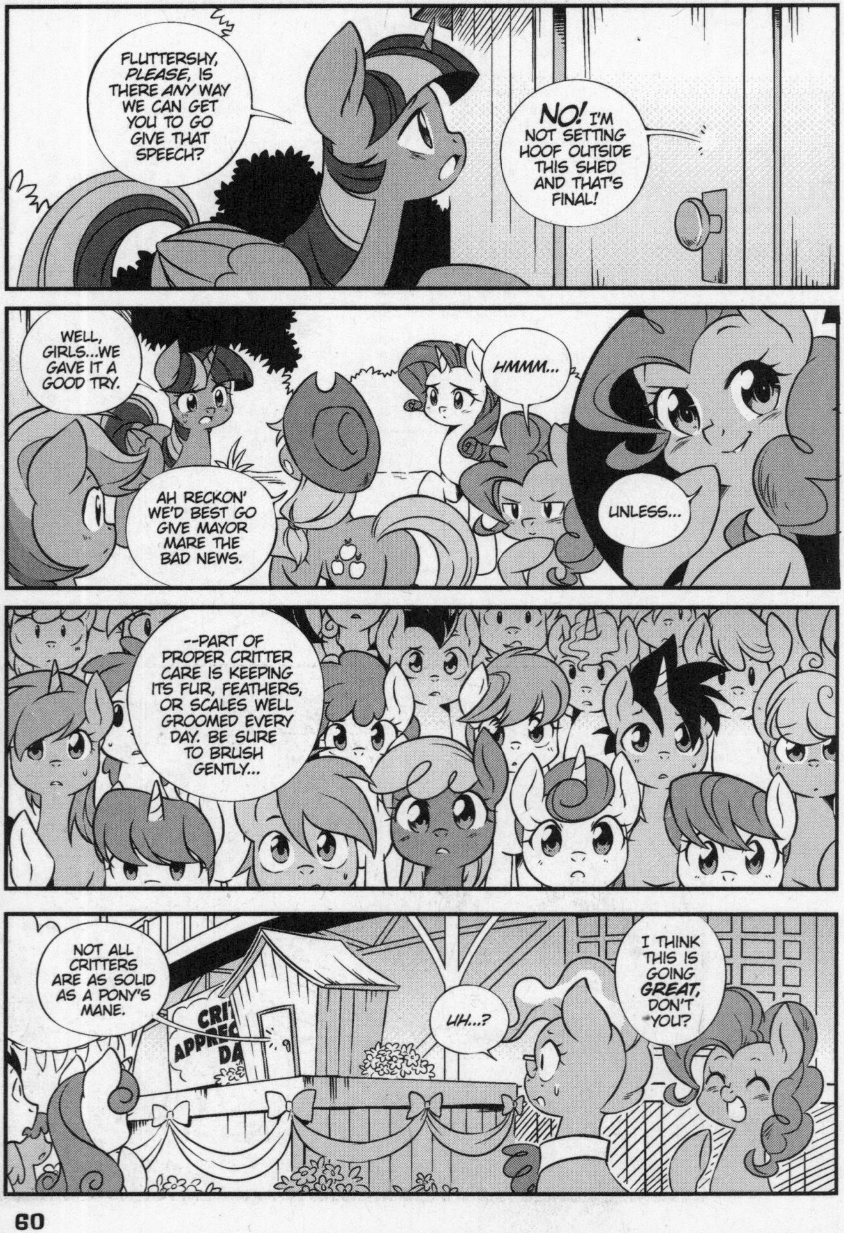
FLUTTERSHY, *PLEASE*, IS THERE *ANY* WAY WE CAN GET YOU TO GO GIVE THAT SPEECH?
NO! I'M NOT SETTING HOOF OUTSIDE THIS SHED AND THAT'S FINAL!
WELL, GIRLS...WE GAVE IT A GOOD TRY.
AH RECKON' WE'D BEST GO GIVE MAYOR MARE THE BAD NEWS.
HMMM...
UNLESS...
--PART OF PROPER CRITTER CARE IS KEEPING ITS FUR, FEATHERS, OR SCALES WELL GROOMED EVERY DAY. BE SURE TO BRUSH GENTLY...
NOT ALL CRITTERS ARE AS SOLID AS A PONY'S MANE.
UH...?
I THINK THIS IS GOING **GREAT**, DON'T YOU?

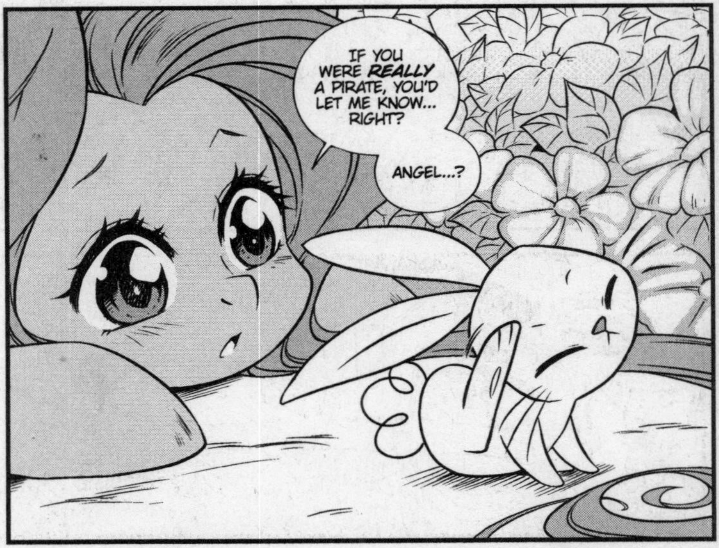
IF YOU WERE REALLY A PIRATE, YOU'D LET ME KNOW... RIGHT?
ANGEL...?

CHAPTER 5

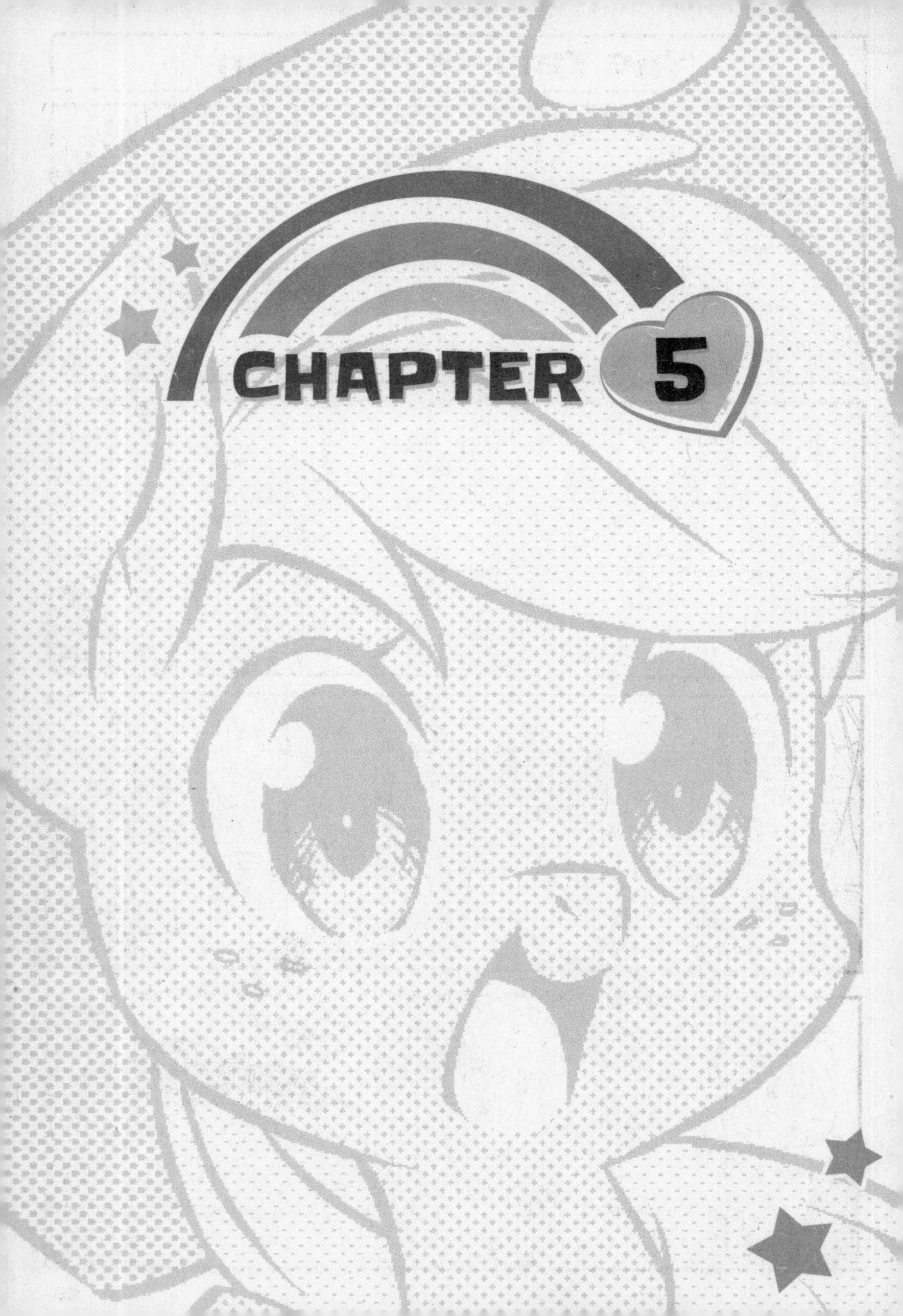

The Farm's in a Jam

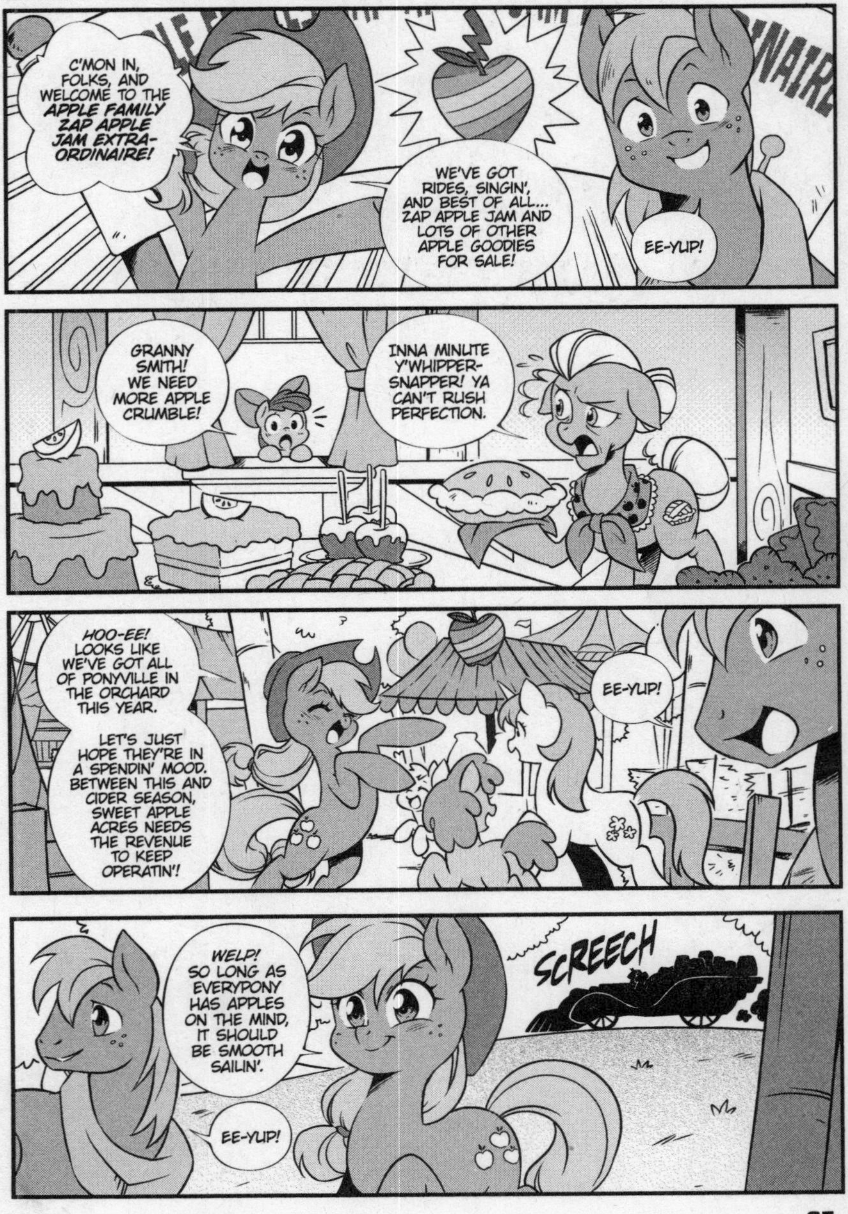
C'MON IN, FOLKS, AND WELCOME TO THE *APPLE FAMILY ZAP APPLE JAM EXTRA-ORDINAIRE!*
WE'VE GOT RIDES, SINGIN', AND BEST OF ALL... ZAP APPLE JAM AND LOTS OF OTHER APPLE GOODIES FOR SALE!
EE-YUP!
GRANNY SMITH! WE NEED MORE APPLE CRUMBLE!
INNA MINUTE Y'WHIPPER-SNAPPER! YA CAN'T RUSH PERFECTION.
HOO-EE! LOOKS LIKE WE'VE GOT ALL OF PONYVILLE IN THE ORCHARD THIS YEAR.
LET'S JUST HOPE THEY'RE IN A SPENDIN' MOOD. BETWEEN THIS AND CIDER SEASON, SWEET APPLE ACRES NEEDS THE REVENUE TO KEEP OPERATIN'!
EE-YUP!
WELP! SO LONG AS EVERYPONY HAS APPLES ON THE MIND, IT SHOULD BE SMOOTH SAILIN'.
SCREECH
EE-YUP!

Orange You Glad He Didn't Say Banana?

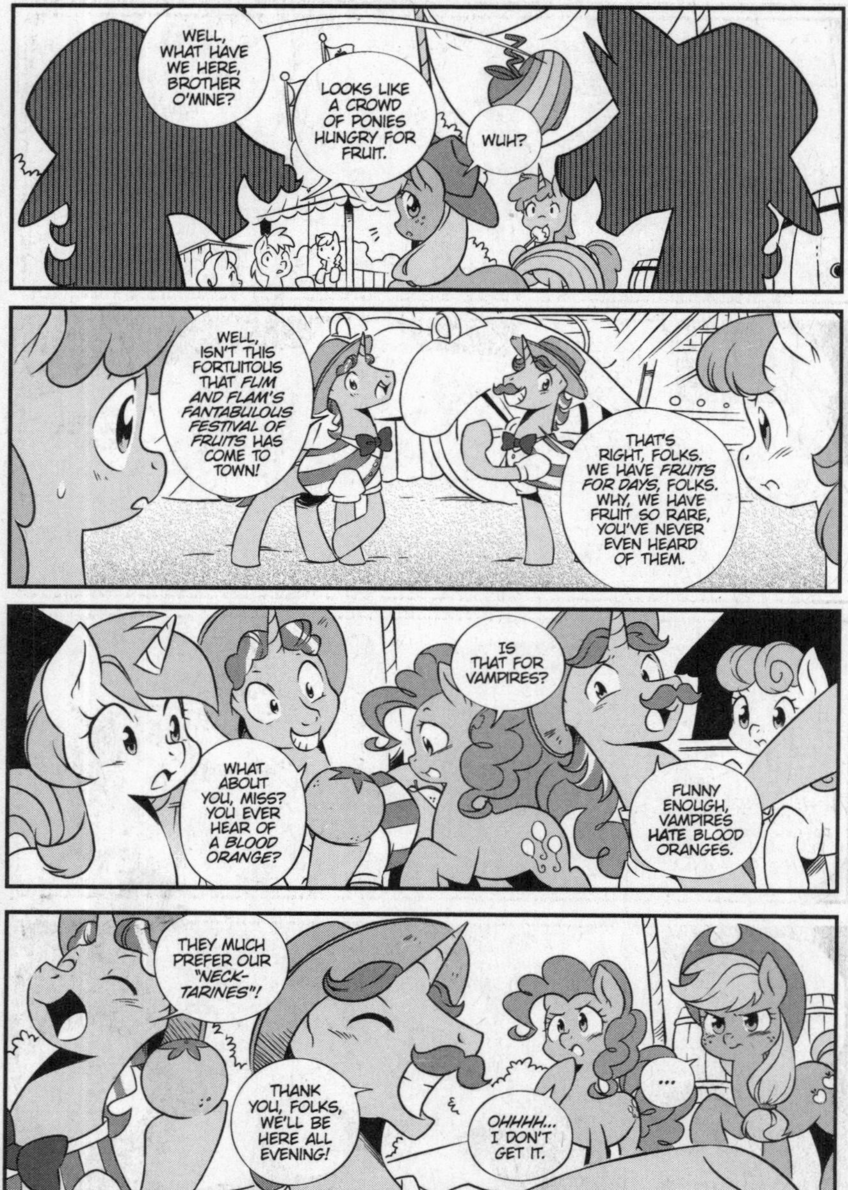
WELL, WHAT HAVE WE HERE, BROTHER O'MINE?
LOOKS LIKE A CROWD OF PONIES HUNGRY FOR FRUIT.
WUH?
WELL, ISN'T THIS FORTUITOUS THAT *FLIM AND FLAM'S FANTABULOUS FESTIVAL OF FRUITS* HAS COME TO TOWN!
THAT'S RIGHT, FOLKS. WE HAVE *FRUITS FOR DAYS*, FOLKS. WHY, WE HAVE FRUIT SO RARE, YOU'VE NEVER EVEN HEARD OF THEM.
WHAT ABOUT YOU, MISS? YOU EVER HEAR OF A *BLOOD ORANGE*?
IS THAT FOR VAMPIRES?
FUNNY ENOUGH, VAMPIRES HATE BLOOD ORANGES.
THEY MUCH PREFER OUR *"NECK-TARINES"*!
THANK YOU, FOLKS, WE'LL BE HERE ALL EVENING!
...
OHHHH... I DON'T GET IT.

There Mangoes the Neighborhood

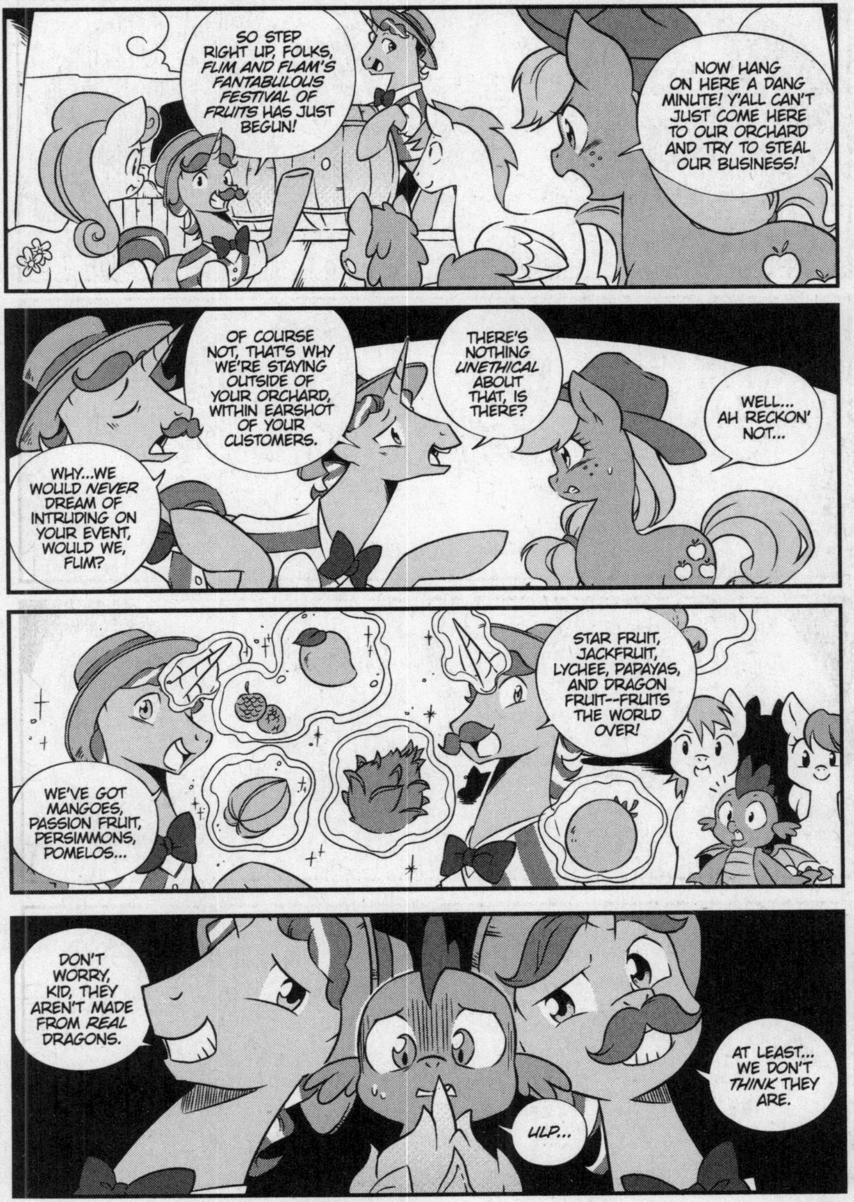
SO STEP RIGHT UP, FOLKS, *FLIM AND FLAM'S FANTABULOUS FESTIVAL OF FRUITS* HAS JUST BEGUN!
NOW HANG ON HERE A DANG MINUTE! Y'ALL CAN'T JUST COME HERE TO OUR ORCHARD AND TRY TO STEAL OUR BUSINESS!
WHY...WE WOULD *NEVER* DREAM OF INTRUDING ON YOUR EVENT, WOULD WE, FLIM?
OF COURSE NOT, THAT'S WHY WE'RE STAYING OUTSIDE OF YOUR ORCHARD, WITHIN EARSHOT OF YOUR CUSTOMERS.
THERE'S NOTHING *UNETHICAL* ABOUT THAT, IS THERE?
WELL... AH RECKON' NOT...
WE'VE GOT MANGOES, PASSION FRUIT, PERSIMMONS, POMELOS...
STAR FRUIT, JACKFRUIT, LYCHEE, PAPAYAS, AND DRAGON FRUIT--FRUITS THE WORLD OVER!
DON'T WORRY, KID, THEY AREN'T MADE FROM *REAL* DRAGONS.
AT LEAST... WE DON'T *THINK* THEY ARE.
ULP...

Hollow Promises

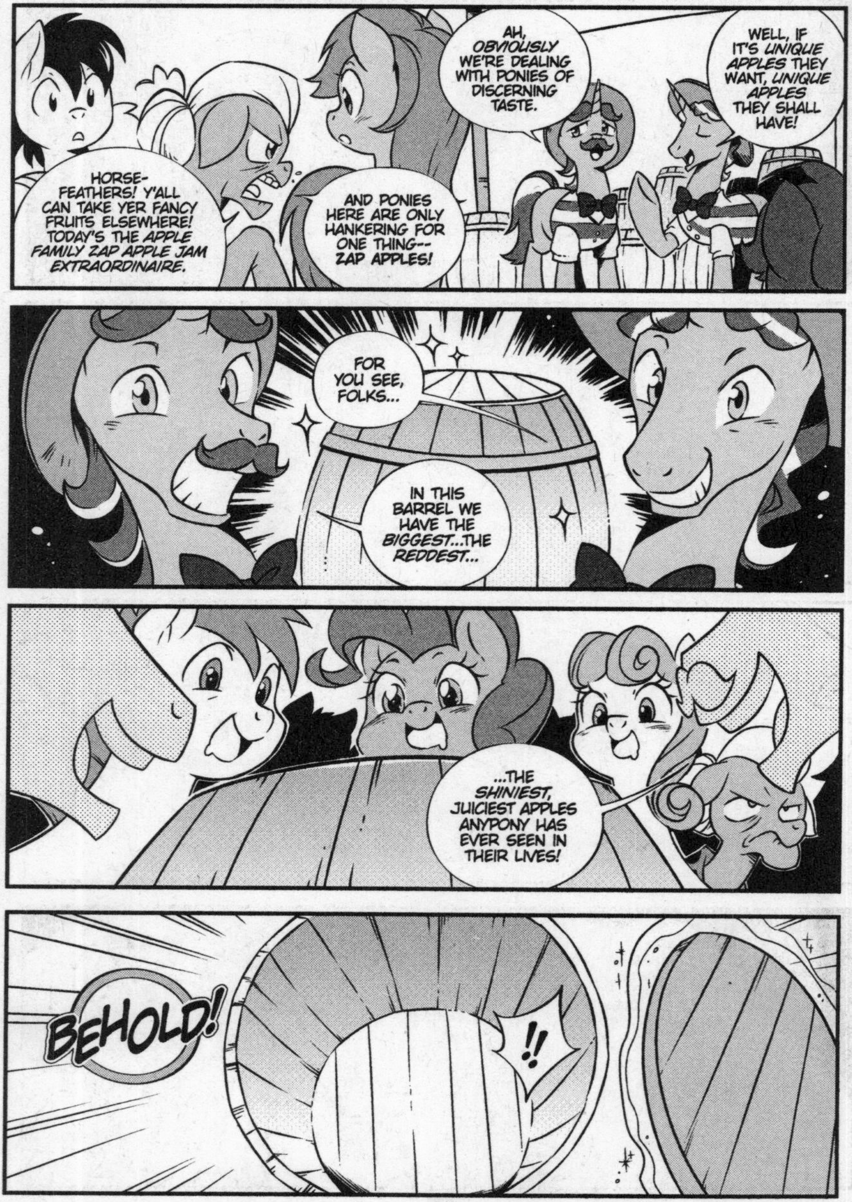
HORSE-FEATHERS! Y'ALL CAN TAKE YER FANCY FRUITS ELSEWHERE! TODAY'S THE *APPLE FAMILY ZAP APPLE JAM EXTRAORDINAIRE.*
AND PONIES HERE ARE ONLY HANKERING FOR ONE THING--ZAP APPLES!
AH, *OBVIOUSLY* WE'RE DEALING WITH PONIES OF DISCERNING TASTE.
WELL, IF IT'S *UNIQUE APPLES* THEY WANT, *UNIQUE APPLES* THEY SHALL HAVE!
FOR YOU SEE, FOLKS...
IN THIS BARREL WE HAVE THE *BIGGEST*...THE *REDDEST*...
...THE *SHINIEST*, JUICIEST APPLES ANYPONY HAS EVER SEEN IN THEIR LIVES!
BEHOLD!
!!

Empty Calories

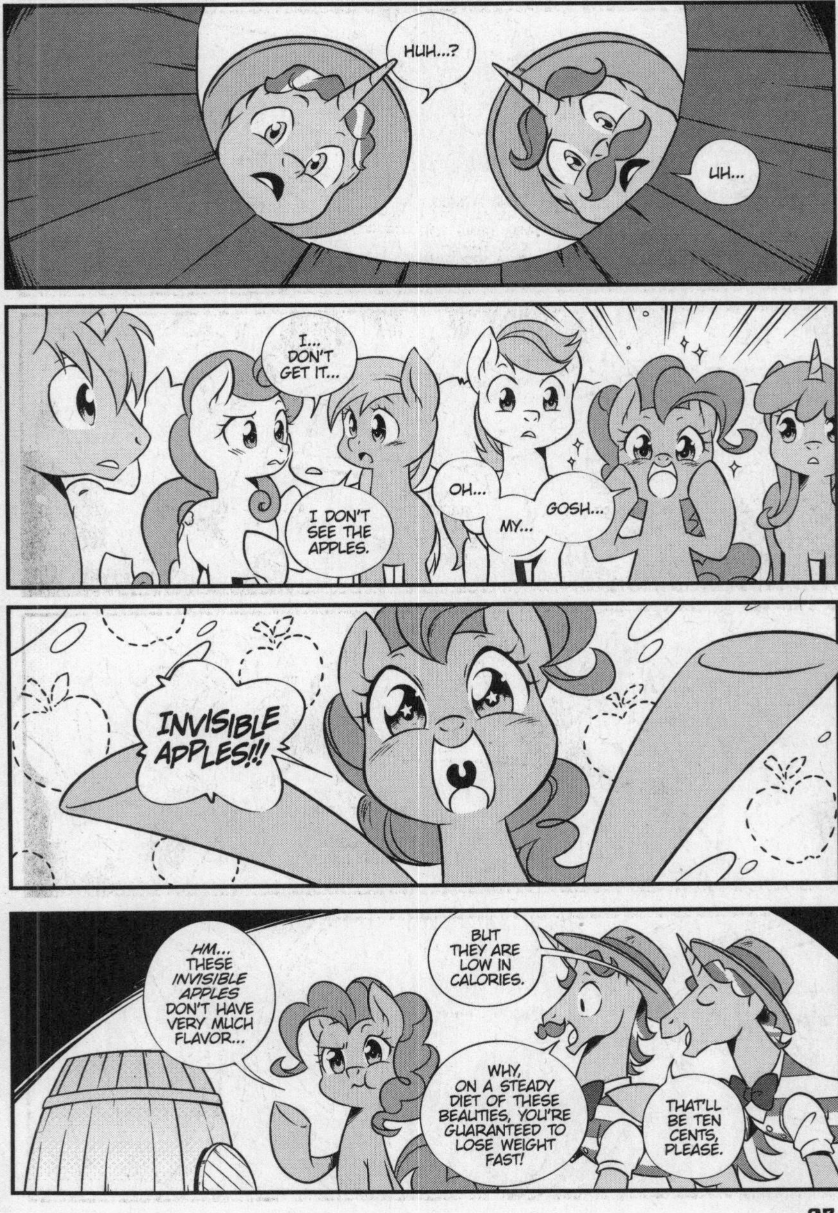
HUH...?
UH...
I... DON'T GET IT...
I DON'T SEE THE APPLES.
OH... MY... GOSH...
INVISIBLE APPLES!!!
HM... THESE INVISIBLE APPLES DON'T HAVE VERY MUCH FLAVOR...
BUT THEY ARE LOW IN CALORIES.
WHY, ON A STEADY DIET OF THESE BEAUTIES, YOU'RE GUARANTEED TO LOSE WEIGHT FAST!
THAT'LL BE TEN CENTS, PLEASE.

Now There's Something You Don't See Every Day!

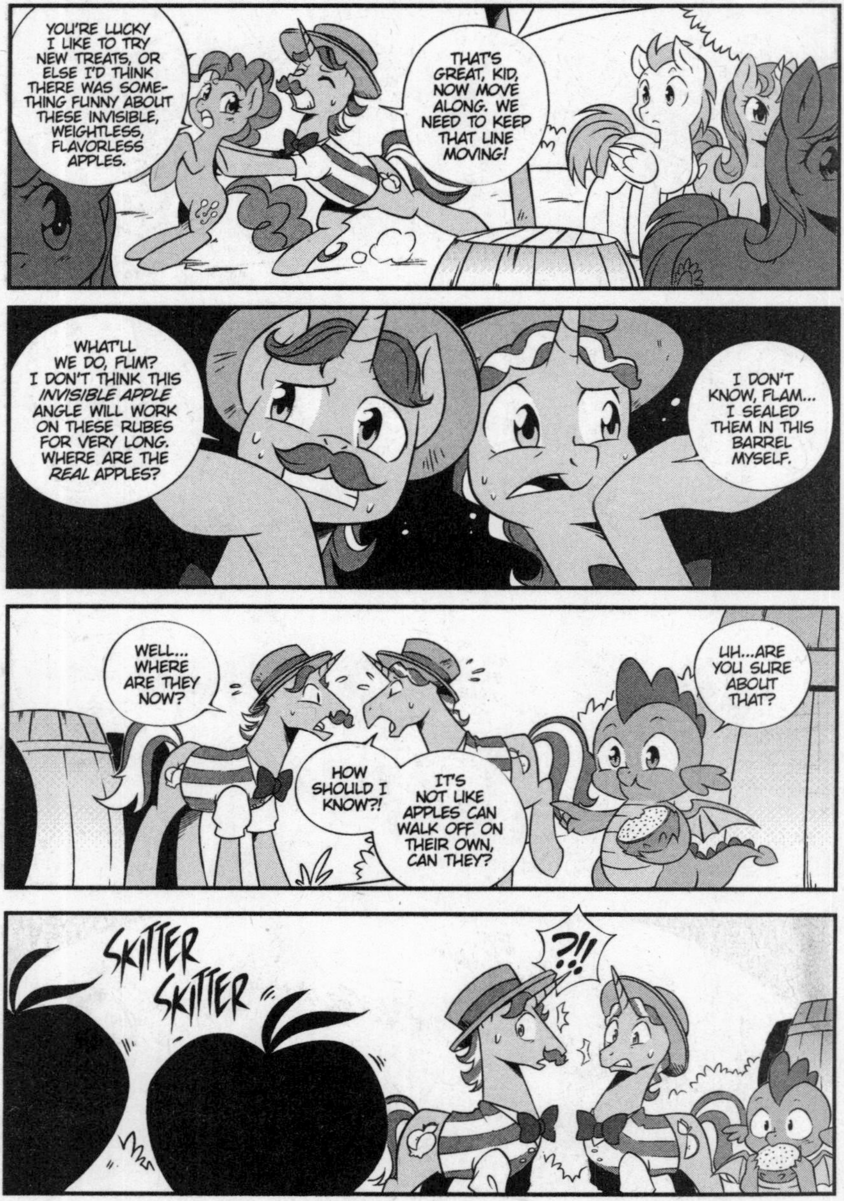
YOU'RE LUCKY I LIKE TO TRY NEW TREATS, OR ELSE I'D THINK THERE WAS SOME-THING FUNNY ABOUT THESE INVISIBLE, WEIGHTLESS, FLAVORLESS APPLES.
THAT'S GREAT, KID, NOW MOVE ALONG. WE NEED TO KEEP THAT LINE MOVING!
WHAT'LL WE DO, FLIM? I DON'T THINK THIS *INVISIBLE APPLE* ANGLE WILL WORK ON THESE RUBES FOR VERY LONG. WHERE ARE THE *REAL* APPLES?
I DON'T KNOW, FLAM... I SEALED THEM IN THIS BARREL MYSELF.
WELL... WHERE ARE THEY NOW?
HOW SHOULD I KNOW?!
IT'S NOT LIKE APPLES CAN WALK OFF ON THEIR OWN, CAN THEY?
UH...ARE YOU SURE ABOUT THAT?
SKITTER SKITTER
?!!

Caught in a Pinch

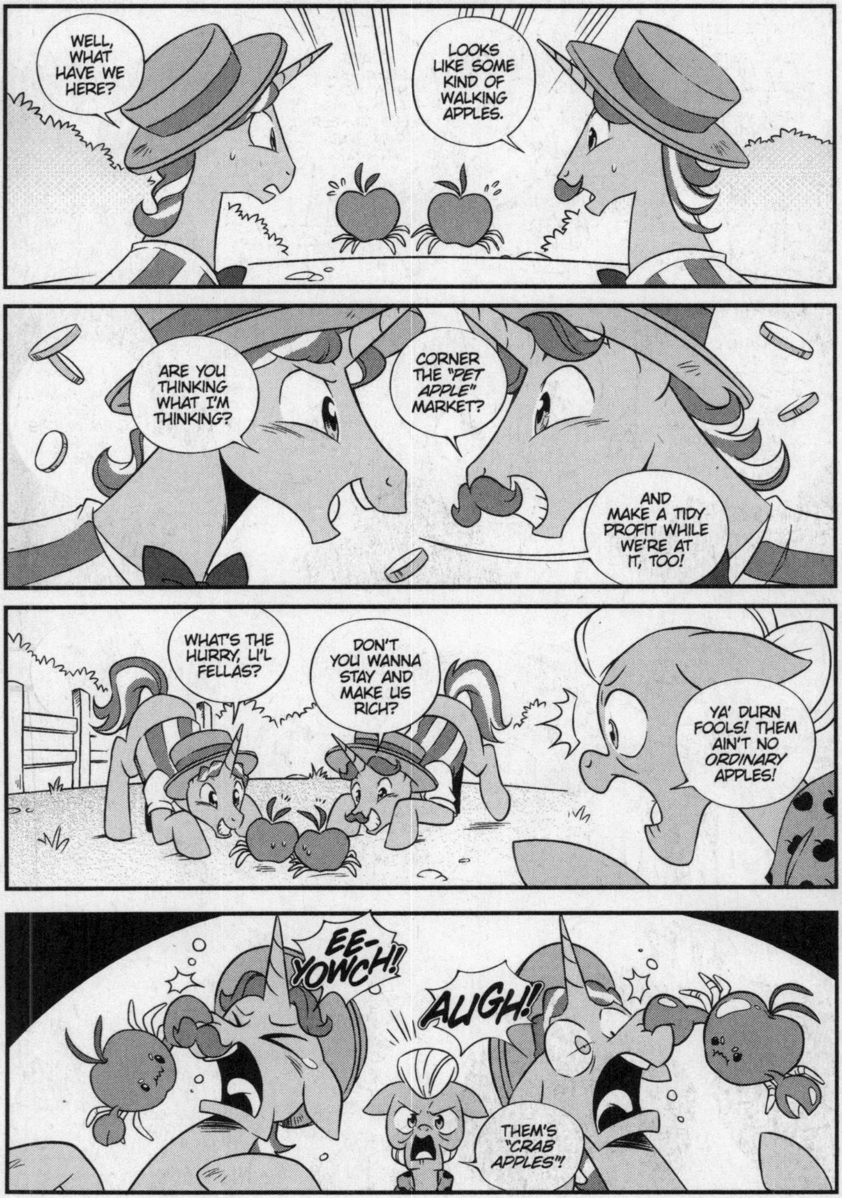

WELL, WHAT HAVE WE HERE?
LOOKS LIKE SOME KIND OF WALKING APPLES.
ARE YOU THINKING WHAT I'M THINKING?
CORNER THE "PET APPLE" MARKET?
AND MAKE A TIDY PROFIT WHILE WE'RE AT IT, TOO!
WHAT'S THE HURRY, LI'L FELLAS?
DON'T YOU WANNA STAY AND MAKE US RICH?
YA' DURN FOOLS! THEM AIN'T NO ORDINARY APPLES!
EE-YOWCH!
AUGH!
THEM'S "CRAB APPLES"!

Pony Pinchin' Problems

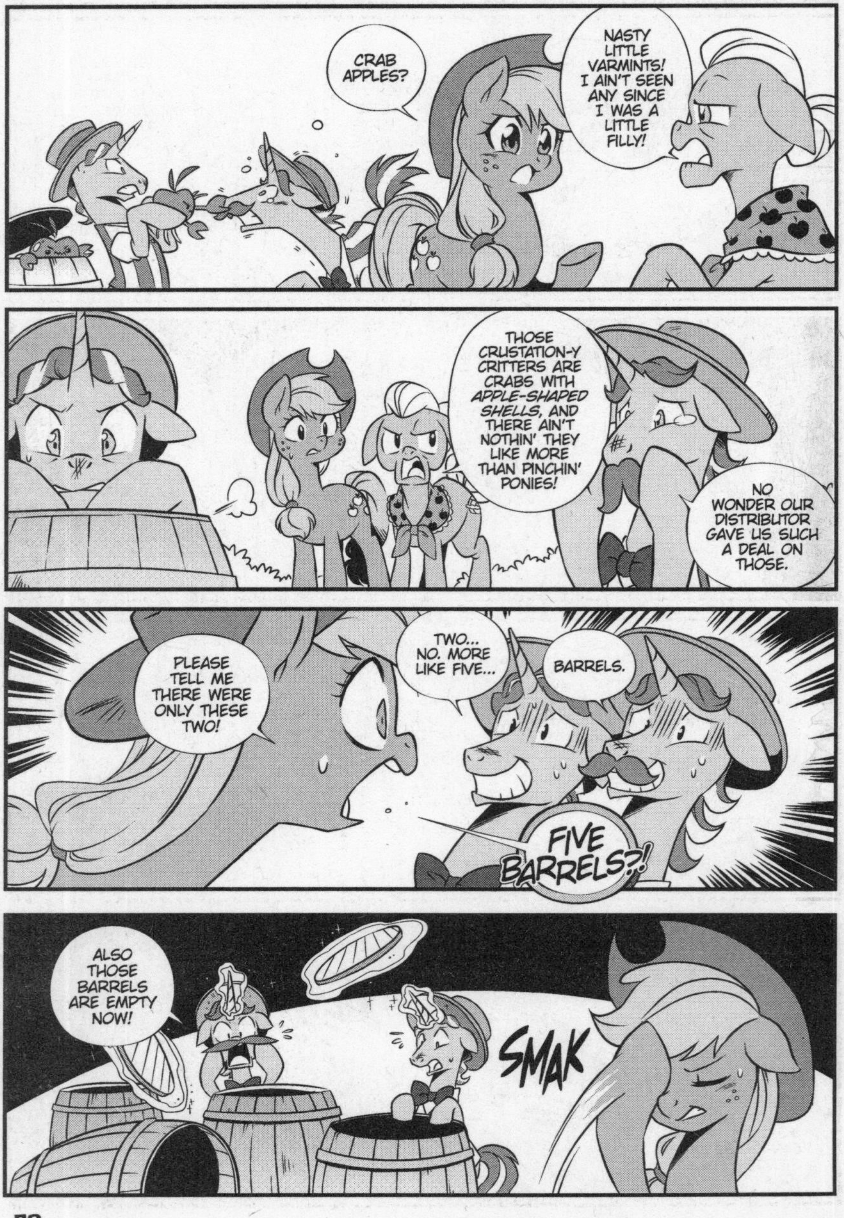
CRAB APPLES?
NASTY LITTLE VARMINTS! I AIN'T SEEN ANY SINCE I WAS A LITTLE FILLY!
THOSE CRUSTATION-Y CRITTERS ARE CRABS WITH *APPLE-SHAPED SHELLS*, AND THERE AIN'T NOTHIN' THEY LIKE MORE THAN PINCHIN' PONIES!
NO WONDER OUR DISTRIBUTOR GAVE US SUCH A DEAL ON THOSE.
PLEASE TELL ME THERE WERE ONLY THESE TWO!
TWO... NO. MORE LIKE FIVE...
BARRELS.
FIVE BARRELS?!
ALSO THOSE BARRELS ARE EMPTY NOW!
SMAK

Practical Retreat

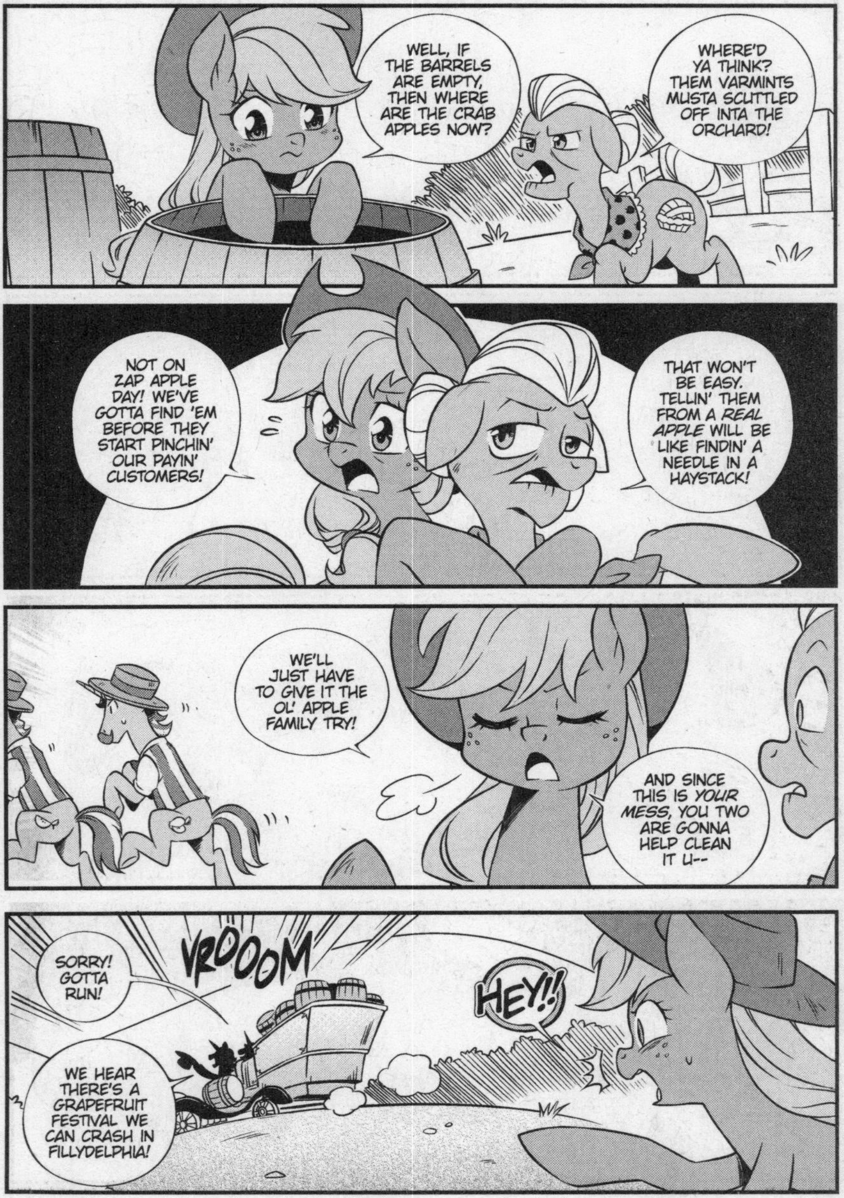
WELL, IF THE BARRELS ARE EMPTY, THEN WHERE ARE THE CRAB APPLES NOW?
WHERE'D YA THINK? THEM VARMINTS MUSTA SCUTTLED OFF INTA THE ORCHARD!
NOT ON ZAP APPLE DAY! WE'VE GOTTA FIND 'EM BEFORE THEY START PINCHIN' OUR PAYIN' CUSTOMERS!
THAT WON'T BE EASY. TELLIN' THEM FROM A *REAL APPLE* WILL BE LIKE FINDIN' A NEEDLE IN A HAYSTACK!
WE'LL JUST HAVE TO GIVE IT THE OL' APPLE FAMILY TRY!
AND SINCE THIS IS *YOUR MESS*, YOU TWO ARE GONNA HELP CLEAN IT U--
SORRY! GOTTA RUN!
VROOOM
WE HEAR THERE'S A GRAPEFRUIT FESTIVAL WE CAN CRASH IN FILLYDELPHIA!
HEY!!

Pinchpocalypse Now

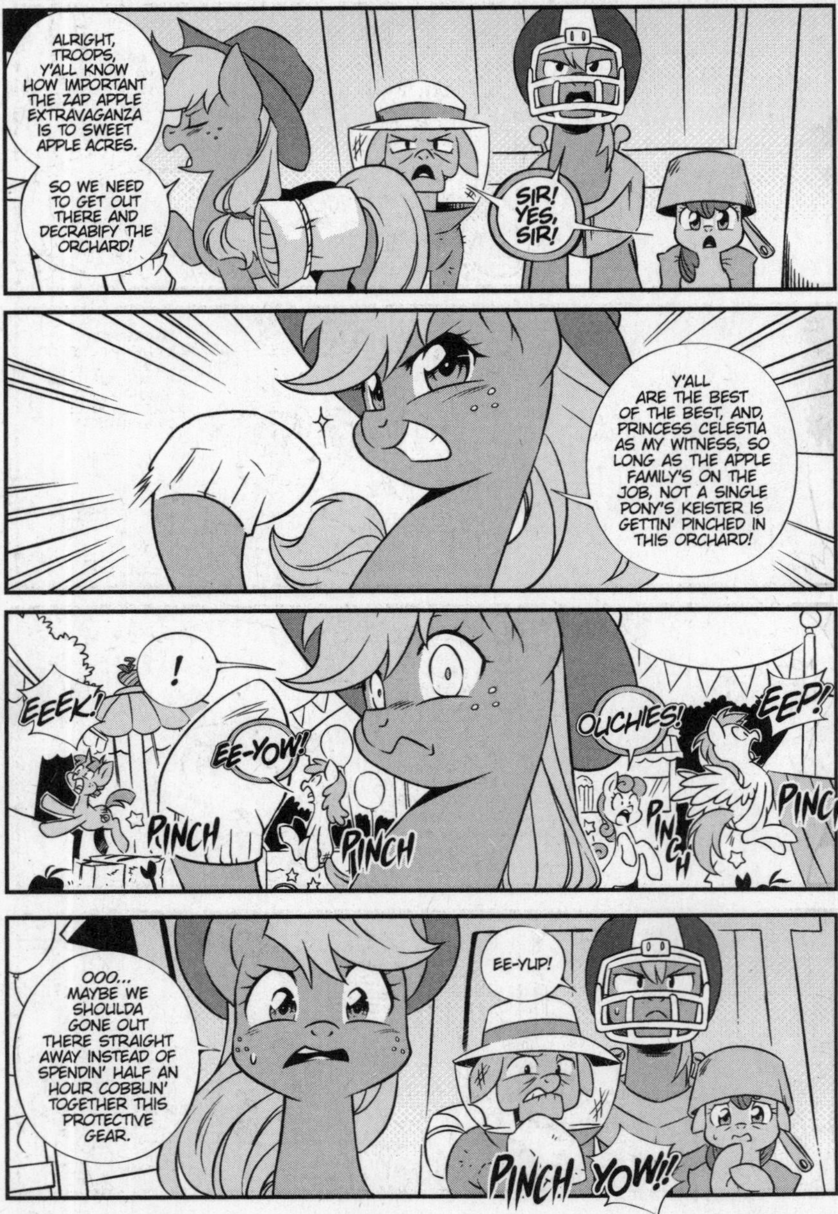
ALRIGHT, TROOPS, Y'ALL KNOW HOW IMPORTANT THE ZAP APPLE EXTRAVAGANZA IS TO SWEET APPLE ACRES.
SO WE NEED TO GET OUT THERE AND DECRABIFY THE ORCHARD!
SIR! YES, SIR!
Y'ALL ARE THE BEST OF THE BEST, AND, PRINCESS CELESTIA AS MY WITNESS, SO LONG AS THE APPLE FAMILY'S ON THE JOB, NOT A SINGLE PONY'S KEISTER IS GETTIN' PINCHED IN THIS ORCHARD!
!
EEEK!
EE-YOW!
PINCH
PINCH
OUCHIES!
EEP!
PINCH
PINCH
OOO... MAYBE WE SHOULDA GONE OUT THERE STRAIGHT AWAY INSTEAD OF SPENDIN' HALF AN HOUR COBBLIN' TOGETHER THIS PROTECTIVE GEAR.
EE-YUP!
PINCH
YOW!!

A Clawful Fate

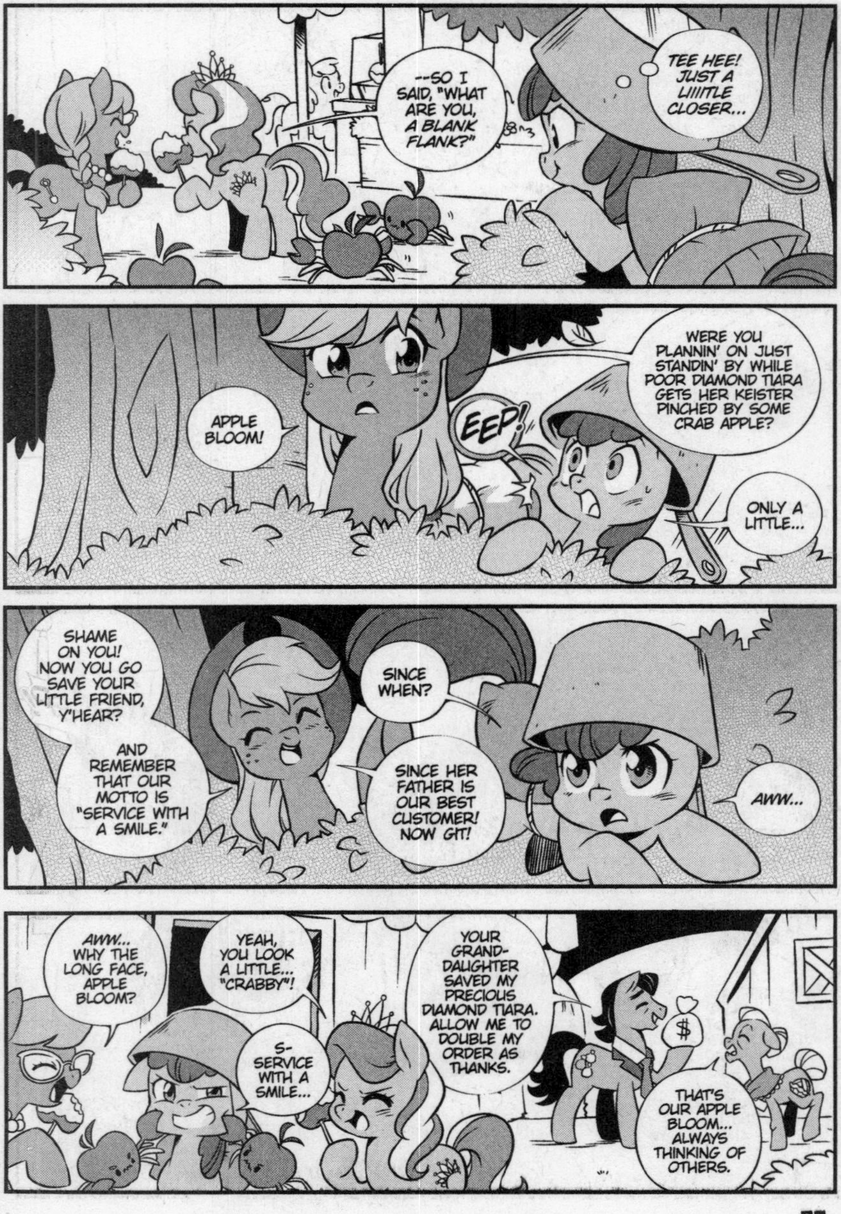
--SO I SAID, "WHAT ARE YOU, A BLANK FLANK?"
TEE HEE! JUST A LIIIITLE CLOSER...
APPLE BLOOM!
EEP!
WERE YOU PLANNIN' ON JUST STANDIN' BY WHILE POOR DIAMOND TIARA GETS HER KEISTER PINCHED BY SOME CRAB APPLE?
ONLY A LITTLE...
SHAME ON YOU! NOW YOU GO SAVE YOUR LITTLE FRIEND, Y'HEAR?
AND REMEMBER THAT OUR MOTTO IS "SERVICE WITH A SMILE."
SINCE WHEN?
SINCE HER FATHER IS OUR BEST CUSTOMER! NOW GIT!
AWW...
AWW... WHY THE LONG FACE, APPLE BLOOM?
YEAH, YOU LOOK A LITTLE... "CRABBY"!
S- SERVICE WITH A SMILE...
YOUR GRAND-DAUGHTER SAVED MY PRECIOUS DIAMOND TIARA. ALLOW ME TO DOUBLE MY ORDER AS THANKS.
THAT'S OUR APPLE BLOOM... ALWAYS THINKING OF OTHERS.

Appleshell Shocked

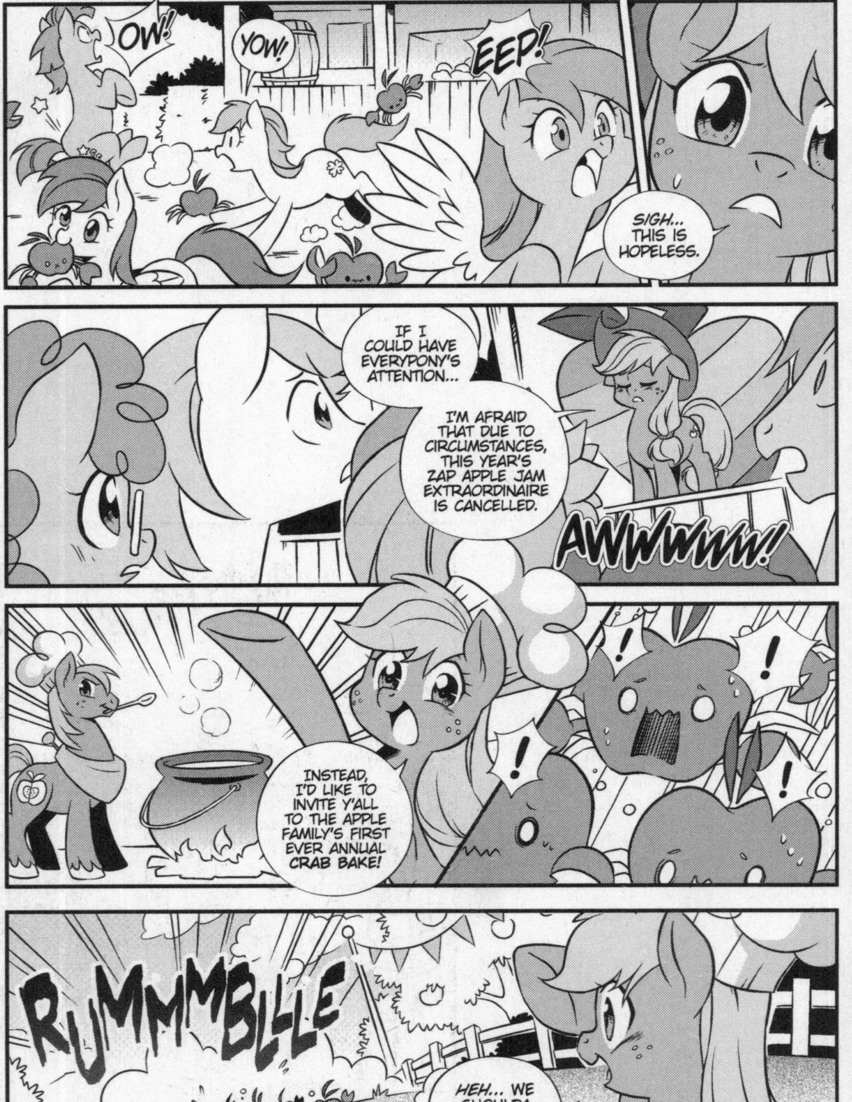
OW!
YOW!
EEP!
SIGH... THIS IS HOPELESS.
IF I COULD HAVE EVERYPONY'S ATTENTION...
I'M AFRAID THAT DUE TO CIRCUMSTANCES, THIS YEAR'S ZAP APPLE JAM EXTRAORDINAIRE IS CANCELLED.
AWWWWWW!
INSTEAD, I'D LIKE TO INVITE Y'ALL TO THE APPLE FAMILY'S FIRST EVER ANNUAL CRAB BAKE!
!
!
!
!
RUMMMBLLE
HEH... WE SHOULDA THOUGHT OF THIS HOURS AGO!

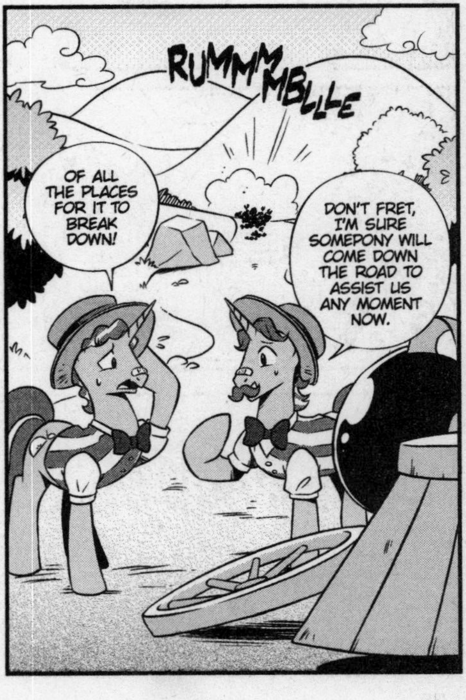
RUMMMMBLLLE
OF ALL THE PLACES FOR IT TO BREAK DOWN!
DON'T FRET, I'M SURE SOMEPONY WILL COME DOWN THE ROAD TO ASSIST US ANY MOMENT NOW.

CHAPTER 6

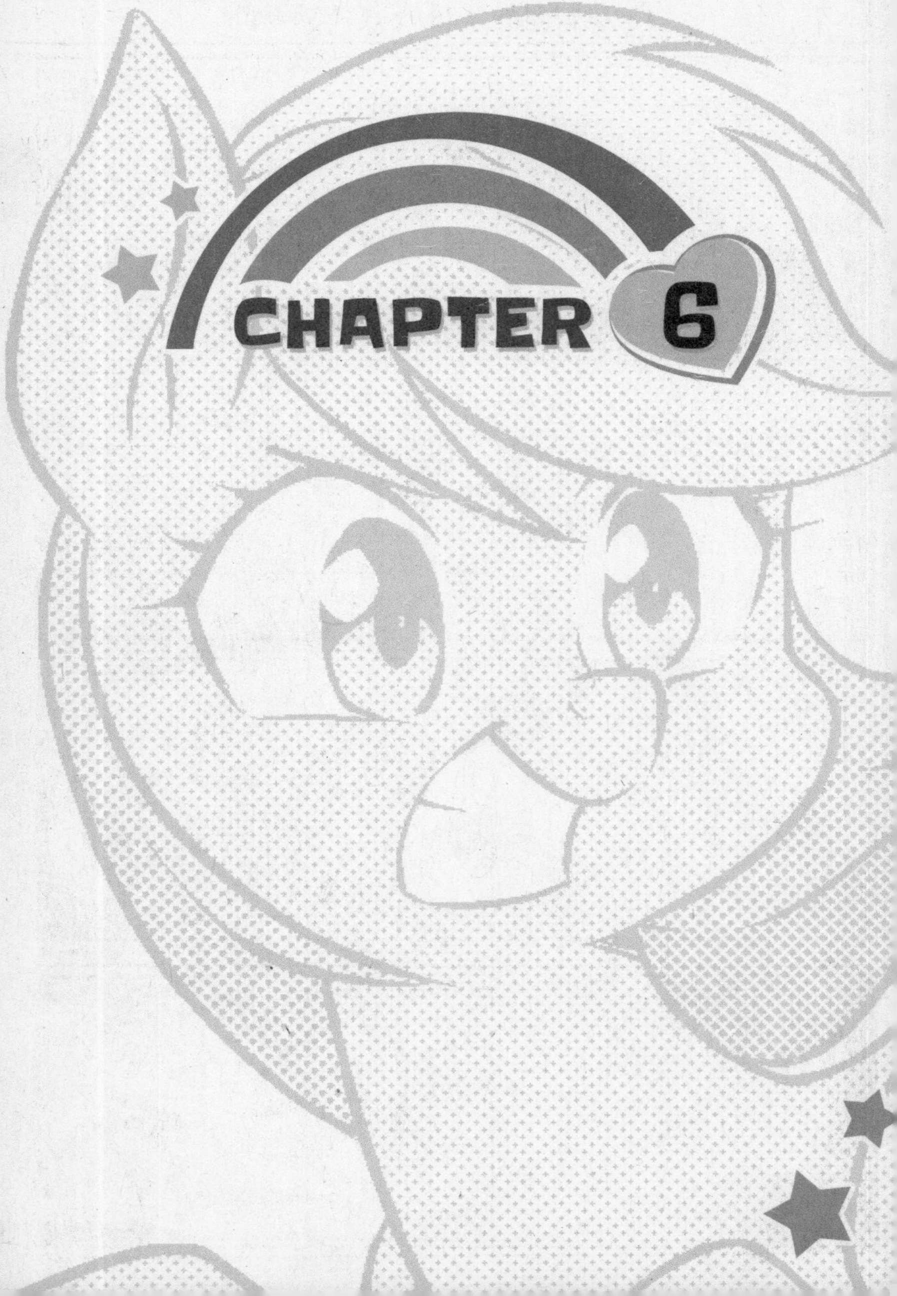

Flee Market

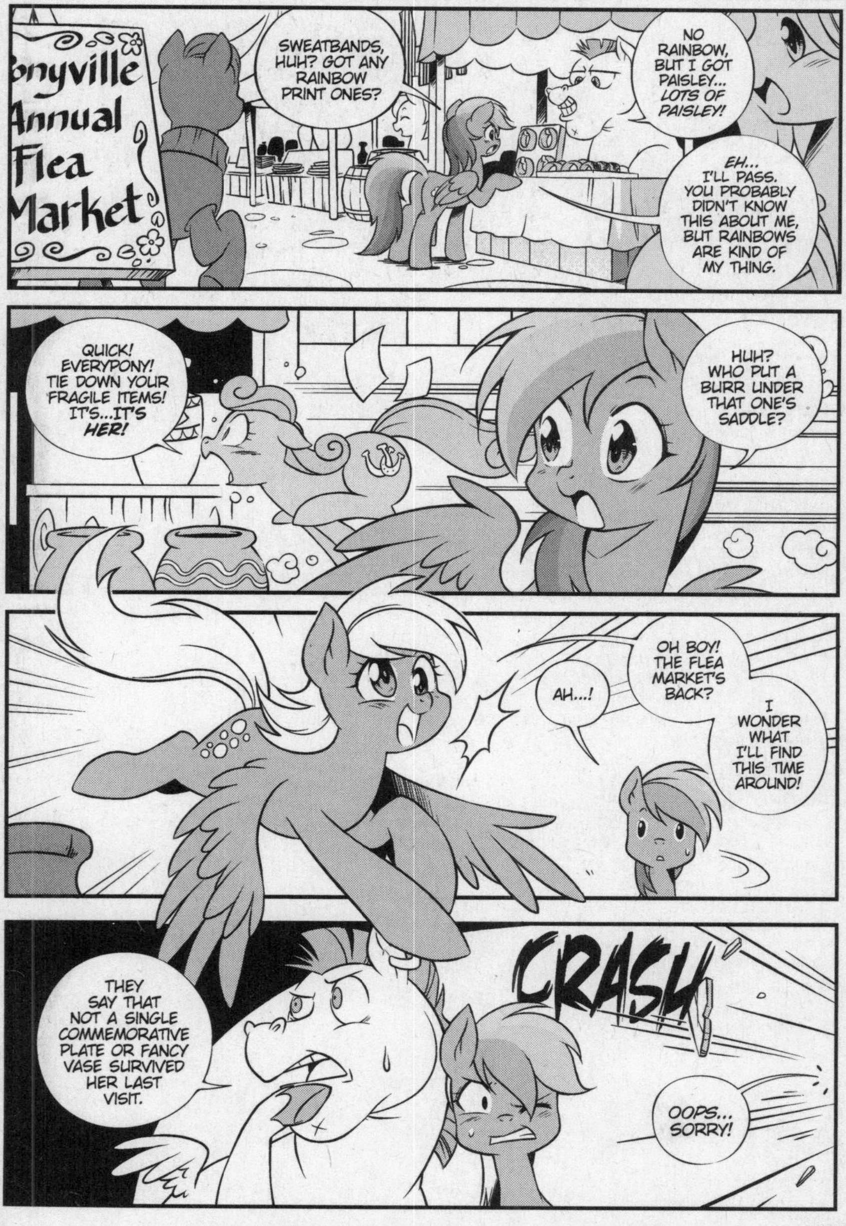
onyville Annual Flea Market
SWEATBANDS, HUH? GOT ANY RAINBOW PRINT ONES?
NO RAINBOW, BUT I GOT PAISLEY... *LOTS OF PAISLEY!*
EH... I'LL PASS. YOU PROBABLY DIDN'T KNOW THIS ABOUT ME, BUT RAINBOWS ARE KIND OF MY THING.
QUICK! EVERYPONY! TIE DOWN YOUR FRAGILE ITEMS! IT'S...IT'S *HER!*
HUH? WHO PUT A BURR UNDER THAT ONE'S SADDLE?
AH...!
OH BOY! THE FLEA MARKET'S BACK?
I WONDER WHAT I'LL FIND THIS TIME AROUND!
THEY SAY THAT NOT A SINGLE COMMEMORATIVE PLATE OR FANCY VASE SURVIVED HER LAST VISIT.
CRASH
OOPS... SORRY!

Slap Not-So-Happy

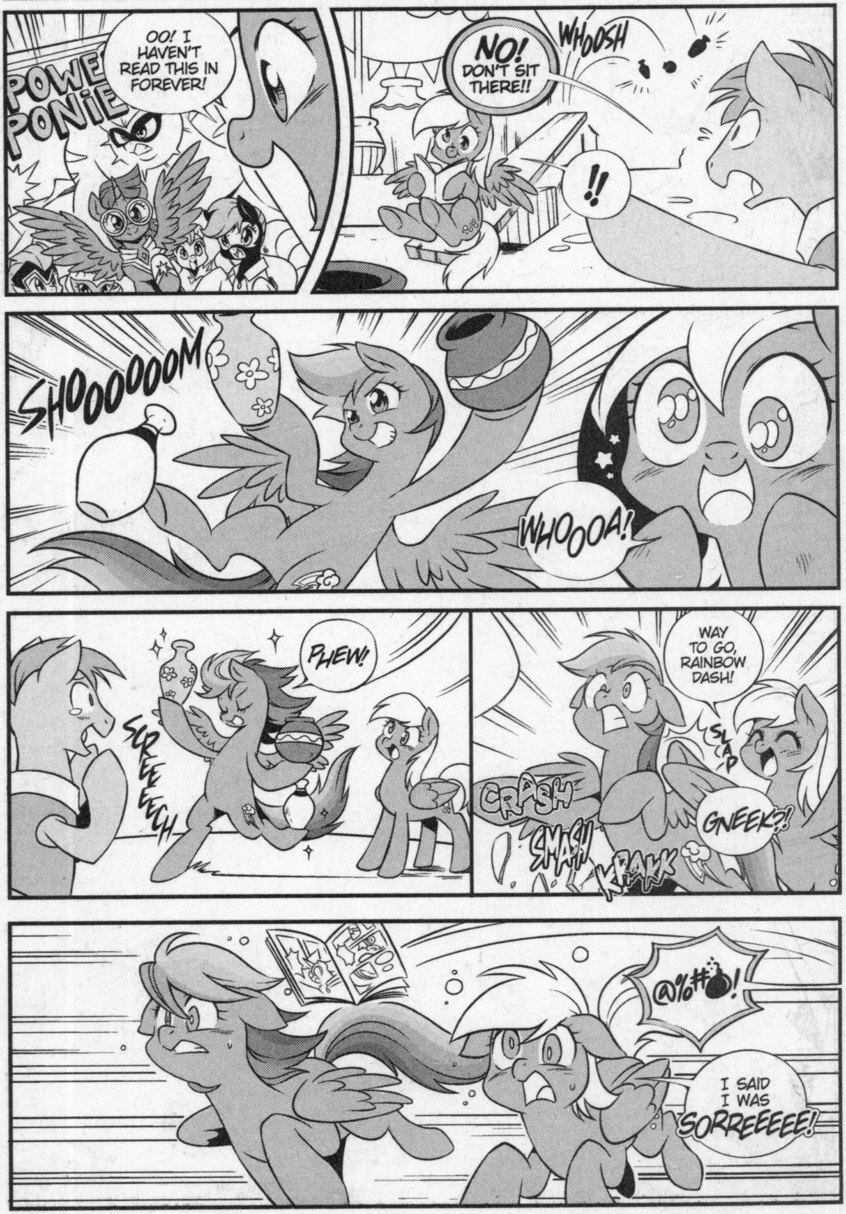
POWE
PONIE
OO! I HAVEN'T READ THIS IN FOREVER!
NO! DON'T SIT THERE!!
WHOOSH
!!
SHOOOOOOM
WHOOOA!
PHEW!
SCREEEECH
WAY TO GO, RAINBOW DASH!
SLAP
CRASH
SMASH
KRAKK
GNEEK?!
@%#!
I SAID I WAS SORREEEEE!

Bringing the House Down

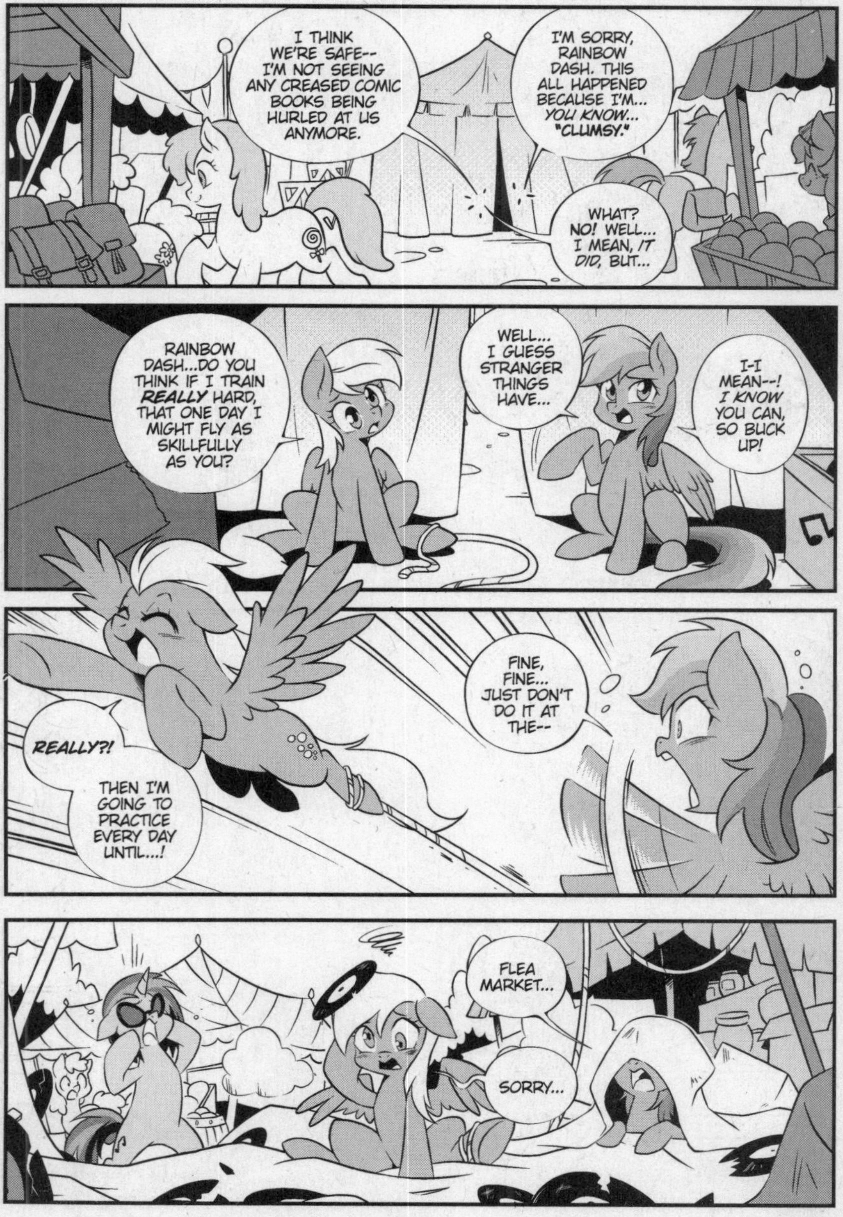
I THINK WE'RE SAFE-- I'M NOT SEEING ANY CREASED COMIC BOOKS BEING HURLED AT US ANYMORE.
I'M SORRY, RAINBOW DASH. THIS ALL HAPPENED BECAUSE I'M... *YOU KNOW...* **"CLUMSY."**
WHAT? **NO!** WELL... I MEAN, *IT DID,* BUT...
RAINBOW DASH...DO YOU THINK IF I TRAIN ***REALLY*** HARD, THAT ONE DAY I MIGHT FLY AS SKILLFULLY AS YOU?
WELL... I GUESS STRANGER THINGS HAVE...
I-I MEAN--! *I KNOW* YOU CAN, SO BUCK UP!
REALLY?!
THEN I'M GOING TO PRACTICE EVERY DAY UNTIL...!
FINE, FINE... JUST DON'T DO IT AT THE--
FLEA MARKET...
SORRY...

Charmed... I'm Sure!

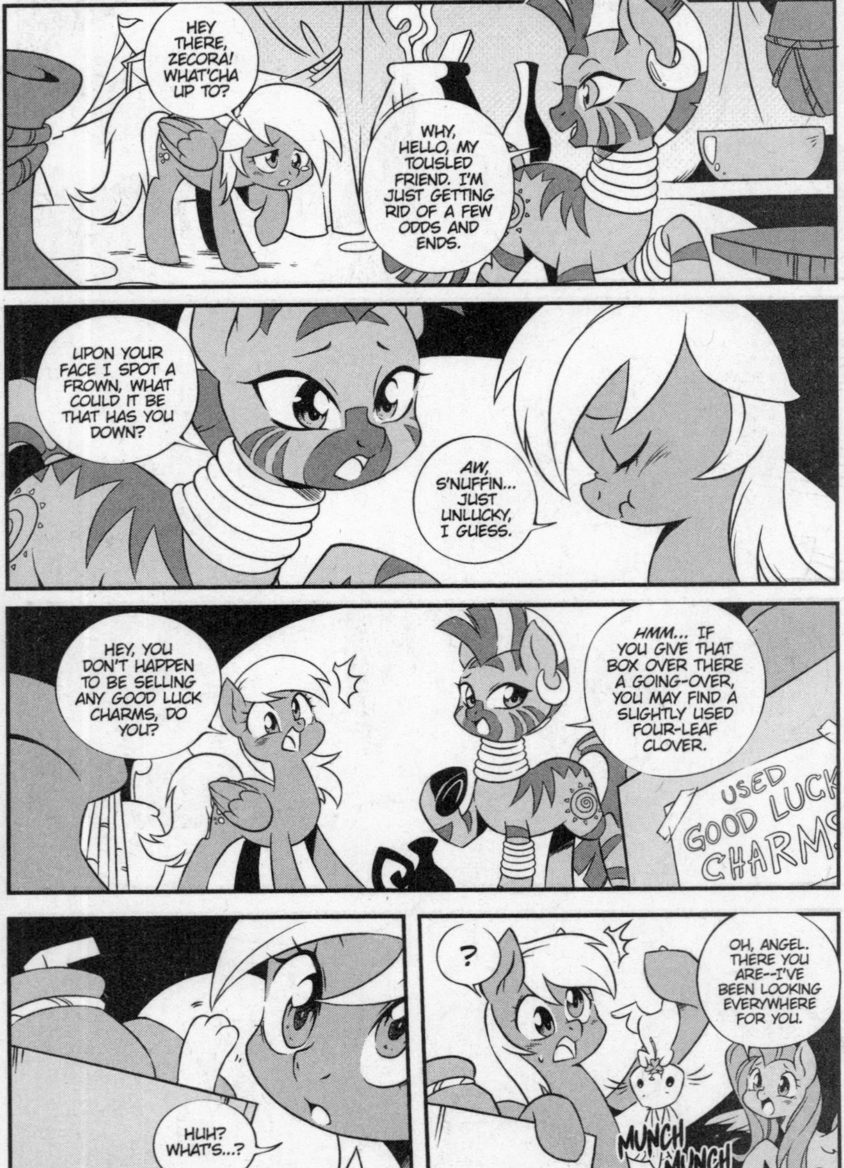

HEY THERE, ZECORA! WHAT'CHA UP TO?
WHY, HELLO, MY TOUSLED FRIEND. I'M JUST GETTING RID OF A FEW ODDS AND ENDS.
UPON YOUR FACE I SPOT A FROWN, WHAT COULD IT BE THAT HAS YOU DOWN?
AW, S'NUFFIN... JUST UNLUCKY, I GUESS.
HEY, YOU DON'T HAPPEN TO BE SELLING ANY GOOD LUCK CHARMS, DO YOU?
HMM... IF YOU GIVE THAT BOX OVER THERE A GOING-OVER, YOU MAY FIND A SLIGHTLY USED FOUR-LEAF CLOVER.
USED GOOD LUCK CHARMS
HUH? WHAT'S...?
?
OH, ANGEL. THERE YOU ARE--I'VE BEEN LOOKING EVERYWHERE FOR YOU.
MUNCH MUNCH

Can I Give You a Hand?

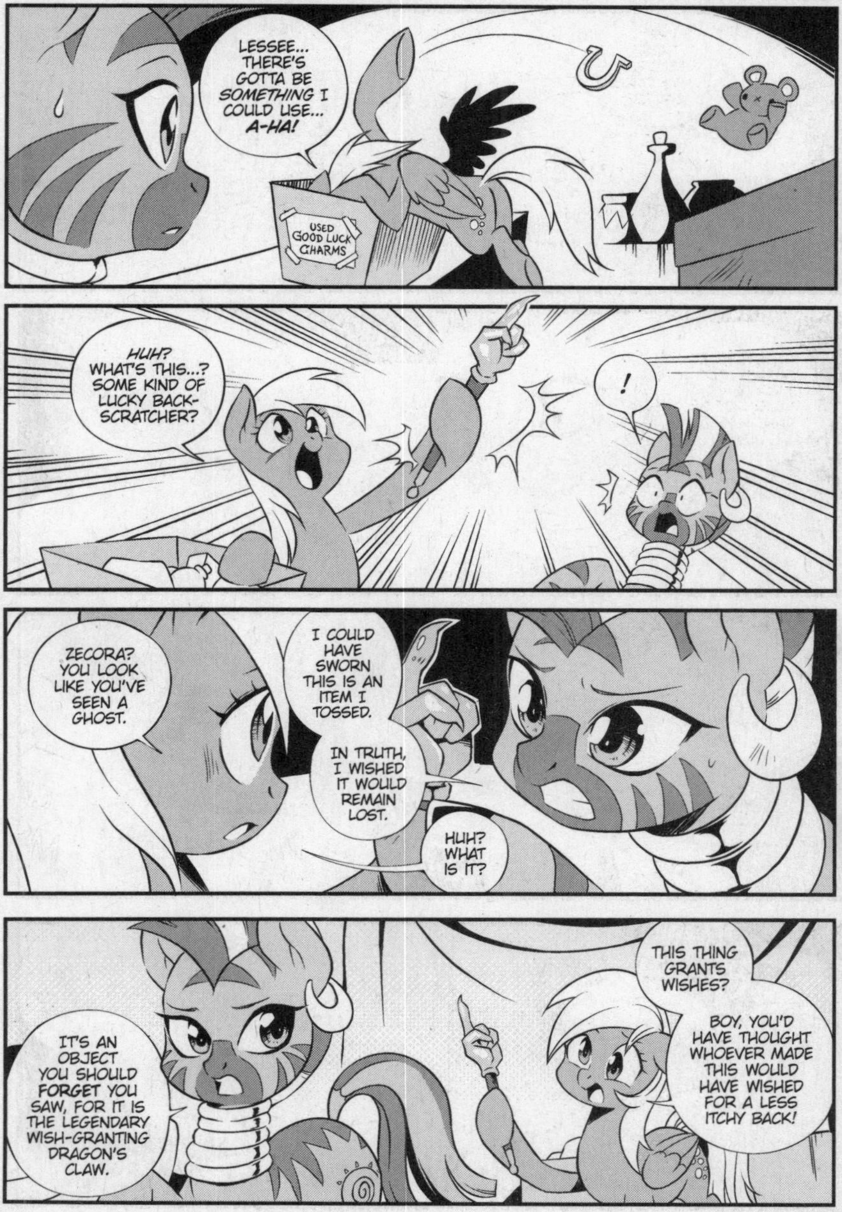
LESSEE... THERE'S GOTTA BE *SOMETHING* I COULD USE... *A-HA!*
USED GOOD LUCK CHARMS
HUH? WHAT'S THIS...? SOME KIND OF LUCKY BACK-SCRATCHER?
!
ZECORA? YOU LOOK LIKE YOU'VE SEEN A GHOST.
I COULD HAVE SWORN THIS IS AN ITEM I TOSSED.
IN TRUTH, I WISHED IT WOULD REMAIN LOST.
HUH? WHAT IS IT?
IT'S AN OBJECT YOU SHOULD FORGET YOU SAW, FOR IT IS THE LEGENDARY WISH-GRANTING DRAGON'S CLAW.
THIS THING GRANTS WISHES?
BOY, YOU'D HAVE THOUGHT WHOEVER MADE THIS WOULD HAVE WISHED FOR A LESS ITCHY BACK!

Be Careful What You Wish For

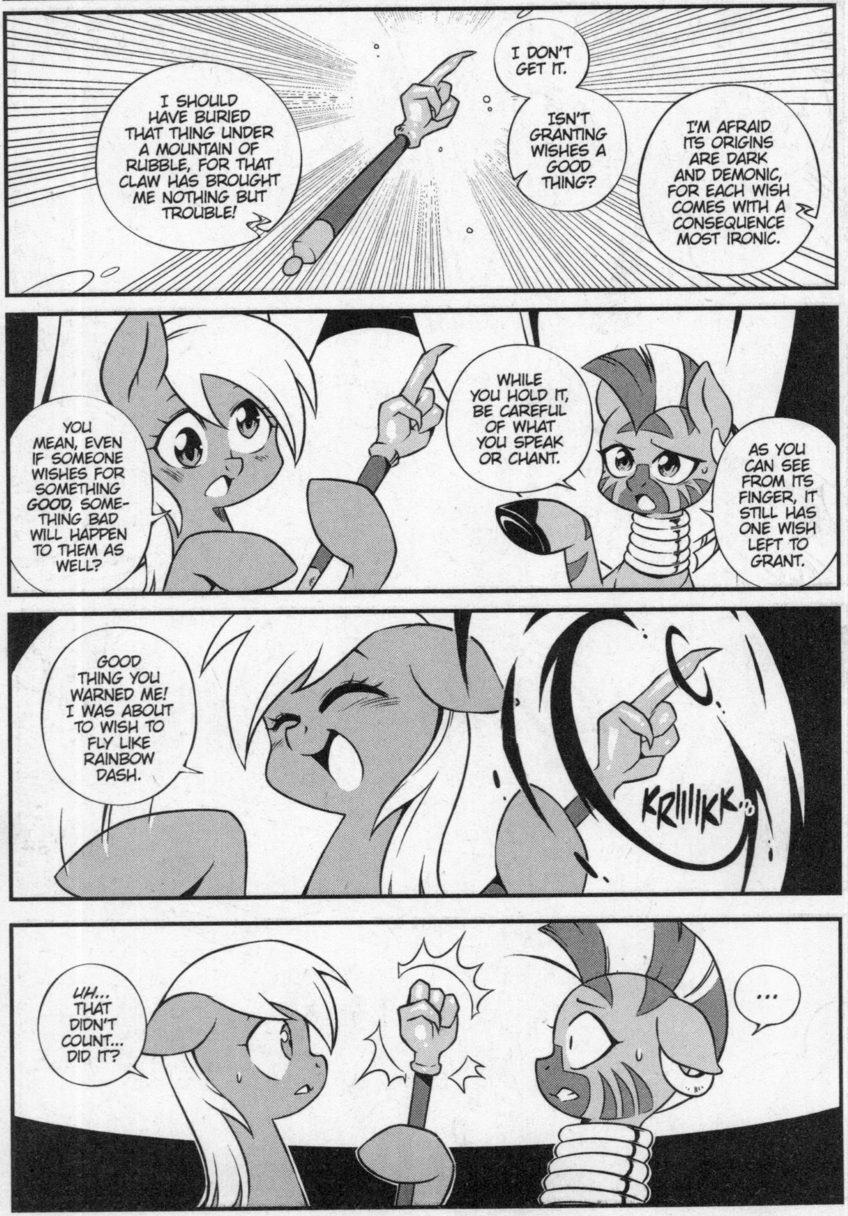
I SHOULD HAVE BURIED THAT THING UNDER A MOUNTAIN OF RUBBLE, FOR THAT CLAW HAS BROUGHT ME NOTHING BUT TROUBLE!
I DON'T GET IT.
ISN'T GRANTING WISHES A GOOD THING?
I'M AFRAID ITS ORIGINS ARE DARK AND DEMONIC, FOR EACH WISH COMES WITH A CONSEQUENCE MOST IRONIC.
YOU MEAN, EVEN IF SOMEONE WISHES FOR SOMETHING GOOD, SOME-THING BAD WILL HAPPEN TO THEM AS WELL?
WHILE YOU HOLD IT, BE CAREFUL OF WHAT YOU SPEAK OR CHANT.
AS YOU CAN SEE FROM ITS FINGER, IT STILL HAS ONE WISH LEFT TO GRANT.
GOOD THING YOU WARNED ME! I WAS ABOUT TO WISH TO FLY LIKE RAINBOW DASH.
KRIIIIKK
UH... THAT DIDN'T COUNT... DID IT?
...

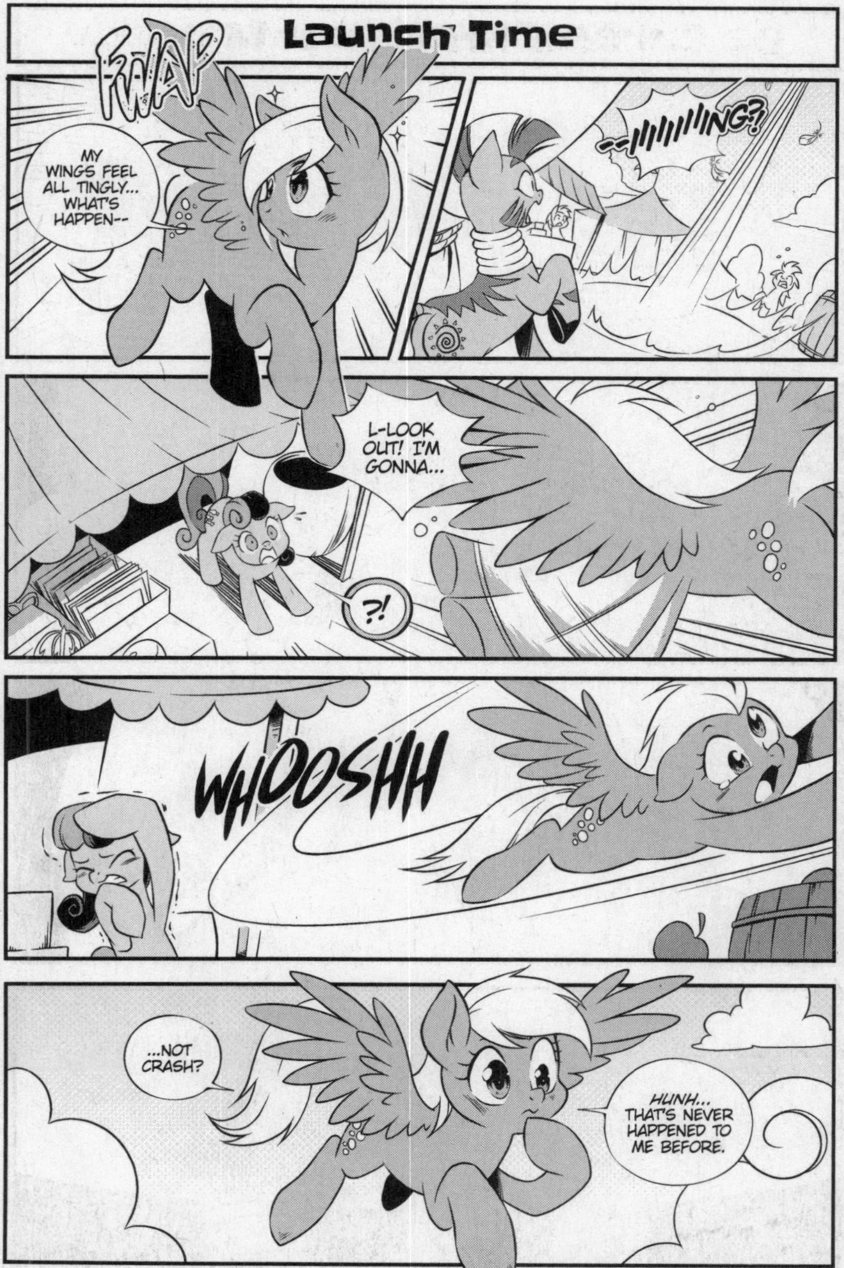
Launch Time
FWAP
MY WINGS FEEL ALL TINGLY... WHAT'S HAPPEN--
--IIIIIIIIIING?!
L-LOOK OUT! I'M GONNA...
?!
WHOOSHH
...NOT CRASH?
HUNH... THAT'S NEVER HAPPENED TO ME BEFORE.

Switching Flights

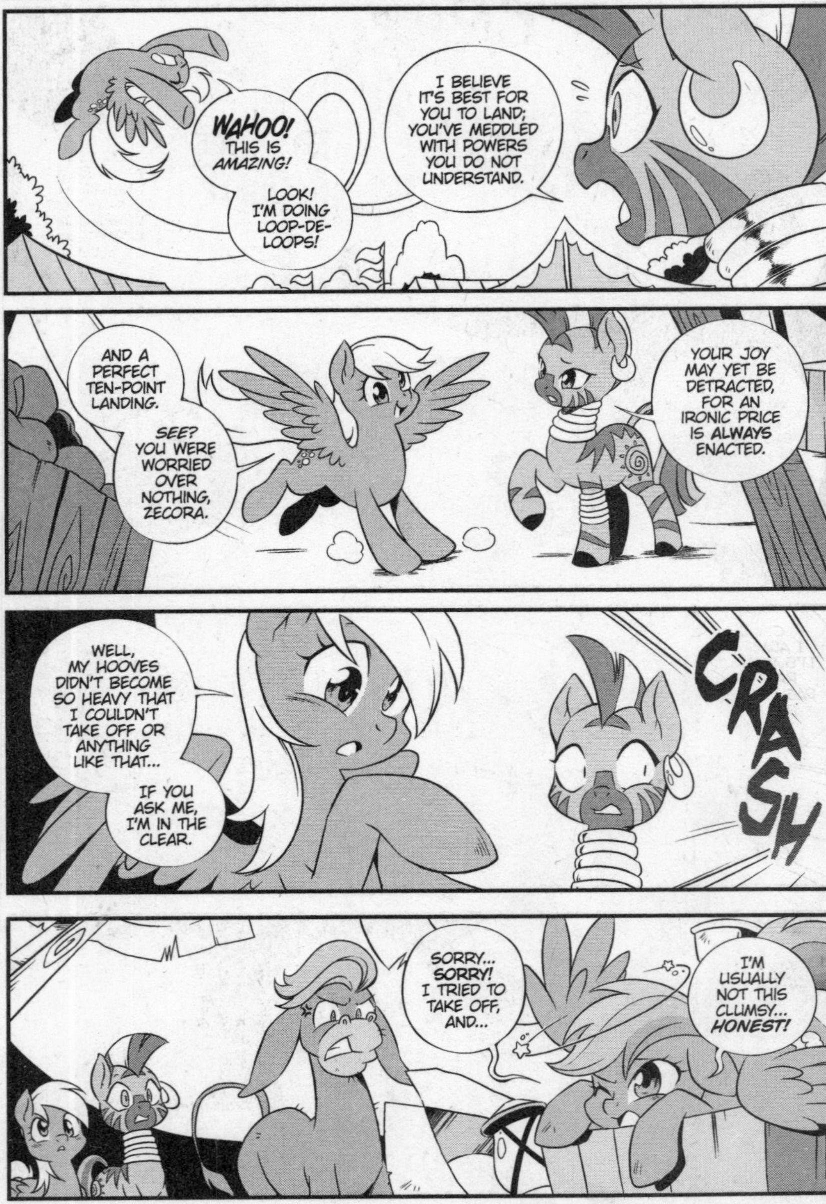
WAHOO! THIS IS AMAZING!
LOOK! I'M DOING LOOP-DE-LOOPS!
I BELIEVE IT'S BEST FOR YOU TO LAND; YOU'VE MEDDLED WITH POWERS YOU DO NOT UNDERSTAND.
AND A PERFECT TEN-POINT LANDING.
SEE? YOU WERE WORRIED OVER NOTHING, ZECORA.
YOUR JOY MAY YET BE DETRACTED, FOR AN IRONIC PRICE IS ALWAYS ENACTED.
WELL, MY HOOVES DIDN'T BECOME SO HEAVY THAT I COULDN'T TAKE OFF OR ANYTHING LIKE THAT...
IF YOU ASK ME, I'M IN THE CLEAR.
CRASH
SORRY... SORRY! I TRIED TO TAKE OFF, AND...
I'M USUALLY NOT THIS CLUMSY... HONEST!

Rainbow Crashed

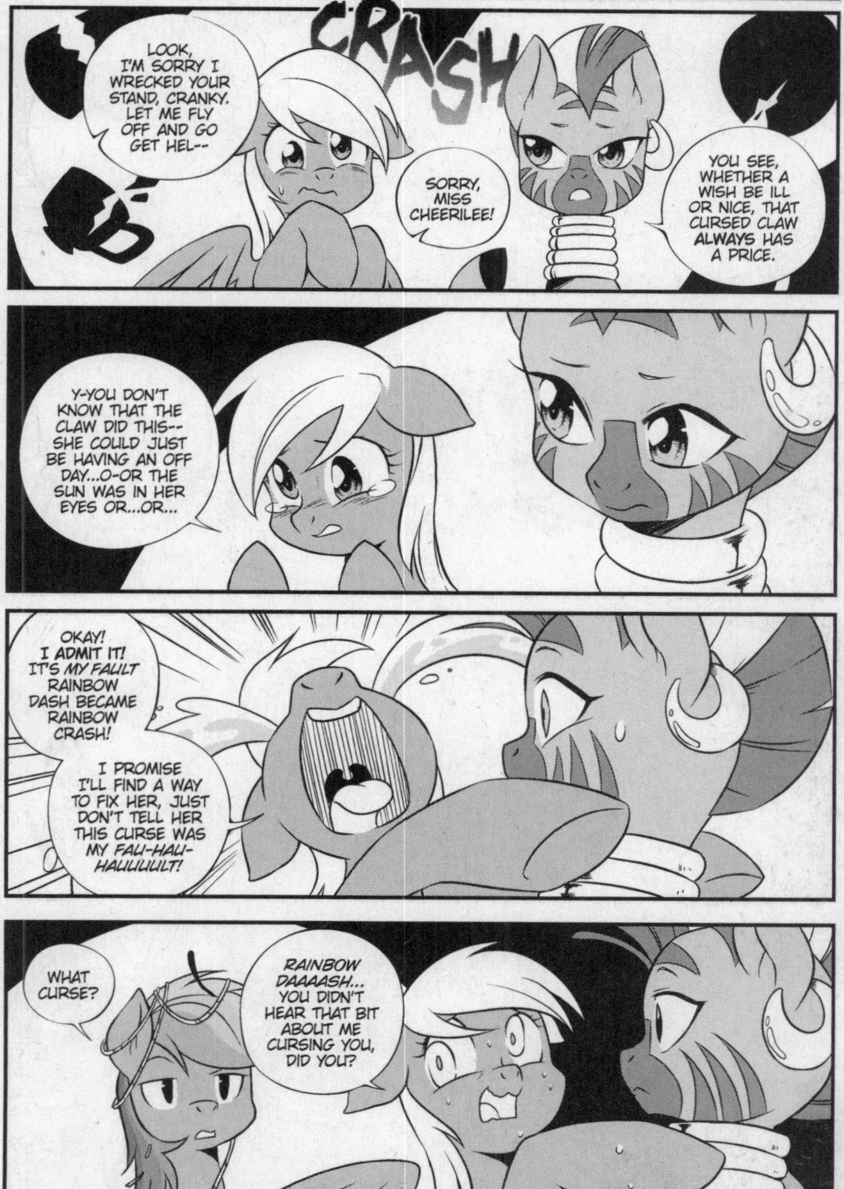
CRASH
LOOK, I'M SORRY I WRECKED YOUR STAND, CRANKY. LET ME FLY OFF AND GO GET HEL--
SORRY, MISS CHEERILEE!
YOU SEE, WHETHER A WISH BE ILL OR NICE, THAT CURSED CLAW ALWAYS HAS A PRICE.
Y-YOU DON'T KNOW THAT THE CLAW DID THIS-- SHE COULD JUST BE HAVING AN OFF DAY...O-OR THE SUN WAS IN HER EYES OR...OR...
OKAY! I ADMIT IT! IT'S *MY FAULT* RAINBOW DASH BECAME RAINBOW CRASH!
I PROMISE I'LL FIND A WAY TO FIX HER, JUST DON'T TELL HER THIS CURSE WAS MY *FAU-HAU-HAUUUUULT!*
WHAT CURSE?
RAINBOW DAAAASH... YOU DIDN'T HEAR THAT BIT ABOUT ME CURSING YOU, DID YOU?

Dash Test Dummy

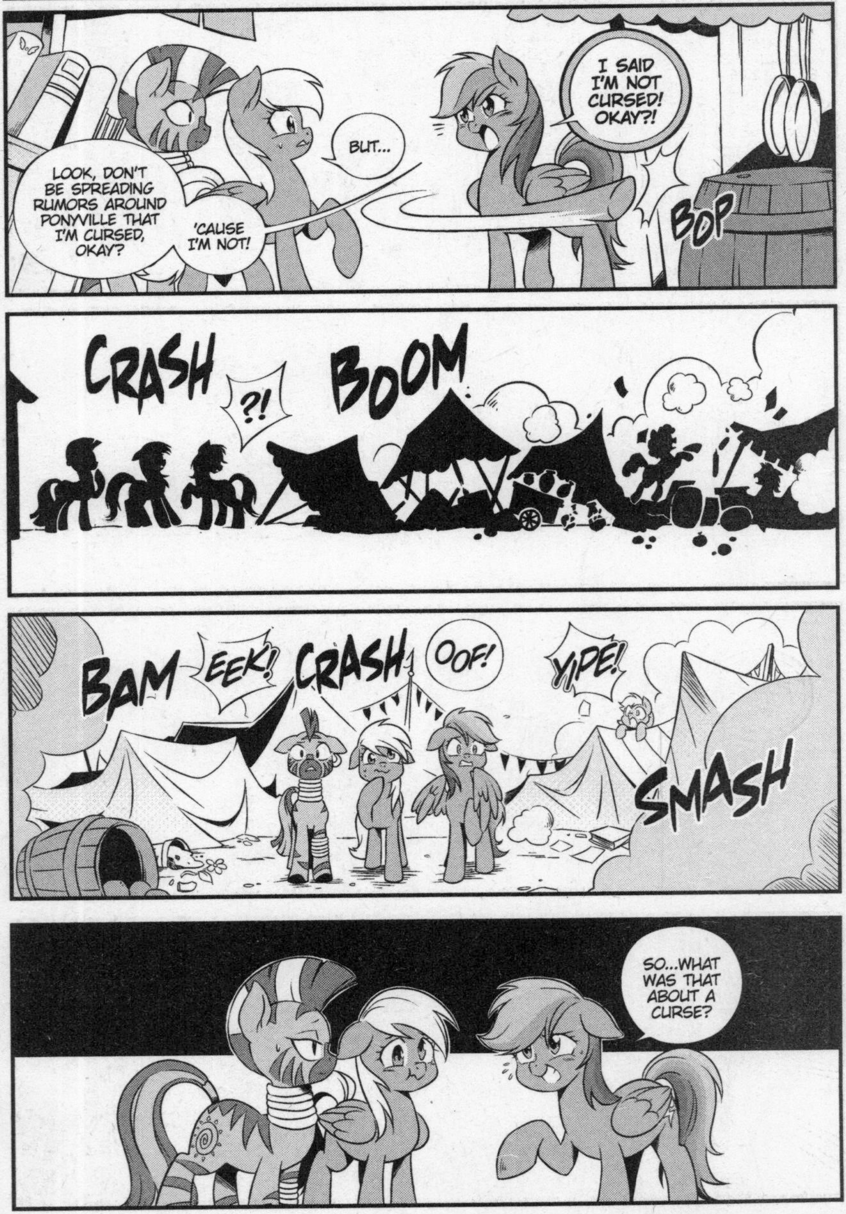
LOOK, DON'T BE SPREADING RUMORS AROUND PONYVILLE THAT I'M CURSED, OKAY?
'CAUSE I'M NOT!
BUT...
I SAID I'M NOT CURSED! OKAY?!
BOP
CRASH
?!
BOOM
BAM
EEK!
CRASH
OOF!
YIPE!
SMASH
SO...WHAT WAS THAT ABOUT A CURSE?

The Solution Is Afoot

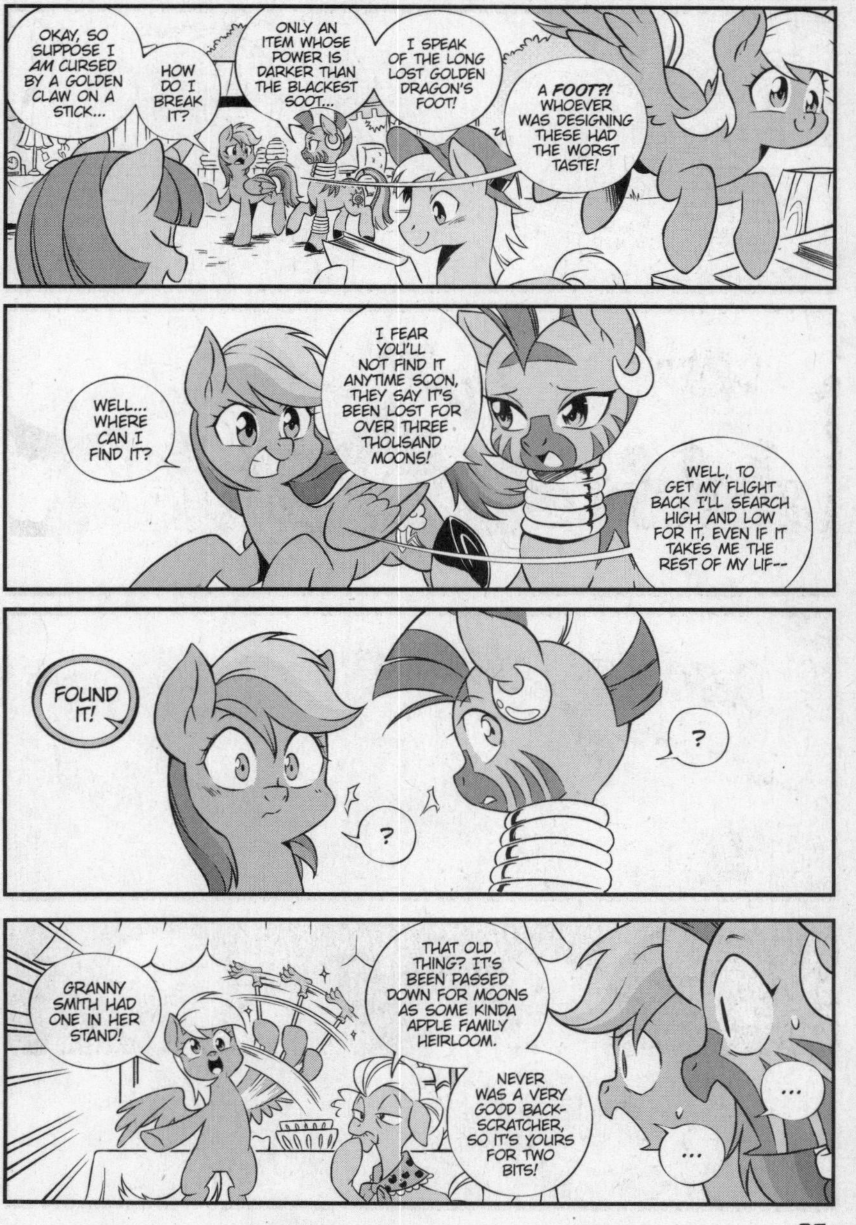

OKAY, SO SUPPOSE I AM CURSED BY A GOLDEN CLAW ON A STICK...
HOW DO I BREAK IT?
ONLY AN ITEM WHOSE POWER IS DARKER THAN THE BLACKEST SOOT...
I SPEAK OF THE LONG LOST GOLDEN DRAGON'S FOOT!
A *FOOT?!* WHOEVER WAS DESIGNING THESE HAD THE WORST TASTE!
WELL... WHERE CAN I FIND IT?
I FEAR YOU'LL NOT FIND IT ANYTIME SOON, THEY SAY IT'S BEEN LOST FOR OVER THREE THOUSAND MOONS!
WELL, TO GET MY FLIGHT BACK I'LL SEARCH HIGH AND LOW FOR IT, EVEN IF IT TAKES ME THE REST OF MY LIF--
FOUND IT!
?
?
GRANNY SMITH HAD ONE IN HER STAND!
THAT OLD THING? IT'S BEEN PASSED DOWN FOR MOONS AS SOME KINDA APPLE FAMILY HEIRLOOM.
NEVER WAS A VERY GOOD BACK-SCRATCHER, SO IT'S YOURS FOR TWO BITS!
...
...

Mob Tactics

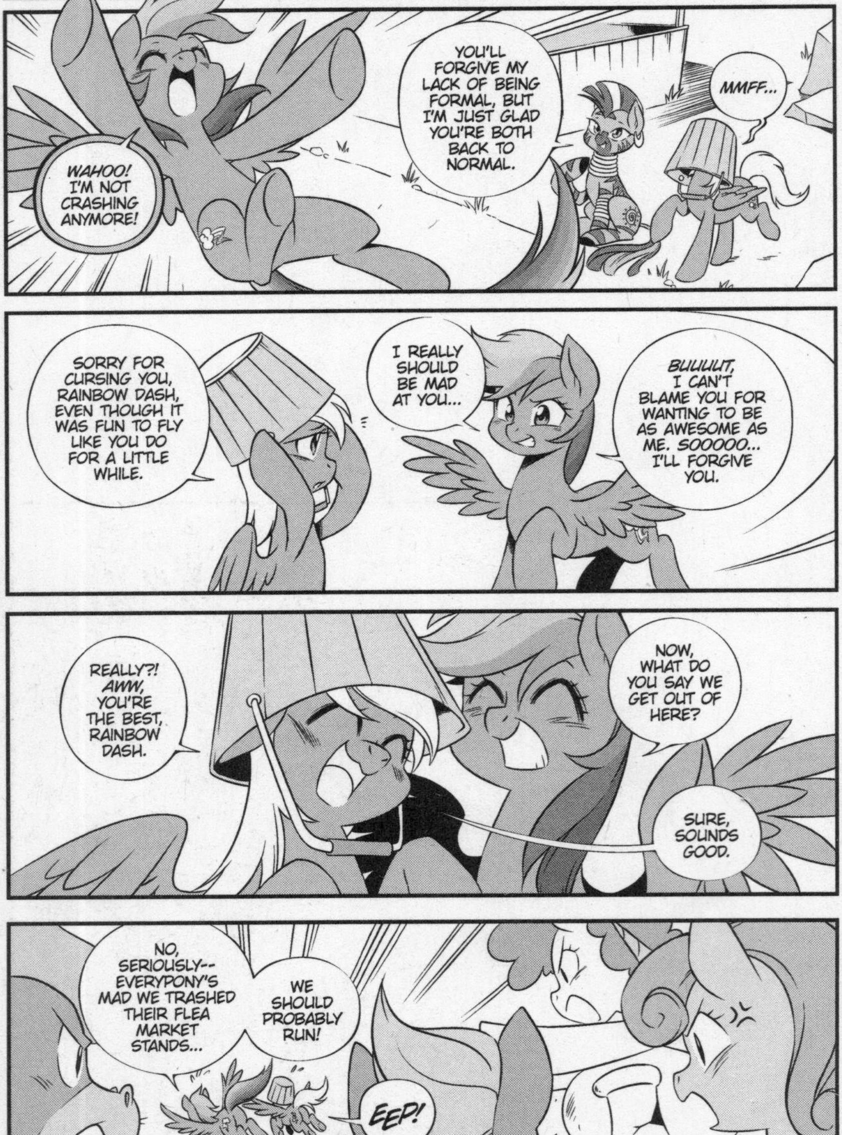
WAHOO! I'M NOT CRASHING ANYMORE!
YOU'LL FORGIVE MY LACK OF BEING FORMAL, BUT I'M JUST GLAD YOU'RE BOTH BACK TO NORMAL.
MMFF...
SORRY FOR CURSING YOU, RAINBOW DASH, EVEN THOUGH IT WAS FUN TO FLY LIKE YOU DO FOR A LITTLE WHILE.
I REALLY SHOULD BE MAD AT YOU...
BUUUUT, I CAN'T BLAME YOU FOR WANTING TO BE AS AWESOME AS ME. SOOOOO... I'LL FORGIVE YOU.
REALLY?! AWW, YOU'RE THE BEST, RAINBOW DASH.
NOW, WHAT DO YOU SAY WE GET OUT OF HERE?
SURE, SOUNDS GOOD.
NO, SERIOUSLY-- EVERYPONY'S MAD WE TRASHED THEIR FLEA MARKET STANDS...
WE SHOULD PROBABLY RUN!
EEP!

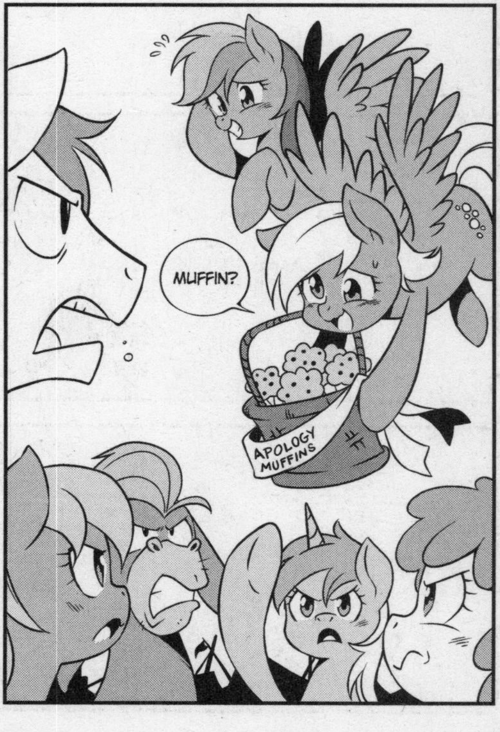
MUFFIN?
APOLOGY MUFFINS

CHAPTER 7

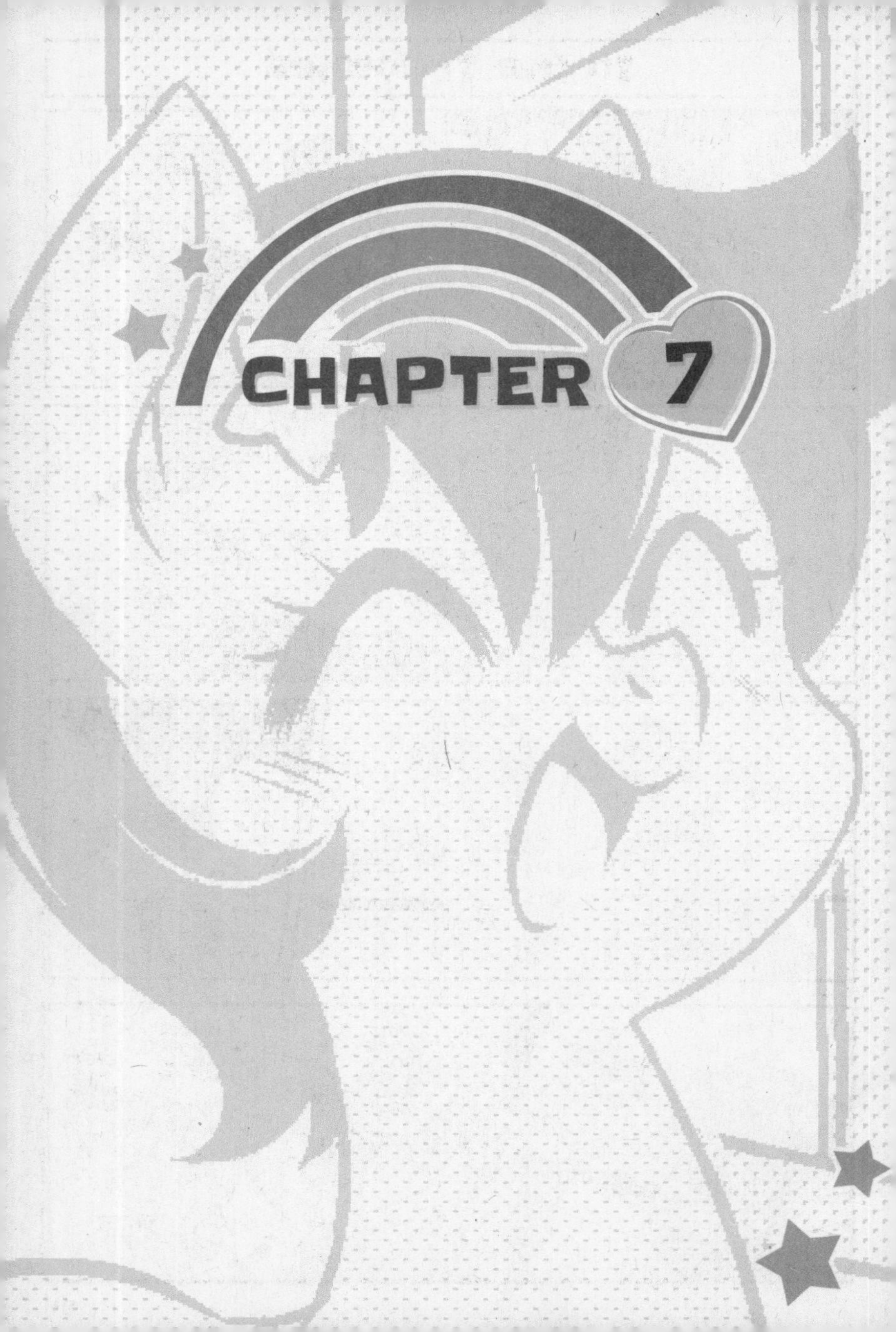

In the Trenches

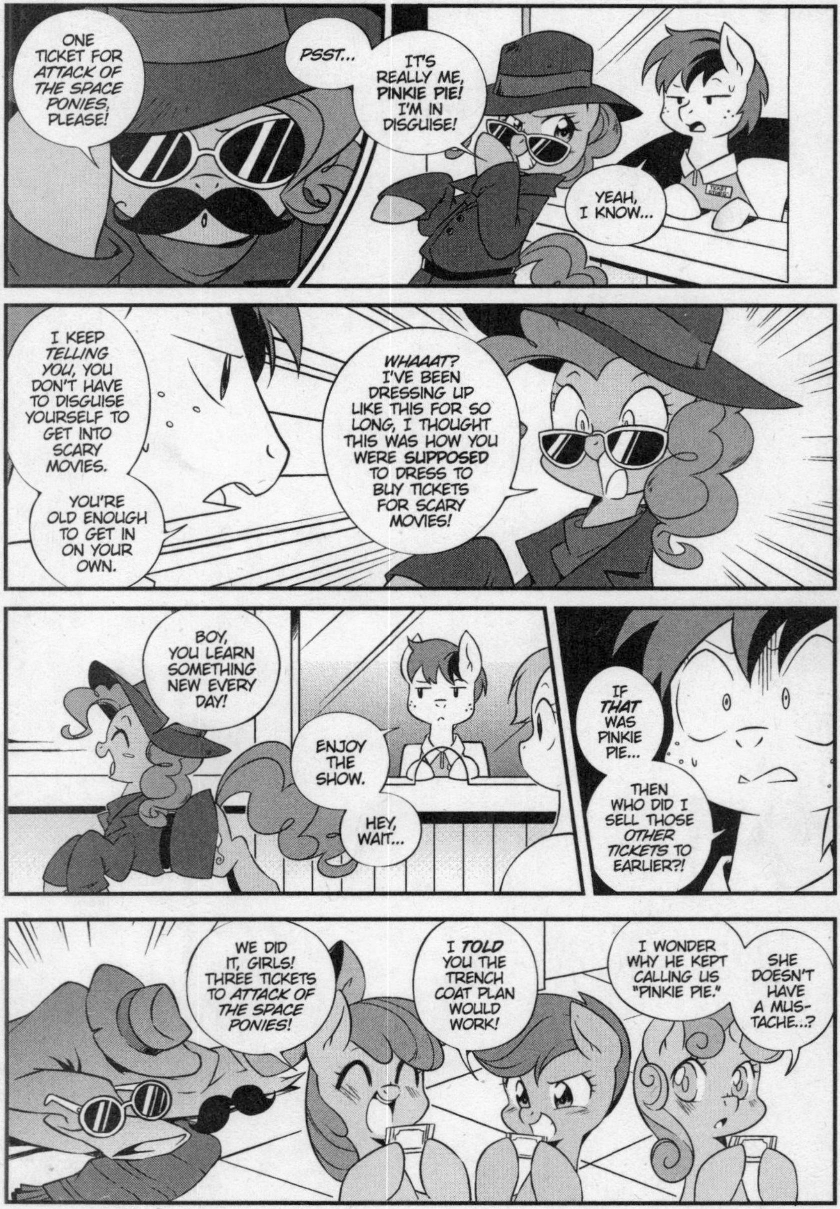
ONE TICKET FOR *ATTACK OF THE SPACE PONIES,* PLEASE!
PSST...
IT'S REALLY ME, **PINKIE PIE!** I'M IN DISGUISE!
YEAH, I KNOW...
I KEEP *TELLING* YOU, YOU DON'T HAVE TO DISGUISE YOURSELF TO GET INTO SCARY MOVIES.
YOU'RE OLD ENOUGH TO GET IN ON YOUR OWN.
WHAAAT? I'VE BEEN DRESSING UP LIKE THIS FOR SO LONG, I THOUGHT THIS WAS HOW YOU WERE **SUPPOSED** TO DRESS TO BUY TICKETS FOR SCARY MOVIES!
BOY, YOU LEARN SOMETHING NEW EVERY DAY!
ENJOY THE SHOW.
HEY, WAIT...
IF ***THAT*** WAS PINKIE PIE...
THEN WHO DID I SELL THOSE *OTHER TICKETS* TO EARLIER?!
WE DID IT, GIRLS! THREE TICKETS TO *ATTACK OF THE SPACE PONIES!*
I ***TOLD*** YOU THE TRENCH COAT PLAN WOULD WORK!
I WONDER WHY HE KEPT CALLING US "PINKIE PIE."
SHE DOESN'T HAVE A MUS-TACHE...?

A Kernel of Truth

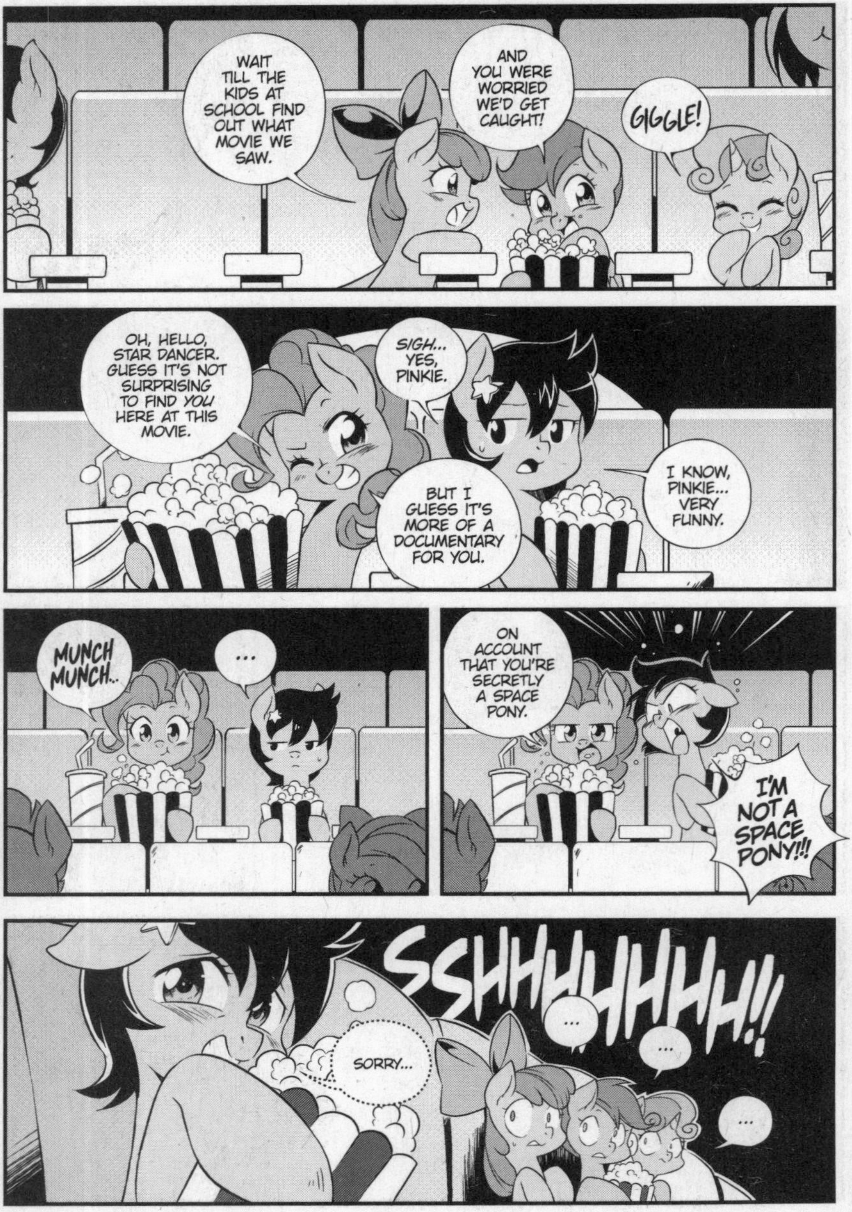

WAIT TILL THE KIDS AT SCHOOL FIND OUT WHAT MOVIE WE SAW.
AND YOU WERE WORRIED WE'D GET CAUGHT!
GIGGLE!
OH, HELLO, STAR DANCER. GUESS IT'S NOT SURPRISING TO FIND *YOU* HERE AT THIS MOVIE.
SIGH... YES, PINKIE.
BUT I GUESS IT'S MORE OF A DOCUMENTARY FOR YOU.
I KNOW, PINKIE... VERY FUNNY.
MUNCH MUNCH...
...
ON ACCOUNT THAT YOU'RE SECRETLY A SPACE PONY.
I'M NOT A SPACE PONY!!!
SSHHHHHHHH!!
SORRY...
...
...
...

The Silver Scream

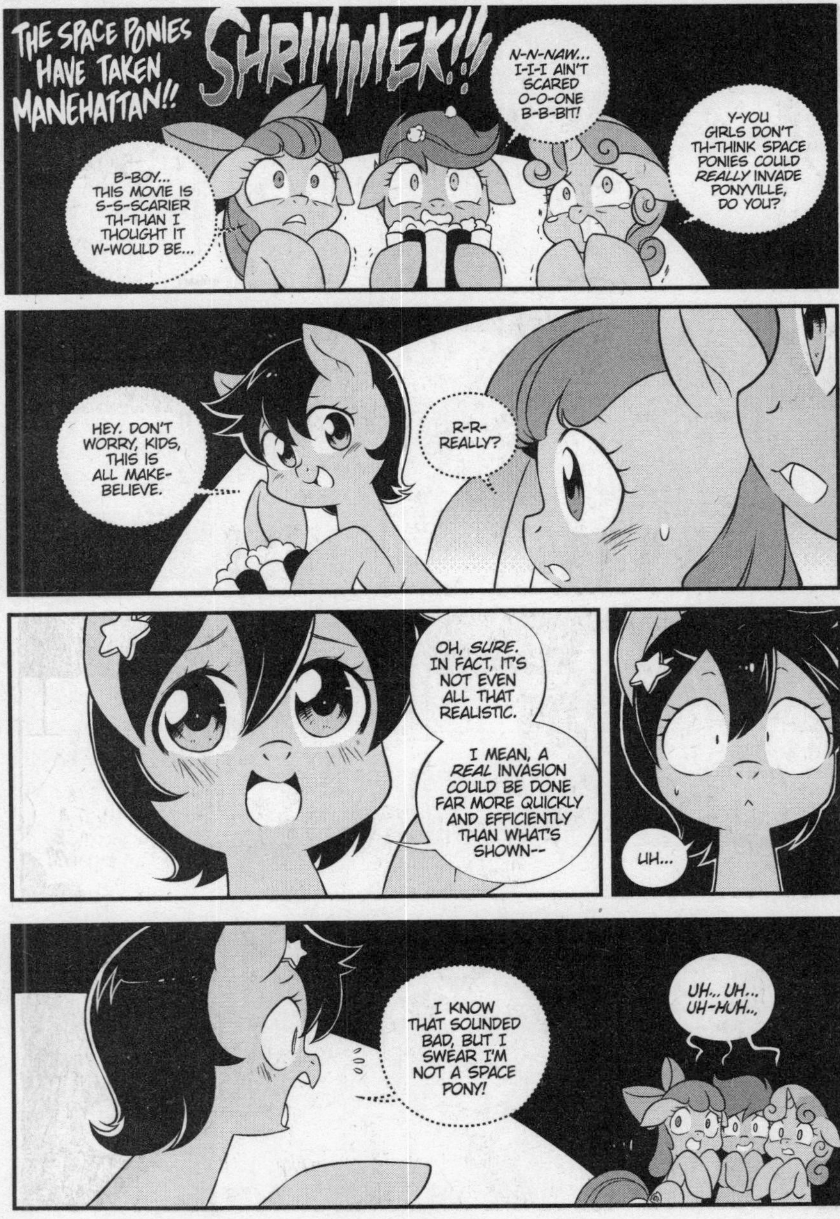
THE SPACE PONIES HAVE TAKEN MANEHATTAN!!
SHRIIIIIEK!!
N-N-NAW... I-I-I AIN'T SCARED O-O-ONE B-B-BIT!
B-BOY... THIS MOVIE IS S-S-SCARIER TH-THAN I THOUGHT IT W-WOULD BE...
Y-YOU GIRLS DON'T TH-THINK SPACE PONIES COULD *REALLY* INVADE PONYVILLE, DO YOU?
HEY. DON'T WORRY, KIDS, THIS IS ALL MAKE-BELIEVE.
R-R-REALLY?
OH, *SURE*. IN FACT, IT'S NOT EVEN ALL THAT REALISTIC.
I MEAN, A *REAL* INVASION COULD BE DONE FAR MORE QUICKLY AND EFFICIENTLY THAN WHAT'S SHOWN--
UH...
I KNOW THAT SOUNDED BAD, BUT I SWEAR I'M NOT A SPACE PONY!
UH... UH... UH-HUH...

Duly Noted

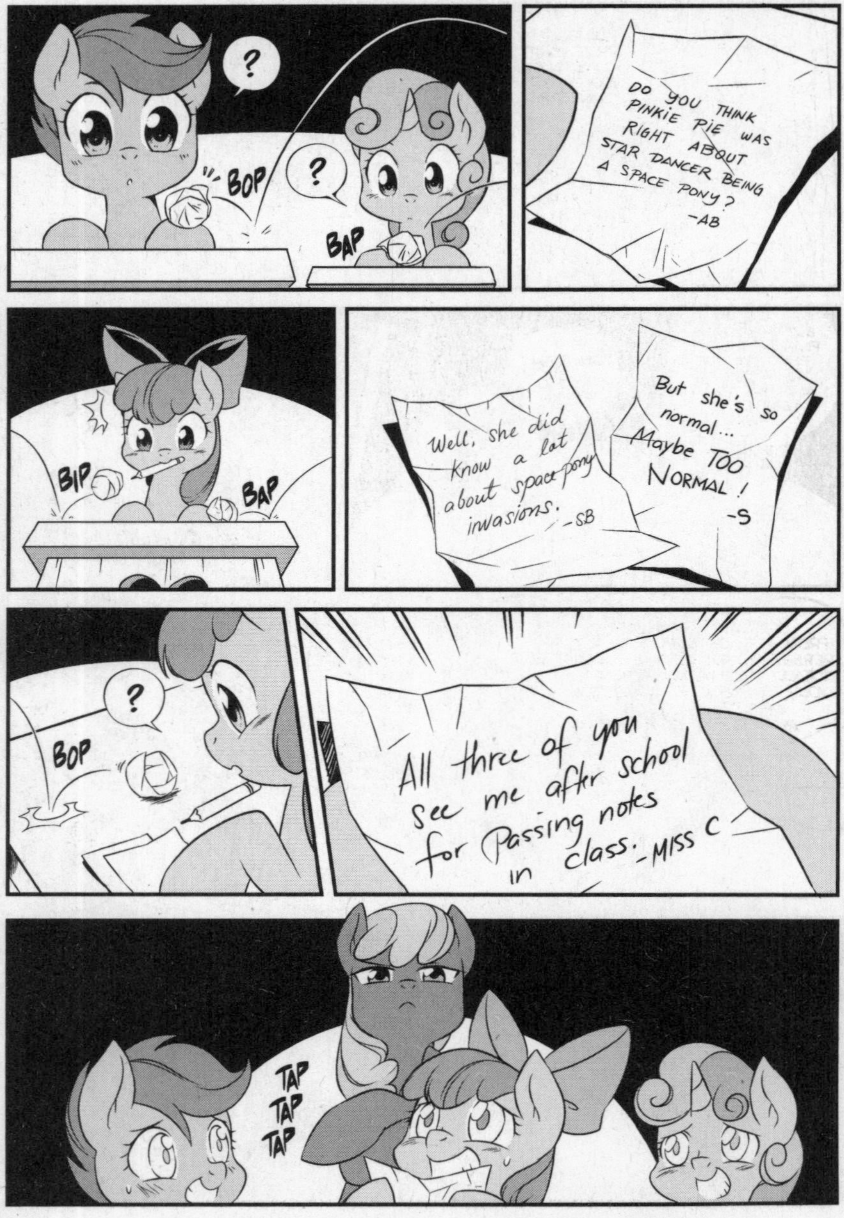
?
BOP
?
BAP
DO YOU THINK PINKIE PIE WAS RIGHT ABOUT STAR DANCER BEING A SPACE PONY? -AB
BIP
BAP
Well, she did know a lot about space pony invasions. -SB
But she's so normal... Maybe TOO NORMAL! -S
?
BOP
All three of you see me after school for Passing notes in class. -MISS C
TAP
TAP
TAP

Scoota-loota-loo, Where Are You?

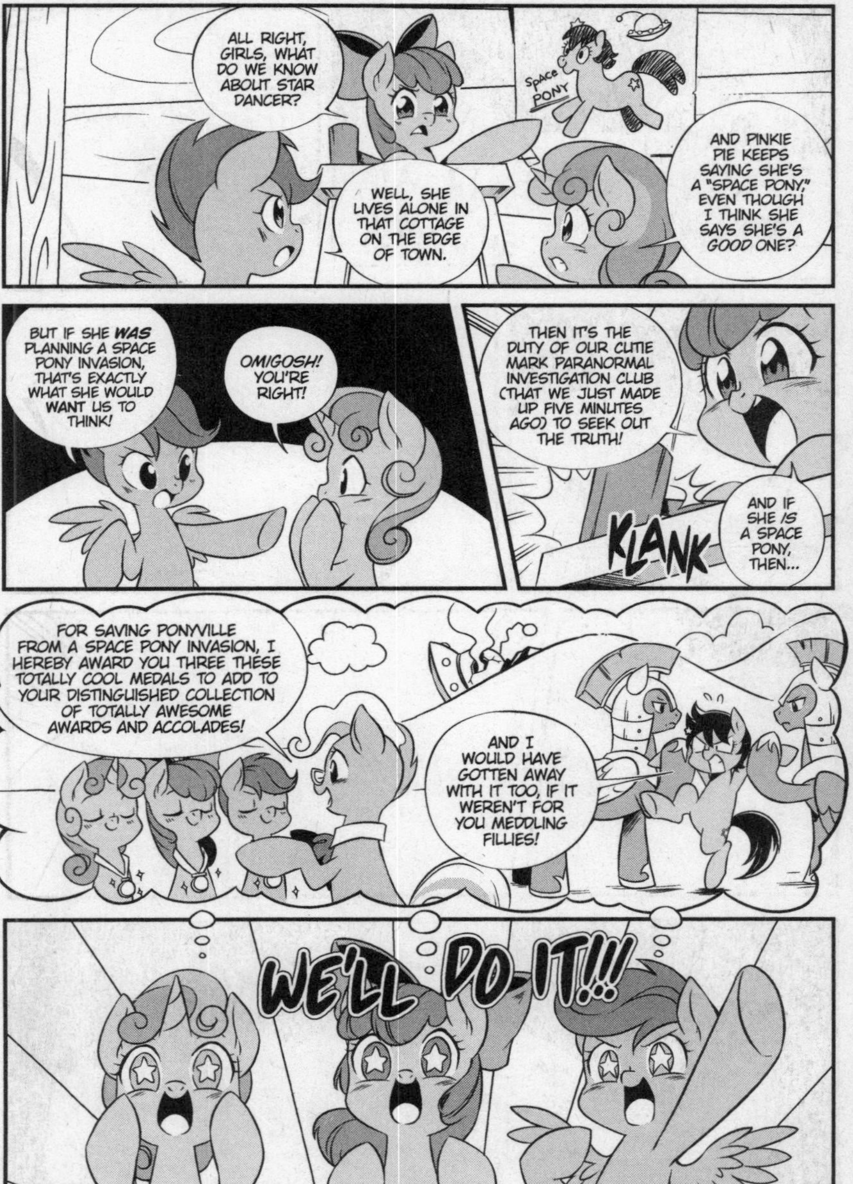
ALL RIGHT, GIRLS, WHAT DO WE KNOW ABOUT STAR DANCER?
Space PONY
WELL, SHE LIVES ALONE IN THAT COTTAGE ON THE EDGE OF TOWN.
AND PINKIE PIE KEEPS SAYING SHE'S A "SPACE PONY," EVEN THOUGH I THINK SHE SAYS SHE'S A *GOOD* ONE?
BUT IF SHE **WAS** PLANNING A SPACE PONY INVASION, THAT'S EXACTLY WHAT SHE WOULD WANT US TO THINK!
OMIGOSH! YOU'RE RIGHT!
THEN IT'S THE DUTY OF OUR CUTIE MARK PARANORMAL INVESTIGATION CLUB (THAT WE JUST MADE UP FIVE MINUTES AGO) TO SEEK OUT THE TRUTH!
KLANK
AND IF SHE *IS* A SPACE PONY, THEN...
FOR SAVING PONYVILLE FROM A SPACE PONY INVASION, I HEREBY AWARD YOU THREE THESE TOTALLY COOL MEDALS TO ADD TO YOUR DISTINGUISHED COLLECTION OF TOTALLY AWESOME AWARDS AND ACCOLADES!
AND I WOULD HAVE GOTTEN AWAY WITH IT TOO, IF IT WEREN'T FOR YOU MEDDLING FILLIES!
WE'LL DO IT!!!

What's Menu with You?

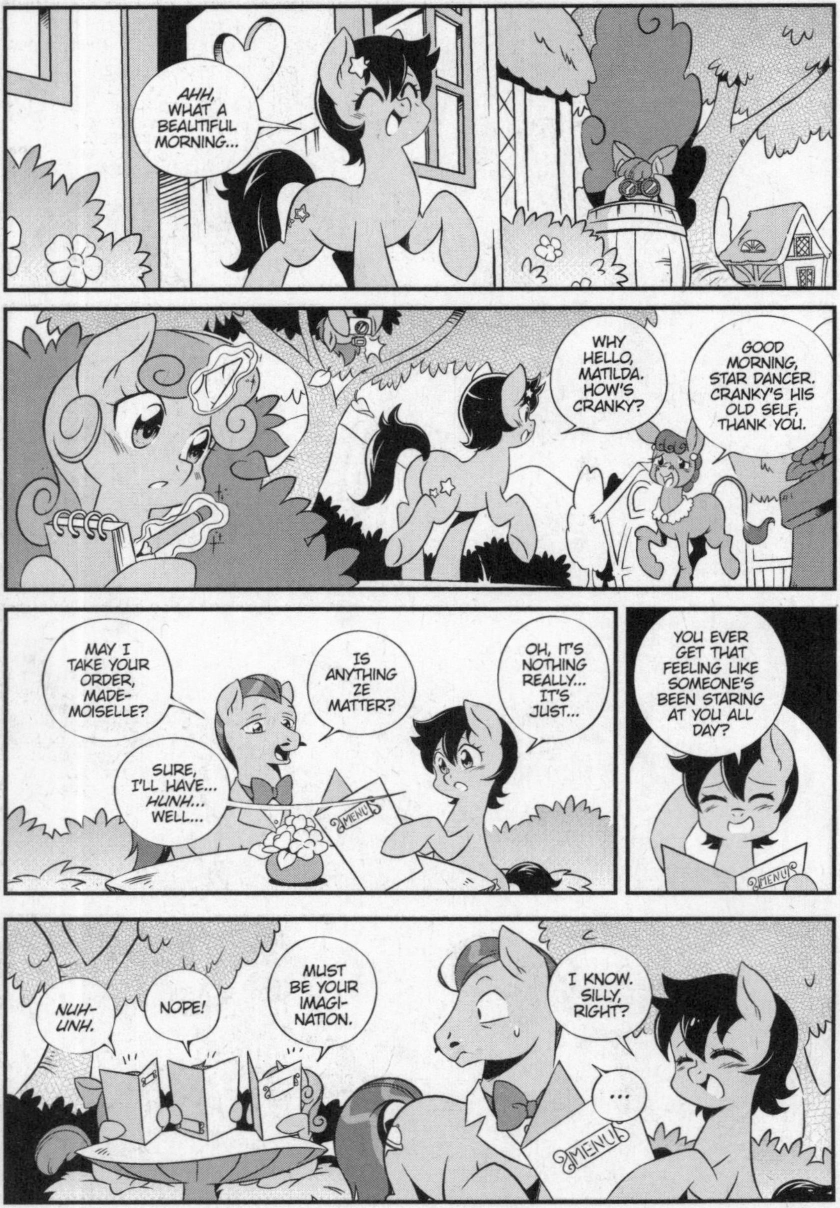
AHH, WHAT A BEAUTIFUL MORNING...
WHY HELLO, MATILDA. HOW'S CRANKY?
GOOD MORNING, STAR DANCER. CRANKY'S HIS OLD SELF, THANK YOU.
MAY I TAKE YOUR ORDER, MADE-MOISELLE?
SURE, I'LL HAVE... *HUNH*... WELL...
IS ANYTHING ZE MATTER?
OH, IT'S NOTHING REALLY... IT'S JUST...
MENU
YOU EVER GET THAT FEELING LIKE SOMEONE'S BEEN STARING AT YOU ALL DAY?
MENU
NUH-UNH.
NOPE!
MUST BE YOUR IMAGI-NATION.
I KNOW. SILLY, RIGHT?
...
MENU

Mare Today, Gone Tomorrow

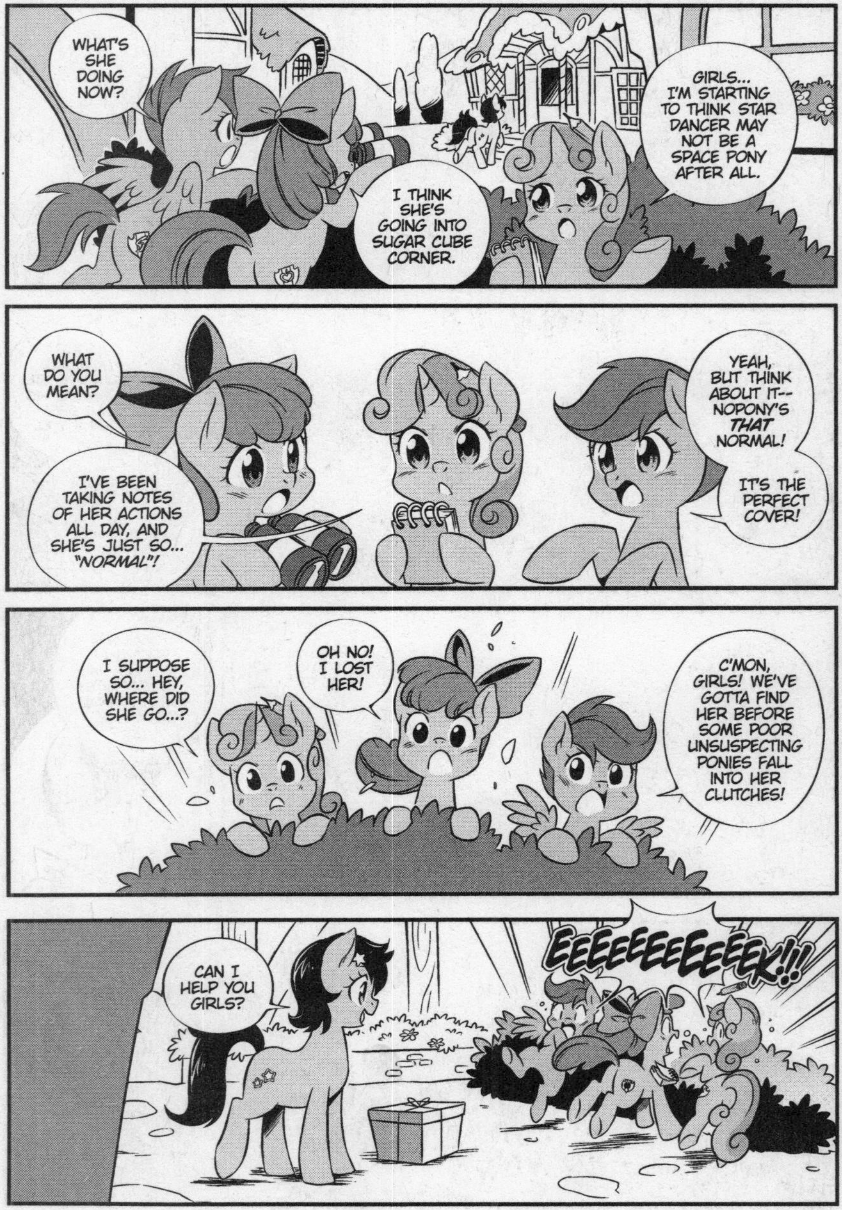
WHAT'S SHE DOING NOW?
I THINK SHE'S GOING INTO SUGAR CUBE CORNER.
GIRLS... I'M STARTING TO THINK STAR DANCER MAY NOT BE A SPACE PONY AFTER ALL.
WHAT DO YOU MEAN?
I'VE BEEN TAKING NOTES OF HER ACTIONS ALL DAY, AND SHE'S JUST SO... "NORMAL"!
YEAH, BUT THINK ABOUT IT-- NOPONY'S *THAT* NORMAL!
IT'S THE PERFECT COVER!
I SUPPOSE SO... HEY, WHERE DID SHE GO...?
OH NO! I LOST HER!
C'MON, GIRLS! WE'VE GOTTA FIND HER BEFORE SOME POOR UNSUSPECTING PONIES FALL INTO HER CLUTCHES!
CAN I HELP YOU GIRLS?
EEEEEEEEEEEK!!!

Piece of Cake

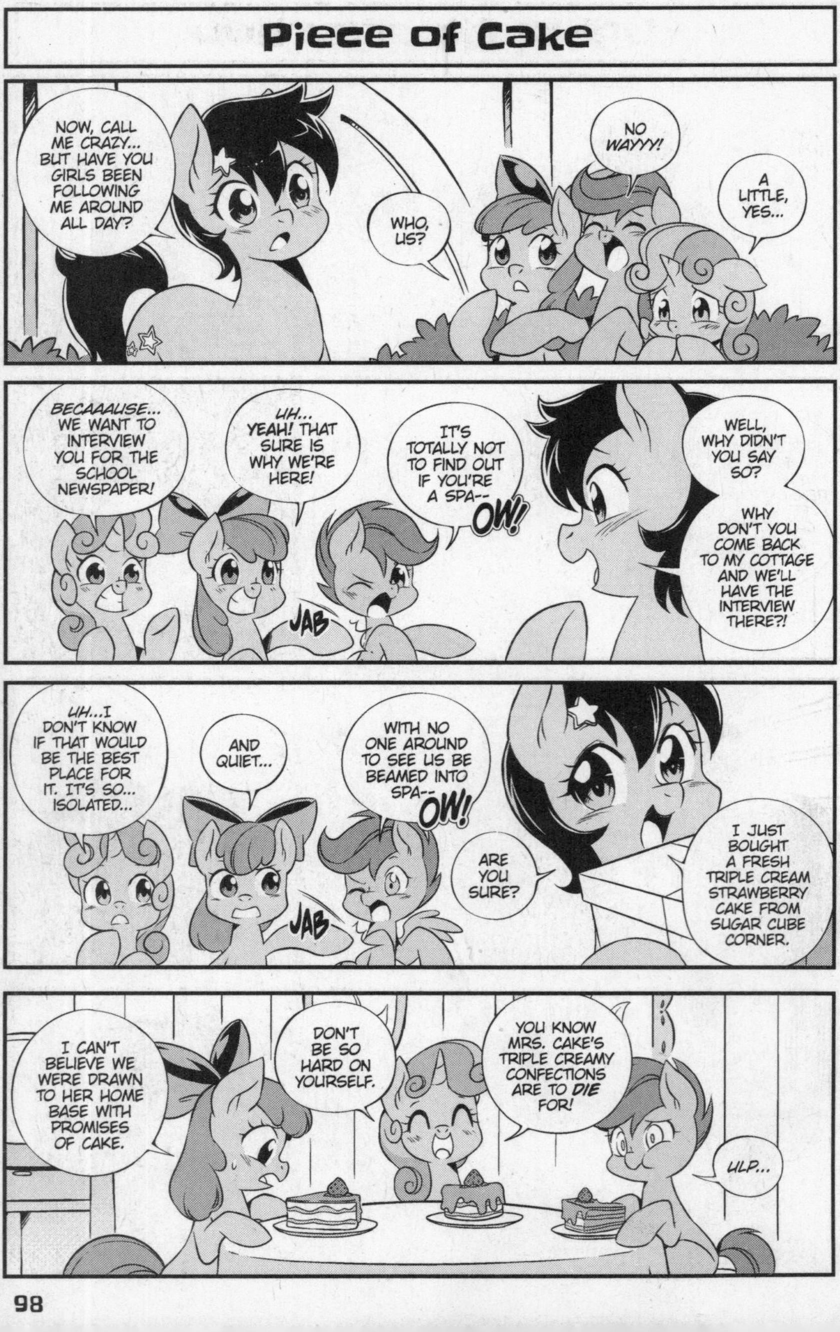
NOW, CALL ME CRAZY... BUT HAVE YOU GIRLS BEEN FOLLOWING ME AROUND ALL DAY?
WHO, US?
NO *WAYYY!*
A LITTLE, YES...
BECAAAUSE... WE WANT TO INTERVIEW YOU FOR THE SCHOOL NEWSPAPER!
UH... YEAH! THAT SURE IS WHY WE'RE HERE!
IT'S TOTALLY NOT TO FIND OUT IF YOU'RE A SPA--
OW!
JAB
WELL, WHY DIDN'T YOU SAY SO?
WHY DON'T YOU COME BACK TO MY COTTAGE AND WE'LL HAVE THE INTERVIEW THERE?!
*UH...*I DON'T KNOW IF THAT WOULD BE THE BEST PLACE FOR IT. IT'S SO... ISOLATED...
AND QUIET...
WITH NO ONE AROUND TO SEE US BE BEAMED INTO SPA--
OW!
JAB
ARE YOU SURE?
I JUST BOUGHT A FRESH TRIPLE CREAM STRAWBERRY CAKE FROM SUGAR CUBE CORNER.
I CAN'T BELIEVE WE WERE DRAWN TO HER HOME BASE WITH PROMISES OF CAKE.
DON'T BE SO HARD ON YOURSELF.
YOU KNOW MRS. CAKE'S TRIPLE CREAMY CONFECTIONS ARE TO *DIE* FOR!
ULP...

Lights Out, For You

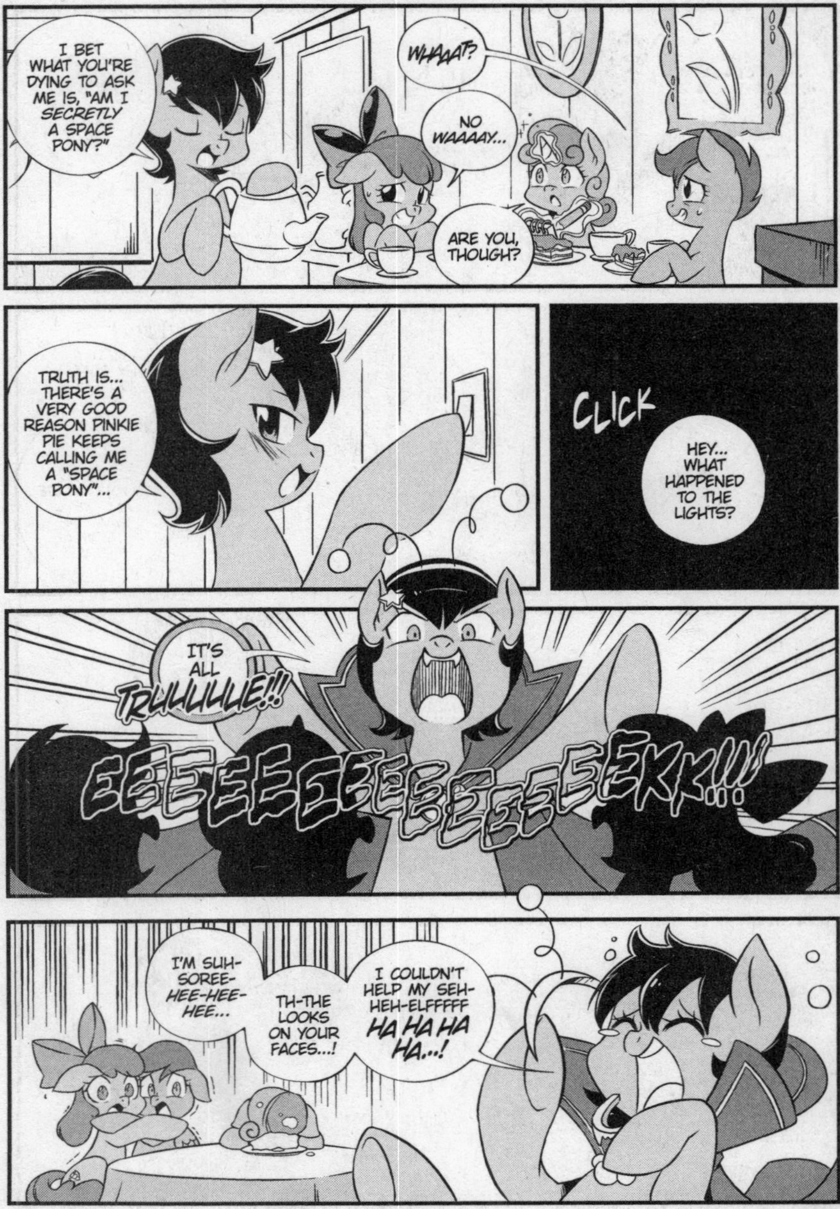

I BET WHAT YOU'RE DYING TO ASK ME IS, "AM I SECRETLY A SPACE PONY?"
WHAAAT?
NO WAAAAY...
ARE YOU, THOUGH?
TRUTH IS... THERE'S A VERY GOOD REASON PINKIE PIE KEEPS CALLING ME A "SPACE PONY"...
CLICK
HEY... WHAT HAPPENED TO THE LIGHTS?
IT'S ALL TRUUUUUE!!!
EEEEEEEEEEEEEEEEEEEKK!!!
I'M SUH-SOREE-HEE-HEE-HEE...
TH-THE LOOKS ON YOUR FACES...!
I COULDN'T HELP MY SEH-HEH-ELFFFFF HA HA HA HA...!

The X-Smiles

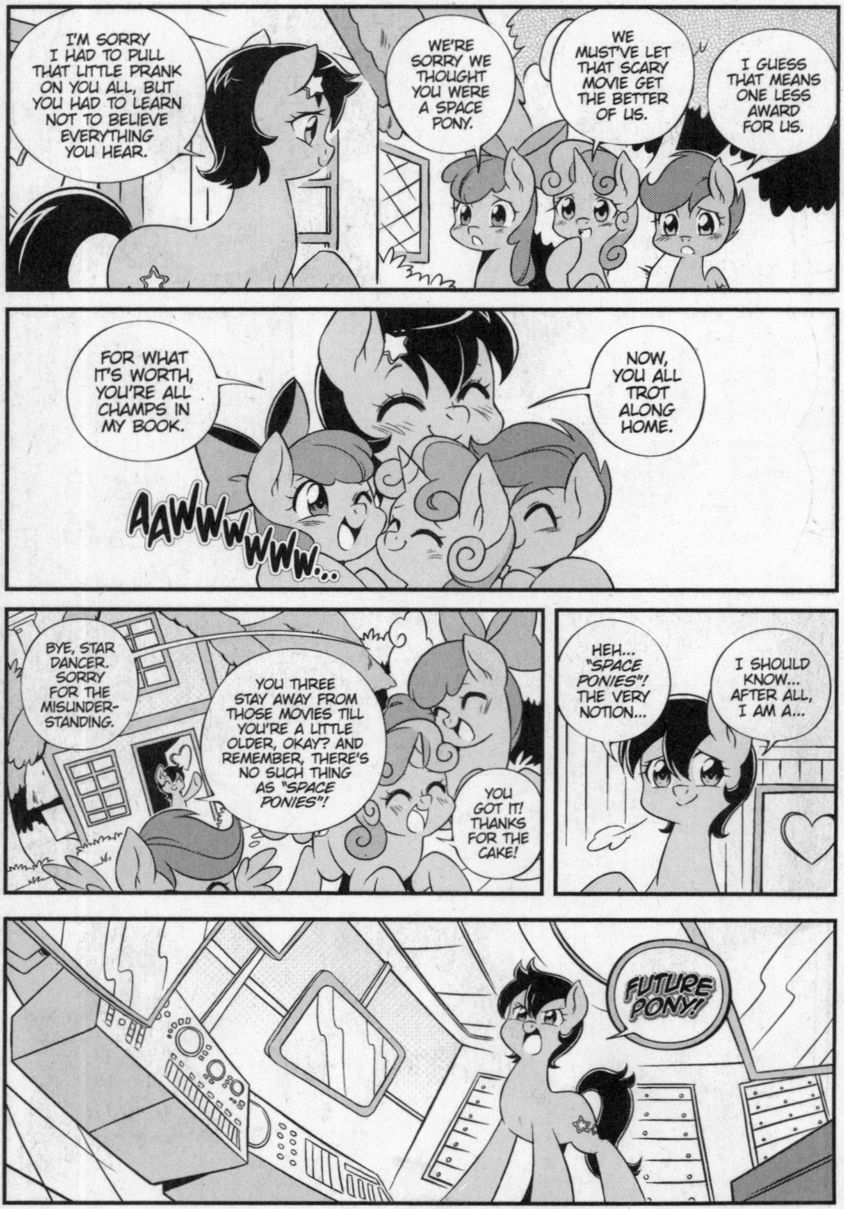
I'M SORRY I HAD TO PULL THAT LITTLE PRANK ON YOU ALL, BUT YOU HAD TO LEARN NOT TO BELIEVE EVERYTHING YOU HEAR.
WE'RE SORRY WE THOUGHT YOU WERE A SPACE PONY.
WE MUST'VE LET THAT SCARY MOVIE GET THE BETTER OF US.
I GUESS THAT MEANS ONE LESS AWARD FOR US.
FOR WHAT IT'S WORTH, YOU'RE ALL CHAMPS IN MY BOOK.
AAWWWWWWW...
NOW, YOU ALL TROT ALONG HOME.
BYE, STAR DANCER. SORRY FOR THE MISUNDER-STANDING.
YOU THREE STAY AWAY FROM THOSE MOVIES TILL YOU'RE A LITTLE OLDER, OKAY? AND REMEMBER, THERE'S NO SUCH THING AS "SPACE PONIES"!
YOU GOT IT! THANKS FOR THE CAKE!
HEH... "SPACE PONIES"! THE VERY NOTION...
I SHOULD KNOW... AFTER ALL, I AM A...
FUTURE PONY!

Explosive Personality

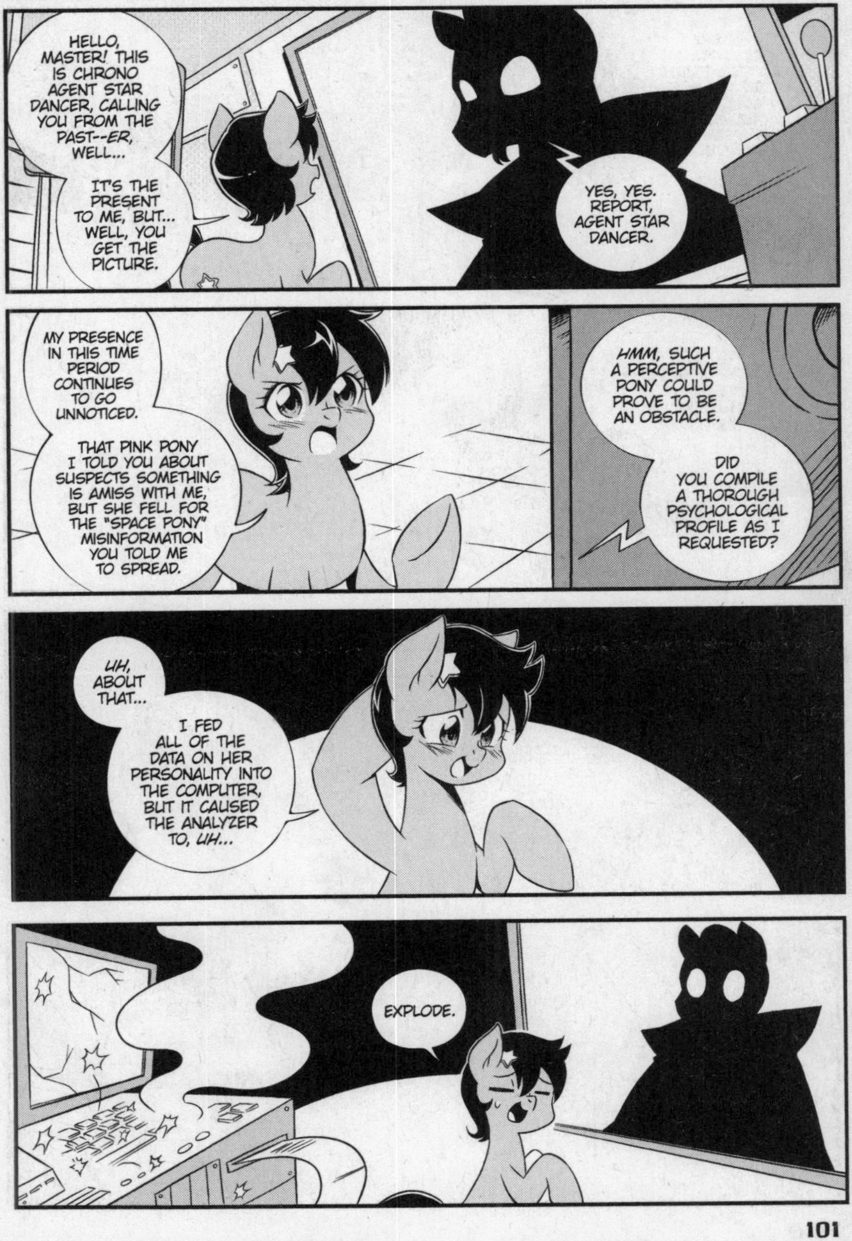
HELLO, MASTER! THIS IS CHRONO AGENT STAR DANCER, CALLING YOU FROM THE PAST--*ER*, WELL...
IT'S THE PRESENT TO ME, BUT... WELL, YOU GET THE PICTURE.
YES, YES. REPORT, AGENT STAR DANCER.
MY PRESENCE IN THIS TIME PERIOD CONTINUES TO GO UNNOTICED.
THAT PINK PONY I TOLD YOU ABOUT SUSPECTS SOMETHING IS AMISS WITH ME, BUT SHE FELL FOR THE "SPACE PONY" MISINFORMATION YOU TOLD ME TO SPREAD.
HMM, SUCH A PERCEPTIVE PONY COULD PROVE TO BE AN OBSTACLE.
DID YOU COMPILE A THOROUGH PSYCHOLOGICAL PROFILE AS I REQUESTED?
UH, ABOUT THAT...
I FED ALL OF THE DATA ON HER PERSONALITY INTO THE COMPUTER, BUT IT CAUSED THE ANALYZER TO, *UH*...
EXPLODE.

This Concludes Our Broadcast Day!

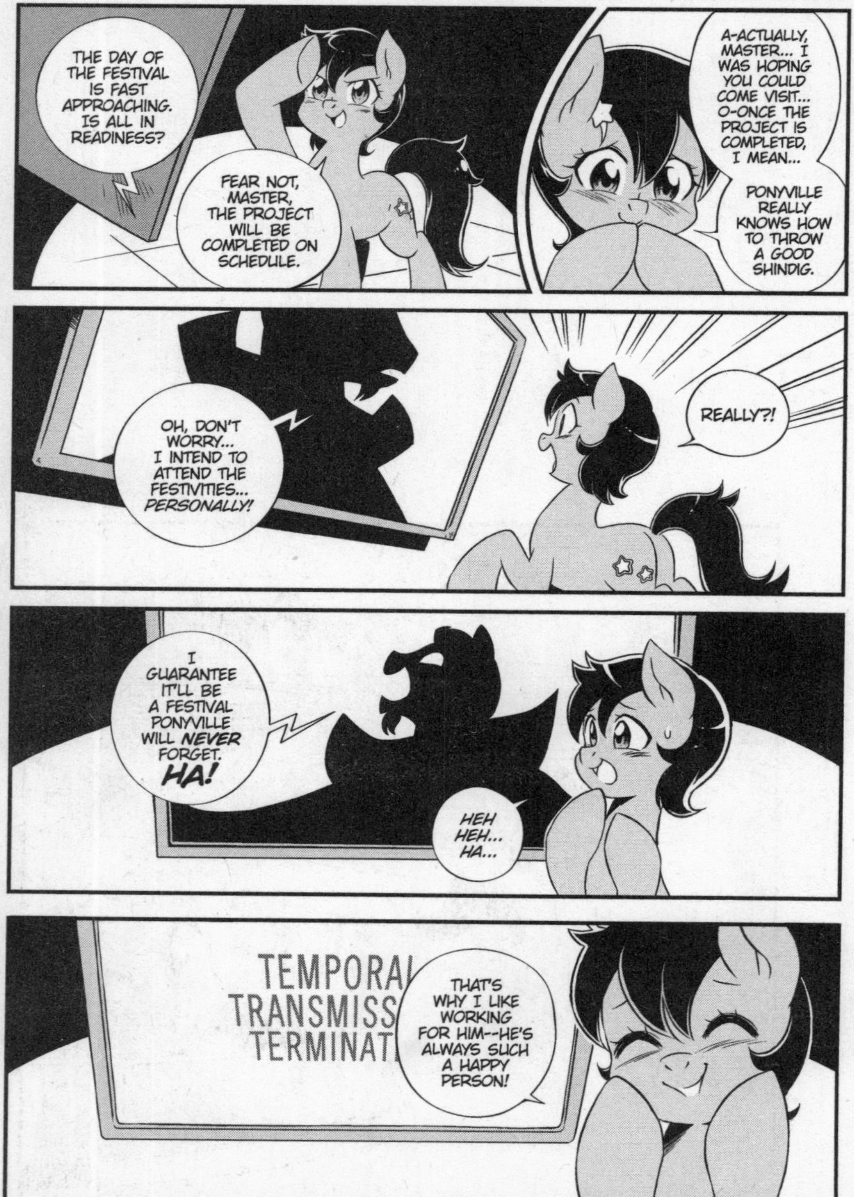

THE DAY OF THE FESTIVAL IS FAST APPROACHING. IS ALL IN READINESS?
FEAR NOT, MASTER, THE PROJECT WILL BE COMPLETED ON SCHEDULE.
A-ACTUALLY, MASTER... I WAS HOPING YOU COULD COME VISIT... O-ONCE THE PROJECT IS COMPLETED, I MEAN...
PONYVILLE REALLY KNOWS HOW TO THROW A GOOD SHINDIG.
OH, DON'T WORRY... I INTEND TO ATTEND THE FESTIVITIES... *PERSONALLY!*
REALLY?!
I GUARANTEE IT'LL BE A FESTIVAL PONYVILLE WILL *NEVER* FORGET. ***HA!***
HEH HEH... HA...
TEMPORAL
TRANSMISS
TERMINAT
THAT'S WHY I LIKE WORKING FOR HIM--HE'S ALWAYS SUCH A HAPPY PERSON!

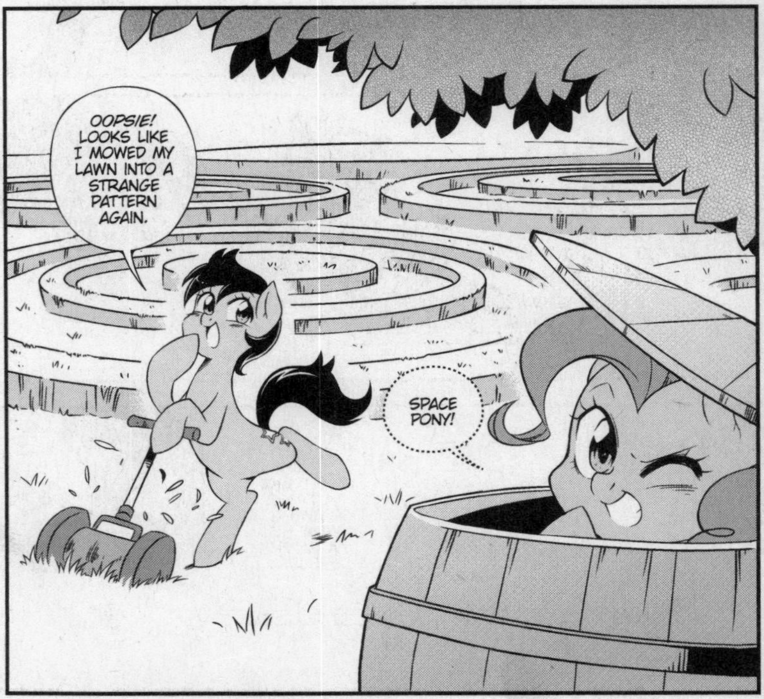
OOPSIE! LOOKS LIKE I MOWED MY LAWN INTO A STRANGE PATTERN AGAIN.
SPACE PONY!

CHAPTER 8

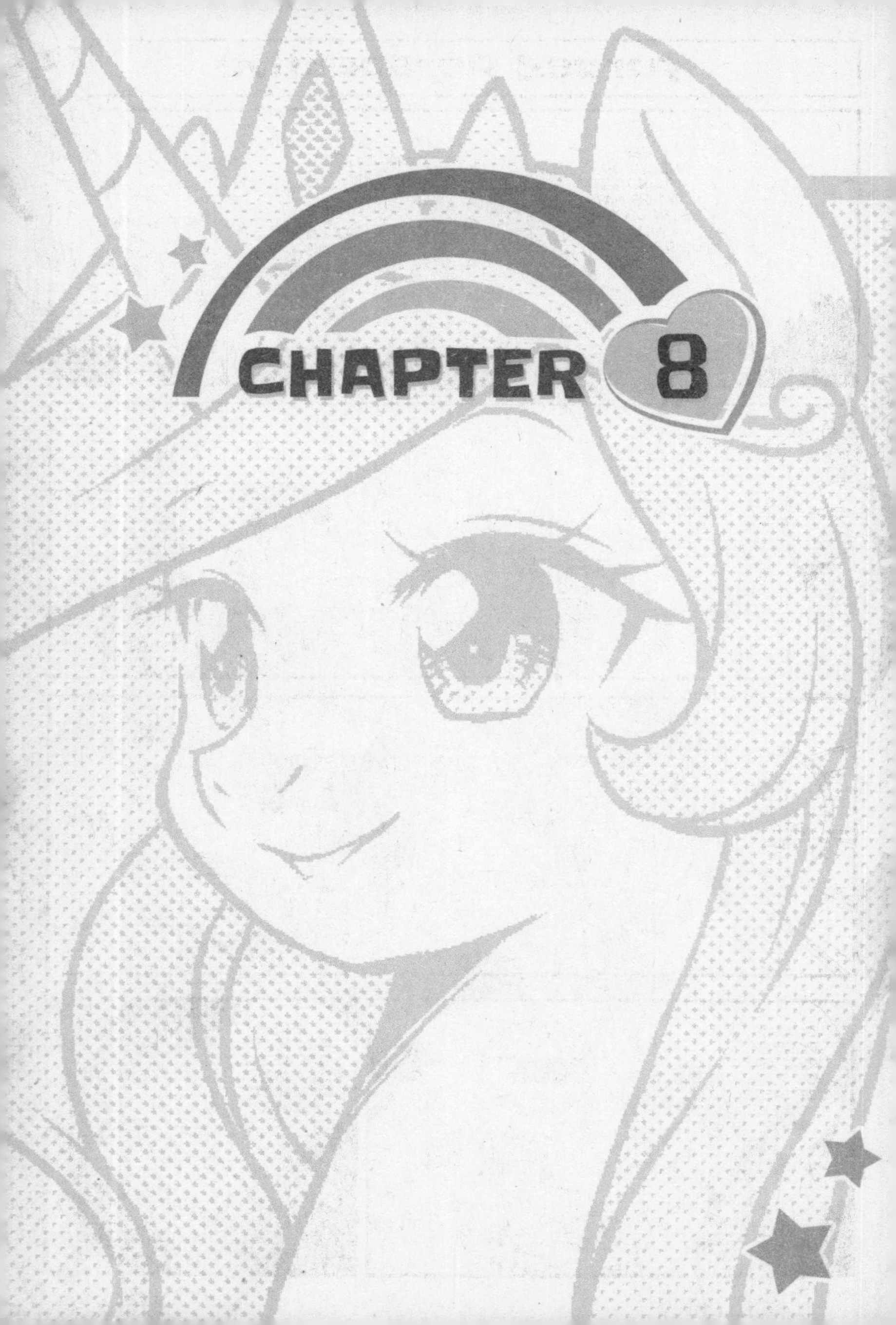

Forced Perspective

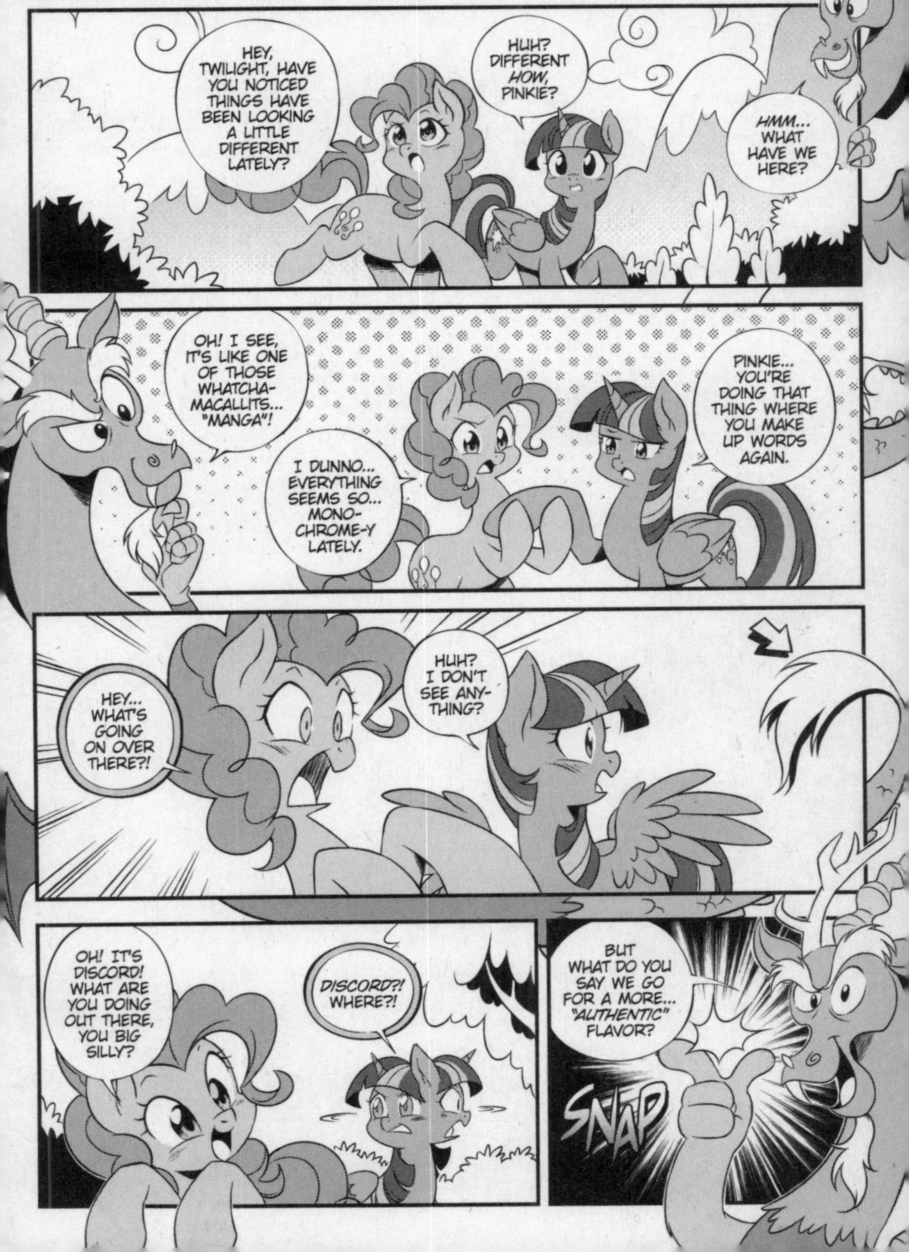

HEY, TWILIGHT, HAVE YOU NOTICED THINGS HAVE BEEN LOOKING A LITTLE DIFFERENT LATELY?
HUH? DIFFERENT *HOW*, PINKIE?
HMM... WHAT HAVE WE HERE?
OH! I SEE, IT'S LIKE ONE OF THOSE WHATCHA-MACALLITS... "MANGA"!
I DUNNO... EVERYTHING SEEMS SO... MONO-CHROME-Y LATELY.
PINKIE... YOU'RE DOING THAT THING WHERE YOU MAKE UP WORDS AGAIN.
HEY... WHAT'S GOING ON OVER THERE?!
HUH? I DON'T SEE ANY-THING?
OH! IT'S DISCORD! WHAT ARE YOU DOING OUT THERE, YOU BIG SILLY?
DISCORD?! WHERE?!
BUT WHAT DO YOU SAY WE GO FOR A MORE... *"AUTHENTIC"* FLAVOR?
SNAP

Astonishing! We're All Manga Style, Now?

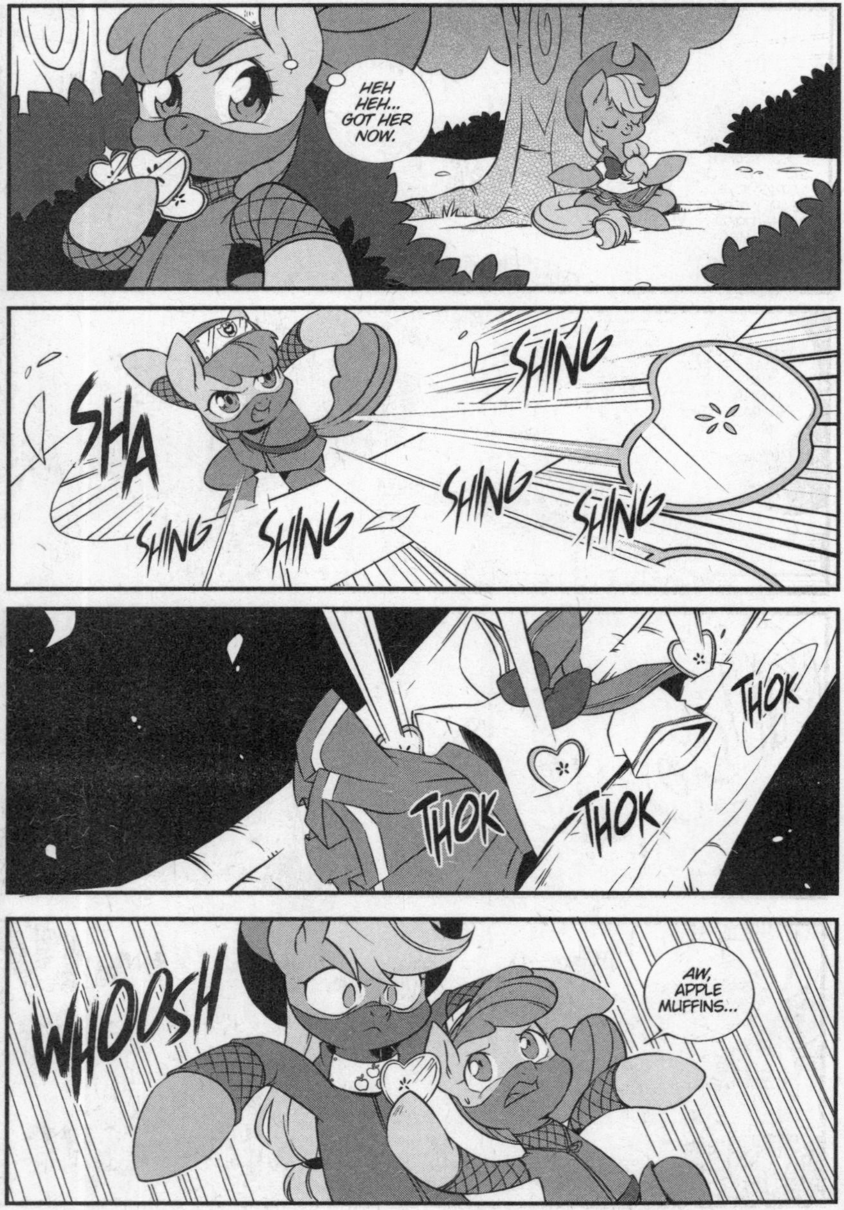
HEH HEH... GOT HER NOW.
SHA
SHING
SHING
SHING
SHING
SHING
THOK
THOK
THOK
WHOOSH
AW, APPLE MUFFINS...

Watch Out! A Rain of Apples from Above?!

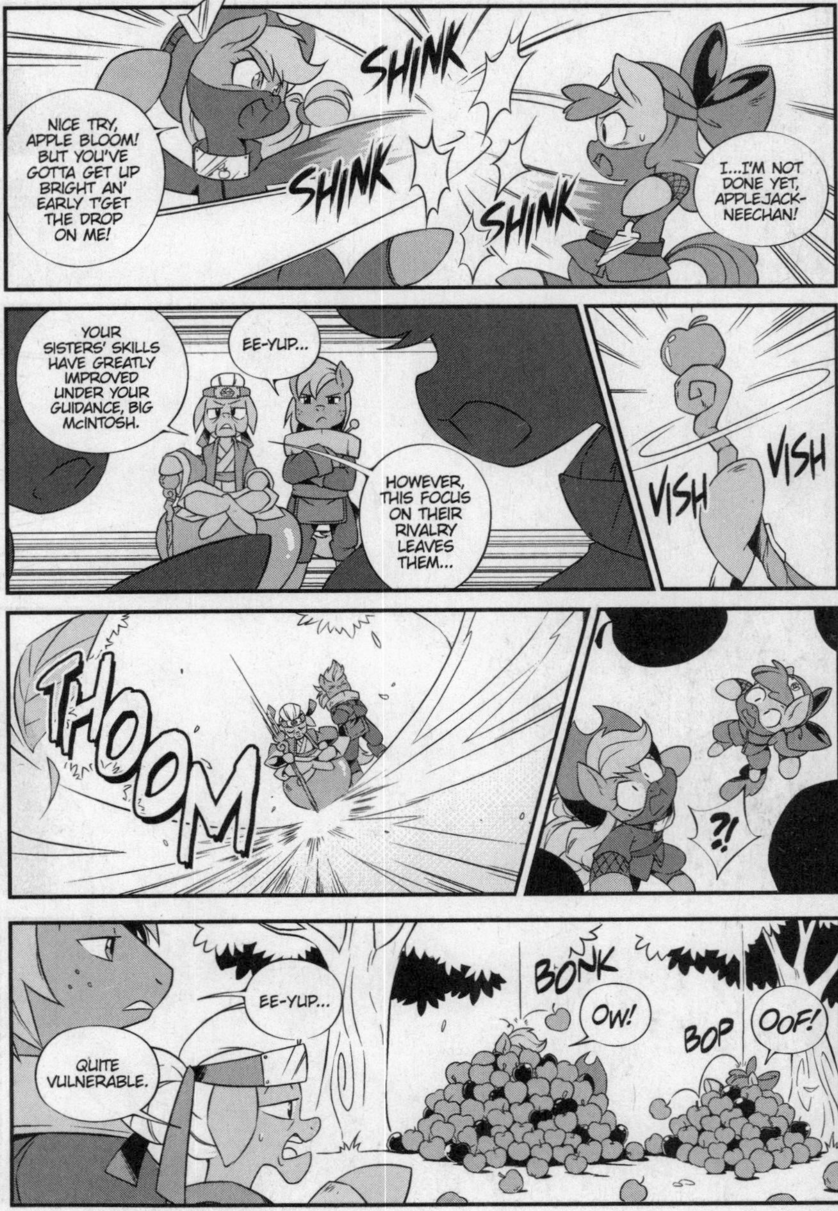
NICE TRY, APPLE BLOOM! BUT YOU'VE GOTTA GET UP BRIGHT AN' EARLY T'GET THE DROP ON ME!
SHINK
SHINK
SHINK
I...I'M NOT DONE YET, APPLEJACK-NEECHAN!
YOUR SISTERS' SKILLS HAVE GREATLY IMPROVED UNDER YOUR GUIDANCE, BIG McINTOSH.
EE-YUP...
HOWEVER, THIS FOCUS ON THEIR RIVALRY LEAVES THEM...
VISH
VISH
THOOM
?!
EE-YUP...
QUITE VULNERABLE.
BONK
OW!
BOP
OOF!

Confusing!
The Ancient Prophecy Is Way Too Specific!

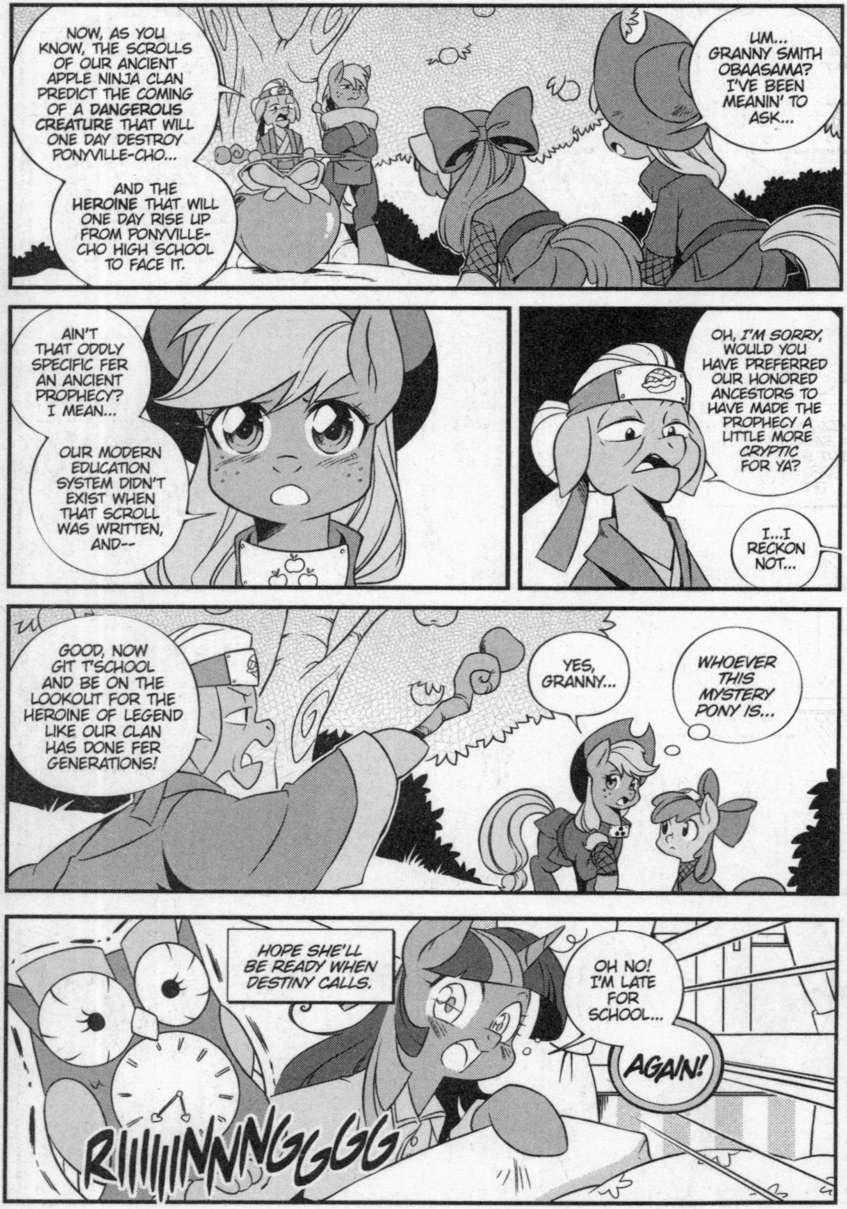
NOW, AS YOU KNOW, THE SCROLLS OF OUR ANCIENT APPLE NINJA CLAN PREDICT THE COMING OF A DANGEROUS CREATURE THAT WILL ONE DAY DESTROY PONYVILLE-CHO...
AND THE HEROINE THAT WILL ONE DAY RISE UP FROM PONYVILLE-CHO HIGH SCHOOL TO FACE IT.
UM... GRANNY SMITH OBAASAMA? I'VE BEEN MEANIN' TO ASK...
AIN'T THAT ODDLY SPECIFIC FER AN ANCIENT PROPHECY? I MEAN...
OUR MODERN EDUCATION SYSTEM DIDN'T EXIST WHEN THAT SCROLL WAS WRITTEN, AND--
OH, I'M SORRY, WOULD YOU HAVE PREFERRED OUR HONORED ANCESTORS TO HAVE MADE THE PROPHECY A LITTLE MORE CRYPTIC FOR YA?
I...I RECKON NOT...
GOOD, NOW GIT T'SCHOOL AND BE ON THE LOOKOUT FOR THE HEROINE OF LEGEND LIKE OUR CLAN HAS DONE FER GENERATIONS!
YES, GRANNY...
WHOEVER THIS MYSTERY PONY IS...
HOPE SHE'LL BE READY WHEN DESTINY CALLS.
OH NO! I'M LATE FOR SCHOOL...
AGAIN!
RIIIIINNNNGGGG

Too Many Choices!
Which Pony Is the Legendary Heroine?!

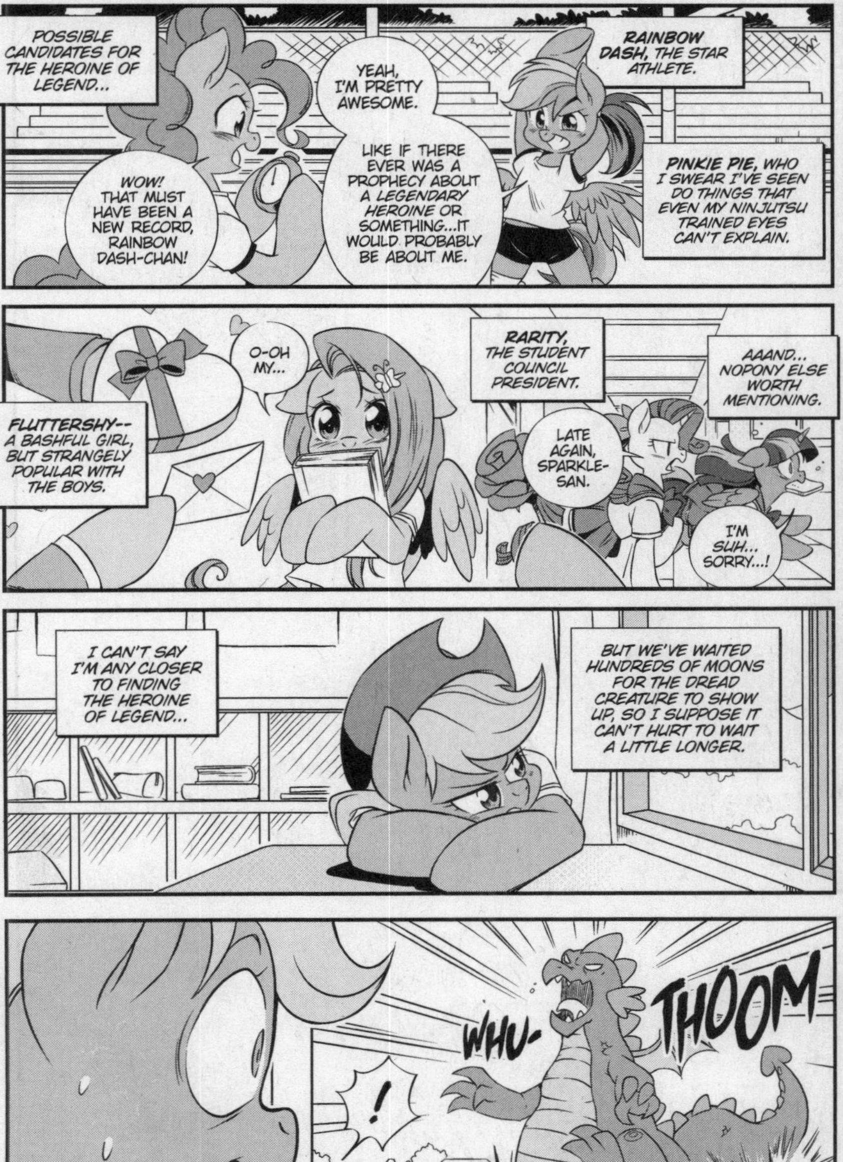

POSSIBLE CANDIDATES FOR THE HEROINE OF LEGEND...
RAINBOW DASH, THE STAR ATHLETE.
WOW! THAT MUST HAVE BEEN A NEW RECORD, RAINBOW DASH-CHAN!
YEAH, I'M PRETTY AWESOME.
LIKE IF THERE EVER WAS A PROPHECY ABOUT A LEGENDARY HEROINE OR SOMETHING...IT WOULD PROBABLY BE ABOUT ME.
PINKIE PIE, WHO I SWEAR I'VE SEEN DO THINGS THAT EVEN MY NINJUTSU TRAINED EYES CAN'T EXPLAIN.
FLUTTERSHY-- A BASHFUL GIRL, BUT STRANGELY POPULAR WITH THE BOYS.
O-OH MY...
RARITY, THE STUDENT COUNCIL PRESIDENT.
LATE AGAIN, SPARKLE-SAN.
AAAND... NOPONY ELSE WORTH MENTIONING.
I'M SUH... SORRY...!
I CAN'T SAY I'M ANY CLOSER TO FINDING THE HEROINE OF LEGEND...
BUT WE'VE WAITED HUNDREDS OF MOONS FOR THE DREAD CREATURE TO SHOW UP, SO I SUPPOSE IT CAN'T HURT TO WAIT A LITTLE LONGER.
!
WHU-
THOOM

Unexpected! The Legendary Wand Appears at Last!

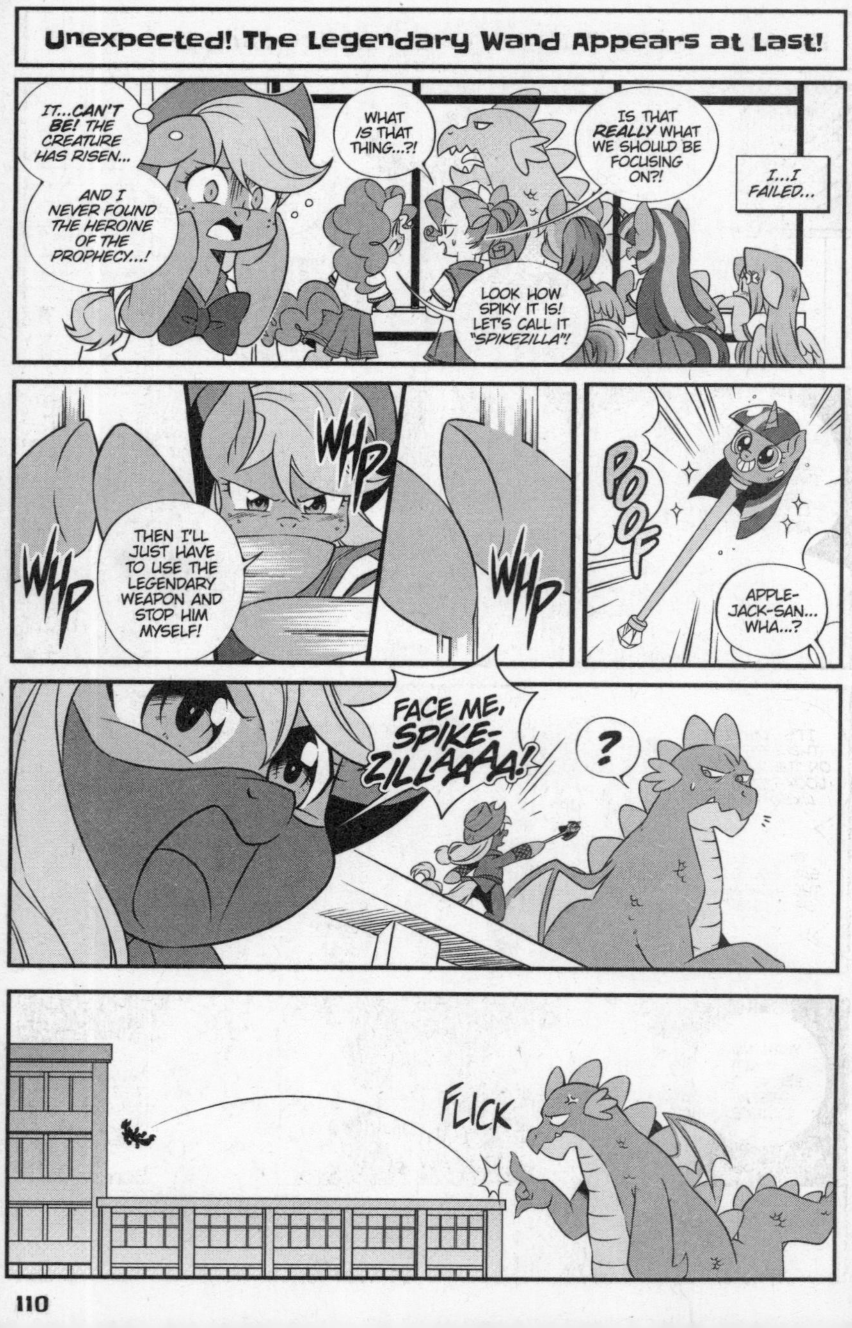

IT...CAN'T BE! THE CREATURE HAS RISEN...
AND I NEVER FOUND THE HEROINE OF THE PROPHECY...!
WHAT IS THAT THING...?!
IS THAT REALLY WHAT WE SHOULD BE FOCUSING ON?!
LOOK HOW SPIKY IT IS! LET'S CALL IT "SPIKEZILLA"!
I...I FAILED...
WHP
WHP
THEN I'LL JUST HAVE TO USE THE LEGENDARY WEAPON AND STOP HIM MYSELF!
WHP
POOF
APPLE-JACK-SAN... WHA...?
FACE ME, SPIKE-ZILLAAAA!
?
FLICK

Sudden Twist! Twilight Is the Legendary Heroine?!

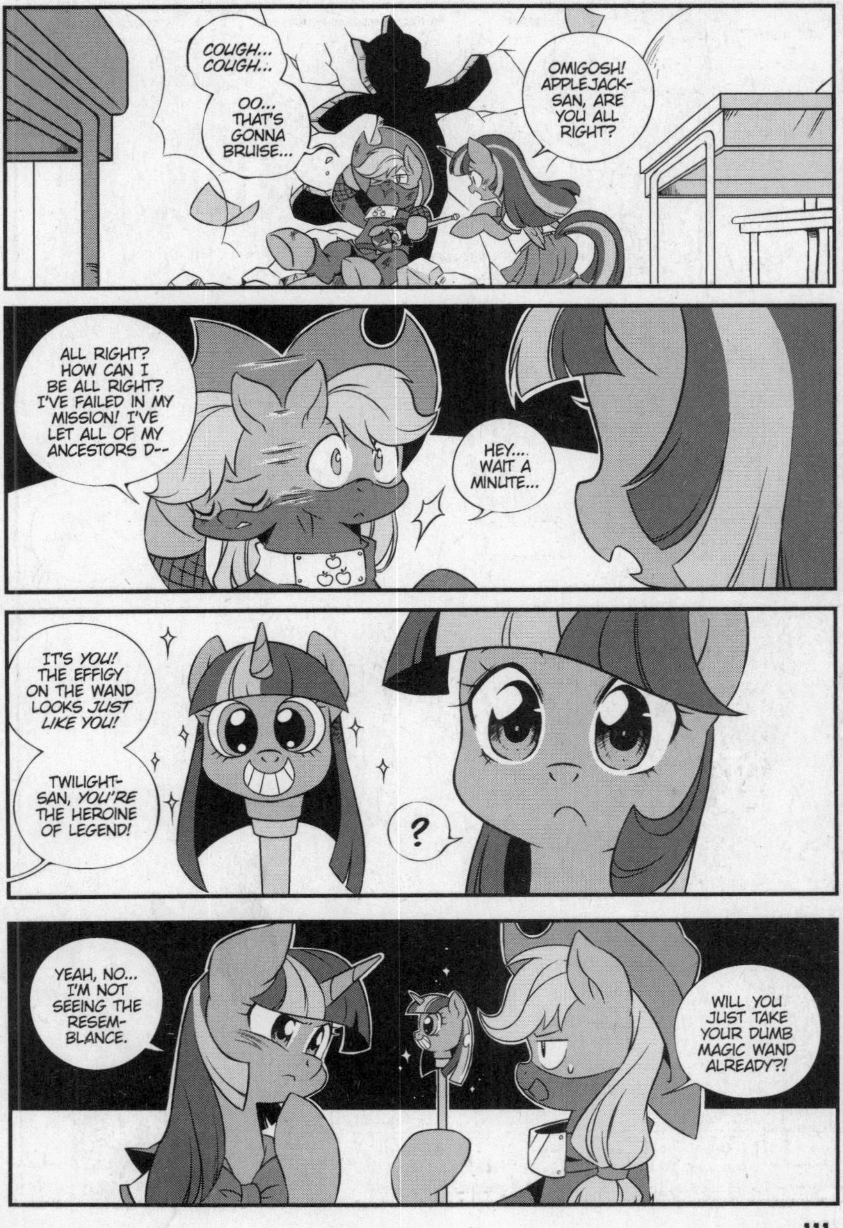
COUGH... COUGH...
OO... THAT'S GONNA BRUISE...
OMIGOSH! APPLEJACK-SAN, ARE YOU ALL RIGHT?
ALL RIGHT? HOW CAN I BE ALL RIGHT? I'VE FAILED IN MY MISSION! I'VE LET ALL OF MY ANCESTORS D--
HEY... WAIT A MINUTE...
IT'S YOU! THE EFFIGY ON THE WAND LOOKS JUST LIKE YOU!
TWILIGHT-SAN, YOU'RE THE HEROINE OF LEGEND!
?
YEAH, NO... I'M NOT SEEING THE RESEM-BLANCE.
WILL YOU JUST TAKE YOUR DUMB MAGIC WAND ALREADY?!

Fabulous! Miraculous!
The Magical Transformation Achieved at Last!

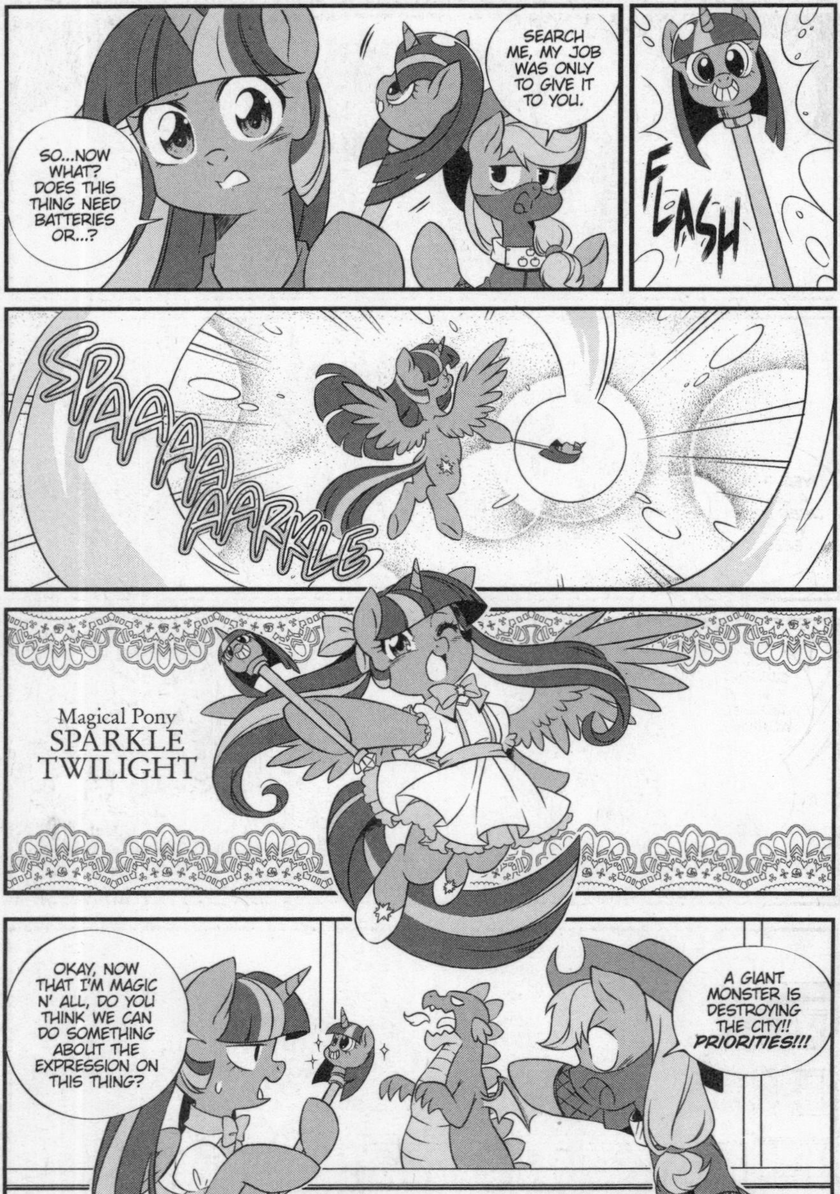

SO...NOW WHAT? DOES THIS THING NEED BATTERIES OR...?
SEARCH ME, MY JOB WAS ONLY TO GIVE IT TO YOU.
FLASH
SPAAAAAARKLE
Magical Pony SPARKLE TWILIGHT
OKAY, NOW THAT I'M MAGIC N' ALL, DO YOU THINK WE CAN DO SOMETHING ABOUT THE EXPRESSION ON THIS THING?
A GIANT MONSTER IS DESTROYING THE CITY!! *PRIORITIES!!!*

I'm Coming for You!
Sparkle Twilight Issues a Challenge!

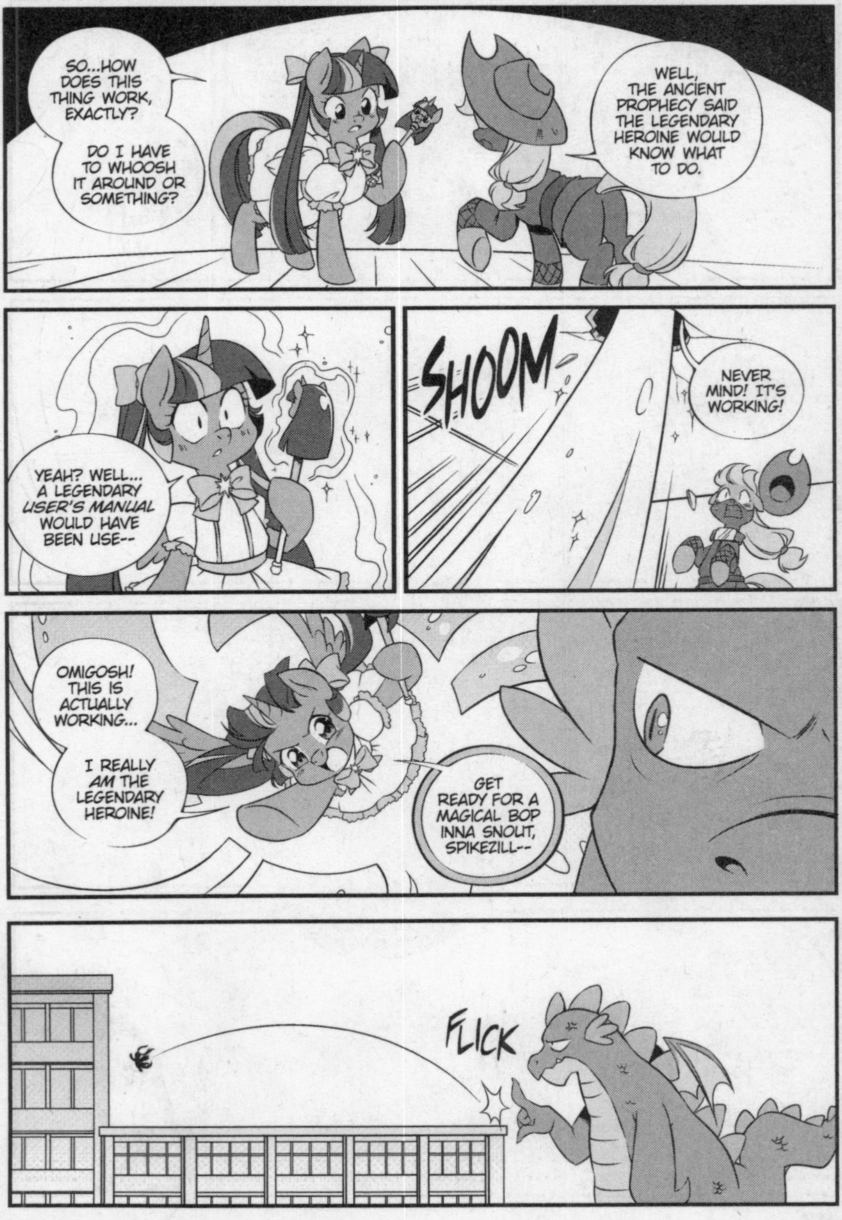
SO...HOW DOES THIS THING WORK, EXACTLY?
DO I HAVE TO WHOOSH IT AROUND OR SOMETHING?
WELL, THE ANCIENT PROPHECY SAID THE LEGENDARY HEROINE WOULD KNOW WHAT TO DO.
YEAH? WELL... A LEGENDARY *USER'S MANUAL* WOULD HAVE BEEN USE--
SHOOM
NEVER MIND! IT'S WORKING!
OMIGOSH! THIS IS ACTUALLY WORKING...
I REALLY *AM* THE LEGENDARY HEROINE!
GET READY FOR A MAGICAL BOP INNA SNOUT, SPIKEZILL--
FLICK

Don't Give Up, Twilight!
The Schoolponies' Desperate Pleas!

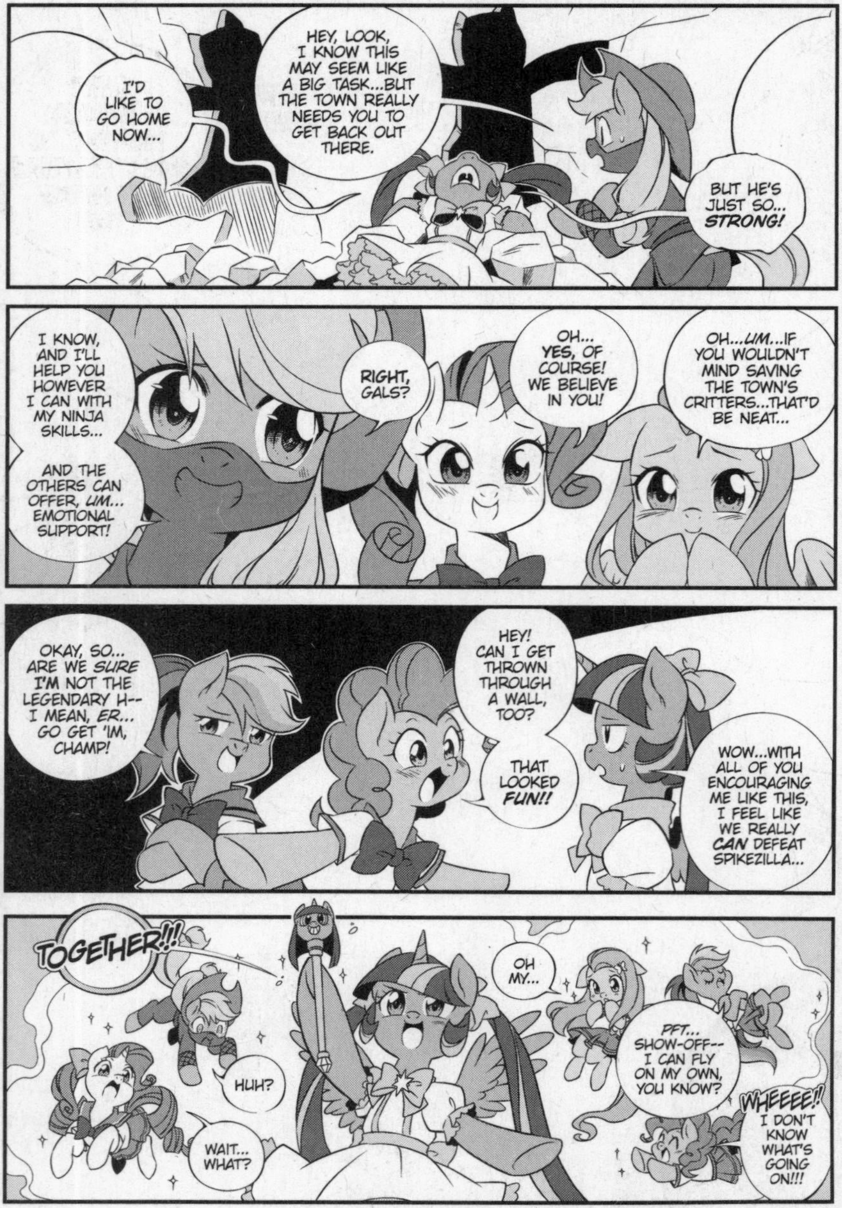

I'D LIKE TO GO HOME NOW...
HEY, LOOK, I KNOW THIS MAY SEEM LIKE A BIG TASK...BUT THE TOWN REALLY NEEDS YOU TO GET BACK OUT THERE.
BUT HE'S JUST SO... *STRONG!*
I KNOW, AND I'LL HELP YOU HOWEVER I CAN WITH MY NINJA SKILLS...
AND THE OTHERS CAN OFFER, *UM*... EMOTIONAL SUPPORT!
RIGHT, GALS?
OH... *YES*, OF COURSE! WE BELIEVE IN YOU!
OH...*UM*...IF YOU WOULDN'T MIND SAVING THE TOWN'S CRITTERS...THAT'D BE NEAT...
OKAY, SO... ARE WE *SURE* I'M NOT THE LEGENDARY H-- I MEAN, *ER*... GO GET 'IM, CHAMP!
HEY! CAN I GET THROWN THROUGH A WALL, TOO?
THAT LOOKED *FUN!!*
WOW...WITH ALL OF YOU ENCOURAGING ME LIKE THIS, I FEEL LIKE WE REALLY *CAN* DEFEAT SPIKEZILLA...
TOGETHER!!!
OH MY...
PFT... SHOW-OFF-- I CAN FLY ON MY OWN, YOU KNOW?
HUH?
WHEEEE!! I DON'T KNOW WHAT'S GOING ON!!!
WAIT... WHAT?

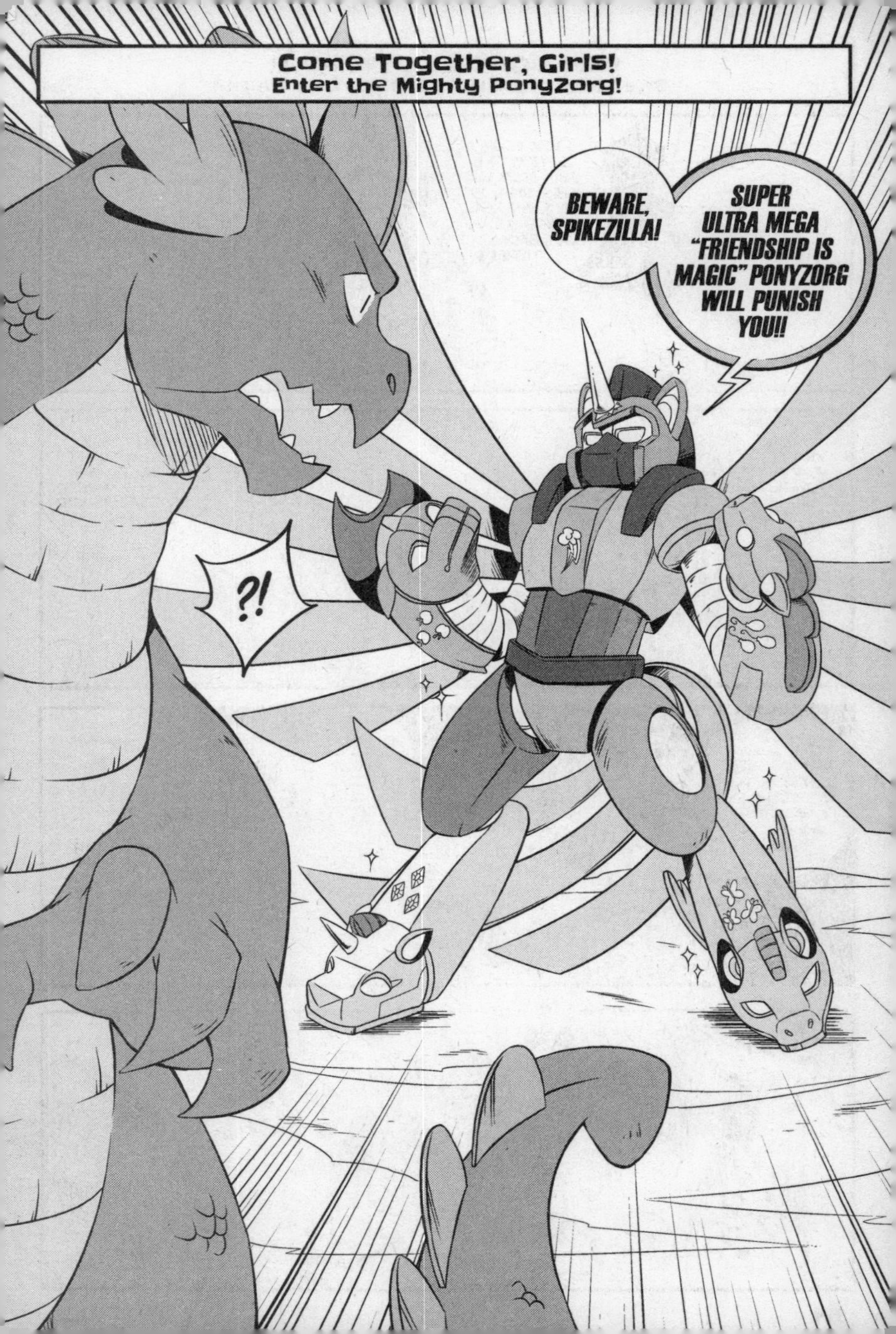
Come Together, Girls!
Enter the Mighty PonyZorg!
BEWARE, SPIKEZILLA!
SUPER ULTRA MEGA "FRIENDSHIP IS MAGIC" PONYZORG WILL PUNISH YOU!!
?!

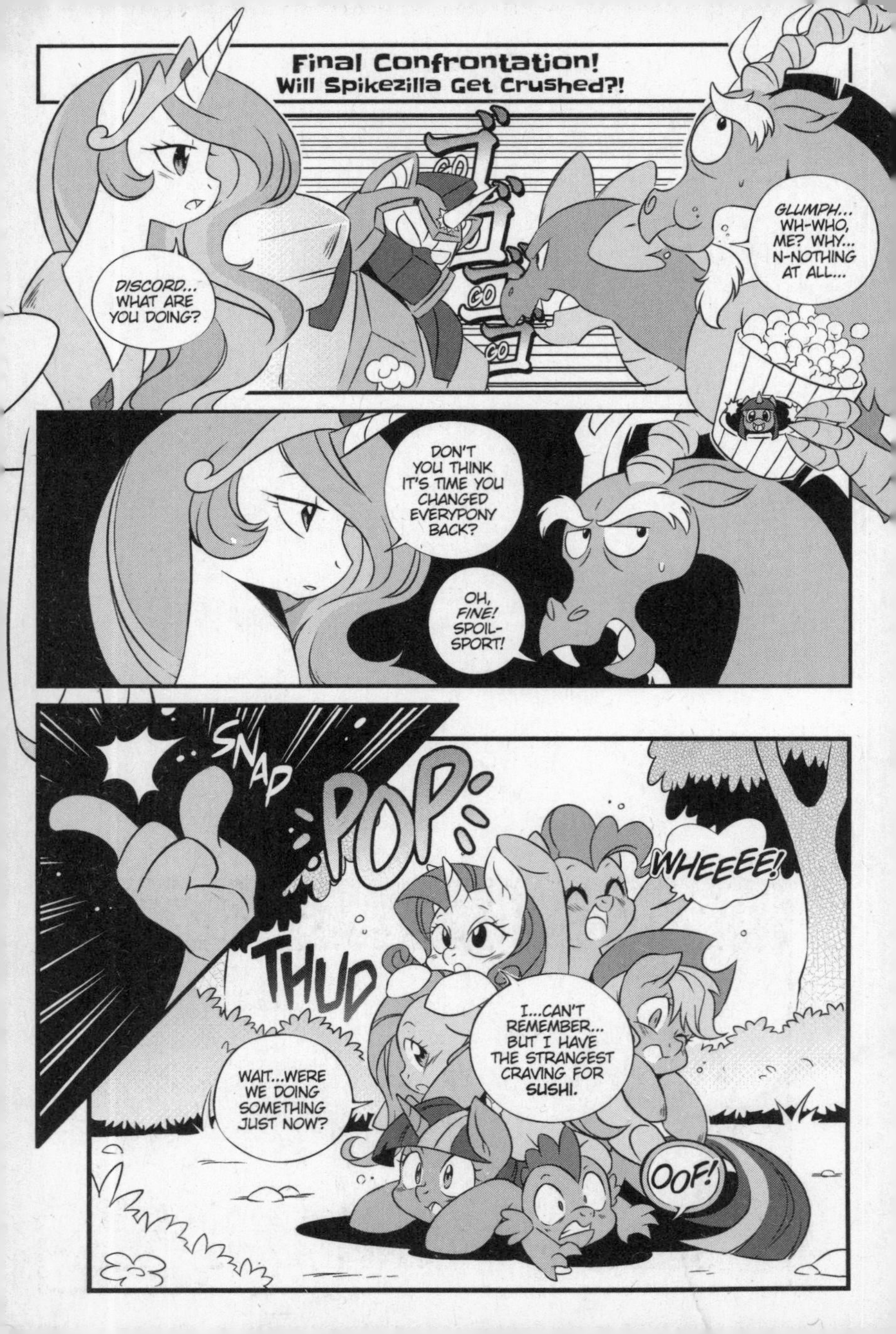
Final Confrontation!
Will Spikezilla Get Crushed?!
GO
GO
GO
GO
DISCORD... WHAT ARE YOU DOING?
GLUMPH... WH-WHO, ME? WHY... N-NOTHING AT ALL...
DON'T YOU THINK IT'S TIME YOU CHANGED EVERYPONY BACK?
OH, FINE! SPOIL-SPORT!
SNAP
POP
WHEEEEE!
THUD
I...CAN'T REMEMBER... BUT I HAVE THE STRANGEST CRAVING FOR SUSHI.
WAIT...WERE WE DOING SOMETHING JUST NOW?
OOF!

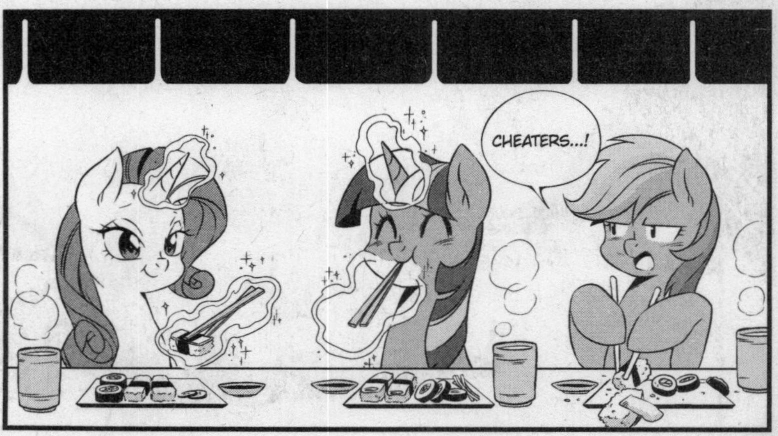
CHEATERS...!

My Little Pony The Manga

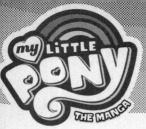

SKETCH GALLERY

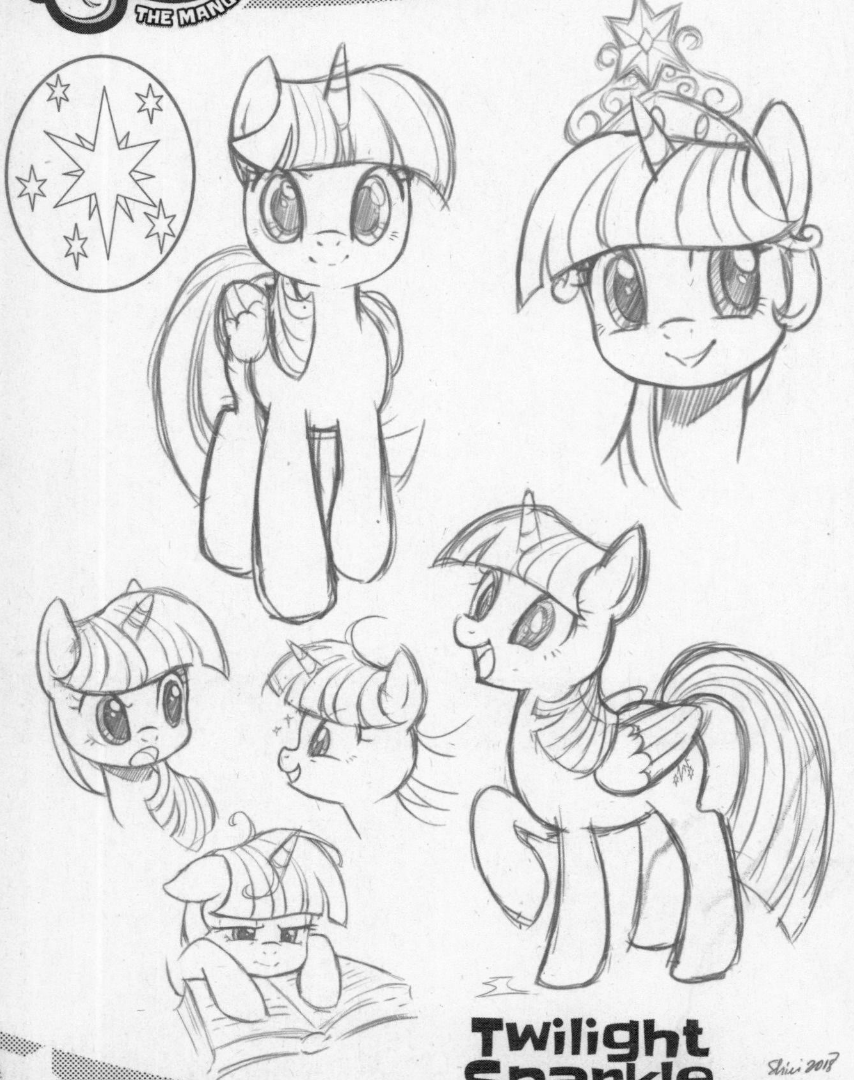

Twilight Sparkle

Pinkie Pie

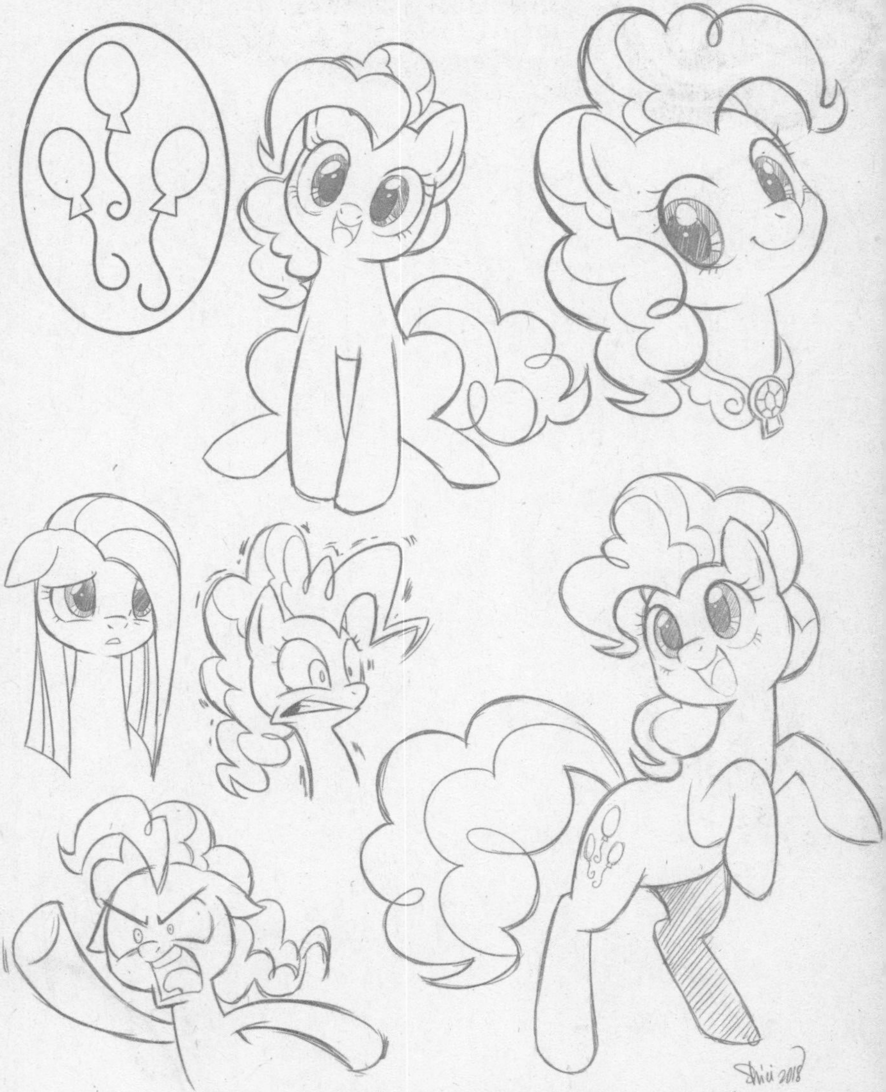

SKETCH GALLERY

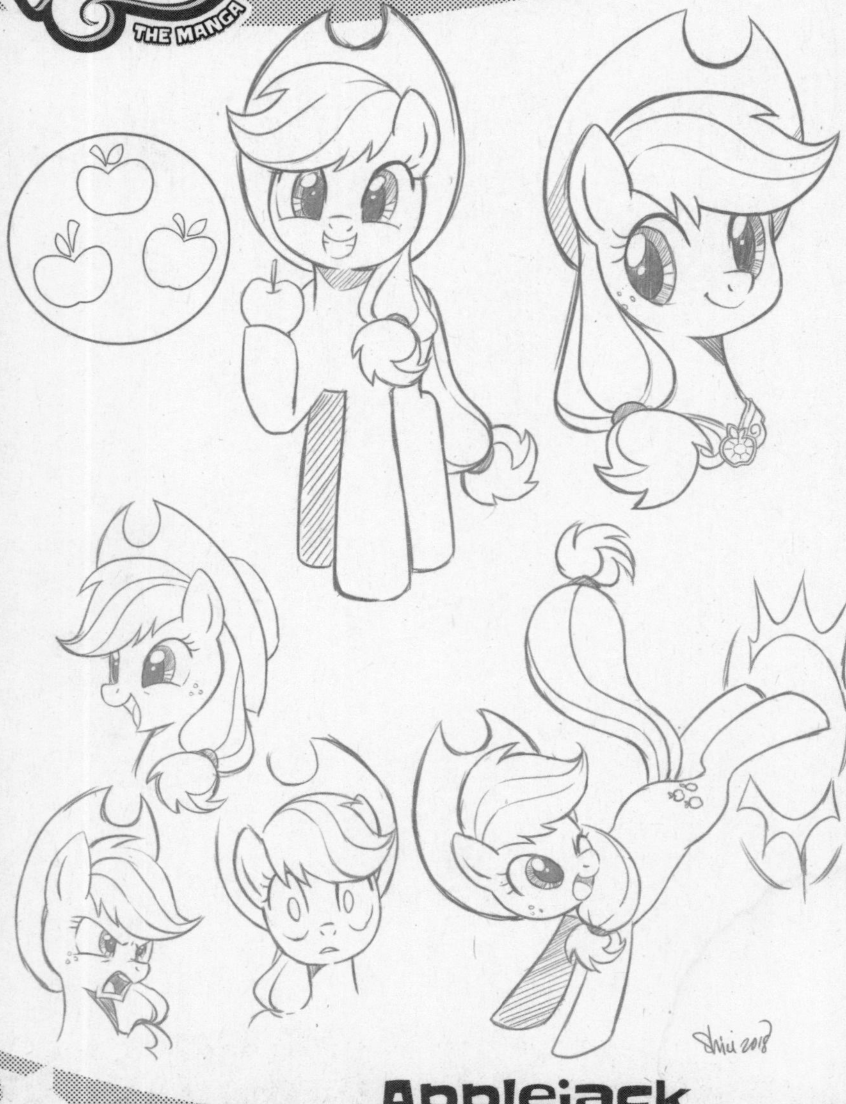

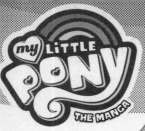

Applejack

Rainbow Dash

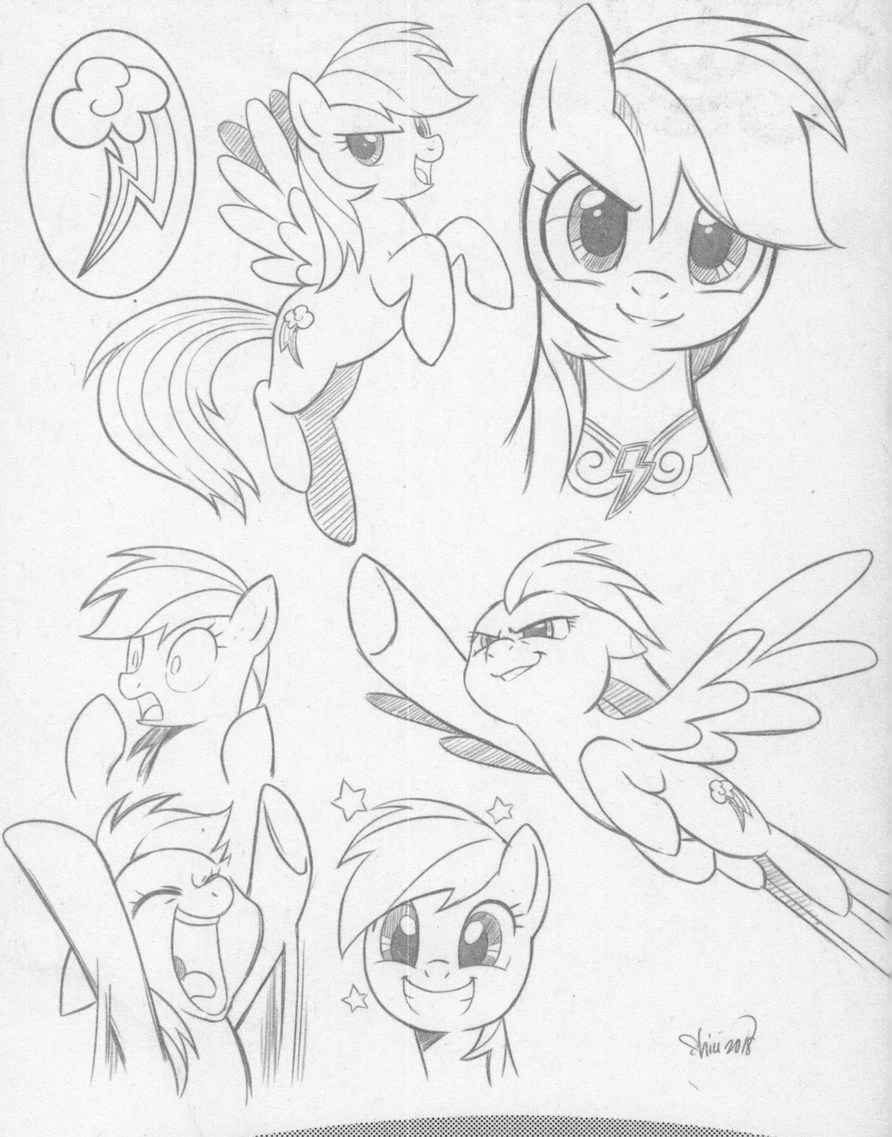

my LITTLE PONY THE MANGA

SKETCH GALLERY

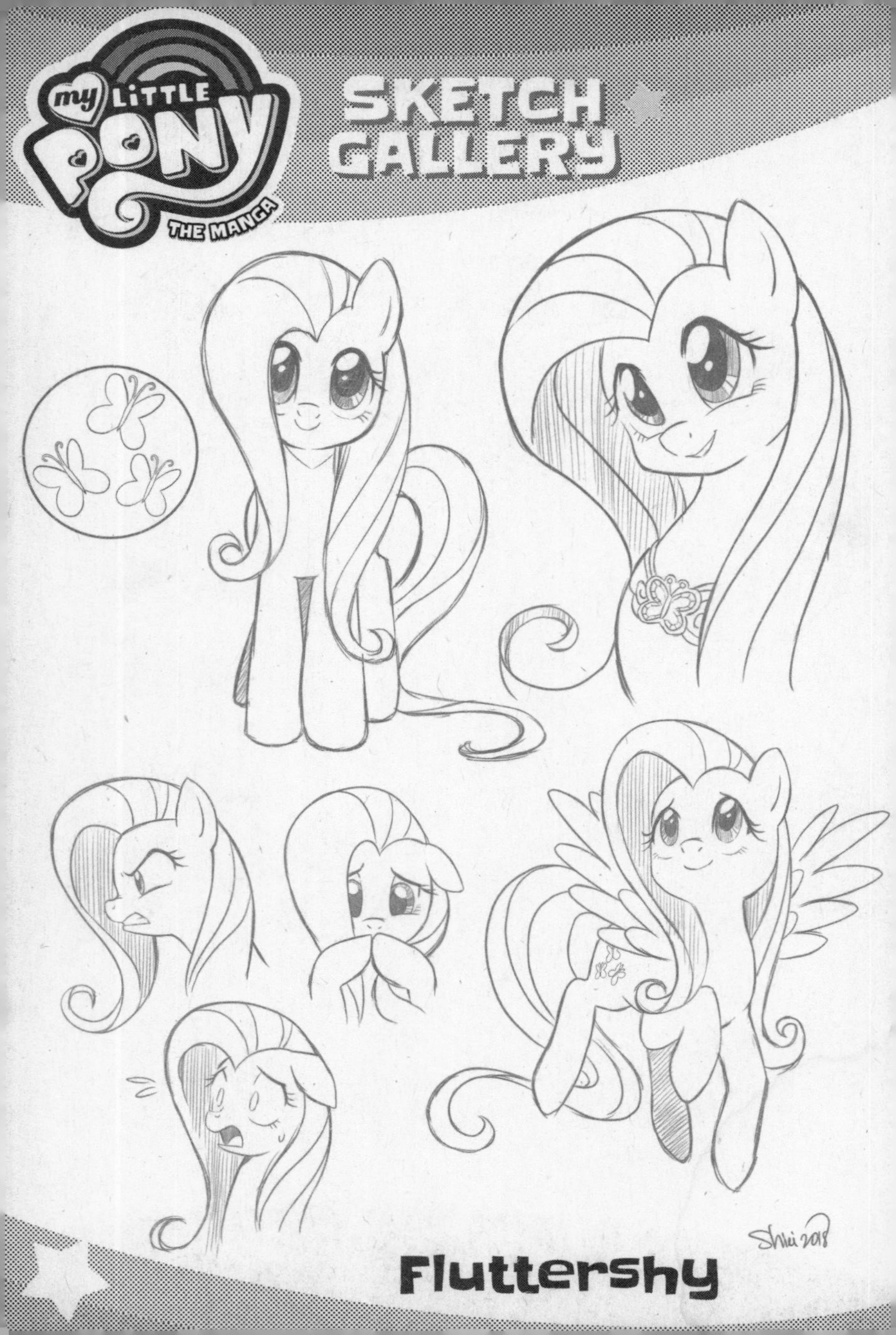

Fluttershy